The series of beeps began counting down, and then, as smoothly as I'd ever felt it, we were seamlessly encompassed in the motionless motion of the roll, its nauseating qualities dissipated as much as a good Lumeship could dissipate them.

Because we had both been lightly stung, Tynnanna, Jemeret, and I knew the instant his consciousness changed, opening into a vastness so great, so awesomely endless, that we were bounced backward from it to escape the threat of pain that underlay such power. Tynnanna said, "You cannot call us from normal space without the metal, whose atomic structure is a focal point, but you may call us here."

I was struggling to form a sentence, but before I could bring the words, *How did you get here?* into proper alignment, the starfire answered. "We live here. That is why we come to you most readily in forms of light. Listen now. There is a danger near which you do not suspect and which may not be evoked. If it is, then you can lose much. It can possibly be repaired from a source you cannot now guess . . ."

By Roby James
Published by Ballantine Books:

COMMENCEMENT
COMMITMENT

COMMITMENT

Roby James

A Del Rey® Book
BALLANTINE BOOKS • NEW YORK

A Del Rey® Book
Published by Ballantine Books

http://www.randomhouse.com

Library of Congress Catalog Card Number: 97-93328

ISBN 0-345-40979-5

Manufactured in the United States of America

First Edition: July 1997

10 9 8 7 6 5 4 3 2 1

For Sima and Steve
without whose love and support
this would never have been possible

And for Becky
who, to my joy, will live to read it

Substance
is what remains
when everything you can think of
has gone

—Eli Siegel

The Story Thus Far

A Factual Account of Emotional Events

Accustomed to the technological sophistication of the great interstellar empire known as the Com, Class A Ronica McBride, newly graduated from lifelong training, awakens on a strange, pretechnological world without the sting—the strongest of her distinctive abilities, called talent—and without her recent memories. Because of her remarkable resemblance to a woman that legend says will unite the normally scattered tribes of the Samothen, one of two opposing factions on this planet, she falls into the hands of Jemeret of the Boru, a man who always seems to know far more about her than a stranger would.

At first determined to return to the Com, which her talent and schooling have suited her to rule, Ronica is reluctantly swept up into the life of the Samothen. She embarks on a series of discoveries about the world which seem to contradict much of what she had been taught, as well as to confirm the legend of her identity as High Lady of the tribes—tribes whose members also possess talent, though not in the levels of power that she herself wields.

Her slowly returning memories lead her to question the values of her past in the Com, where, as one of only two Class A's among millions of citizens, she was expected to be crucial to the maintenance of the empire. Eventually, it becomes obvious to Ronica that Jemeret is also a Class A talent. She is puzzled and angry, but learns to trust him, and as time passes finds herself falling in love with him. Although their relationship is not a smooth one, it is confirmed by an entity called the starfire, a powerful collective intelligence worshiped by both factions on this world. The starfire seems to be manipulating events toward an end that is slowly revealed as pivotal to the future of all humanity, whether talented or talentless, on this world and throughout the Com.

After Ronica's attainment of the position of High Lady, Jemeret triggers in her a final revelation of how her memories were lost and why he knows so much about her, and the starfire tells them that they must return to the Com, where the ability of humankind to continue evolving will be determined.

The story, told through Ronica's journal, continues.

1. A Question of Memories

Whatever it is that makes someone decide to risk everything is, I think, different for everyone. But there is a moment of commitment, a particular moment in which the scales slip from wanting life more than anything else to wanting something that can only be gotten at the risk of life. That microsecond is the same for all of us, no matter what it is we're striving after.

When someone in the Com began trying to kill us, we could have turned back; it never occurred to us. When the choice we had to make balanced on the pointed edge of possible suicide, we could have refused it; we chose to risk everything. Were we fools or heroes? Is it the same thing, really?

Once he knew I was keeping this journal, my Lord Jemeret said it was imperative for me to tell the story, or else in a hundred years, or two hundred, people will insist on making us more than we were. "We don't need to be larger than life," he said to me. "Life is large enough as it is."

The link between the story when I first found myself on Caryldon and the story that follows was, appropriately enough in my view, an eftel. I'd been so convinced that the wilderworld was self-contained, untouched. And yet I'd lived the winter in a house that hid an eftel—the comlink operating in real-time between worlds. It was something that was part of the Com, not part of the Samothen.

Coney had told me that the Com had proscribed Caryldon, but that wasn't any kind of surprise. I'd known from the time I was a child, in training in the School for Talent on Werd, that wilderworlds were proscribed. We thought it was because the government used them as receptacles for the malcontents, the misfits, the ones who couldn't or wouldn't fit into the Com. We were only partly right.

"We are a very tolerant society, Ronica McBride," Jara Deland once said to me, "but only within bounds." The Com's liaison to the MIs was being pedantic again. "Every tolerant society must have bounds, and we set them in places where they can preserve the essence of what we are."

I believe telling people who can't hear you that they're wrong is about as useful as taking a bath in mud. So I didn't tell Jara that I thought she was a hypocrite. The Com was only infinitely tolerant of *itself*, in the variations it agreed to accept. Bring it a variation of values beyond the boundary, and the Com closed ranks to stamp it out.

Ah, well. Perhaps we are all the same when it comes to that.

We had gone to Salthome, where the Marl lived, to have me declared High Lady of the Samothen, so we'd brought all the members of the Inner Council with us—chiefs of their tribes and their designated co-Councillors. The starfire had come to us after the Council confirmed me, not only to verify the confirmation, but to warn us that our responsibility went further than this world, and that we risked a great deal if we failed in it. I didn't think I understood the full scope of what the starfire was saying, but Jemeret seemed to. Some things became clearer before we left Salthome to return to our own village, Stronghome. Jemeret and I met again with Ashkalin, Lord of the Marl and the father of one of my two oldest childhood friends, Kray, whom I had killed almost three years earlier in another life.

Most of Ashkalin's tribe had not gotten to their beds until dawn, and so when he appeared at the campsite we were sharing with Coney and Sandalari, he came alone. He was wrapped in a cloak against the damp chill of morning fog that lay like a curtain over the cove around which the houses of Salthome clustered. The sound of the sea seemed hushed and far away.

Jemeret either sensed or heard him before I did, and I awoke when I felt my lord stir. Ashkalin stood on the other side of the firepan, his cloak held tightly around his lean body, his dark brown eyes—so like Kray's had been before I took the life from them—fastened on the two of us. I felt Jemeret sit up, shaking off the last remnants of sleep. "My Lord Ashkalin," he said.

"My Lord Jemeret," Ashkalin said, then to me, "My Lady Ronica. I'd like a few moments to speak with you before you break camp."

I pushed off the blanket and got to my feet, feeling a little shaken, and amazed that I had actually been able to sleep at all. The revelations of the day before, while dumbfounding, had been somehow a relief. After months of trying to remember what had happened to me before I arrived on Caryldon, the retrieved memory, while terrible, was somehow comforting, because even though it raised questions, it destroyed anomalies.

Jemeret swung easily to his feet behind me. We had slept fully dressed, so it took only a second for the three of us to move across the village square and back to the house in which Jemeret had triggered my repressed memories of Kray's killing and my own self-maiming. I wasn't certain, before I walked into the house again, that I could. But after a single misstep at the door, a single tremor that ran down my spine to remind me of the upheaval, I found I could enter it as if it were any other place.

A tall, graceful woman with rich red-gold hair had built up the fire in the hearth and was stirring a hanging pot with a ladle. She looked up at us as we came in, smiling at Ashkalin, nodding respectfully to Jemeret and me.

Jemeret said, "How are you, Delazi? We missed you at Convalee."

"I had a tribe to run in my brother's absence," she said to him, a little tartness in her voice. "And considering we can't make our normal long-water runs this winter, it's a damned good thing I made sure we were stocked way over the water line. You have your choice of good grog or bad shilfnin."

"Take the shilfnin," Ashkalin said. "The Honish know the

Inner Council is here, and they've mobilized at the neck of the peninsula."

Jemeret swore, the first time I'd ever heard him do that. "We were so damned careful, crossing in!"

Ashkalin nodded. "I'm sure you were. Krenigo sent one of his guards home last night. My guess is the man didn't go to Columbary." He eyed the anger on Jemeret's face and added, more softly, "We have no real evidence against him, you know."

Jemeret took a long breath. "I know. Delazi, we'll serve ourselves."

She glanced at Ashkalin, who nodded almost imperceptibly. "I recognize 'Get out' when I hear it," she said, then bowed to Ashkalin and left the room.

As soon as she was gone, Jemeret spoke. "I couldn't challenge Krenigo even if we had evidence. I won't provoke a war among the tribes just before I have to go off-world."

"And if you're not back by Convalee next summer?" the Lord of the Marl asked, ladling out mugs of shilfnin for us. I sipped mine—Delazi had been right; it was awful.

Jemeret's eyes narrowed as if he were weighing all sorts of parameters somehow joined to Ashkalin's question. Then he said quietly, "You know the stakes I'm going to play for. We've talked about it long enough."

Ashkalin's reply seemed to me to be indirect. "Sabaran and I will allow no one to menace your tribe until your return. It would be dishonorable, like attacking the unarmed."

"As far as anyone's concerned, Ronica and I will have taken one of your ships and gone in search of the Isle of the Wise."

The Lord of the Marl nodded. "My own private vessel, the *Starwing*, is supposed to be meeting you at the Outside Cove."

"What's the Isle of the Wise?" I asked.

"It may be a legend," Jemeret said. "Or it may be real. It's said to be a repository of all the wisdom of the ancient ones, the masters of a civilization that existed here long ago. We've never been able to search for it before, because there was never time. Now that we have a High Lady, we should have the information in that repository, too. Legends say it will provide us with guidance for the future."

"Is this another legend the starfire told your na-sire and Venacrona to create?" I asked him.

Ashkalin looked at me curiously.

Jemeret shook his head, not bothering to explain the basis for the question. "The legend of the Isle of the Wise is much older than the meteor shower that occurred just before the starfire appeared here."

Ashkalin seemed to debate asking, but didn't. It's interesting how people who understand something about secrets often don't ask questions they might otherwise pursue. It's as if the very recognition that you have a secret—and Ashkalin shared with Jemeret, Venacrona, Sabaran, and Sandalari the big secret of the existence of the Com—prepares you to accept that other people have secrets, too. Instead, the Lord of the Marl said, "My ships have looked for the Isle of the Wise on their long-water runs, but even then we don't seem to have gone far enough to find it. The ocean stretches much farther than we can go when we're fishing. As far as I know, it's never been fully explored." He turned back to my lord. "And if you're not back in time for Convalee?"

"If we aren't at the Plain of Convalee in latesummer next year, then hold all of the normal activities except the Day of the Bell and agree to meet again two years later. But –" He paused "—we'll send you word if it doesn't look like we'll be here."

I wanted to say that we were sure to have returned by the second summer from now, but then it occurred to me that I had little right to be sure of very much. And, though Ashkalin seemed to know what Jemeret meant by the stakes he would be playing for, I didn't.

"So how are we going to get you back across the Honish lands when they've got an army waiting on the border?" Ashkalin asked.

"Can't we go around them, by ship?" I asked, looking from one of them to the other.

"*We* can't," Jemeret said, "but it may be better for us if

Ginestra, Lyrafi, and Tatatin go that way. It's not just that the sea roads would delay us nearly a month and I want to be off-world as soon as possible. It's that I feel we have to give the Honish a lesson, and if Krenigo—or some agent they placed with the Vylk—arranged for them to pick this spot and time, I'm for seeing they get it."

Ashkalin masked his surprise, but I was reading him fairly steadily, and I recognized its depth. "You will not convince me that you want a war with the Honish now any more than you want a war in the tribes of the Samoth," he said.

"I said a lesson," Jemeret corrected him, "not a war."

The two men looked levelly at one another for a moment and then slowly smiled, as if sharing an understanding. Ashkalin asked, "You're truly going to try to shut down the machines?"

My body jerked as if I'd just received an overload, which, in a way, I had. Jemeret's gray eyes swiveled to me even as he nodded to Ashkalin. "Oh, yes," he said. "I'm tired of giving them our children and having them throw back the broken ones. When I couldn't save Zitten—the young man from the Resni who wanted the sting so much he took all those drugs about fifteen years ago—when I recognized that your son had paid with his life, when I saw what had happened to Ronica, I swore there had to be a way to break the Com's hold over us, and if I have to break it over everyone else to accomplish that, then that's what I have to try to do. They rely on the MIs for everything. They've given the machines too much of what belongs to us."

I stared at him. He sighed. "And then when the starfire told us that the Com isn't letting talent evolve the way it should, that the entire human race is in jeopardy because of that enforced restraint, I had even more reasons to want to act."

I was utterly flabbergasted. I'd known for some time that my Lord Jemeret was a confident man with great power, but I had never believed him to be reckless. Indeed, in the time I'd been on Caryldon, he'd been extremely cautious, almost conservative. But he'd just made several of the most foolhardy statements I'd ever heard, and I knew from the way he was watching me that he was waiting for my reaction.

I took a swallow of the really terrible shilfnin and asked slowly, "Did I understand you? You want to go up against the power of the Com? You want to shut off the MIs?"

He didn't answer directly, just watched me.

He was a powerful man, but the Com was—the Com. The MIs were—I didn't know I believed it until then—overwhelmingly powerful. And I knew the Com. It had raised me. It was two hundred and fifty worlds, their resources and people, supported by a union of human and machine intelligences governing the far-flung empire with economic, technological, political, and military persuasion. The unity of government and MIs was the greatest force imaginable, seemingly impregnable, its methods as subtle as the offer of scientific upgrading, longer life and greater wealth, or as gross as the clone army called the Drenalion. All it asked was that the populations contributed as required and never created problems.

"It can't be done," I whispered.

"The starfire says it may be possible," Jemeret told me calmly. "You were standing right beside me when they said it."

"Your wish was that the Com be—" I found I couldn't say it, as if speaking it and making it real would bring the whole weight of the Com down on us.

Jemeret smiled at me. "Don't panic, love. We won't be doing anything until we have a course of action we can follow. And I don't have any notion of trying to destroy the government as such, if that's what you're worried about. I just want to rewrite a treaty. To do that, I only want to turn off the MIs." His smile widened; it almost reached his eyes. "Someone, sometime, turned them on, you know."

He sounded as if he were explaining it to a child, as if the vulnerability of the MIs was a given, a concept I simply didn't grasp. I was fighting not to become angry, not to sting him in utter disregard for his point of view. I was convinced that the MIs were entirely invulnerable. They were so much larger than we were, so far-flung, so *complete*, that it would be tantamount to suicide to threaten them.

I remembered an incident when I was only eleven, when a group of crazies from Selleran, of all places, under the influence of an insane leader little better than a witch doctor, got passage to Orokell, strapped themselves up with fullnite smuggled in from Teraton, marched up to the demographics center, and ate the fusings to blow everything to bits. While the Drenalion sponged up the mess of people and circuitry, the engineers shifted the data and workings to extra capacity elsewhere in the system. The MIs never even said ouch.

After that attack, the government ordered work to begin on a major program simulating judgment in humans when they were in danger. I didn't know if it had been completed and activated, but I thought it very likely.

Jemeret would be putting himself in mortal peril by his goal, which to me was infinitely foolish. And yet I couldn't say so. Most of my history with my Lord Jemeret was as student, as surely as I had been Mortel John's student. And now that I had come to love the man who had braceleted me, I recognized that I couldn't just tell him how wrong he was, couldn't just say, "What you want isn't faintly within the realm of possibility. Don't be ridiculous. Give it up." I thought I owed Jemeret too much to argue with him. I thought he'd been wiser than I for too many months now. Even though his wisdom was Caryldon wisdom, I thought I should not—well, enough. I didn't say anything.

Ashkalin took a sip of the shilfnin, made a face, and poured his mugful into the cold fireplace. "Will you want any of the Marl going with you to the border?"

"I think not," Jemeret said. "Where I'll hope you and Sabaran come through is in convincing your tribes that an absent High Lady is a High Lady all the same."

The leader of the Marl nodded once, then looked at me. "When he wasn't sent back, I thought my son was doing well."

"He was doing well," I said. "He just had a blind spot when it came to me. If I'd known then what I've learned since—"

"But you didn't," Jemeret said smoothly. "Keep remembering that. The Com mishandles talent to the point of outright abuse; the greater the talent, the worse the abuse. It's got to stop."

I wasn't certain that I could accept this premise. I didn't blame the Com for what I saw as my own flaw. I had thought that if I failed as a Class A, it must also be the failure of all those men who had trained me. But the killing—that had to be on my own head, because I did not know how to be moderate, because for me it was all or nothing. Jemeret insisted it was the Com that had the ultimate responsibility for everything, and, even though he had never lied to me—except once, for a few hours, about something I had to arrive at the truth of myself—I thought that his love for me made him unwilling to tie to me the wrong of which I was guilty, just as my love for him made me forbear to tell him he was crazy to take on the MIs.

No matter what had come before it, no matter what directly motivated it, I had killed my friend Kray, and I thought I ought to have been able to avoid that. It made me angry that he had raped me, but I'd hurt myself worse than he had hurt me, and the only reason I was a "normal" person again was because Jemeret had committed himself to healing me.

I cleared my throat. "I understand the need to alter how the Com deals with Caryldon," I said carefully. "But they're very powerful, and I am under oath to them."

"I'm not," Jemeret said strongly, "and neither is Sandalari." He drank half his shilfuin off without grimacing. "And I'll remind you now—but probably not again—that you're under oath to me, too."

He was right. I had sworn submission to him when I formally became a Boru, joining my life to his as inevitably as any other member of his tribe, and then even more because we shared the same kind of power—power we were about to take to a Com that was nearly starved for it.

Some instinct made me say, "I don't think I'll tell them about the second oath. They might not like the conflict of interest that implies."

"You'd better come to terms with it yourself," Jemeret said quietly, then looked at Ashkalin. "If you want to come to the border with us, you're welcome to. Just don't bring too many guards. And if, while we're gone, Venacrona sends for you, get to Stronghome as fast as you can."

Ashkalin nodded. "I've never failed to respond to the code words. I want them to leave us alone as much as you do."

"What code words?" I asked.

"We have to try to keep the secret, even though this absence—and whatever it causes to happen there—will stress it far more than anything else has," Jemeret said to Ashkalin, ignoring me. "Whatever happens, things will probably change, one way or another, and we may not be able to come back here. We'll try to send word to Veen when we can."

It was the first time I had ever heard him admit that a return from the Com might not be possible. I knew how much that admission would have distressed him, and I knew then, if I had had any doubts, how determined he was to try to do what I considered undoable.

"What code words?" I repeated.

"Whenever we have to deal here with the world outside, we signal one another by saying, 'The need is great,' " Ashkalin said, obviously deciding that one of them should answer me. "It means the survival of our way of life is endangered, and we had better be aware of it."

Jemeret set down his mug. "We've got to get started. I want to be across the Honish lands by tomorrow morning."

"What kind of plan do you have?" I asked him. "If there's an army at the border—"

He reached over and took my hand. "Don't worry about the Honish army. We'll get past it. This is just something that needs a scenario."

I squeezed his hand, still unused to his easy command of Com jargon, and without the slightest idea of what he might have in mind.

It is a basic fact of life on Caryldon that the Honish are deeply, inherently superstitious. They live in a world of propitiation or punishment, and the darkness around them is peopled with spirits more powerful than themselves. Their fear gives us powerful weapons over them, the kind of weapons Jemeret loves to use most—those that persuade rather than destroy. I think he was already trying to formulate a bloodless scenario when we left Salthome.

Tatatin objected to being shipped off the long way, but Lyrafi and Ginestra of the Dibel had no such misgivings, and eventually the Chief of the Elden gave in. We had decided to pack the Ilto off with them, ostensibly to guard them, since the ship had to sail through Honish waters, but in truth it was because Jemeret suspected that the Ilto's chief, Ustivet, was just as capable as Krenigo of betrayal. We all agreed we'd be better off without them. Ustivet protested. Jemeret stung him, and he went.

Lyrafi looked a little puzzled at the strength with which I hugged her in parting, but she didn't ask questions, and I deliberately forced myself to ease up. I had begun, unavoidably, thinking that I might never see her again, that I might never be returning to Caryldon. It was what I'd devoutly wished for when I first arrived here; now it meant a depth of loss I did not want to explore. Sometime during my stay of less than a year on this world, the acceptance that my exile here was inevitable had turned into happiness to be a part of it. Now, going back to my former life was not a prospect I could view without trepidation. But it was nothing I could avoid, either.

My klawit companion, Tynnanna, leaped out in front of us as we started up toward the high plateau that led away from Salthome. He was eager to be on the move again, for the great hunting cats of Caryldon were accustomed to ranging over large areas. As we reached the plateau itself, we gave our tivongs their heads, and I glanced around at the group of people nearest us. Coney was riding just beside me, looking as if he would like to say something. When we slowed the animals to a walk for the first time, partway through the morning, he drew his tivong up beside mine, and Rocky rubbed his head against the neck of Coney's mount, establishing dominance with one gentle scrape.

"Ronnie, I heard there could be trouble at the border," Coney said in a low voice. He was always careful not to be overheard when he called me by my nickname or when we talked about the empire outside Caryldon.

I nodded, lowering my own voice to match his. "There probably will be some disturbance." I smiled at him. "You haven't seen Jemeret handle trouble yet." And I told Coney how we'd averted a war after Convalee by drawing strength from the assembled tribes to keep the Honish troops asleep until the three tribes from the peninsula had crossed the Honish lands.

"Can you do it again?" he asked me.

"I wasn't the one who did it. And I'd guess we can't, because there aren't enough of us now to affect the numbers that must be in the army the Honish are bringing. Besides, even if we could establish a cap, we couldn't hold it for the seven or eight hours it will take to cross over."

He thought about that as we rode in silence for a while. Then he said, "I'll be fascinated to see what he tries."

So will I, I almost said, and then mentally shook myself. I needed to try to think of scenarios myself. I'd been depending on my Lord Jemeret to solve problems since I got to this world, and I knew it was at least in part because he was wiser than I. Not only did he know far more about Caryldon than I did, but he also knew something about the Com, and he'd been building scenarios for decades longer than I had. However, I *was* officially High Lady of the Samothen. I would have to start acting like it.

Sandalari rode up on Coney's other side and, still in the low voices that meant they would be discussing the Com, asked him some questions. I didn't augment my hearing to intrude on their privacy. She was, I thought, a little nervous about the idea of going back to a Com she'd failed to find a place in before, but I admired her determination to go with us—and I would be grateful for her company. Once she took Coney's attention away from me, I started thinking about the approaching problem, wondering whether I could come up with a scenario to prevent an incipient ambush.

The morning sun glinted for a moment, dazzlingly bright, off Jemeret's silver brow-crown, which put me in mind of the brow-crown I was wearing. Mine was not made of silver, though that was its color, but of the metal from which the starfire appeared to us. Wearing it was already so familiar to me that I didn't notice I had it on. Now, reminded of it, I was struck by a curious whimsy, and I pathfound my crown directly through the skin on my forehead. It was truly whimsical; I'd never before tried to understand and influence something as small and simple as a circlet of metal. It had no moving parts, no overt use other than as decoration, but it did have several unusual properties. First, it was the starfire's chosen way to manifest itself; second, when I'd been declared High Lady of the Samothen, the starfire seemed to leave a tiny piece of its substance inside the crown, which even now was writhing subtly with the star colors. Since I knew that the starfire was a living, sentient creature or creatures, that implied something extraordinary about the circlet I was wearing, and dozens of additional questions about the nature of the starfire.

As with all basically primitive objects, the crown was very sluggish about responding. Mechanical systems are quicker, technological ones faster still. The more complex the system, the easier it is to get it to reveal itself.

Riding under the great bowl of sky that arched over the plateau, I pathfound the crown, asking it to reveal its structure and its properties, and as the morning wore on toward afternoon, and we speeded our pace to reach the boundary of the Honish lands as quickly as possible, it slowly opened itself to me.

The metal itself was not a vastly unusual substance. In molecular weight and shape, it was much like the silver it superficially resembled. Its molecular bond was, however, slightly more frangible, and it had more than twice the conductivity. It also had a property of containing and concentrating energy in the spaces between its atoms, as though creating a reservoir, so that when touched by an outside, motivating force, it looked as if it could behave like a laser weapon.

Like all inanimate structures or objects that harbored life, it couldn't tell me anything about the life-forms within. For a fleeting moment I was tempted to try to sting that life-form, but

Jemeret had warned me not to, and I couldn't convince myself that the tiny piece of the starfire currently resident in my crown was actually isolated from the huge volume of fire it produced when it appeared during our ceremonial rites. I wondered if the starfire's energy could be turned into a beam; I wondered if I could do it. I filed it away, an unanswered question among so many.

We camped for the night about six kilometers from the border, far enough so that the Honish would not know our position. Our sensory scouts had shown they had only two spies on the plateau, and those two were relatively close to the boundary itself. We'd sent Krenigo and his guards back to Columbary, and Zunigar had taken the Resni south across the moors to the Hive. That left a party comprising the Boru, the Genda, the Nedi, and Ashkalin of the Marl—twenty-seven of us all told, against an army of several thousand of the Honish.

It might have daunted a more weak-willed group of people—or a more cautious or more sensible one—but Jemeret obviously had something in mind, and I told myself I would never underestimate the power of that brain. I remember wondering if he overestimated it, if that was why he felt he could take on a technological force I perceived as far beyond his ability. I didn't pursue it.

The guards built a fire in a hollow and set up the lean-tos, but no one left the encampment to hunt. We would live on the biscuits we'd brought from Salthome until we were back on Samish land again.

Sandalari and I were the only women remaining now, so when we had to go a considerable distance to find a small copse of trees to relieve ourselves, we went together. On our return, she said to me softly, "I never thought I'd be going back."

"You don't have to," I said.

She flashed me that radiant smile. "Oh, yes, I do. There's a greater purpose here, and the stars intend us to try to pursue it. I even—" She stopped walking and lifted her tunic, so that the lower part of her back was bare. "Raise my cloak and look."

Even before I gathered the material and held it out of the

way, I knew her back would be entirely scarless. I let the cloak drop, and she slid the tunic back down. "I never understood why you didn't heal that last scar when you healed all the others."

She turned back to me. "We all of us keep some of our scars, Ronica. Some of us keep them on the inside, like you; some of us on the outside, like me."

"Jemeret?" It came out as a whisper.

"He has scars, too," Sandalari said immediately. "He's just infinitely better at hiding them than anyone else alive."

"I don't see him as having scars," I said. "I see him as the Class A the Com wanted me to be—perfect, powerful, and brilliant."

She smiled again. "You love him," she said. "You're entitled to see him that way. But always remember your idea of perfection and the Com's may be vastly different now." She cocked her head to one side and a lustrous golden curl fell out of her hood. "I think it's going to be very interesting."

"Risky, too." I was tentatively broaching a subject I wasn't sure she'd understand; she had only been eight years old when she left the Com. "He thinks he can do something to them—something impossible."

She frowned. "Jemeret doesn't tackle what he sees as impossible, but he's always done very difficult things. I trust his choices."

I heard an implied reproach, as if she'd added, *So should you.* I told myself to listen to her; she had known him longer than I. He had healed her just as he'd healed me, taken her from that battered child I remembered to this luminous beauty.

Suddenly I was frowning, too. "Sandalari, Jemeret says all talent arises here on Caryldon."

"So?"

"But when they brought you to us on Werd, you'd been badly abused *because* you had talent. That doesn't make sense."

She looked down at the brown, mosslike grass that covered the rolling plateau. "I was the only child we know of in the recent history of Caryldon who was born with power to the Honish, not to the Samothen."

I stared at her. "How?"

She shrugged, a fluid movement under her cloak. "We don't know. My parents were obviously people of some means, or I might have been killed outright. If there were others like me, they must have been dispatched as soon as the power was discovered. I suppose my parents thought that if I just didn't *use* the power I had, then it would be as if I didn't have it. But how do you teach a child not to see when her eyes are open?"

We had nearly reached the campsite. "How did you get to the Com?"

"There are factions among the Honish, just as there are among the tribes of the Samothen. Someone got information about me to Lord Sabaran, and he bought me. I'm told it was about the time the Com demanded another child—they'd just lost someone—so the men decided to see if the Com had any chance of healing me."

I flushed. "And we both know how that worked out."

She rested her hand lightly on my arm. "You know I don't hold you at fault. Put it behind you."

We parted at the edge of the hollow in which the lean-tos had been set. She went to help with the attempt to heat up some shilfnin; I went to take care of the tivongs.

Ashkalin found me there and stood quietly, watching, until I had finished. I stroked Rocky's nose before I walked over to him. "My Lord Ashkalin, can I help you?"

"I would like you to tell me about my son," he said.

Something twisted inside me, but I knew what he was saying, and I could agree at once that it was possible I owed it to him. It wouldn't be easy. "We were three, Kray and Coney and I. I can tell you about him better if Coney helps me. Is that acceptable?"

His deep brown eyes seemed to weigh me for a moment, and then he nodded.

So that evening, Coney and I sat with Ashkalin at some distance from the shrouded fire, cross-legged, hands folded in front of us. For the next several hours, as the stars appeared and slowly circled above us, Coney and I gave Kray's childhood and adolescence back to the father who had never seen them. We discovered all over again the things that had made Kray one of us, and I found myself remembering what I loved, what made me angry, and what had, at last, terrified me so. Coney's memories differed from mine, because he had never been in competition with either of us, and because he was a gentler person than I. Between the two of us, sometimes laughing and sometimes crying, we reconstructed our friend. It was almost possible for me to forget that our friend had slipped me an experimental drug in order to rape me, and that I had killed him as he accomplished, but did not complete, the act he intended. Before Jemeret came to call us for a strategy meeting, I think I had forgiven Kray for his inability to refrain from the rape, which had killed him and cost me my sanity and almost three years of my own life.

There were still questions I hadn't asked. Revelations have their own resonance, and I'd allowed them to surround me, to cushion me from the time I didn't remember fully, the time I spent without a functioning brain. Now, remembering Kray with Coney, watching Ashkalin, I was ready to look at that empty time, and it had to be through eyes other than my own.

Jemeret had posted all the guards, including our own, on our chosen perimeter around the hollow, leaving Henion, Henion's co-Councillor and cousin Lenape, Sabaran and Sheridar, Venacrona, and Sandalari still in the hollow. Coney, Ashkalin, and I found them all near the fire as we returned.

"I never really believed it would come to a fight when we wouldn't have all our guards with us," Henion was saying as we came up to them.

"There are all kinds of fights," Jemeret said. "Sabaran, you probably know more about the Honish than any of the rest of us. How unified are they actually likely to be? Who is most likely to be leading them?"

The big Gendal stroked his blond beard thoughtfully. "There are two main factions, one answering to the Lewannees and their allies, the other answering to the Beckanees, who are the most unyieldingly hostile to the Samothen. I've heard the

Beckanees added a lot of adherents when they learned the Lewannees had Lady Ronica in their hands and let her get away."

Jemeret grunted with something like satisfaction. "So we're likely to be facing Beckanees."

"It's logical," Venacrona said. "The Lewannee stonehouses are at the opposite end of the Honish lands, and the Beckanees' are near here, just north of the peninsula neck."

"Do you have a plan?" Sheridar asked Jemeret.

"I have five or six plans," Jemeret replied. I saw that he didn't use the Com jargon "scenario" in front of anyone who wasn't aware of the secret. "In at least three of them, we don't get to the Samish lands alive."

"Concentrate on the others," Sabaran said dryly, and Jemeret threw him one sideways glance.

"I'd like to get through quickly and without casualties," my lord said. "But that would take negotiation, and we don't have a lot of time. So I can't give that option much chance of success."

"I'd hoped you were going to tell us about the promising plans,"Ashkalin said.

"That *is* one of the promising plans." Jemeret toyed lightly with the hilt of his shortsword. "It's just not quite as promising as I'd like."

I cleared my throat. "I don't know what the other plans are," I said almost shyly, "but I'd like to try something."

"What?" Sheridar asked, his eagerness and youth bursting out.

I didn't look at him, never took my eyes off Jemeret's face. I'd become accustomed to using his reactions, his responses, as guidelines for my own behavior. At the outset I'd been angered by the tribal rules that mandated my needing his permission for things I wanted to do; now I needed him to confirm me, and I knew he sensed that need. I know now—much later—that I'd made Jemeret my touchstone, that I'd gone from a disastrous need for control to a potentially disastrous need for his approval, once again swinging from one extreme to the other as if no territory at all lay between them. Old patterns are the easiest to slide into, because they're the most comfortable, the most familiar. I'd learned to use my shields on a sliding scale instead of reflexively, all up or all down. But I hadn't learned, and wasn't then aware, that my entire behavioral architecture operated in extremes, too. Jemeret had shown me how wrong the need for complete control of everything was for me, and I'd accepted that. I'd punished myself for it horribly. Now I had retreated to the opposite extreme and gratefully gave Jemeret the right of approbation. He'd always told me I would have to trust him; I had grown to trust him perhaps more than I trusted myself.

He touched me lightly with his sting to tell me to go ahead. I closed my eyes and made myself aware of my brow-crown, just as months before I'd made myself aware of the bowls of starfire metal sunk into the altar in the temple at Stronghome. And just as I had then called the starfire by remembering my encounter with it on the Plain of Convalee, I called it now by remembering how it had come to us in Salthome the evening before.

The gasps would have made me aware that something was happening even if I hadn't seen the shapes and shadows of sudden phantasms on my closed eyelids. My eyes snapped open and I was dazzled by the light, which surrounded us like a living, glowing mist. It was not normal starfire; the red and blue colors were entirely absent. The gold and white had diffused from their ordinary state of fire to something more like smoke. And then it all vanished, presumably back into my brow-crown, leaving everyone gaping at me, stunned. My lord glowed with pride and some very real gratitude.

In the silence, I irised my eyes wide open again to compensate for the sudden darkness, broken only by the now-comparatively weak firelight. Sandalari said appreciatively, "A weaponless weapon."

"I didn't know it would do that," I said in a low voice.

"What did you think it would do?" Henion asked, his expression nearly one of awe.

I shrugged. "I just wondered if it could release its energy in a way that might help us to get home. It—" I wasn't really sure how to say it. "—it made its own choice."

Jemeret had been smiling at me. "And it's made a very good choice," he said. "Now I think I can develop a plan that has a chance of working. As a matter of fact, you could say it's brilliant."

Ashkalin stifled a snort.

As we had the night before, Jemeret and I shared our campsite with Coney and Sandalari. I honestly didn't know if they were intimate yet, but they were plainly in love. We'd gone over Jemeret's scenario twice. Then, when the latewinter night was at its height, we retired to our separate campsites. The four of us sat cross-legged around a tiny spark of campfire. We were aware, without consciously addressing it, that we four were the ones who would be going to the Com. We were starting to spend more time in each other's company; we were going to become a team.

And I resurrected my decision to pursue the last of my vanished time, a decision that had been sidetracked by the creation of the next morning's scenario. I'd reached the point where my desire to know surpassed my fear of knowing, where my trust of the three people with me was greater than my dislike of negative self-revelation. So I looked at Jemeret. "Will you tell me what happened to me from the time I lost my mind until I—woke up here on Caryldon?" I asked softly. I glanced at Coney, then back again at my lord, repeated the motion, waited. Reaching out to read them, I felt caution, rather than reluctance, and that encouraged me. I went on, "I've remembered what I can remember, but it's not the whole story, and I know that it's not. If I can get the fragments tied together, the holes filled in, then I'll have the materials to go on building with." I didn't have to say that they could fill it in for me; that was something we all knew, even Sandalari.

Into the silence, she said, "I'd like to hear it, if I may. It'll help. I've been away from the Com a long while, and I'm a little nervous about going back."

Coney and Jemeret studied one another for a while longer in

the weak, flickering light from the campfire, and then Jemeret spoke. "I didn't come into it until quite late in the process. You'd better start it."

My gaze flew back to Coney's face, and he drew a deep breath. "The morning Kray raped you, the MIs broadcast the sound of your screaming throughout the Residence. If they hadn't, we mightn't have gotten to you in time to save you."

Shock must have shown actively on my face.

Coney's expression was abruptly sympathetic, and Jemeret reached out and drew me back against his chest, but he didn't sting me. I think he trusted that I'd reached the point where unpleasant news would not pain me beyond my capacity to bear it.

If the MIs had registered the fact that I was screaming, the MIs had been monitoring my suite. Therefore, the MIs had recorded everything that went on in that suite. They'd recorded Class A Jasin Lebec's visit, when we probed each other and he wished me good service. They'd recorded Kray's arrival, and the subsequent rape and killing, and they had either not analyzed the material or their analysis had shown the events to be of little importance—until it became clear to them that they were going to lose me. Only then had they initiated action.

The realization was devastating. And the fact that the MIs had broadcast it meant I had not projected my distress outward to get anyone to come to me. I had not sought help, I'd merely reacted, keeping the situation between Kray and me, and handling it badly.

The MIs could have summoned somebody and prevented the rape. We move in human time, but they can react in microseconds. They had done nothing until I was in danger of losing my life. *They had done nothing.*

I gathered and controlled hard to keep my breathing regular. "I see," I said as steadily as I could. "Go on."

Jemeret's hands tightened briefly on my shoulders.

Coney told me that everyone had come running, and I was at the emergency med and into the radiant fluid tank less than two minutes after they found me. "Jasin Lebec was beside himself," Coney said. "He'd seen Kray going toward your suite, cheerfully greeted him, and never bothered to read for his feelings. They shoved Kray's body into postmortem preservation and just left him there. He was clearly more expendable than you were."

To the MIs, too, I thought bitterly. "And I was in the tank for—"

"Close to two years before they realized they would have to send for Jemeret." He glanced at the man behind me. "Jemeret Cavanaugh."

I accepted he'd have had a finame; everyone in the Com did. Coney was actually—no, not actually, only in the Com—Shems Conewall; Sandalari was a Gregson; I was Ronica McBride. "Did I just float in the tank? Didn't anyone try to heal me? In two whole years?"

"Jasin Lebec tried about twenty times," Coney answered. "They eliminated all his other Com assignments and never even bothered to give me any assignments at all. It was like they thought my presence would somehow help you—or something to that effect." He glanced upward once at the stars, among which, some distance away, the worlds of the Com hung. "I used to come to the room where your tank stood and try to talk to you, but the meds all warned me against it. They wanted you close to stasis. They didn't know what was going on behind your eyes."

I looked at his set jaw, then looked down at his hands. "Jasin Lebec should have been able to find out."

"He tried," Coney said.

Jemeret stirred slightly behind me. "He was too old," he said. "He could still do a great deal, but you're very strong, Ronica, and you were fighting him."

Coney nodded. "He told them repeatedly that it was futile for him to go on trying, but the Tribunal kept insisting he try again and again. Petra Chantrey had some of the professors do a calculation on your declining strength ratio, and she predicted you'd be weak enough for Jasin Lebec to handle in another year's time. The MIs didn't disagree. So they waited. And when we got to the two-year point, he tried again, and you were still as strong as ever. That's when Mortel John told them to send for Jemeret. They argued with him until the MIs kicked in and said they wanted to salvage you enough to risk asking Jemeret to come into it."

"I'm not popular in the Com," Jemeret said dryly.

"I called up his biodata in the library after they started arguing about contacting him," Coney said. "The information was very interesting."

"They didn't proscribe the data?" Jemeret asked, surprised.

Coney shook his head. "I was fascinated by the part that said you were 'unwilling to continue' your Com training. I never realized we could quit—either we graduated or we failed."

"Or both," I said in a whisper.

"Let's not dwell on me," Jemeret said. "We need to get some sleep before we go up against the Honish tomorrow. The Tribunal sent for my help, and I never refuse when talent's involved." His hands stroked my arms and shoulders. "I wasn't prepared for the strength of this particular talent."

"How did they reach you?" I asked him.

His answer nearly floored me. I began to think that he would never be done surprising me, even though I prayed he would, and soon. He said quietly, "There's an eftel in our house, and another in the temple."

"An eftel?" I repeated disbelievingly. "You have an eftel?"

I felt his motion when he nodded. "It's the one piece of Com technology we ever agreed to. They had to be able to reach us to avoid any full-scale landings."

"An eftel." I murmured it again. All through the uphill winter I'd been living with an eftel and I'd never known it. If I had, would I have reached for it? I wondered. Would I have called them?

Coney went on, "We moved your tank and a bunch of the rest of us to the station above Caryldon—it's called Markover Station, by the way. Ah—"

He'd seen my memory jangle. I remembered one of the classes in the politics, economics, and geography of the Com that Mortel John had conducted endlessly for Coney and Kray and me, the politics and makeup of the empire being the cornerstone on which the Com purported to base its rule.

The network of stations had been chosen as a way of monitoring the worlds that fell into three categories: those that might soon be drawn into the Com; those that were having problems with Com rule and seeking what we euphemistically called "uncommitted" member status; and those that had earned, for whatever reason, proscription.

Kray had asked for specific numbers. There were, at that time, 236 worlds in the Com, and there were twenty-three stations—eighteen watching worlds the Com might want to encourage to join, two surveilling Com member worlds with problems of one variety or another, and three over-proscribed worlds. Naturally, Mortel John most wanted to talk about the first two categories, and Kray most wanted to talk about the last. He pushed, as only he could, trying to find out what got a world proscribed, whether the three worlds in question were a threat of any kind, what their names were.

Mortel John had answered, "Proscribed worlds are always nameless; only the stations have names. Wilderworlds are proscribed, but most of those don't need our surveillance. Those which have drawn our attention for any reason, we watch." He paused, eyed Kray. "And no, I will not tell you why, so ask another question."

So then of course Kray wanted to know the names of those stations and where they were, and he kept asking with a dogged determination that refused distraction of any kind until Mortel John gave in. "I cannot imagine why this information would be of any use to you," he said in his most pedantic voice, "but it's clear we'll never get any work done. Prada Station is in the F-2 cluster. Barone Station is in the Jann-Bime cluster. Markover Station is in the Far Arm."

All three of us had been startled by that, and we looked at one another. Kray opened his mouth to pursue it, but I cut in, "How many rolls' journey is the Far Arm?"

"A dozen from Orokell," our teacher answered.

Nobody made dozen-roll trips. They were very costly, and each roll increased the chances of error by an order of magnitude.

"Are there other worlds in the area of the proscribed one?" Coney asked, frowning.

"We have closed the subject," Mortel John said definitively, and returned to his discussion of the politics of placement, the relative strengths of centrist worlds versus those farther out from the core.

Later, the three of us sat in the courtyard under the shade trees, which counterfeited protection from Koldor's sun as if the filter shields didn't exist, and tried to think of why the Com would bother to proscribe a world that no one would ordinarily go anywhere near anyway. We failed that day.

Now, in the feeble firelight, watching Coney, I understood. "The question is," I said to him as if he'd been privy to my entire interior memory, "however did the Com find Caryldon in the first place?"

Coney looked inquiringly at Jemeret.

Above my head, my lover said slowly, "That's an excellent question, and one I never bothered to ask. We can slip it in when we get there."

I heard the tone of controlled fury in his voice, and all at once I knew what that swirl of anger was that I encountered when I probed him, the hot knot that he carried around inside him. "You hate them, don't you?" I asked him.

"No," he said. "I hate what they do to people like you and Sandalari and your classmate Kray. I hate it that the MIs have taken over the responsibility for human things. I hate it that they use a tool like the Drenalion against people. But I don't hate them. They've forgotten what humanity was supposed to be without talent. As a result, they make it almost impossible to be human *with* talent." His voice went low and hard. "We have to find a way to stop it."

"Part of the problem, I think," Coney said, "is entrusting the training of people with talent to Mortel John."

"Why?" I asked. I was about to argue that Mortel John had been a good teacher, that he'd certainly been able to train me successfully, but Jemeret broke into my thoughts.

"What brought you—finally—to that point of view?" he

asked Coney. "My sense of you was that you were defending him the last time we argued about it."

"He has a new class of talent now, you know," Coney said.

"I know damned well," Jemeret said. "They're the two children the government demanded to replace Ronica and Kray, and the new one who's part of the treaty quota. I sent the three of them out there. A girl from the Genda—she'd be four now—and a boy from the Nedi, who'd be almost six, and then the new Boru boy."

"The older two are dead," said Coney.

I felt Jemeret's shock and anger wash over me, picking up on my own. I was rocked by the deaths of two children with talent in the Com. Just as shocking as the fact that they were dead was the conclusion that the Com had lost four talents in less than four years, when they were supposed to value talent so highly. It seemed inexplicable.

"Why didn't you tell me?" Jemeret demanded. Sandalari sat up, startled.

Coney's voice was infinitely gentle. "Because I know you, Jem. You're the fairest man I've ever known, but you love Ronnie so much that I was afraid . . ." He paused.

We all waited.

Coney drew in a long breath. "If you didn't heal her, you wouldn't have to send her back to them," he said at last.

I was so surprised at him that some of my shock dropped away. His new hardness, the changes that had become part of him since I'd killed Kray—these were deeper, stronger things than I'd previously guessed. I squirmed around a little in Jemeret's arms, so that I could see the expression on his face. I didn't try to sting him.

For a long moment Jemeret didn't speak. Then he said, "When you told me why they'd sent you down here, I was tempted to keep her. But not very, and for less than a minute. Because I do love her. Do you seriously think I'd leave her broken when I had the power to heal her?"

"Sorry." Coney's voice was barely a whisper.

My lord shook his head. "If I hadn't agreed to bring her back, they never would have let her come here," he said. "And so now you can tell me what happened to the two older children in Mortel John's new class of talent."

Coney tried to hold his tone carefully expressionless. "Someone penetrated the School for Talent on Werd and cut their throats," he said. "Whoever it was missed the new child, Tial Borland, they're calling him—I assume he's the child Tal that I heard mourned at Midwinter Song. He's fine, and they moved him from Werd to Koldor when they sent me here. The killer almost decapitated the children, so they wouldn't have the time or the chance to begin to heal themselves." A vein jumped in his cheek. Sandalari put her hand on his arm and stroked him, but she was close to tears. I felt a cold wash on my spine as the horror and anger began to grow stronger.

Coney went on, "Mortel John's reaction was to say regretfully, 'We lose so many. Another setback is not unexpected. At least we hadn't yet invested much in their training.' " The bitterness had crept into his voice anyway.

Jemeret's rage washed over me and then faded as he masked it.

Now I was as astounded as I was horrified. "I don't understand," I said. "What happened to Mortel John? How did he grow so—callous?"

Coney said calmly, "Jemeret told me that Mortel John isn't human any longer. He's a cyborg created by the MIs for the specific purpose of indoctrinating talent into the Com."

While I was gaping, Sandalari—who seemed to have a much greater capacity to accept and adapt to shocks than I did—asked, with a tartness I was totally unused to hearing from her, "Does it occur to no one that he hasn't done a particularly praiseworthy job of it?"

"Oh, they know that," Jemeret said, his voice tight, but no overt edge of the hot rage in it now. "They simply can't arrive at a better approach. They've been arguing about it for almost thirty years."

I had started to tremble, and I gathered and held it fiercely down. At least momentarily, this new revelation minimized my pain at the slaughter of children. I had been raised by a machine. And I'd thought it a mistake that I had been formed just by men! I fought to put it behind me with the kind of determination I'd learned earlier in life to avoid confronting anything disturbing, then dredged it back again and made myself look at it and say, *All right, live with it and go on. It's more bearable than a lot else has been, and you bore that!*

I concentrated on the murders, looking at Coney. "What did the MI surveillance records show? Surely they would have identified the killer—or killers—by now, from the holos."

Coney shook his head. "They haven't any suspects at all. There was no surveillance, Ronnie."

I stared, open-mouthed again.

He said, "Surveillance is expensive, and highly consumptive of energy and resources, and there are a lot of troublemakers who need it. Until some substantial investment's been made in talent, the children are a renewable resource, that's all. Remember, before our Tenday, Mortel John told us the Com was willing to spend our lives? We thought he was saying it to keep us alert by making us furious over the gall of the government. But it turns out to be completely true."

"Why haven't they demanded replacements from us?" Jemeret asked. "Since they clearly consider talent disposable, I should have thought they'd have been asking for some more to dispose of."

"You had Ronnie," Coney answered. "They want her back more than they want a new class of talent. She's supposed to replace Jasin Lebec for them, and they wanted to stay in your good graces until you returned her."

Sandalari said softly, determinedly, "They're going to get back more than they bargained for."

I suddenly had a completely inappropriate urge to laugh, recognized it as the outer edge of hysteria and pushed it away, even as Jemeret was making himself dissolve his active anger back into the knot I had sensed from the first time I probed him.

"I think many of us are getting more than we bargained for," he said.

We were all silent for a time. I watched Sandalari gently stroke Coney's arm, felt Jemeret's familiar touch on my shoulders and upper back. Then he went on with what I'd asked to hear. "At any rate, thank the stars, they called me to come up to Markover and assess the scope of the damage you'd done to yourself. I put Tuvellen in charge of the tribe and took a lander up to the station."

I could almost imagine it—not completely, but well enough. I had seen someone afloat in the radiant fluid before. I would have been naked, mindless, staring through the sparkling gold curtain, but seeing nothing. "I must have been—" It was little more than a hiss, but in spite of muting the emotions, I still couldn't find the words for what I must have been.

Jemeret turned me so that I could see his face, even as he stung me with the complete sincerity of what he was saying. "You were amazingly strong and beautiful," he said. "From the moment I saw and felt the woman you'd grown into, I wanted you."

Suddenly I couldn't seem to do more than whisper. "Were you the one who gave me to them?"

His gray eyes glittering, he slowly nodded. "All three of you," he said, and then waited.

I sensed, without probing him or receiving any kind of projection from him, that he feared I would condemn him for having been the one who took me from my tribe and put me in the hands of a society that had almost destroyed me. But of course I couldn't do that; I needed his approval, his guidance, too much. I needed to understand, to forgive. I actually smiled a little, laid my hand on his cheek. "I wouldn't be who I am if you hadn't done—all the things you did," I said. "Now please tell me how you put me back together again."

He relaxed almost visibly, and then he talked for a while. My mind, when he had first entered it, was complete chaos. "It was like a war zone in the middle of a thunderstorm," he said, tapping my brow lightly with one forefinger. "There was so much raw power flinging itself around that I had to withdraw almost at once, because I just wasn't prepared for it."

"I can't imagine that," Sandalari said. "You are so much more powerful than the rest of us."

Jemeret nodded, neither flattered nor inclined to deny what the Samothen had for twenty-two years accepted as truth. "I was used to being far more powerful than anyone else. When I first power-tested her, she showed promise, but nothing extraordinary. When the treaty demand for children came due, she seemed a good bet. On Markover, I was stunned by what I found."

It gave me a thrill of pride to hear him say that, and at the same time I was a little embarrassed. He sensed it, and pulled me back against him.

"It's like falling into a nest of dissociated communicator wires," he said over my head. "Each wire is broken and is spewing data furiously out the broken end. The power of the information flow makes all kinds of noise, along with the sort of electrical impulses that bounce back off each other, like sparks flying. Every broken end matches another end somewhere else in the nest, but with more than a million severed connections, there's no way of matching them up by chance. I had to keep trying connections until I made a match, then I had to pull the two ends together through the mess, seal them, and force the seal to hold. You kept trying to rebreak the connections again."

I was almost overwhelmed by the patience and determination he must have had. "How did you ever have the strength—even you?" I asked him wonderingly.

"I borrowed some of Coney's reserves every day," he answered, "and I spent four months inside your head, rebuilding."

Coney stirred. "Sometimes as much as sixteen hours at a stretch," he said. "I'd never even imagined such a thing was possible." He paused briefly. "I'm not sure it would have been, for anyone else."

I felt again the deep admiration of Jemeret's power, coupled now with appreciation that he'd chosen to share so much of it with me.

As always, he seemed to know what I was thinking, a vestige, I knew now, of the extraordinary amount of time he'd spent inside my brain. "I told you before that some things have very high prices," he said softly. "I decided immediately that you were worth whatever I had to pay for you. I haven't had any cause to regret that decision." His hands wandered down my sides, his fingers almost absently teasing, and I shivered at his touch. "And I charged a price for healing you, as well. I forced the Com government to agree to allow you to choose between a life here and one there."

I was grateful that he had ensured I be given that additional gift, and I closed my tear ducts before my eyes could fill.

"The snag," Coney said, "is that you'll need to live that life—the life of a Class A—for a sufficient time to make a reasoned comparison. That's how the contract reads. I'm sure the government can't imagine that once you have that kind of power, you would ever be willing to give it up."

"Well, it's not as if we haven't work to do there," Jemeret said in a low voice.

"How did you find out Mortel John wasn't—isn't—human?" I asked, finding my way back to a question that hadn't been fully resolved. "In all the years I was with him, I never suspected."

"You never tried to sting him?" my lord countered.

I shook my head. "Not since I was a baby. He stood up to me then, and I couldn't shake him. Somehow I never tried again."

"I, on the other hand, tried to sting him when I was about fourteen and discovered that I simply couldn't get to all of him. Back when I was being trained, he taught physical defense techniques as well as all the classroom subjects. One afternoon in the exercise yard, I ducked under a swing and stung him to weaken him. His response was so fragmented that I knew something was very wrong. For whatever reason, I decided to pathfind him, grabbed his arm, and the rest of his brain was there, but it wasn't precisely his."

I couldn't imagine how that must have made him feel. I didn't know how I would react when—if—I saw Mortel John again. He'd been the closest thing I'd ever had to a father, and he'd turned out to be an MI. Or, at the very least, the half-machine instrument of the MIs.

"It's—amazing," I said. "I keep expecting that life will become simpler, more balanced, now that I've got my memory back, now that I understand what happened, what it caused, but it doesn't settle."

"It won't," Jemeret said. "Not until—one way or another—we're finished. And perhaps not even then. As a matter of fact, it just got more complicated."

I knew what he meant. "We're going to the Com, taking talent to a place where someone or something is *killing* talent." I flushed, bit my lip. "Someone besides me."

All three of them made some sounds of dismissal, demurral, or reassurance.

"Will we be in danger?"

"I shouldn't think so," Jemeret said. "Anyone cowardly enough to attack babies isn't likely to come after full-grown talents." He seemed to ask Coney for confirmation.

"Sinet, Lage, Camla, Lendo, Vazhny, and Jasin Lebec were all very well when I left," Coney said. "And if the Tribunal was concerned about our being attacked, surely they'd call and tell us to stay here until they find out what's going on."

Providing they're even trying to find out, I thought. After all, Mortel John hadn't sounded overly concerned about losing two-thirds of his class.

Jemeret shrugged. "We need to get some sleep. We'll need our reserves at full strength in the morning."

Something began nibbling at me at that moment, something I couldn't quite get my mind around. "One more question, Jemeret." I pulled back so that I could see his face again, irising my eyes to make his features clearer in the now fading firelight and the pale starlight from the huge bowl overhead. "The sex—" Abruptly, I didn't know what to ask.

He understood instantly. He seemed to consider what he wanted to say. Coney and Sandalari had frozen in place, but we'd nearly forgotten them anyway. At last the level gray eyes rose to meet mine directly, and Jemeret said, "You had never learned that sex and power are not the same thing. You used it as power on Coney; Kray used it as power on you. I had to help you see that ideally the two aren't really related at all."

That rattled me, and he saw it. "I would have wanted you even if it hadn't been vital to healing you," he said. "I'd spent too much time inside your head not to need to be inside your body as well. But you'd blown out on a sexual trigger that tore your control of yourself away. Healing you demanded a sexual solution that ultimately gave you the control back and then taught you how to share it. That's where health lies."

He had, I know now, used sex to teach me about sharing. At the time, however, I'd learned the lesson very incompletely. I know it's a difficult lesson. I always thought I could learn the hard things as quickly as the easy things. It isn't so.

"The Com couldn't have healed you," he said, "because the MIs fail to understand that what they consider the wasteful irrationality of emotion is an integral part of human life. We need our emotions. You were deeply harmed emotionally. But the MIs see emotions as an inconvenience, and the government has unfortunately subscribed to the gospel of the MIs."

"I never thought about health," I said with surprise. "I always thought I'd just continue to be any way I wanted, and everyone else would have to accept me, because I was the Class A."

"You're still the Class A," Coney said. "Jemeret's presence won't change that."

"What's changed," Sandalari said, "is that you aren't the Com's Class A any longer."

If I'd said aloud at that moment what I distinctly remember thinking—*It's true, I'm not the Com's Class A, now I'm Jemeret's Class A*—if I'd actually verbalized it, maybe I could have become sooner what I would ultimately have to be—*my own* Class A. Maybe not. But once again, I didn't say anything. I think now I was somehow never destined to grow quickly enough into the responsibilities laid upon me.

"Did someone say something about sleep?" Sandalari asked.

Jemeret shifted position, stretching out under the canvas lean-to, drawing me along with him. "It would be best," he said. "Tomorrow won't be easy." His lips brushed my neck and ear, and he tightened his arms around me.

Once you get into the habit of introspection, it can become overwhelming. I reflected on sex and power as objectively as I could long after I thought he'd fallen asleep. If we never made love again, I would still love him with every bit of my strength for healing me. If we never probed each other again, it might hurt me, but it wouldn't affect what I felt for him. I'd been convinced one of the reasons I loved him so much was the sex—the physical act had been both my perigee and my apogee. It was of vital importance in my life up to now. And yes, it was tied up with power, but also with place. In the Com, it hadn't worked out. Jemeret thought that was a power issue. I wasn't confident enough on the topic to doubt him. Here in Caryldon, it had been pretty damned splendid. What would happen when we were back in the Com again?

"Make yourself relax, and go to sleep," Jemeret said in a low voice.

I burrowed back against his chest and complied.

11. Going Forward

Early the next morning, we parted from Ashkalin, who would seek high ground, watch what happened when we crossed the border, then return to Salthome to report to his people and—via Paja messenger—to the other tribes that we had safely boarded his ship and sailed off in the calm between Severance Storms. He mounted his tivong, and Jemeret and I went to bid him farewell.

The Lord of the Marl leaned down from his mount and offered Jemeret his hand. "May the stars give you solid ground again," he said gruffly, an old seafarer's blessing.

Jemeret nodded his thanks and clasped the hand. When he released it, Ashkalin looked at me. I read him quickly and knew his feelings toward me were still mixed: composed of a small portion of sexual desire; a larger portion of unavoidable anger, well contained; some admiration; and a healthy amount of simple hope.

"I'll try to see that your son didn't die for no reason at all," I said.

He blinked once, taken by surprise, then held out his hand to me. "I hope we meet again, Lady Ronica."

"So do I."

He held my hand a moment longer than he needed to, then dropped it, straightened, turned his mount, waved his guards to follow, and started his journey home. In ten minutes we had packed up and started ours.

Tynnanna reached the border first, bounding down off the high plateau into the edge of the Honish forest, which gave some camouflage even on this side of the boundary. We followed him.

Our advance guards had already placed the army for us, and Jemeret and I used the Honish's gross emotions to pinpoint the Beckanees and the Lewannees in the mass of people. We had decided—for reasons that remained unclear but felt right—that I would concentrate on the Lewannee men and Jemeret would take the Beckanees. We would use the starfire smoke like a fog to obscure all the view possible, but especially around us. The location was far enough from the sea marshes so that morning fog was a relative rarity, and until we created it, there had been no hint of any.

The Honish men were confident; they had no reason not to be. They far outnumbered us, and what they called the "Samish arts" had never been known to stop a projectile.

I read our own people as we approached the border, and without exception they were all feeling a calm determination, a trust in my lord and me which I found almost unbearably touching. It was not beyond the realm of possibility that some of us would die here, and yet I sensed no fear in anyone. How much of it was simple disbelief in that possibility, the human failing of thinking ourselves immortal, and how much something entirely different, I didn't know. I would feel the same sense of ineffable gratitude each time this precise situation arose, when people with faith in us put themselves in peril because of that faith. In many ways, I still find it inexplicable.

I glanced back up toward the plateau, looking for Ashkalin and his men on the Samish side, but not finding them by sight and not willing to cast for them. I wished them well, hoping they were wishing us the same. Everyone was prepared to move as soon as we signaled. We wanted no hesitation, no chance for the Honish—slower than we were simply by virtue of their numbers—to try to move on us while we stood still.

As the sunlight gilded the crowns of the trees, we reached the frontier itself, and Jemeret and I looked at each other from the backs of our tivongs, touched each other with our stings, and acted.

I pathfound my brow-crown, asking it to release its energy,

and the fog spread out, glowingly bright. At precisely that moment, Sandalari began to sing.

Like most agricultural societies, the Honish were very superstitious about the weather. Their rituals to propitiate the natural forces of sun, rain, hail, and wind, to magnify times of plenty and lessen times of want, had evolved into elaborate, often beautiful, prayers which they sang in worship services in their fields and pastures. Sandalari's voice was priestess-trained, and it was as strong and as lyrically exquisite as Lyrafi's. I sensed that the fog would also lift it and carry it along, magnifying its sound in the same way the cave on Zuglith played with sound.

When Jemeret first suggested stinging the families of the Honish leaders, I had wanted to imbue them with the sort of panic that would make them need to break and run away. Jemeret smiled and said, "You still have a tendency to think in terms of all or nothing. When superstition is at work, a little distress should be more than enough. We don't have to do it all. We can let them work for us."

So as the smoke spread out, a glowing fog in the otherwise clear morning, and Sandalari sang the Honish Song of Punishing Weather, Jemeret and I projected the kind of anxiety that arises in a religious person at odds with his deity. They would feel uneasiness, guilt, a sense of failure, of wrongness.

And as they tried to deal with that, bathed in the almost subliminal pathos of a prayer that they feared the need for and tried to avoid, we moved forward slowly, shielded by the fog.

We made it the entire way through the army of Honish guards and a good distance through the forest before we urged our mounts into a gallop. We knew, from maintaining contact with them, that the Lewannee men were actually less fearful than those of the Beckanees, but the latter were so determined to assert their own superiority that they forced the issue. The argument, blessedly, took a long, long time. Superstition, internal rivalry, and bewilderment are a powerful combination.

Venacrona crossed into Samish lands far ahead of the rest of us, and, traveling alone, managed to sneak past the scattered Honish patrols on this side of their lands. When he signaled back to us that he was safe, Jemeret pulled me in and used my reserves, along with his own, to bubble us. Sandalari's singing was halted by the bubble, but that was probably a good thing, because she'd been singing steadily for almost eight hours, and the sun had already gone down.

Once Jemeret took my reserves, I had to let the starfire's smoke return to the crown, and for the first time we could clearly see where we were. We had, of course, left the bulk of the army hours behind us. Unfortunately, the Honish guard patrols at the border saw us coming and knew who we were. The bubble meant they couldn't hear us, but they showed up just as the fog dissolved.

I discovered firsthand that a bubble had no effect on an agerin pellet. One of the men, weapon already nocked and ready, fired before Jemeret or I, near exhaustion from the long drain on us throughout the day, could sting any of them.

Time slowed down and I was able to gauge the trajectory of the pellet as it headed for my chest. Then Tynnanna roared and, almost too fast to see, sprang at Rocky, who reared, startled. The pellet dug into my thigh. I damped down my pain receptors, though not soon enough to stop the stab.

Jemeret's rage swept out past me, and a full quarter of the patrol dropped. Gundever, Henion, Sabaran, and Sheridar, along with most of the guards, were firing back almost at once. For a few moments the air seemed thick with arrows and pellets. The bubble had dissolved, Jemeret knowing it was useless once the firing started, and needing to conserve his rapidly waning energy.

Then the opposition was still, and we were pounding furiously across the scant remaining distance to our own lands. Three of us had been injured, Sheridar the most severely. As we all pulled to a halt, on our own territory at last, flinging ourselves from our lathered tivongs, Sabaran supported his son's weight down off his mount.

Jemeret touched me long enough to ascertain that I was all right, then stumbled down off Vrand and went to Sheridar. Coney had helped Sandalari, who was as good as exhausted herself, then came to me. "Jemeret needs you more," was all I said to him.

Venacrona and Gundever came to help me. I'd shut off the pain immediately, and I forced myself to concentrate on my own leg. The pellet had lodged against my thigh bone, but had fortuitously not shattered it. I diagnosed a hairline fracture and took the time to knit the bone cells back together again before I looked up at Venacrona's anxious face. "Get the guards set up in case they come after us," I said to him, and he gestured to Henion to see to it. I took a moment to glance quickly around, and only one of the Nedi guards had been hit, but the wound was clearly mortal. In the Com, he might have been saved. Here, there was neither technology, time, nor energy to accomplish that.

"Gundever, can you use your shortsword to dig the pellet out?" I asked him. "It won't hurt me."

The young guardsman drew his smaller sword and knelt next to my leg, sliding his gloved hand most of the way down the blade and pausing briefly. "Should I burn the blade first?" he asked. "I may have to go pretty deep."

"My body will automatically act as an infecticide," I said. "Just dig."

Venacrona clasped my hand in his. "You're trembling. You draw strength from Gund. I'll get the pellet out."

Gundever gratefully surrendered the blade, sat down beside me and took my hand out of Venacrona's. "He'll do a better job anyway," he said to me. "Take as much of my energy as you need to hang on."

Until his words actually registered, I didn't realize how apt a description "hang on" really was. My reserves were nearly all depleted without my realizing it—the result of pathfinding the crown, stinging the Lewannees, yielding my strength to Jemeret, and then taking the pellet. I grasped at Gundever's currently greater strength and drew in enough to stabilize myself before I could do the reserves any further injury. I'd been talentless once for a tenday; I didn't want to have to confront that situation again. Gundever rocked a little, and I hastily scaled back my demands, embarrassed.

"Almost there," Venacrona said distractedly, and a moment later, "The pellet's out." I began to rebuild the shattered cells, vessel and muscle both. Only when I thought I had done enough to avert serious injury did I draw myself back and, exhausted, lie panting.

Sheridar was fully conscious now, working on himself, and he nodded to the men around him. Sabaran briefly embraced Jemeret, and he and Henion bent to pull my lord to his feet. Jemeret looked over at me, his own weariness evident. "Hard as it may be to go on," he said, "I think we have to put distance between us and the border." For a moment he was almost angry again. "I didn't want anyone to die, so I'm sorry, Henion, about Medio. And I think I may have blasted one of the Honish guards too strongly. I lost my temper when they almost succeeded in killing Ronica."

I wanted to say I hadn't been in any real danger, but memory conjured the picture of the pellet headed for my chest, and Tynnanna making Rocky leap to move me out of death's path.

We buried the Nedi guard, but there was no time for ceremony over him. Then we stripped the gear from the tivongs wounded in the attack, for they had suffered more than we, being larger and easier to hit. When we remounted, Sabaran and his son rode double, as did Coney and Sandalari. Henion mustered the remaining guards and brought up the rear, protecting us as we went northeast, deep into the night.

By the time we stopped at last, near dawn, we were almost at the end of our strength, and it was threatening an icy winter rain, not, thank the stars, a storm. No one bothered with food. We just found a relatively sheltered clearing in the forest north of the Plain of Convalee, set up all the canvas shelters, fed the tivongs, rolled ourselves into our blankets, and slept or deeped, depending on our individual power levels. Sabaran gave the guards only one-hour watches, to ensure their continual freshness, but we were undisturbed for the long hours we needed to rest.

Avoiding war is sometimes more costly in talent than allowing war to be fought. We had been taught that in the Com, where we were carefully instructed in the process of balancing the costs of scenarios. There on Caryldon, we could not have fought the Honish army simply due to the strength of their numbers, but we could have eliminated the patrol with relative ease. Jemeret had chosen to try to avoid the killing, and had failed at the border. We paid a pricc for that in our own bodies and in the life of one of us. I don't think I realized it then, but I was coming to believe it was the only price we had the right to pay.

When I swam upward from deeping into sleep, then snapped alert, my back was nestled against Jemeret's chest and my nose was buried in the fur of Tynnanna's shoulder. I snorted, and the cat rolled away from me, stretched elaborately, and got to his feet. Jemeret stirred, wakeful, too.

"Are you all right?" he asked, touching me with his sting.

I moved around to face him, still lying in his arms, touching him back. "Reserves full again," I said. "You?"

He nodded. "I keep wondering how long I'll be this resilient," he said in a low voice. "Someday I'll reach the point where one day's deep won't fill me. I wonder how old I'll be when it happens."

"You can ask Jasin Lebec," I said, "when you see him." My own voice suddenly shook, and I gathered and controlled it.

He tensed briefly when I mentioned Jasin Lebec. Then he raised himself on one elbow, watching me. "What just happened?"

I debated what I really wanted to say. "Sandalari keeps talking about 'going back to the Com' as if it's some sort of adventure. She's looking forward to it. And I know I'm going because I'm oath-bound to. Jemeret, I think I can go to the Com, but I don't think I can go *back*."

He smiled. "If you can't go back, love," he said, "then go forward instead."

Sheridar was almost completely well when we left thc Gendals at the Forge, and Henion and his people had already returned to the Nedi. I had healed my wound completely after all my strength was back, and was able to help Sheridar see how to continue with his own healing. I was beginning to learn not to try to do everything myself, just to guide and teach, as I had Shantiah at Midwinter Song. Jemeret watched me, but said nothing. Sometimes I thought Tynnanna watched me, too.

Only the Boru and Sandalari made the long run north. She'd taken leave of the Genda before we departed and was now an incipient Boru herself, though we would have no time for a formal induction ceremony before we went off-world. Another Severance Storm was due, and we raced it the final days, doing the steep climb into the valley that sheltered the home of the Boru at a speed that made footing treacherous. Tynnanna raced along ahead of us, his fur ruffled by the rising wind. He was capable of traveling much faster than we were; indeed, he could have gotten to the top in a fraction of the time it took us. He stayed with us, however, sometimes running up the nearly vertical walls beside the flatter track and then returning to pace us again. I expected him to peel off from us before we reached the village proper, for he never spent the storms with us, but this time he stayed close to my stirrup.

Jemeret had called ahead, stinging Tuvellen, his second-in-command, and Sejineth, the tivong keeper. In the face of the storm, which was nearly upon us, they met us in the deserted village. Everyone else was locked in their homes or at their assigned tasks, sheltered from the violent weather. Wordlessly, the two men took the tivongs from us and went to put them away. Venacrona spoke to both of them quickly before he, Coney, and Sandalari ran to the temple, closer to the tivong barns than our house was. The guards split off for the house of men, and Gundever ran for his home. Even before the guards and Gundever reached their destinations, Jemeret and I had stung them carefully to eliminate the memory of our skirmish with the Honish and implant the false memories of returning to Stronghome alone, of seeing the four of us departing with Venacrona toward the cove containing Ashkalin's ship.

When we reached the porch of our house, my lord paused for a moment in the face of the powerful wind and made certain that Tuvellen and Sejineth had understood Venacrona's swift orders to say nothing about our return. He was, I knew, ready to sting them as well, but he seemed satisfied by what he learned. I didn't try to probe them along with him, because I wasn't at all certain what he was looking for.

He signaled me to get inside just as the wind was threatening to push me over, and Tynnanna, who had, surprisingly, accompanied us all the way to the house, used his powerful body, his shoulder the height of mine now as he reached his full growth, to block the strongest gusts. Nevertheless, I was still almost lifted off my feet and slammed into Jemeret. My lord caught my arms and jerked me back upright as he swung the door open for us. Tynnanna followed us in.

Numima wasn't there tending the house. She, like the others in the village, had not known when we would return; if we worked our visit here correctly, no one would know we'd been here at all except for Tuvellen and Sejineth. Somehow, Jemeret and Venacrona would make certain that they told the same story Gundever and the guards did: that Gundever had come back with the guards but without the rest of us—Venacrona would be returning from the Genda later, and Jemeret and I had gone in search of the fabled Isle of the Wise at the request of the starfire.

We left our boots and cloaks by the door and Tynnanna settled on the hearth, waiting for someone to light the fire for him. We went into our bedroom to change into dry clothes while the house shivered in the wind. Jemeret pulled on a loose pair of leggings and his robe, then watched me brush my travel-tangled hair in front of the polished metal mirror above the trunk in our dressing room. For a few minutes I brushed vigorously at the light brown mass, but then my motions slowed. I stared at his reflection, burnished by the mirror as he lounged negligently in one of the fireplace chairs, his eyes on me.

"What?" he asked when I stopped moving, the hairbrush cradled in one palm.

I turned toward him. "I was just thinking how happy I am to be back here, that I finally have someplace I can call home, and it's ironic that just as I feel that way, we're leaving."

I expected him to say we'd be back, but he didn't. Instead he shifted in the chair and swung one of his legs over a chair arm.

"We need to talk a little about that, Ronica. If I know the Com at all—and I think I do—there's a strong possibility that once we get there, they'll try to separate us."

The words thrust a stab of fear through me. I thought that I could face anything at all if he were with me. Alone, I wouldn't be his Class A any longer, and then who would I be? But I knew he was right. We were both Class A's. It was government policy to use talent on separate assignments once their training was complete, except of course for Sinet and Lage. "We can't let them separate us," I said as steadily as I could.

"I agree." He nodded once. "I've thought of a number of different scenarios, and I believe our most effective approach will be to tell them we're married."

Knowing the reputation of the Honish institution of marriage among the tribes of the Samoth, I was vastly surprised, but it did make sense. Braceleting was unique to the Samothen, and it was a largely spiritual and emotional bond. Neither of those qualities was valued by the Com politicians or the MIs. Spirituality was to be publicly tolerated and privately disparaged by those in power. The MIs found such feelings disruptive rather than valid, viewing them as a problem to be overcome, not a factor to be weighed in the forecasting models. Marriage, on the other hand, was a legal bond with economic overtones and political consequences, and that the Com understood very well.

Jemeret watched me conclude that he was right, then went on, his voice a little gentler. "And since you're under oath to the Com, and I'm not, I believe I'd better be the husband."

I felt a smile pull at the corners of my mouth. "I used to wonder if I'd ever marry," I said, a little apologetically, "and I'd always conclude I wouldn't, but if by some chance I did, I was certain *I'd* be the husband."

He smiled back, his expression slightly amused. "I guessed that," he said. "And for anyone except me, man or woman, you probably would have been. For purposes of what we want to try to do in the Com and this marriage, however, you have to agree to be the wife."

In a second or two I'd considered all the arguments, all the options, and I knew he was once again right. I lowered my head and went back to brushing my hair. "Yes, all right," I said. "I suppose I do already think of you as my lord; you might as well be my husband, too." I tried not to sound grudging.

He got to his feet and came to put his arms around me, taking the hairbrush from my fingers and brushing the last tangled section of my hair. His hands were gentle, and I felt that he was trying to master a sadness I hadn't previously been aware of. He felt my inquiry.

"At the border," he said, "I lost my temper, and I used an unmodulated stroke of the sting. I may have killed one of those soldiers. I was too tired to control it, but if I hadn't been so tired, I might have killed more. And Medio died, too."

I recognized all the symptoms. "Jemeret, you did the best you could, and you know it. You've taught me to try and forgive myself when I do something—" I searched for the right word. "—flawed. Don't tell me I have to remind you."

"No," he said, still smiling, his hands moving steadily over my hair. "I just need to stop at the temple before we actually leave for the spaceport. I want to perform the starfire ritual for expiation. It's a sure antidote to sorrow over the misuse of power, and when talent dies as well as the untalented, it's absolutely necessary."

In the mirror, I met his gaze. "You mean there's a ritual I can use to help me say I'm sorry I killed Kray?"

"If you're so inclined." He gathered my hair into his left hand and held it. "Just decide what you're really sorry about before you perform the ritual."

I thought about that as he put the hairbrush down and let go of my hair. I wasn't sorry I had defended myself against the attack or tried to keep the rape from happening. I wasn't sorry I had recovered from the suicide attempt, and I would never need to ask for expiation for that. But I had known, somewhere inside, the moment I hit Kray with the sting, that my action was inappropriate, even immoral. A physical kill was something entirely different; other people could do it, too. It was not so shameful an act. Killing with the sting was an abuse of power unlike any the human race had ever seen. I had to think more about that, so I filed it at the back of my mind.

Memory nudged me. I turned to face Jemeret, unwilling to look only at his reflection. "You killed Kowati with the sting without falling into this kind of remorse."

"Kowati betrayed the tribe," Jemeret said evenly, "and the tribe is more important than any individual." He paused for a moment, but I sensed he wasn't done, so I waited. "And there was another reason. You hated yourself because—at least in part—you believed no one else had ever used the sting to kill. I knew it would help you to accept your action if you knew I'd done it, too. But I did the expiation ritual for it later."

Once again his wisdom came as a surprise to me. I said, "I think it'll be an interesting experience to be in the Com with you, even as your wife."

From the other room there was a crash, and we went out to find the scattered pieces of a large bowl in which Tynnanna had hoped to find something to eat. We took some meat from the cold storage box, whose small openings admitted air from outside, put it in another bowl, and let the klawit retire to the hearth with it. He was large enough now so that his body blocked half the fireplace, and he was not gentle about devouring his dinner. While he ate we picked up the pieces of the first bowl.

"We ought to have some food, too," I said.

He nodded, and Tynnanna snorted in our direction and went on eating, adjusting the meat between his paws.

Jemeret fished up some dried fruit and biscuits. "Sit down and take some of this," he said. "Then I have to make a call."

The eftel was right in our house, in a recess beside the main room fireplace, disguised as part of the wall. There was something entirely incongruous about the sight of my lord easily holding an example of the best and most expensive technology the Com had to offer, a symbol of the strongest empire in millennia. It put me back in touch with everything I thought had been lost to me forever, and neither the storm nor the distance was an obstacle to it, as they were to so many other things.

"There's a storm here now," my Lord Jemeret said to

whomever was on the other end of the connection, up on the station. "Confirm it on your tracers, and when you see it move away, send a lander with room for four."

Some instinct prodded me unexpectedly. "Six."

He glanced at me, not understanding.

"Six," I repeated. "Please tell them that."

He hesitated a moment, then said, "Correction. Room for six."

I felt immediately better, confirmed.

"Excuse me," Jemeret said abruptly, in the kind of tone that implied he was impatiently overriding some sort of stupidity, "but I wasn't asking you for anything. I'm telling you to send down a Line-2 lander when the storm is over." He broke the connection, shaking his head, and sealed the eftel back into its compartment. "Six?"

"You, me, Coney, Sandalari, and Tynnanna, who needs room for two. He saved my life when the Honish guards shot at us. We're going into a situation where I want that kind of loyalty with me." He smiled, nodded a slow agreement, took my hand in his. I didn't add that where Tynnanna went, the voice of the starfire went also.

The cat was washing his face, fastidiously unconcerned. Jemeret kissed my wrist, moving on from there. I put aside the thought of being his wife in the eyes of a Com whose only real knowledge of me was not to my credit, and slid closer to him.

The storm lasted five days, and when it broke, Jemeret left the house at once to speak with Tuvellen about his approaching absence. The cover story Venacrona would tell, of our sailing to find the Isle of the Wise, he and Sejineth would reinforce; Gundever and the guards would also stand as proof. We believed our tribe would want their leaders to discover the ancient secrets; it would cement our leadership of the Samothen as little else could have. It might have given the tribes additional leverage with the Honish, as well. I thought that they would probably have found it hard to believe the truth of the secret we already knew, but it bothered me that we were not willing to trust our people well enough to tell them that truth.

"When I've finished with Tuvellen, I'll go on to the temple," Jemeret said. "It's still early enough so that most of the tribe won't be awake, and we can be away before there's much activity to stifle. Coney's out walking around—Venacrona couldn't stop him—and he should get here before I get back. You two meet me over there."

Tynnanna rose and stalked out after him. The klawit had gone out every day of the storm, in any stray lulls, but he'd always returned quickly, and by the last day we knew he was as careful about not being noticed as if he knew that we didn't want it known we'd returned to Stronghome.

"I keep feeling that I should pack things, but then I wonder what," I said as Jemeret fastened his cloak. "I think it would probably be ill-mannered to take the crowns."

He smiled. "Just the nomidars and Tynnanna," he said. I was pleased we were taking the stringed, sympathetic instruments with us. I smiled back at him. "Dress warmly. It's hours to the spaceport." Then he and the klawit were gone, Tynnanna's huge shoulders momentarily threatening to push out both sides of the door frame.

I was alone in our house. I dressed in thick leggings and a laba-fur tunic that made me feel a little like a child's bugbear. I draped my hooded cloak over one of the couches, put the two nomidars on top of the cloak, and then I had nothing else to do.

We were really going to the Com, leaving Caryldon, the wilderworld I'd grown so used to. Leaving home. I wandered from room to room, running my fingertips lightly over the surfaces, impressing on myself the dimensions and textures of the place. It felt safe, and I nearly laughed. I'd always thought my safety would be automatic, coming from my own talent and from the esteem in which the Com held Class A's. Now I knew it had to come from deeper within me than talent alone, and I was infinitely grateful that Jemeret was coming with me.

Coney rapped on the door and opened it as I was coming out of the kitchen. He was dressed much as I was, his cloak already fastened. He had never looked entirely comfortable in the clothing of Caryldon, and he was a little uneasy now. I kissed him lightly on the cheek. "Even when I knew there was a way off this world, I didn't think it would actually come to this," I said.

"I did," he said. "Trying to make it happen more quickly was the only real doubt I had. When you set foot on Markover Station, I've completed my first Class C assignment."

"Congratulations." I didn't mean it to sound sarcastic, but he flushed, and I looked down at my cloak and the pair of nomidars. "I suppose they'll give you another, and that will take you away from us." I had to look up at him again.

His light brown eyes went thoughtful. "Perhaps," he said slowly, "but I think there's a chance that they may want to use me to try to influence you. And Jemeret. If that's the case, they'll send us on the same assignments." He glanced at the door, as if expecting Jemeret to come in. "Or they may want me with you, and Jemeret somewhere else."

I shook my head. "I'm his wife," I said deliberately. "I accepted the role, and he would have to relinquish his authority. He won't do that."

Coney smiled. "Clever," he said appreciatively. "I suppose Sandi and I could do something along those lines. The Com's a big place."

"Sandi?" I repeated.

"It went with 'Coney,' " he said. "Are you nervous?"

I was, and I saw no reason to deny it, not to him. "Some. I know more about the Com and the government than I used to, and I'm beginning to feel that may be a detriment."

He nodded once. "I know what you mean." His mouth twitched a little. "I keep telling myself that I know how to do this. I know how to deal with the people, at any rate, and I don't have to deal with the MIs."

"Except for Mortel John." It was out before I realized I'd said it.

Coney shook his head in disbelief. "I still can't accept that, even though I'm sure it's true."

"Oh, it's true. No wonder he could hold out so well against

my sting that time I stung him. Next time I'll pathfind him and be done with it." I must have sounded angry.

Coney said softly, "Easy, Ronnie. I think you'd better hold back—at least at first. They don't have any reason to believe you're personally hostile to them, and I've seen how they act around Jemeret. The dislike is mutual, so they're very wary. It's a measure of how much they want you back that they're willing to deal with him at all."

I felt a rush of the old pride in my self-importance, the feeling the government completely encouraged in me the whole time I was in training. Now I laughed at myself.

Coney was watching me closely. "You have to be careful. They remember how you were. They were afraid all along that Jemeret might change you, but it would probably be better if you didn't let on how much."

"You've changed, too," I said on impulse. "I felt it from the very first."

His expression was serious. "Yes, well, with you in the radiant tank and Kray in postmortem preservation, I lost my innocence pretty damned quickly."

"Not entirely." I whispered it. "You're still an Epicyclist, after all."

Coney's face altered swiftly. "Ronnie, my faith is not a result of innocence. It grows out of hope. There is a considerable difference."

I didn't want to respond to that; I still couldn't see faith the way he saw it. "Jemeret said you went out walking. Why?"

He grinned at me sheepishly. "I love this place," he said softly.

I realized that I wasn't the only one who wanted to stay. It somehow embarrassed me. "We'd better get over to the temple now," I said. "Jemeret said he'd meet us there, and it's almost false dawn."

Coney took the nomidars while I pulled my cloak on, and with only one glance backward at the warm little house, barely visible against the beginning of the light on the snow, I followed him down the path toward the temple.

Sejineth waited outside with five tivongs and Tynnanna, and

at the door of the temple itself were Sandalari and Venacrona, cloaked for travel. Jemeret was coming up from the village, moving quickly and quietly. Coney went to stand by Sandalari, who smiled up at him, then looked at me.

"How long do you think it will take you to find the Isle?" Sejineth asked me.

"We don't know where the Isle is," I said, avoiding the question. "We'll be back as soon as we can."

Jemeret had joined us by that time. "Wait here," he said to the others. "There's one last thing to do inside."

Venacrona led the way up to the starfire chambers on the second floor, and Jemeret took my arm and steered me along with him. Without hesitation, the two men turned and walked into the chamber where thin sheets of blue mica surrounded the overhead lamp. I stood uncertainly in the doorway for a moment, for my own instinct had been to go into the central chamber, the one for all the star colors.

"Here," Jemeret said, holding out his hand to me.

Venacrona was setting out a small wooden bowl with a sweet-smelling spice powder in it. "I'll leave you," he said, "and I'll be outside."

"Thank you," my lord said softly.

It was, I realized, the first time he and I had been alone in the calm quiet of the temple. "Why the blue chamber?" I asked him. The walls and the altar played with the sound in strange ways, just as the cave of the starfire metal had.

"Blue is the color of life," Jemeret said, "in our color lore, at any rate. But if you think about it, the blue worlds are the best to settle on. The blue stars have the longest lives ahead of them." He took off his cloak and dropped it against one of the walls. "It's in the face of life that I need to atone for taking life."

Before he'd quite finished the last word, the whoosh of the starfire's arrival permeated the room, and a faint blue glow colored everything. It surprised me, because it was warm, and I'd never associated heat with the starfire before.

Jemeret took a handful of the powder and tossed it into the blue flame, his eyes fastened on the pale brightness. "I've come to acknowledge that I took a life which was not mine to take," he said. "I've misused the power of which I am caretaker, and the one I harmed is beyond my reach. As he cannot give me forgiveness, I place my fault in the hands of the force which created that power."

He rested his palms flat on the altar top and bowed his dark head until the column of starfire nearly touched his hair. A tendril of the flame emerged beneath his lowered face and caressed his forehead. The heat seemed to ebb out of the flame, sinking downward in cavalier defiance of physics.

Jemeret straightened as the tendril retreated, his soft gray eyes looking blue in the reflection from the starfire. Even without making any effort to read him, I knew that the pain he'd been feeling had gone out of him, and he'd come to an acceptance of what he'd done.

"Do I do that?" I asked him.

"If you want to."

I nodded once, tossed my cloak on top of his, and crossed the chamber to stand beside him in front of the glowing altar. The spice powder felt gritty against my palm. As I scattered it into the blue column, the warmth seemed to return to the fire.

"I've come to acknowledge that I took a life which was not mine to take," I said, but before I could say anything else, the entire chamber seemed to reverberate as the starfire column shook.

Jemeret said quietly, "Lives."

"What?" I looked at him, surprised. I had only Kray on my conscience.

"You cannot just atone for one when you carry two," he said. "When I was healing you, I studied a great deal about your past. I wanted to rebuild the correct brain. When you were barely nine, you used your sting to kill a man who attacked the three of you with a nerve blaster."

The hitch. I'd killed him with the sting, and they'd never told me. They'd shielded me from the knowledge, and my ignorance had probably made it easier for me to use against Kray a weapon I'd already used once with impunity. And I'd only been a child.

Jemeret watched me adjust to the new knowledge. "Even as a child, you were stronger than they thought you'd be."

"But not smarter."

"The potential was there," my lord said, his voice as gentle as his eyes.

I swallowed, told myself to accept it, and repeated the phrases Jemeret had spoken to the starfire, but in the plural. The words resonated within me, shaking me at a cellular level, and I drew in a shuddering breath as I leaned on the altar. The resonance inside me was painful, making me ache in response to it.

The starfire's blue tendril rose and touched my forehead. The ache and the resonance drained away in a cool, soothing glow that sank into me. I still recognized that a misuse of power was a shameful thing, but I could understand that flaws did not of themselves invalidate a person's worth. I could resolve to try to keep from repeating my error. I could depend on Jemeret to help me. And I could recognize intellectually that I might fail in that attempt without needing to destroy myself. I almost added "again" to that, but I had been saved from self-destruction by the man who stood beside me. It wasn't visceral knowledge yet, but it was a beginning. The tendril withdrew, and the blue light vanished as the starfire slid back into its bowl.

I blinked away unexpected tears, and reached out to put my arms around Jemeret. "Are you all right?" he asked. I nodded against his chest, which moved under my cheek as he spoke. "We may not be able to perform this ritual in the Com."

"Do you think we'll be killing anyone?"

"I hope not, but all things are possible."

We picked up our cloaks and left the temple.

Sejineth had turned over the reins of the tivongs to Venacrona, and now he nodded briefly to Jemeret, a bit longer to me, and then looked back at the Lord of the Boru again. "I wish you well," he said a little stiffly. Jemeret nodded in return.

I couldn't help feeling he deserved a little more, as Shantiah had deserved it. "Tuvellen will depend on you for help," I said.

"We won't forget, and when we return from the Isle of the Wise, you will be suitably rewarded."

The lean, rough-faced tivong keeper I had known since my first days on this planet nodded once again at his chief, then looked back at me. "You'll be sailing in strange waters, Lady Ronica," he said. "Have a care."

I almost told him he was more right than he might ever know. "Thank you," was all I said.

He turned and disappeared into the slowly lightening dawn.

"Power?" Coney asked Jemeret.

"More than he uses," Jemeret said. "He's one of those Boru who could do more than they choose to or learned how to. When his father lost the chieftainship, and Sejineth knew he wasn't strong enough to challenge me, he stopped trying to use a lot of his power, except with the tivongs." He looked momentarily thoughtful. "I might have encouraged him more than I did." He took Vrand's reins from Venacrona. "Let's get away."

I mounted Rocky, calming my abruptly racing heart. In a way, it was ludicrous. I was returning to a world I'd been raised to influence and rule, and I was nervous and uncertain, because I was no longer who I'd been. I fiercely put it down. As Coney had said, I could do this.

In point of fact, I *had* to do it. Somebody was trying to destroy talent, if the murders of two small children were any indication, and the MIs—which had not stopped me from killing Kray—were unlikely to be applying much in the way of resources to the problem. Jemeret might well be right that the rest of us were not in danger, but the third child, Tial Borland, clearly would be. And Jemeret had shown me that one of the purposes of talent was the protection of talent. I wanted to do that.

Then, too, I wanted the government, especially the members of the Tribunal, to see that I was not the mindless, helpless wreck they remembered. I had enough pride remaining to want their good opinion; I think I felt I still deserved it, had worked hard to earn it. I knew Jemeret didn't care what they thought of him, but I hadn't reached that point yet.

There was another reason, too, in its own way even more compelling, though I hadn't fully faced it yet. If there was any way to keep Jemeret from committing suicide by trying to eliminate the MIs, I had to be there to save him. He had saved me.

I used to think you could judge people best by what they had: their power, their decorations, the possessions they valued, the company they kept. And I still think you can know something about them by those criteria. But I think when you truly want to know someone, look first at their debts. People are to a great extent what they recognize they owe. When someone tells you he owes nothing to anyone, you know instantly who he is.

III. Markover Station

With Venacrona in the lead and Coney bringing up the rear, the five of us took the now-familiar road around the village, keeping ourselves slightly hidden in the trees. We made it onto the mountain track that led up Harrilith before the first rays of light gilded more than the uppermost peaks.

No one was moving in the houses yet, and if someone looked out the window and saw movement in the trees, they would think it was some forest creature seeking food before the onset of the next storm. If we returned—I made myself change that to *when* we returned—the entire population would turn out to greet us, but this was very different. As far as our tribe knew, we were not here at all.

We didn't talk much. Tynnanna had raced out ahead of us and vanished, as usual, but he was waiting for us at the crest of the track. We stopped there, and Jemeret and Coney dismounted immediately. Sandalari and I quickly followed. Venacrona uncoiled a length of rope from his saddle and we tied our tivongs to it, so he could lead them. He would take them on to the Genda, then return to Stronghome with a guard from Sabaran, as if he were only now, belatedly, returning from the peninsula. He would expound at length about our departure.

Only he was mounted now. "I'll see you safely to the second ledge before I continue down," he said.

"Be careful on the road south," Jemeret cautioned. "Tuvellen should do well enough, and I'll try to call you if I can. Follow me." The last was to the rest of us, and it sounded uncharacteristically brusque. I read him as we started to walk along the track, and he was tense and apprehensive. His normal confidence was there, but it had acquired a patina that contained it.

Suddenly he stepped to the left, onto a hidden trail entrance upslope of one of the huge boulders that lined that side of the track and which had concealed the trail quite effectively. We four could slip onto the trail and then into the narrow mouth of what turned out to be an equally narrow tunnel, but there was no way Tynnanna, with his wide shoulders, could follow.

The klawit was not deterred. He gave one growl as I lingered at the entrance watching him, and then he crouched, sprang upward over the boulders, and dashed straight up the slope, heading for a destination he already seemed to know.

The tunnel was long, but never completely dark, for it climbed gently upward, away from the descending track, close enough to the ground above it so that tiny shafts rose to the surface of the upper wall of Harrilith and provided, at intervals, light and fresh air. In addition to climbing, the tunnel curved toward the north, following the outer slope of the massive mountain.

In less than an hour we'd reached a thin ledge which also curved around one of the mountain's high faces. We couldn't see the track below until the point at which it reached the floor of the valley. Sandalari gave a small, nervous giggle, utterly unlike her. "The ledge will hold," Jemeret said almost absently. "It's just built to look as if it won't."

I glanced around, looking for Tynnanna, but he was nowhere in sight. We turned sideways and, balancing our nomidars, edged along the ledge to the narrow slit of another tunnel mouth. This one curved upward even more steeply. It was clear to me that the spaceport was at a much higher altitude than anything else on this world, perhaps because there would be significantly less chance of anyone seeing the flash of a lander.

By the time the second tunnel ended, more than an hour later, I was expanding my lung capacity to take advantage of every bit of oxygen in the rarefied air. I was certain the others had done the same.

The ledge the second tunnel gave onto was much wider and a little icier, though not considerably, and when we came out onto it, Jemeret turned and stared back and down the way we'd come. I looked where he was looking, altering my focus to see the barely discernible speck of dark against the white and gray background. That spot was, I knew, Venacrona with the tivongs, patiently waiting for us to arrive here, at this place. I felt Jemeret's signal to the priest, who probably would not have been able to see us, and the dark spot moved off, toward the crest of the pass leading to the rest of the world beyond Stronghome.

Coney put his arm across Sandalari's shoulders and hugged her briefly against his side. Jemeret touched me with the sting, and I felt his inquiry even before I saw it in his eyes.

"I'm all right," I said.

A smile flickered at the corners of his mouth, and he turned to lead the way across this ledge and around a peak of Harrilith into a flat area hidden on all sides by a bowl of other peaks. There was no snow on it, so I knew the material was not natural. In its center sat a Com lander, as shiny in the afternoon sun as any government vehicle I ever remembered; beside it, incongruous and imperturbable, sat Tynnanna, nearly tall enough so that his ears were level with the vehicle's roof. Now that the footing was secure, we accelerated into a run, all four of us keeping pace easily.

In less than fifteen minutes we were at the lander. It must have been programmed to admit anyone, for its door slid open at once, and Jemeret ducked inside to expand the opening to the "cargo" setting. By the time we climbed in, he had retracted two of the seats to make a cargo space that Tynnanna could fit into. The klawit didn't hesitate, just stepped inside and curled up as if he were in front of the hearth at home. By that time the other three of us had activated the seat fields while Jemeret sealed the craft for liftoff.

"It feels strange," Sandalari said. "I have a vague memory of things like this, but the recollections have become almost dreamlike. And now—here I am."

"Here we all are," Coney said. He looked at Jemeret. "Do you want to take it up, or should I?"

"Change first," my lord said. "Then you take it. I have to shave."

"I won't *hear* of it," I nearly shouted.

All three of them stared at me, and Jemeret laughed. "You know as well as I do that no one wears a beard in the Com."

"Set a new fashion." For some reason, I was very upset by the idea of the beard vanishing. He'd had it since the first day I'd seen him on Caryldon. The only time I remembered him without it, I had been in the tank, and I didn't want to be reminded of that. Inspiration struck, and I spun on Coney. "Grow a beard. Now. Sandal—Sandi, you don't mind, do you?"

Coney started to speak, then seemed to think better of it.

"Why should I mind?" Sandalari asked. "He's the same man with or without a beard."

"But it's not the same statement," I said, suddenly certain. "Jasin Lebec always did whatever the Com wanted. He was the perfect Class A. I will not be an unquestioning instrument of theirs anymore, and they already know that Jemeret won't be. We want them slightly off balance, and they *need* us. Coney . . ."

He studied me for a few moments, then looked at Jemeret. Incongruous as it was, because I considered the Com my ground, not Jemeret's, I waited to see if my lord would approve my choice.

"I am the husband," he said softly, "but I'm not a Brochidian husband. Coney, grow the beard. I'll change first, and I guess I'll take the lander up." He slid open the flight locker and looked at the jumpsuits hanging there. The Com had specified gold and bronze, indicative of our respective ranks. Jemeret made a small noise of disgust and pulled the nearest off its hanger, thumbing the label on. "Dark blue," he said. The color flowed downward from the collar. Jemeret carried the suit into the minuscule eliminatory, emerging a minute later fully dressed, his close black beard still intact.

Coney followed, first turning his jumpsuit to the same dark

blue. When he emerged, his new beard was just past the stubble stage. I wondered what they'd done with the tunics, leggings, and cloaks. The eliminatory would be too small to start piling them up.

"What's a Brochidian husband?" Sandalari asked while Coney was out of sight and Jemeret was taking the control readings prior to launch.

"Brochid is one of the many Com worlds where the local customs were very different when the Com took over," I answered, pulling out a jumpsuit and handing it to her, then taking another for myself. "Only men could be husbands, and they could only marry women. The women had to be completely subservient to the commands of their husbands, fathers, and brothers."

"Sounds like the Honish," she said, wrinkling her nose with distaste. "I wonder if all primitive, powerless societies structure themselves that way."

"Not all. Just the ones where the men can't bear competition from us." It was simplifying, and I knew it, but I was more nervous than I was willing to admit. "Anyway, the Brochidian men objected strenuously to the changes that being part of the Com would bring, and about half their women supported them. The other half went into revolt. By the time the Drenalion were sent in, a quarter of the women on the planet were dead. Ever since then, the term 'Brochidian husband' has been used to mean a person who demands obedience at all costs."

I pressed my jumpsuit label and said, "Dark blue." I didn't tell her that there was also an expression, "Brochidian marriage," which meant a marriage in which the husband—male or female—totally dominated the wife, to the point where obedience was no longer an issue and submission was automatic. It was a term of contempt among the people in the Com. Jara Deland had once told me she would never permit anyone to come to power in the government if she discovered they had an inclination to be Brochidian.

Sandalari nodded, and we took turns changing into our jumpsuits. Then, as it turned out the men had done, we fed our Caryldon clothes into the disposer. To me it was one more step away from my tangible ties to that world, leaving only the nomidars and the extremely tangible klawit lying on the cargo platform. I smiled. Whatever the Com might be expecting, we were unlikely to be it. Jemeret joined us in the seats and anchored the seat fields. The vehicle rose smoothly off the surface. I didn't turn to see how Tynnanna was taking the lift, and he made no noise.

Once we were under way, Jemeret threw the lander back on its own devices and rose, smiling at the three of us in our dark blue clothes. The choice of color puzzled me, and I asked him about it. He nodded approvingly at Coney's slowly thickening sandy beard, which was now as well-shaped as his own and only needed filling out.

"Dark blue's the color I've always worn in the Com," Jemeret answered me. "It was my student color when I was in training, and when they first offered me the right to wear gold, I laughed at them." His gray eyes slid down the form-fitting cloth on my body. "They'll wonder at your choice."

"You're my husband," I said as lightly as I could. "I can only be expected to follow your lead."

"Coney, you have the right to wear bronze," my lord said to the other man.

Coney grinned, and Sandalari cleared her throat. "Ah," she said, "that may be true, but we decided he should follow my lead in our marriage, and of course they have no hold on me."

We all grinned at one another then, and I beat back a pang of envy that she'd gotten to be the husband. Jemeret sensed it. "You're still High Lady," he said. "Think of the responsibility more than the honor."

"I'm trying to," I said. I'd been raised not to shirk responsibility, and Jemeret had shown me that responsibility was not synonymous with tyranny. The Com hadn't realized that yet.

We docked at the station with barely a bump, even though Jemeret had refused to let the lander dock itself and resumed control for the actual approach. Moments later I was plunged into the technological world of the Com.

I'd never been on a station before—not while I was aware

of being on one. These were not quite the marvels that the rollships were, but they were marvelous all the same, self-contained little worlds, though not self-sufficient. Markover Station was especially vulnerable, for its supply lines stretched a long way off. The smoothness of the deck under my jumpsuit boots felt very strange, almost disorienting, because the plasteel was perfectly flat. Only the familiar feel of my nomidar's neck against my palm—Sandalari was carrying Jemeret's—seemed to stabilize me as I stepped out of the lander onto the perfect surface. Jemeret widened the doorway, and Tynnanna uncoiled himself and padded out onto the landing deck beside us.

I swept the surrounding area and felt shafts of surprise from some of the station staff monitoring our landing. As I completed the sweep, I was brought up short by encountering someone I knew very well. Jasin Lebec was here on the station, and that was a stunning discovery. It meant that, contrary to all conventional wisdom, the Com had put both its Class A's, and Jemeret, whom it knew to be a Class A, in the same place.

Jemeret's head came up sharply, and I knew he'd discovered that Jasin Lebec was here as well.

A young woman in the tan jumpsuit of the Merchant Fleet guard, which was responsible for order in all but conditions of unrest, came up to the four of us. Her shoulders were squared, chin lifted, and she was full of bravado, but unable to keep her eyes from sliding continually to the furred bulk of Tynnanna, who seemed completely imperturbed by his surroundings. The MF guard glanced from me to Sandalari and back again. "Ronica McBride?"

"Yes?" I was almost astonished to hear the automatic arrogance that flavored the single word. This was a citizen of the Com, and I had been trained since just about birth to be entirely superior to such as she. It slid back around me with amazing ease, and I let it have its way.

She nodded to me in the required gesture of respect. "We greet you with all due honor," she said. "An eftel vid conference is being set up for you. Will you follow me, please?"

"I assume you are speaking to all of us." As I said it, I stung her a tiny bit to increase her uneasiness, and as a result she stuttered over her reply.

"Y-Yes, of course." She signaled, and a door irised open. She gestured toward it. I took one step, felt Jemeret's gentle sting, stopped and let him precede me. Sandalari and Coney followed me, and Tynnanna, who had been licking a massive paw with a nonchalant disdain which exceeded my own, rose to his feet, yawned elaborately, and trotted after us into the corridors of the station.

The MF guard had paused inside the irisway, and she was openly surprised when Jemeret was the first one to enter the station proper. "I can show you the way—" she began.

He cut her off. "I know my way around this station," he said sharply. "I assume it's in the conference room?"

I didn't reach out to see if he'd stung her; my guess was that he didn't have to. She looked a little frightened as she nodded, remembered herself, and stepped aside.

We followed him as he strode unerringly through the corridors until we reached a set of double doors, made of some sort of highly polished but artificial wood. There had been no other guards along the way, and the room itself was unguarded. I guessed that Markover was very lightly populated, which made Jasin Lebec's presence even more remarkable.

Jemeret stepped deliberately into the doors' range, and they slid smoothly and noiselessly back. The fact that they were planetside doors, not space irises, said a lot about the confidence that, though not heavily inhabited, the station was not at risk of any kind of attack.

Jemeret walked into the room, and I heard Jasin Lebec say calmly, "Hello, my boy. It's good to see you again."

I moved into the conference room and around my lord's broad shoulders, so I could see the Com Class A whom I was supposed to replace. Jemeret had not spoken.

Jasin Lebec had aged in the years since my last encounter with him, in my suite of rooms on Orokell. He looked far older than he had then, and some of his nearly youthful vigor, the purposefulness, was gone. His gold jumpsuit seemed to fit him more loosely, but I knew that had to be an illusion, because jumpsuits perfectly fit whoever wears them. His dark eyes flew to me, rich with sudden affection. "So you've come back to us, Ronica McBride." He did not try to disguise any of his relief or satisfaction.

I nodded once, not trusting myself to speak to him.

Coney and Sandalari came into the conference room, and behind them, Tynnanna stepped lightly over the door track.

Jasin Lebec did not even try to mask his surprise at the cat. Then he looked at Jemeret and chuckled. "You are determined to make everyone as uncomfortable as possible, then."

"As always," Jemeret said, almost lightly, though he could have said honestly that the klawit was my idea. "Ronica, this is my na-sire."

I had thought there would not still be surprises to come; I realized I'd made a foolish assumption. I stared from one to the other of them for a few moments, then fastened on the old man. "You're Jemeret's grandfather?"

Jasin Lebec nodded. "In an effort to breed more talent, I went back to Caryldon to sire a child, but—"

Jemeret overrode him smoothly. "My father didn't test as having a great deal of power. He seemed to develop as he grew older. The Com contented itself with several other children when he was young."

Jasin Lebec started to say something to Coney, but the clear bell tone announcing the completion of the eftel vid link sounded in the room, and the other side of the table from which we stood momentarily opaqued out as the transmissions balanced themselves. Jasin Lebec pulled out one of the chairs and sat down on our side, but the rest of us didn't sit. We did take advantage of the pause to set the nomidars down on the floor behind us.

The room sprang back into vision, and suddenly there were ten people on the other side of the table: five women, four men, and Mortel John. One of the women gasped at the sight of Tynnanna and half rose, then hurriedly resumed her seat, embarrassed at having forgotten we were many light-years apart.

I recognized Pel Nostro and his wife Jara Deland, the MI

Liaison, at once, and I made no attempt to look at anyone else, not even my old teacher.

"Are you well, Ronica McBride?" the Com Counselor asked with some hesitation, his face wary.

"Well enough, Pel," I said immediately. "My memory is back, my mind is intact, and I'm here."

Jara Deland seemed to hiss something at him, her lips barely moving. I wished we were all in the same room, so that augmented hearing and my sting might work effectively. I'd never felt the old saying, *Talent needs presence,* so keenly before.

"Please, sit down," Pel urged us.

Coney immediately did so, and Sandalari followed so quickly that they seemed to move simultaneously. I waited until they were seated between me and Jasin Lebec, and then I drew out a chair and perched on the edge of it, trying not to seem uncomfortable. After a long pause, Jemeret turned a chair to face him and straddled it, his arms across its back. We were both tense, both disguising it.

"Whyever did you bring the animal with you?" one of the other women asked.

I looked at her, realizing it was Science Bureau head Marga Morena.

"Marga, please," Pel said.

"No, I'll answer her," I said firmly. "We brought him because we thought we might want him. Hello, Marga."

She nodded at me, glanced at the others of us.

"Who's the blonde?" one of the men asked in a whisper meant to be heard.

Sandalari repressed a laugh without it ever appearing on her face.

"I suppose introductions are in order," Pel said as smoothly as he could.

Coney said, as if Pel Nostro had not spoken, "This is Sandi Gregson, my husband."

They gaped, except for Mortel John, as Sandalari said graciously, "It's very—interesting to be back."

It was Mortel John who said, "Exile has agreed with you, Sarai Gregson."

Her brilliant, musical laugh filled the room. "Is that what it was? Truly, I hadn't noticed."

A man I didn't know by sight, younger than the man who had asked the brusque question to begin with, gave a small, appreciative whistle. I knew then that while talent needed presence, beauty and vivacity transcended distance.

Pel Nostro regained his equilibrium before he spoke, a true diplomat. Then he perfunctorily introduced Mortel John, who of course knew all four of us, and my old teacher bowed his head in our direction. In his presence I could not think of him as anything but a man. He was the only one wearing a plain black jumpsuit, unbroken by any of the stylish decorations that sophisticated people affected to follow the changing trends in a largely jumpsuited society. Everyone else on their side of the table wore either gold or silver, and that meant Mortel John looked most like us. That was odd; odder still was that it made me feel almost fond of him.

The women at the table, besides Jara Deland and Marga Morena, were Petra Chantrey, head of the Universities, and the two Class B women I'd met when we were younger, who had slept joyfully with Kray—something I couldn't do. Sinet Coleby was almost fifty now, a breathtaking redhead with high cheekbones and a generous mouth. Lage N'Verre was in her mid-thirties, dark haired and voluptuous. My nod to them was colored by memories, and I read in their eyes—accustomed as I'd become to reading people without the sting—the knowledge of the man I'd killed.

Everyone else seemed willing, even eager, to forget it. But Sinet and Lage had known Kray intimately, shared his designation of Class B, and it was something more to them. In a way, I hated their being there, and at the same time, in another way, I was grateful for it. They were not ongoing members of the Tribunal, the Com's human governing body. Jasin Lebec would have informally represented talent, had he been there rather than here with us. As talent could only have nonvoting delegates on the Tribunal, the Class B women probably would not speak.

Also at the table was Anok Luttrell, head of the Merchant

Fleet, a clever man in his late sixties, who had danced with me at the gala after graduation, and who invariably kept his cleverness hidden until it was needed. He was the man nominally in charge of providing for the citizens of a provider society, working through the largest staff of deputies and subheads anyone had ever assembled.

The man who had whistled softly at Sandalari was introduced as Faucon Oletta, Chief Justiciar, interpreter of the Com laws. He had recently replaced the Chief Justiciar I remembered, and he seemed quite young for the responsibility.

The man who'd asked about Sandalari had cold eyes and heavy muscles. He was probably nearing fifty, and though I knew his name immediately, I'd never seen him before. He was Terrill Guthrie, the human in command of the regiments of the Drenalion. He had not been at graduation; he spent more time with the clones and the small science staff, on loan from Marga Morena, that celled, tanked, and grew them. His greeting to me was one of surface respect, but even with the barrier of the eftel vid, I sensed the darkness below the surface, as I'd sensed it in Krenigo of the Vylk. The two men in no way resembled each other physically, and yet the resemblance was real.

Jemeret was suppressing a genuine restlessness, which didn't lessen when I said calmly, "It's a pleasure. I'm sure you know all of us except Tynnanna. He's a klawit, and our companion."

All ten of the people shifted their eyes to Tynnanna, and Mortel John looked back at us first. Then Pel Nostro moved his gaze to my lord. "Jemeret Cavanaugh," the Com Counselor said formally, "you have fulfilled the terms of your contract with us, and we therefore release you from your obligation. You are free to return to Caryldon with our thanks."

Jemeret smiled, his eyes shooting silver sparks. "Not this time, Pel," he said, his shields up. "I'll be staying this time, at least until Ronica has been given and has made the choice you agreed to. You see, she's my wife."

If the announcement of Coney's relationship had caused astonishment, this declaration was world-shattering enough to allow a great deal of vid cost to accrue without anyone saying anything. Then Jara Deland choked back something she was about to say and Jasin Lebec chuckled, a tendency he quickly repressed.

We let the silence continue for a while longer. Then I broke it. "I understood you had an urgent need for my return. Coney was quite explicit on that point. Perhaps you might want to explain the urgency to me."

Pel Nostro moved suddenly, as if emerging from stasis, but before he could speak, Marga Morena asked sharply, "Ronica McBride, did you marry this man without compulsion and make a free choice of your role in the marriage?"

I raised my chin and looked at her directly. "Of course, Marga. You don't honestly believe I could be forced into such an arrangement, do you? Not honestly."

Jara Deland spoke then, her voice close to vitriolic. "You didn't have a mind when he got his hands on you. How can you be sure?"

For a split second anger overwhelmed me, but I fought it back, careful to hold my face neutral. I said as calmly as I could, "I distinctly remember both the marriage and the role choice, Jara. That indicates to me that I had a mind at that time. All indicators would point to the presence of a mind now, and I'm quite content with my status." I made my voice go low and hard, which wasn't at all difficult. "If we were in the same room, I have no doubts I could convince you." The threat was overt, palpable. I was quite proud of myself for having made it.

Jara Deland sat back in her chair, her hands in her lap, her brown eyes glittering. I fancied I saw a small movement, and thought that she'd just kicked Pel under the table.

"There is a Class A assignment which we wish to offer you," the Com Counselor said. His voice seemed rough, and he cleared his throat before continuing. "It concerns Barbin 3, where a segment of the population is in open revolt against the legitimately constituted planetary government, and there has been—" He was suddenly unable to look at our side of the room. "—an unfortunate loss of life. We need superior Class A talent to stop the rebellion without incurring a greater decrease in resources than has already occurred. We hope you will accept the assignment, Ronica McBride." He looked up, his nearly lashless eyes hopeful and wary at the same time. "If you choose to, Jasin Lebec will see that you're fully briefed."

I had already made a decision, long before the question was asked, in anticipation of this moment. I'm not certain when the notion had crystallized in my mind—probably sometime during the journey back to Stronghome from the peninsula. "My team and I will accept the assignment," I said, gesturing to my right, where Coney and Sandalari sat, trying not to look surprised. "I have no right to speak for my husband." It took all of my control not to stumble over that sentence. I might have been feeling somewhat submissive to Jemeret, but I didn't want to show it to the Tribunal.

Jemeret drawled almost lazily, "I will accept the assignment."

Jasin Lebec looked away from us, and I didn't have to touch him to know that he was vastly amused.

Pel Nostro repeated, "Your team?" He glanced at the other people on his side of the table. "I'm afraid—"

I overrode him as swiftly and smoothly as I could. "Pel, you're going to have to humor me. I've gone through a great deal since graduation, and I cannot allow you to cut me off from the people I need for support. You'll have to trust me enough to think that I know what I'm doing."

"I should think the beast would be more than enough," Terrill Guthrie said in another whisper clearly meant to be overheard.

"Perhaps for you," I shot back at him.

Jasin Lebec tapped his palm against the table several times. I realized he was indicating approval openly, not, as he could have, by projecting. I was grateful.

"Talent in teams?" Pel Nostro asked. "Jara, how do the MIs see that development?"

"Application," Jara Deland said.

There was a click that we all clearly heard even though it originated in the background of the other conference room.

The click was the equivalent of the MIs clearing their throats. Jara Deland seemed to snap to attention in her chair.

"It is our analysis that chances of success without further undue waste of resources are improved 64.3 percent by allowing this team approach to the problem," a disembodied voice said with the expressionless tonalities of every machine in the galaxy except Mortel John. "That is a significant enough margin so that we advise you to approve."

"Well done!" Coney hissed under his breath.

I hadn't expected the MIs to weigh in on my side, and I knew from the consternation Jemeret was projecting that he hadn't expected it either.

Anok Luttrell shifted in his chair, a half smile on his face. "We'll provide a Lumeship for you." He lifted a transit tracker from the table surface in front of him and pressed several keys. "We'll divert the *Megalume*, and it should reach you in forty-two hours, station time." He set the tracker down and let the table surface reabsorb it.

Pel Nostro rose. "We hope to see you on Orokell at the completion of your assignment, Ronica McBride," he said, adding as an afterthought, "And the rest of you."

The vid contact broke, and abruptly the other side of the room was empty. None of us moved for a very long moment. Then Sandalari asked gently, "Am I wrong, or did the MIs just agree to our staying together?"

Jasin Lebec cleared his throat. "The MIs do not agree or disagree, child. They compute percentages and make suggestions."

Jemeret made a sound of disbelief, and Jasin Lebec leaned forward to see his grandson around the three of us. "It's true," he said mildly. "If I've discovered only one thing in nearly a century of government service, it's that the machines make no decisions we don't ask them to make."

I felt my lord's anger, and I wanted to at least blunt it a little. "Jasin Lebec, why didn't you take the Barbin 3 assignment?"

He looked down at his hands, which were just beginning to show the unavoidable slackening of age that even his abilities and the technology of the Com could combat only so far.

Jemeret's anger ebbed; his voice was surprisingly gentle. "He's beyond it now, love. He lost a lot of his strength in the years they tried to use him to heal you."

I felt that keenly, tried to make it easier by accepting it as my due or seeing it as not truly my fault, but ended up pushing it aside. I got up and stepped over Tynnanna's tail to walk around Coney and Sandalari to the old Class A, who rose automatically. "Jasin Lebec, will you permit me to probe you?" I asked seriously.

He started to refuse; I felt it in him. I said, "Don't."

He shrugged then, and I sensed his assent. Instantly I formed a probe and used it to begin to explore for the weaknesses in his system. Jemeret had taught me more about brain physiology and function than Mortel John ever had, and I wanted to use it.

It was a brain that had wielded power for a hundred years, and the connections to the sting—which I could now locate with ease—seemed only a little weak at the acting end, but tapered to almost nothing as I followed them back. Cell regeneration was not something I could do in any brain except my own. I withdrew.

Everyone was watching me, and Tynnanna had risen and was pacing, slowly but with meaning. I'd been gone longer than I thought. I looked inquiringly at Jemeret.

"Just over an hour," he said, adding, to Coney, "Let the guard in now."

Jasin Lebec caught my wrist. "Tell me what your perception is," he ordered. "I find it somehow impossible to—" He broke off, unable to find the words he wanted.

I knew what he meant. I'd been unable to diagnose the absence of my own sting until Jemeret showed me where to find it. As under our own control as it was, there was something nonvolitional about Class A talent, something inherently unstable and unpredictable. Jemeret did not appear to find it so, but then it was not a topic he and I had ever really discussed.

I looked at the old man I'd spent most of my life determined to imitate. "It's a question of reserves," I said.

He frowned. "But my reserves are full." He sounded a little bewildered. "I can feel that they are. I can use them for Class C functions and for pathfinding, so I know they're as good as they ever were—all right, almost as good. I've lost some flexibility, but that's all."

I didn't contradict him. "As nearly as I can assess, the connection between your reserves and your sting has been lost. I don't know if that's a normal effect of aging—and since it involves your sting, you're the only one who could repair it."

"That's something of a problem," he said. "I'd need the sting to rebuild the connection, but I can't use the sting unless the connection is rebuilt."

Sandalari frowned. "Does that mean it can't be fixed?"

I said, "Yes," and after a moment Jasin Lebec nodded.

Tynnanna gave out a demanding roar which echoed off the walls of the conference room and startled all of us. I spun around.

"I think he needs to relieve himself," Jemeret said dryly.

Coney had gone into the corridor and returned with the MF guard, who overheard the last remark and looked understandably uneasy as she blurted, "That creature isn't going to fit into any of the eliminatories, and we don't have a stock storage option, like the ships do!"

Jemeret was trying not to grin. "I suggest you let him back onto the dock area, and then clean up after him," he said.

The guard's jaw dropped. "Do what?"

Jasin Lebec said absently, "That sounds like a good idea."

"Do what?" repeated the guard.

Tynnanna roared again, extended his claws and ripped up a square meter of carpeting, the klawit equivalent of bouncing up and down.

"Soon," Jemeret advised mildly.

The guard flung open the conference room doors and Tynnanna bounded past her, almost knocking her flat.

"I'd better follow him," I said to the others as the guard caught her balance.

"Meet us in the food dispensary," Jemeret said, bending to pick up both nomidars. To Jasin Lebec, he added, "Any change in station command since I went planetside?"

I took the gaping guard by the arm and propelled her along

the corridor in the wake of the klawit, who unerringly found his way back to the lander deck and availed himself of the space to create a mess that was no doubt a great relief to him.

"Gebbish!" the guard swore, wrinkling her nose.

"You wouldn't smell any better to him," I told her as haughtily as I could.

Tynnanna finished and stalked to the doors as if he bore no relation whatsoever to what he was leaving behind. The guard activated the automatic cleansing facilities. "With all respect intended," she said to me as I watched her program the cleansers, "how long will you be staying on the station?"

"Just over forty hours."

"Is he likely to do this again?"

The cleansers were, at least, efficient. Tynnanna watched them curiously as he washed his belly.

"If we feed him." Before she could make any other comment, I went on quickly, "And if we don't feed him, he'll find his own meals."

The cat raised his head and eyed the guard, giving her a full dose of his fiery stare.

"I'll show you to the dispensary," she said. "I'm sorry I ever thought of this as dull duty."

I studied her as she walked around Tynnanna and into the corridor, then I asked curiously, "What's your name and what are your stats?"

She looked surprised that I would take so much notice of her. "My name is Keli Idana. I'm a Merchant Fleet guard of the sixth rank, and a Com citizen. I was born on Veroun twenty-six standard years ago, and I was sent here when I was demoted from fourth rank." She flushed a bright red as she said it, and I realized that she had hair almost the same shade as the blush. It peeped out of her helmet.

"Demoted for what reason?" I asked her softly as we walked side by side. It was clear she was embarrassed by the incident, but it made her more interesting to me.

"I disobeyed a direct order from my superior," she said.

"Why?"

Her answer came almost defiantly, as if she were prepared to incur my contempt. "I'm a Macerate, and I considered myself to have been given an immoral order."

I stopped walking, and she turned to face me, fists clenched at her sides. "Tell me what the order was," I said.

She looked suspicious, but didn't dare challenge me. "I was on a freighter picking up a consignment of telusite coils from the refinery on Nogdala 7 when the local citizens protested. It was something about the terms of the trade agreement. I don't know the details, but they aren't likely to tell anyone at my rank what's going on. They armed us, and they told us to fire on the protesters if they didn't disperse."

"You refused to fire?"

She nodded. "They weren't armed, the protesters. So I refused, and I ended up here." She pointed to the iris at the end of a side corridor. "That's the trough—pardon, the food dispensary."

"You're dismissed, MF Idana," I said to her, and she braced in response, turned and walked away.

Tynnanna had to go through the iris one shoulder at a time, for it was half the size of the door at the dock. I followed him in and saw the dark blue jumpsuits at a long table near the dispensers. There were two other people in the room, both men, both in beige jumpsuits, and both trying to look as if a klawit were a perfectly normal, ordinary phenomenon.

Then I was distracted by the smell of coffee, and I instantly salivated. I hadn't had coffee in months—years, really—and while shilfnin was good, it wasn't as rich or as dark as the bean beverage. Sandalari rose and went to the dispensers as soon as she saw me. When the near dispenser began to produce a massive amount of meatlike protein, I knew she was getting Tynnanna's meal. I went to join the three men at the table.

Jemeret shoved his cup of coffee over to me as I sat down, and I took it gratefully. "What started it, then?" he was asking Jasin Lebec. "There's always a trigger."

The old man was drinking some kind of liquor, and that surprised me, because I hadn't thought he drank. "The trigger was a request from a pair of mine managers on Barbin 3 to renegotiate the terms of their contract with the Com."

Jemeret smiled humorlessly, looking at me. "I suspect it always starts with a desire to renegotiate," he said.

Jasin Lebec nodded. "People want to join the Com, get the benefits it offers, and are grateful at first. Then their perceptions change, and they think they should receive more than the original agreement. When we're on the rollship, I'll set up a conference with the authorities on Barbin 3. They'll be better able to tell you what the situation is at this moment." He paused, then said, "I never thought I would live to see you accept a Class A assignment."

Jemeret's smile grew a little warmer. "I've been accepting assignments since the Com destroyed Zitten Talt. This is just the first one that hasn't involved the need to heal talent, and the first I haven't charged a price for."

"Who was Zitten Talt?" I asked him, setting the empty cup down in the refill circle on the table, which drew it down, filled it with more hot coffee, and raised it again so I could take it back. "I know you healed Sandalari and me. Who else?"

Jasin Lebec looked away. Coney toyed with his own cup. Jemeret was quite serious now. "He was a young Resni. He had been rated Class B by the Com, but he couldn't believe or accept the classification. He got hold of some drugs he thought would boost him to Class A, and despite the danger, he took them."

"But—how old was he?" I was feeling stupid. I'd been seven when Jemeret must have been healing Sandalari, and the only talents I'd known were Coney, Kray, and Jasin Lebec until we were adolescents.

"He was almost twenty years older than you," Jasin Lebec said, "older than Lage by a few years. He could never accept being—lesser."

Kray had had the same problem, but turned it outward instead of inward. I thought I had caught the brunt of it.

"I couldn't save him," Jemeret said with real regret. "The drugs had melted his brain, and there was nothing there to rebuild with."

"One failure isn't so terrible," Jasin Lebec said softly. "Not with the kind of assignments you take on."

Jemeret lifted the cup out of my hand and drank off most of its contents. "What were your failures, na-sire?" he asked.

Jasin Lebec looked sad. "You know, you can be very cruel," he said to my lord. "I used to think that streak didn't run in our family. I met Kray going into Ronica's room that morning—that last morning. I read him in passing, perfunctorily. I didn't catch it. I might have. I blame myself."

Half of me expected Jemeret to apologize; the other half wanted to tell Jasin Lebec what I couldn't tell him—that if he had stopped Kray, I would never have begun growing, and I'd never have met Jemeret. Neither of us said anything.

Coney looked up, waiting to see if we would speak. Sandalari returned to the table, curious, but silent, sensing strain. At last Coney said, "We can't be sure that there isn't a pattern to things, a pattern we can't see or grasp, but which figures into everything. It could be that even if you had caught it, you couldn't have stopped it."

"You always did have a spiritual bent," Jasin Lebec said with a distracted smile. "Some of the Tribunal wanted to wash you out of training because of it."

"Why didn't they?" Coney asked, with more curiosity than hostility.

Jasin Lebec rolled his glass between his hands. "Mortel John recommended you be retained, and the MIs backed him up."

I found it vastly surprising that he spoke of Mortel John separately from the MIs, when I had only recently begun trying to fuse them.

"The MIs again," Sandalari said. "Strange. I hadn't expected them to be on our side."

"Side?" Jasin Lebec asked it with a sharpness much like his old self.

I knew I needed to change the subject. "Am I entitled to a staff?" I asked him. "I mean, does the government make any accommodation if I want to, say, take on a guard?"

Jasin Lebec did not try to mask his surprise, though I thought everyone else at the table masked theirs quite well. "You already have a team," he said. "I suppose that's a precedent of some kind. Do you expect an army as well?"

"Not an army. A guard."

The door irised open and a man in a bronze jumpsuit came in. The two beige jumpsuits at the other table jumped to their feet and braced. The bronze waved them down and came to us. "It's a pleasure to welcome you to Markover Station. Your quarters have been prepared for you."

"How about the klawit?" Coney asked.

The station commander—for command here would be a bronze responsibility—looked over at Tynnanna, who had devoured all the meat and tried to eat the dish as well, and was now delicately washing his huge face and whiskers. "He can sleep wherever he wants to," he said. "We're not equipped to keep animals, let alone cater to them."

"Will you join us for a meal, Commander?" Jasin Lebec asked.

The commander accepted.

In short order I realized that compared to planetside food, station food was perfectly dreadful. I almost asked the commander what he'd done to get sent here. As soon as I'd eaten, I became aware that I'd been gathering at a low level for the past hour because I was tired. I glanced at the others; only Sandalari was showing signs of weariness. I wanted to see the quarters, but there was something else I wanted first.

"Is there a planetview?" I asked the commander.

It was Jemeret who said, "I'll take you there. Which quarters did you give us?"

"Level one, suite five for you and Ronica McBride," the commander answered. "Suite seven for Class C Conewall and his husband."

Jemeret got to his feet as the table absorbed the used dishes, and I rose, too.

On a ship or a station, day and night are matters of whim rather than matters of nature, and by station time it was well past midnight. We said good night, went to the nearest force-lev vertical, and let it raise us two levels. Because the verticals had to move fixtures as well as people, this one was big enough for Tynnanna. It was fairly clear to me by this time that the klawit was not too willing to let me out of his sight yet, and that was fine with me. If the starfire was to speak with me again, it would be through the cat, and I was eager for that to happen.

Level one was far more spacious than the third level had been. Jemeret knew his way around here quite well. He was still carrying both nomidars, and I reached out to take my winewood one from him, but he kept it and said, "In the lounge."

When we passed suite five, he gestured with his own nomidar, and I irised the uncoded door open, barely glancing inside before Tynnanna went in, blocking the view with his shoulders. I closed the door after him and followed Jemeret farther along the corridor to a generous observation lounge that showed the breathtaking blue curve of Caryldon, its winter clouds heavy enough in one place to make me think it might have been another Severance Storm.

I had seen a planet from space before, but while arriving or leaving on a ship, and the world always seemed to be moving. The station was fixed relative to Caryldon, so the planet hung motionless in the huge viewport. I felt a tug toward it. I almost said something, but Jemeret stung me lightly before I could get my mouth open. He was, I knew, reminding me that we were as thoroughly in enemy territory as we would have been among the Honish, but this territory was more treacherous because it was infinitely more devious. We had to be more devious in response.

The lounge was deserted except for us. We sat on the long, curved couch and played a quiet song of serenity. It was his choice, but I welcomed it. We both needed calming.

When the song was finished, we took a final look at Caryldon—at home—and went back to our suite. We made only a cursory search for surveillance; it was too expensive and Markover too remote for it to be a serious possibility.

The bed was huge and created a temperature field that allowed us to use no blanket, even though the room itself was cool. Tynnanna had curled up right in the middle of the sitting room floor, and we could hear his deep breathing as we slid naked into the warmth of the field, which immediately lessened to compensate for our body heat.

We were both tired. Jemeret drew me into his arms, tucked

my head beneath his chin, and we fell into deep almost at once. I didn't deep long, but when I rose to simple sleep, something woke me, and I found him already awake, watching me.

"Is something wrong?" I asked.

"I keep thinking about those two children," he said, his hands automatically caressing my shoulders and breasts. "I want to find out what happened. I want to get a feeling for the emotional levels of the Com regarding talent. I want to—do so many things."

"I want to do those things, too—and more," I said to him. "I want to make whoever did it sorry. But you're worried about something having to do with me. I can read it from you." I turned and snuggled back against him, spoon fashion. "What is it?"

I felt his chest move against my back as he took a deep breath. "Ronica, for nearly a year I've been able to build my life around you," he said against my ear, "and I believe it's made you happy. We can't be as central to each other here as we were among the Samothen. I don't want that to hurt you."

I recognized what he was saying, understood that even if we kept from being separated, we would both have separate obligations, separate goals. I would find it different to be in the Com, and to be the most important person in the Com, than it had been among the Samothen.

"It won't hurt me," I said. "We'll have plenty to do. Carrying out assignments in—" I hesitated, then went on. "—what Sejineth called 'strange waters' should be preoccupation enough."

"I hope so." His voice was firm, and before I could say anything else, he rolled me onto my back and captured my mouth with his.

IV. Building a Team

As *Megalume* was reported in docking orbit, I sought out the station commander and formally requested transfer of MF guard Keli Idana to my personal service.

He stared at me in such surprise that I was sure it would never have occurred to him that anyone might make such a request. Then he said hesitantly, "Guard Idana serves the Merchant Fleet, Ronica McBride," as if it were something I was somehow unaware of.

I nodded at him. "And I am asking the Merchant Fleet, through you, to reassign her to me." I paused to see if he'd say anything. When he did not, I added, "I would regard it as a friendly gesture."

He thought about it, thought about the limits of his own authority, and glanced toward his comsole. I knew he was wondering if he needed to consult a higher-rank officer. I stung him to help him decide that Keli Idana was an unimportant creature, and that pleasing a Class A was more important than punishing a once-insubordinate guard. He registered the transfer order in the next minute, and then he sent for Keli.

I watched her come cautiously into his office, stepping as if she found the ground uncertain. It occurred to me that she was expecting to be reprimanded, that anytime she was noticed by someone in authority, it was bound to be bad news. When he told her she was now my personal guard, her eyes widened and slid to me, asking for confirmation. When he added that the guard of a Class A could hardly be sixth-rank and therefore she could take it that she was immediately reinstated as fourth-rank and promoted to third, she gaped.

Once she seemed to absorb that, he handed her the rank epaulets to replace those she was wearing.

She took them from him slowly, then remembered herself, turned to me and braced.

"We're leaving on the rollship *Megalume* in less than an hour," I said to her in a formal tone, trying not to let my mouth twitch. "Get your kit and report to the dock before departure."

She practically ran from the office. I graciously thanked the station commander for making the wise decision I had just about compelled him to make, and I left also.

I couldn't have said what motivated me to take her with me when I left Markover. I told myself that it was only an instinct, and I would not regret following it.

Rollships went into docking orbit and remained there, sending either a cargo or a passenger shuttle to make contact with the station. It was a very rare spaceport, like the home port on Orokell, that could actually bring one down for repair or storage. We'd requested a cargo shuttle from *Megalume*, and the captain had been completely horrified at the idea of Class A's arriving on his ship on such an unsophisticated craft. He was convinced someone on Markover Station was trying to humiliate him by giving him information that would anger us. Since he knew neither Jemeret nor me, Jasin Lebec made an eftel call and confirmed the order directly. It also let us know that he was leaving Markover with us.

The maneuvering left me time to attach Keli to the team.

We had requested that there be no honor guard to see us off, and the station staff complied gratefully. So when the automated shuttle docked and the doors dual-irised, the six of us and Tynnanna walked aboard. Tynnanna lay down in the middle of the empty cargo area, and Sandalari immediately sat cross-legged beside his shoulder, smiling unselfconsciously at me. "Jumpsuits are so much more practical than the talma."

"Didn't you like leggings and tunic?" I asked her, sitting down beside her.

She wrinkled her nose. "I really am a proponent of jumpsuits."

Keli stared at us as Jemeret lazily stretched out beside me, leaning on Tynnanna.

"Haven't you any belongings?" she asked us.

"Two nomidars," Jemeret said, nodding toward the instruments in a holding field near the wall. "What more do you think we need?"

She glanced down at her own regulation kit, bulging at the sides.

Jasin Lebec was also looking at it. "I'd like to sit on that, if I may," he said to her. "I'm a little too old to be down on the deck plates."

"Please." She was almost overwhelmed to be asked a favor by a man she'd been in awe of her entire life.

Coney sat down beside Sandalari, his arms around her.

The doors shut and the cargo shuttle pulled jerkily away from the station. A passenger shuttle would have moved without any discernible vibration, but the cargo craft didn't have to be nearly so well-stabilized. Keli sat down quickly on the deck.

Jemeret reached out and laid his hand lightly on my arm. I smiled at him.

No one had said a word about Keli joining the party, not even Jasin Lebec. If they had asked me why I'd taken her, I could only have said that I thought I would need her.

It was less than a five-minute trip to the rollship, and we didn't talk. When we were settled in the receiving bay and the door opened out, I was stunned to see what appeared to be the entire watch complement lining the corridor, in full dress uniforms, one woman holding a huge bouquet of white superblooms. We had forgotten to let the ship know we required no pomp, so pomp was what greeted us.

I was tempted to send Tynnanna through first, but I bit back the impulse and looked at Jasin Lebec, who moved smoothly into the lead. I felt Sandalari's surprise and realized that, of all of us, she was the only one who had never been exposed to the Com at its most ceremonious. We'd been taught that these ceremonies were toned down from earlier days, when the rites were more elaborate, more decorative, and lengthier. I wondered if that had been the truth or just someone's idea of something they should tell us to justify the expense in time and resources.

Jemeret took my arm and we walked off the shuttle onto *Megalume*, only the second superluminal vessel I remembered riding. None was necessary among the core worlds, but the first had taken Mortel John and me to Sargasso to meet a representative of the protodolphins while I was still in training. The woman with the flowers held them out to me and introduced herself as the ship's high watch first officer. "I speak for Captain Distan and the entire crew, high watch and low, when I say what an honor it is to have you on board, Class A Ronica McBride," she said, shaking the flowers a little as if to remind me that I hadn't accepted them.

Since I had my nomidar in one hand and Jemeret's hand in the other, I had to hesitate a moment longer until Sandalari reached out and took the instrument from me. I cradled the flowers. "Convey my thanks to everyone."

The first officer repeated a welcome for Jasin Lebec, but she plainly thought all the others were just members of my party. "I'll show you to your cabins," she said. "We need to get under way as soon as possible."

"I'll need the use of your conference room and the eftel vid on highest government priority," Jasin Lebec said to her.

"It's at your disposal," she said quickly. "Please follow me."

We followed her through the assembled ranks of the high watch crew, with me remembering to nod occasionally and distantly. Every so often one of the younger crew members would stare at Jemeret's beard, since its deep black made it much more noticeable than Coney's fawn-colored one. We felt the almost subconscious vibration of the ship getting under way before we'd made it through the ranks, and I wondered if the captain was running the ship himself or if he'd kept some of his bridge crew out of the reception committee.

Lumeships were built like a cross, with another arm intersecting the first two at right angles, and the control room was at the center, where all the arms met. Two arms were considered high watch and two low. The last two were for cargo, and it was at the end of one of those two arms that our cargo shuttle docked. We actually passed through the bridge surround to get to the passenger section on the high watch side, which also contained the conference room and the med.

"Are there any other passengers aboard?" Jemeret asked.

The first officer glanced at him as if she considered the question somehow improper.

I said sharply, "Answer my husband!"

Her eyes flew, startled, to me, and then shot back to Jemeret again. "We were directed to debark all passengers on Robin's World when we were diverted to Markover Station," she said quickly, glancing at me again as if fearful that I would sting her.

"Fine," Jasin Lebec said smoothly. "Then I'm sure there'll be no possible problems about the conference room." Keli was pulling her suspended kit in front of Tynnanna, who stalked with menacing dignity between the assembled crew as if it were beneath him to rip off anyone's head at the present time. The MF guard looked uneasy, almost out of place, and I turned and gestured to her. We had just completed our passage through the lines of crew, the last of whom was ducking what seemed to be a deliberate swipe of the klawit's tail. Keli immediately stepped between Coney and Sandalari and braced for a microsecond before walking along beside me. She let her kit proceed on its own, which would be fine until we had to turn into any side-branching corridor.

"Keli, you're disturbed about something," I said. "Tell me."

She hesitated, partly because she was uncertain about me, and partly because everyone else on the team was listening. Then she said, "I'm a guard, but you appear not to be in any danger, and would certainly sense it if you were. I'm not sure what my duties are."

"We can work out specific duties later," I said to her, soothing her uneasiness with the sting at the same time.

"This way, please," the first officer said as we entered the bridge surround, where all six arms opened into the bubble.

Keli caught her kit and steered it to the left after us.

There were six luxurious cabin suites along this arm, three to a side, then some of the crew quarters. Jasin Lebec glanced into his and said, "I'll be in the conference room. Join me in about ten minutes, if you would." He knew his way quite well around Lumeships; he had spent much of his life on them.

The first officer gave Coney and Sandalari the suite next to Jasin Lebec's, and as she was about to gesture to the one beside that, Jemeret said smoothly, "I'd like to put the guard here, and we'll take the cabin across the corridor. Then the central cabin, beside us, can go to the klawit."

She was taken aback, but was well-trained enough not to show it overtly. "Can that beast use the facilities?" she asked calmly.

"We'll see that he doesn't wreck the place," I said with equal calm. We both appeared not to notice Keli stifling a giggle. "But since he can't fit the lockscan or punch in a code, we'd appreciate your simply unlocking his door."

The first officer had the courage not to ask if that meant Tynnanna would wander in and out at will; she merely opened a panel and keyed in a code. The door spiraled wide, and Tynnanna walked in. Jemeret handed me his nomidar and I juggled both instruments and the flowers long enough for the door to read his retinal patterns. He went into Tynnanna's suite as I let the door to our cabin read my own patterns, then waited for it to open so I could enter and relieve myself of the instruments and the bouquet. I set the nomidars on the long cushioned bench that passed for a couch shipside and laid the flowers on the table, which read them and created a water pocket in its center. I dropped the stems in and took the time to look around.

The luxury, the spaciousness, almost astonished me. The first room could have contained the assembly hall of the temple at Stronghome. The carpet underfoot was plush enough to show footprints before it sprang back into place. The long couch, wide enough to sleep on, took up one part of the cabin. I went to the cabin design template just inside the door, moved the table and its seats out of the way, toward the comsole, and elled the couch so that instead of a long bar, it made a right angle to itself. The comsole had been left in its wall slot, but there was so much available space, I had it come out.

"I didn't know you had a need to redecorate." Jemeret's voice was faintly amused.

I turned in time to see him wave the door closed. Without consulting one another, we each immediately laid a palm flat against the cabin wall. Despite the fact that I knew we were both doing the same thing, I kept pathfinding through the wall panels, which responded so quickly it was almost dizzying. I'd become accustomed to pathfinding nontechnological things, and they were sluggish. I read the circuits of the cabin very quickly, identifying the purpose of each, from the wall panels, to the couch, table, and comsole, to the workings of the bed and the huge eliminatory.

When I was certain, I took my hand away. Jemeret had already completed his survey. We smiled at one another. There was no surveillance. "They weren't expecting us to be on this ship," he said. "It was diverted at the last moment."

"How is Tynnanna fitting in?"

Jemeret grinned, the boyish expression I loved and had seen very little of recently. "There's almost enough room for him to race around in there. I called him up some meat and showed him the eliminatory. He'll be using the bath, I suspect, but it's self-cleaning." He studied me for a few moments, his gray eyes going more serious. "How are you fitting in?"

"Easily," I said. "Jemeret, I was raised in this society. I fit into it really well, and now that I've seen the Tribunal, I know I can stand up to them. I was worried about that."

"Were you?"

"A Class A shouldn't show weakness." It was meant as much for me as for him. "They remember what I did—and what was done to me. They'll always have that knowledge. I don't want to—falter again."

He nodded once, accepting that without comment.

"Shouldn't we be going to the conference room now?" I asked him.

"Probably. Come along." He held out his hand.

All conference rooms look alike, even those of the governing councils on Orokell. Only the Tribunal conference room is significantly larger, but it often unites four different groups around its huge, square, open-centered table. The conference table on *Megalume* was a normal rectangle, but two different eftel vid images had been integrated around it by the time we got there. Jasin Lebec was seated on the near side of the table, and the image of Pel Nostro was at the table's head. The image on the far side was an old woman in silver, between two younger men in bronze. All but Jasin Lebec rose as we walked in. The door irised shut behind us and the bar at its top flared to show that it had been secured.

Jasin Lebec glanced at the two of us. "This is Planetary Governor Gayli Hatlo and her Assistant Governors Caffel Jet and Bok Melanez." The three strangers nodded solemnly at us.

Pel Nostro resumed his seat at the table. "Speaking for the central Com, I feel I must apologize for the delay in our response, Governor Hatlo," he said. "We hope to make that up to you by the unprecedented step of offering you the services of three Class A's. In addition, of course, to Class A Jasin Lebec, you are to receive the attentions of Class A Ronica McBride and Acting Class A Jemeret Cavanaugh."

I raised an eyebrow at the "acting" and glanced at Jemeret. He shrugged.

"We are pleased to see you so recovered from your illness, Ronica McBride," the Planetary Governor said formally.

I inclined my head to recognize the sentiment without responding to it.

She sat down as Jemeret and I did; a full five seconds later the young men on either side of her sat as well. The governor went on, "We're so very grateful you've come. We cannot stop the fighting. Our planetary enforcement corps consisted of a hundred thousand men and women. All but fifteen thousand have been lost. The rebels have six plasma disruptors." Plasma disruptors were forbidden weapons; their possession alone would have incurred the severest penalty the Com meted out. Plasma disruptors not only had completely debilitating effects on humans, but were shielded against blasts from orbit. The Com had outlawed them when it discovered that someone inside a disruptor was nearly invulnerable from outside attack as long as the weapon's atomic power source continued to function.

"Where did the rebels get the weaponry?" Jemeret asked.

One of the assistants answered. "We believe they were flown in disassembled in contraband shipments from one of the Nogdala worlds. The planetary administration in the Nogdala system is notoriously lax in controlling its populace." His voice took on a level of disdain that completely ignored the fact that his own world was currently in revolt.

"Is there a leader of this rebellion?" I asked. It was a standard first question in a Class A problem. Tactics said it was best to sting the leadership.

"We believe," said the other assistant—I never did discover which was which—"that there are two brothers involved. They received an unfavorable judgment—"

"But a fair one," interrupted the first assistant.

"—a fair but unfavorable judgment," amended the second, "in the Planetary Court when they petitioned for a reevaluation of their contracts. The judgment seems to have embittered them."

I thought that was putting at least 85,000 deaths a little mildly.

"How did they persuade others to join them?" Jemeret asked. "I am assuming here that even with plasma disruptors two men would have some trouble wiping out an entire army."

Gayli Hatlo chose to reply herself. "There are a number of our citizens who object to the Com's payment schedule for our telusite."

"We have a mutually beneficial trade agreement signed ten years ago," Pel Nostro said, his calm voice belying the agitation I felt certain he was experiencing, even though I couldn't use the sting to read him.

"Some of the citizens feel that the Com benefits more than we do," said the assistant on the governor's right. "*We* are certain the agreement is eminently fair, you understand, but some of our citizens have chosen to disagree."

I wished I could have read him. The eftel vid showed that he looked entirely sincere, but then no one with any degree of political sophistication could make a statement like that in complete sincerity.

"When we lost most of the planetary corps and could not secure the services of a Class A, we were forced to appeal to the government for other assistance, and that resulted in a division of Drenalion attempting to quell the disturbance," Gayli Hatlo went on. "Of course, they could not touch the people in control of the plasma disruptors, and so they—" She was choosing her words carefully now. "—attempted to dissuade those supporting the rebels."

I felt a chill run through me. A division of Drenalion could, in theory, destroy the population of an entire world before they were stopped. Jemeret turned to look at Pel Nostro, who had discovered something interesting in his tabletop. "Exactly how much of this planet is in revolt?" my lord demanded.

"About a third," the Com Counselor said, not meeting his gaze.

"How much was in revolt before you sent in the Drenalion?" I asked, laying a hand on Jemeret's thigh under the table.

Pel Nostro cleared his throat, but didn't answer.

Gayli Hatlo spoke. "About two percent."

I felt Jemeret's anger sweep over and through him. Jasin Lebec must have felt it, too. "It was an error in judgment, sending in the Drenalion," he said softly. "The Com won't make such an error again, but you see, they could not send me."

I realized something, and I was certain that Jemeret must have seen it, too. The MIs did not know how to deal with human beings any longer without a Class A or wholesale murder. I looked at Pel Nostro closely. He was obviously uneasy. All at once, almost inexplicably, I wanted to talk with Mortel John, but there would be no chance to do that in person unless he came to Orokell, or unless we had an opportunity to go to Koldor. Providing, of course, we survived Barbin 3.

Jemeret was speaking to the three people planetside. "You will see to it that your latest intelligence information and maps are on board *Megalume* before we enter orbit."

They assured us they would. Then one of the assistants

described the general progress of the war so far, and it amounted to only one thing: as long as the rebels had the plasma disruptors, the war could not be stopped without using wide-beam pulses against the planet itself. The Com was against such action, not because it would have an unreasonably high cost in innocent human life, but because it would have destroyed the planet's stock of telusite. The people were, of course, less of a consideration than the mineral, because they were a more easily renewable resource.

The other assistant then took over, reporting on the destruction of climate controls, leaving the world prey to unleashed storms that had destroyed a great many of the surface-grown crops. Agricultural, medical, and transportation equipment had been destroyed or damaged, and could not be replaced as long as the war continued. Power-generating facilities had been lost. I could almost imagine that the only things on Barbin 3 that were fully operational were the weapons.

"Are there Drenalion still on the surface?" I asked suddenly, interrupting the report.

"No, Class A," the Planetary Governor answered, sounding a little nervous.

"Is the planetary corps still involved?"

"No again," she said. "We pulled our skeleton troop out well before the government division landed. They're in orbit now, as we are, on subluminal ships."

"Then who are the rebels fighting?" I asked.

Pel Nostro cleared his throat again and replied. "They're fighting those members of the Barbin 3 population who have remained loyal to the Com."

Jemeret leaned forward, resting a deceptively relaxed hand on the tabletop. "If the rebels have plasma disruptors, what are the Com loyalists fighting with?"

"They have been armed with cephalic rays," the Com Counselor said.

I was stunned, but before I had a chance to express my outrage, Jemeret's voice went low and hard. "Those are just as illegal as the plasma disruptors. Did they come from Nogdala as well?"

"No," Pel Nostro said evenly. "We could not leave our friends unarmed, so we armed them."

Jasin Lebec made a quick motion of his hand, under our side of the table. Both Jemeret and I read it as a request not to pursue the matter; Jemeret pressed his lips together and looked down at the tabletop to mitigate the power of his sudden glare.

I was equally angry; I just wasn't surprised. Giving the population cephalic rays meant that the Com had decided not to make repeated futile attempts to destroy the plasma disruptors; they would just ensure that the power to destroy all those rebels outside the weapons, on the ground, existed in the hands of the loyal population. It was not necessarily a humane solution, but it would ultimately be *some* sort of solution. Over a long enough period, without allies on the outside to supply them, the people in the disruptors—and there were usually two to a disruptor cabin—would probably die of thirst or starvation. If very little of the indigenous population remained, the Com would move people in to repopulate the world. The telusite would be untouched.

"Please continue with your report, Assistant Governor," Jasin Lebec said emotionlessly.

The young man continued, almost gratefully, from where I'd interrupted him, as if dealing with unrehearsed questions was a process completely alien to him. The recitation began again, and I thought about the MIs' logic: if the rebels could not be disarmed, the loyalists would have to be given sufficient weaponry to hold Barbin 3, or the telusite would be lost to the Com. It was a very logical decision, the kind the MIs could make without a single quibble about legality or morality.

The image of the three administrators on Barbin 3 began to waver, which could have indicated anything from a radio-generating source coming too near the transmission, to the planetary government having indicated in advance the maximum they were willing to spend on the vid call. Governor Hatlo made a hasty, professionally hopeful farewell, and that part of the conference room was suddenly unoccupied. Only the Com Counselor remained.

Jemeret turned to Jasin Lebec. "How long until we orbit?"

"Six days," Pel Nostro said before the older man could respond.

Jemeret acknowledged the answer.

"Then we have some time to build a scenario," I said.

"Let's get something to eat and some sleep first," Jemeret suggested.

"Do you think it's solvable as a Class A problem?" Pel Nostro asked, his voice showing his hesitation.

I was nodding thoughtfully when Jemeret spoke. "I think it's *only* solvable as a Class A problem. When's the first roll?"

"Within the hour," Jasin Lebec answered, nodding at the unobtrusive roll chronometer near the door. It was counting backward from 00:52:12.

Pel Nostro cleared his throat again. "Ronica McBride, to the best of your own ability to analyze the situation, can you tell me if it is also your belief that this problem is solvable?"

I debated several possible replies, ranging from the insupportably arrogant to the obviously ingratiating, and then I decided to simply tell the truth. "There's a team working on the assignment, Pel, not just me."

His reply showed how completely he devalued those of us who were not Class A. "Jasin Lebec has served with great distinction for years, but he has not the strength or quickness that was his in his prime. And Jemeret Cavanaugh—" He censored himself. "Well," he said to me, "I have confidence in your ability to do the best possible job, and I'm gratified that you feel the Barbin 3 problem will yield to solution. Some of the Tribunal members have expressed grave concern over your ability to complete a Class A assignment." He lowered his head in the seated equivalent of a bow, then vanished as the eftel vid link was cut from his end.

"That old ashadophed," Jemeret said with an ironic grin. "I think he doesn't trust me."

"I'm amazed that he seems to trust *me*," I said to him. "All he knows about me any longer is that I took the government oath, and that I love you."

Jasin Lebec leaned on the table with both arms. "He has no choice. You are his best chance for dependable Class A talent.

Even if he doesn't believe what he's saying, he has little choice but to say it."

"You may not be what you were, but the Tribunal still has you. You've been loyal to them for decades." I watched him shake his head even as I said it.

"I've lost touch," he said wearily.

His words sparked something in me, and I gasped. "Lost touch," I repeated to the old man. "That's it, you know. That's literally true. You've lost touch with your reserves, and you can't work the sting without them. And once that connection's disintegrated, it's irreversible. But you use an entirely different faculty to touch other people. What if—"

I reached out and let him recognize my touch. Jemeret guessed just before his grandfather did, and then Jasin Lebec followed my touch back to me. As soon as he contacted my reserves, he nodded. It was something he could not have done had I not initiated the joining, because I was a Class A, but since I had laid the path, he could follow it. It was, I realized, the same kind of action that had allowed Jemeret to save my life those months ago—a two-part match that permitted one Class A to use the reserve energy of the other. Such groundwork would not be necessary if he were to try to avail himself of the energy of a lesser talent, not now that the demonstration was over and he could clearly see the path he needed to follow into another mind's reserves.

"Now I think I know what Concy and Sandi are doing here," Jasin Lebec said with satisfaction. "With their reserves at my disposal, I can still do the work I was trained for."

"So then you won't mind if we give you a large part in whatever scenario we come up with," I said lightly, drawing back my own sting and letting him linger for a moment, memorizing the open pathways with a deliberate slowness born of age and declination.

When he withdrew, he looked at me very closely, but did not respond directly. "I sleep between rolls," he said. "The second one will be about seven hours later than the first. I suggest we meet an hour after the second roll ends, and I'm happy to offer my cabin for that purpose."

"What will that be, ship's time?" I asked.

"Fifth hour, low watch," Jemeret said. "Come along, love. Let's spend some time in our own cabin."

Keli was waiting outside our door, her own irised open, looking worried. She relaxed when she saw us. I touched her lightly with the sting to make her feel more confident. "Get yourself something to eat and some sleep, Keli," I said to her as our door read Jemeret's eye and opened for us.

"Perhaps you should let me know when you're going someplace, Ronica McBride," she said to me hesitantly. "It's my duty to know, even if you don't want me to accompany you."

"How do you like your cabin?" Jemeret asked her gently.

She nearly started, but caught herself in time. "It's more space than the entire barracks on Markover," she blurted, then colored sharply.

"I've never had a guard before, Keli." I had to work to keep my tone from sounding apologetic. "I'll try to keep your responsibilities in mind if you'll do something for me in return."

She nodded once, as if that were a given.

"You have to call me just Ronica." Now she did look startled. I couldn't help smiling. "You'll get used to it. My team has privileges I extend to no one else. Agreed?"

She nodded again.

"Keli, one thing you can do for us is keep an eye on Tynnanna when you're awake," Jemeret said. "He'll probably stay put, but if he doesn't, wake us." He began to turn to go into our suite, and I guessed that he must have read her, because he almost immediately turned back. "You are not to stay awake staring at his cabin door. We need you rested."

"Yes, sir," she said.

He gave her one of his genuine smiles, and I touched him lightly, both by laying a hand on his arm and by using my sting, to show him how pleased I was that he seemed to approve of my impulsive choice to take her on.

In a minute we were inside our suite with the door shut, and I nearly fell into his arms. He laughed at me and lifted me up off my feet. "You're doing fine."

"We're not even through the first roll yet," I said. Events would at some point, I knew, begin to draw me into the inevitable vortex of having to act, and I was already fearful that if I started acting without thinking in advance, I was likely to react in ways I'd learned on Caryldon, which was almost as bothersome as thinking I'd react in ways I'd learned in the Com. I wasn't at all certain what effect Caryldon-learned manners might have, and I hadn't begun to come to terms with whether I could deal with that effect.

Jemeret kissed me. "Exactly," he said. "So stop worrying until it's appropriate behavior. We have about half an hour before the roll. Let's order something to eat."

I told the comsole what we wanted, and the table presented it to us. We took the dishes to the angle of the couch and sat cross-legged on the rug, eating and drinking small helpings of the various Com foods I'd ordered. I hadn't been aware of how much I'd missed some of them until I tasted them again.

We were just finishing when the five-minute chime sounded, alerting us to the imminence of a roll. Jemeret shoved the dishes back onto the table, and I bolted the last of a lesser Ludurn wine and tossed him my glass. Then the two of us, without talking about it, moved swiftly out of our cabin and into Tynnanna's. The klawit would never have experienced the disorientation of roll before, and while we could have stung him from our own cabin, it seemed we both reached the conclusion that he would be infinitely more comforted by seeing us while the roll was going on.

Tynnanna had curled up in a major ball in the center of the front room floor, having challenged the carpet's self-cleaning facility by devouring his meat in typical klawit fashion. He raised his head as we came in, his eyes burning with recognition. We sat down on either side of him and I slid against his shoulder, feeling the coarse-soft fur under my cheek. The double chime of the second warning sounded.

"Do you know how long it's been since I had to go through one of these things?" Jemeret said softly.

"I doubt they've improved the experience much since then," I said a little regretfully. "We come through it uncomfortable, but unharmed, so why should the Com devote any resources to experimenting with the Lume technology?"

"The roll technology hasn't changed since they discovered it," Jemeret said. "They might be able to make it more comfortable—it was one of the major research projects at the Universities back when I was in training—but they couldn't ever find a way to make it less consumptive of resources. And they wouldn't do the one if they couldn't do the other."

The last warning sounded, and the Lume field generator activated with the subliminal hum that made my hair stand on end. Tynnanna growled, a low rumble that vibrated in me as I sat pressed up against his rib cage.

We waited until the beep cycle began, and then I glanced at the viewport. Watching the light waves drop into the realm of sound, vanishing from the visual, was, as always, irresistible, just as was counting down the seconds until activation.

Rolls seem timeless, so I never know how long we're in them, even though their actual length varies widely. They are rarely long enough for us to recognize that we can move or think, but after they end, there is a memory of time having passed. The nausea builds after the ship has become the only speck of light in the universe; the weird, discordant harmonies that resonate in the bones must do so over some span of time. And yet, entering and emerging from rolls somehow seems to happen outside normal time and space. We were told, in our classes, that some rolls were long enough for the nausea and disorientation to pass and a quasinormal feeling to return. Then movement and conversation were possible, but I personally never experienced one of those, nor did we expect any on the trip from Caryldon to Barbin 3.

As we dropped into normal space a long way from the initial roll point, I found myself wondering if time lost in the radiant tank was like time lost in the rolls; it passed, leaving shadows but no tracks, a silence with echoes.

Tynnanna roared, full-throatedly, shaking his head with such violence that he knocked me partway across the cabin. I rushed to sting him, but found Jemeret there first, already calming him. "We'd better put him to sleep for the other rolls,"

I suggested, climbing to my feet and banishing my own nausea as best I could.

Jemeret got up as well. "I think he'll be all right," he said. "Come on. We need some sleep ourselves."

And of course that wasn't the first thing we did when we got into our cabin's wide bed. I was, as always, amazed by his ability to move me, by the power of the passion. He was endlessly imaginative and endlessly strong. When I could think again, before I slept, I was overwhelmed by gratitude.

V. A Class A Assignment

We had completed the last of the rolls and were in normal space for the final time before we would orbit Barbin 3 when Jasin Lebec came to get Jemeret and me to tell us Pel Nostro was in the conference room by eftel vid.

In many ways it had been a seductive trip. I was rediscovering the joyful luxury of sonic cleansing, electrolyte shampoos, and holotainment. I'd been able to use the ship's library to renew my acquaintance with some of the great music and drama of the Com, both past and present. Jemeret watched me without any visible evidence of concern, but I sensed it was there without needing to read him for it.

One high watch, Coney and I spent a few hours watching status reports on the current Com statistics—he had stayed somewhat in touch through the years before Jemeret arrived on Markover; I was three years behind on information. Most of the reports were glowingly positive, the language typically Com-proud, but I sensed some hints of things not said. I wasn't at all sure how to process missing information that I couldn't quite identify.

Another high watch, Jasin Lebec told us his observations on the changes occurring in the Com in the absence of Class A talent. The picture, completely disregarding the toll from the war on Barbin 3, was far from attractive. A number of the Planetary Governors had registered requests for Class A service to help sway delicate negotiations. Suffering under the inability to exploit that talent, they had, in not a few cases, begun flirting either with repression or with illegal means of control, even assassination.

I was horrified. The MIs seemed to have given up any attempt at persuasion or bargaining in the absence of Class A talent, and lacking persuasion, only some permutation of coercion remained. That meant the Com needed me intensely, and my oath would save lives. I began to wonder how Jemeret had abrogated that responsibility. Granted, he was young—scarcely fifteen—when he rebelled against training and got himself returned to Caryldon, but Jasin Lebec had been younger and more vital then. Now he was weakening, aging, and probably in need of a well-earned rest, and I was the central point on which his future pivoted. I saw that the environment in which I'd been raised was in itself a powerful habit, a habit I could sink back into with very little trouble, a habit that had taught me I could do a lot of good.

Jemeret was rarely with me in the time between rolls, for he was working on some sort of project. I think he might have been waiting for me to ask him about it, but I plunged into relearning the world of the Com, seeking out Coney's company or Sandalari's, or even Keli's, before I sought his. We'd been through the eight rolls it would take to reach our destination, and I'd spent the last low watch exercising Tynnanna in one of the cargo holds instead of coming to bed in our cabin. I felt Jemeret sweep for me as the high watch began.

I was sitting in Keli's cabin, playing scattergies with her, the two of us engrossed in the combination of skill and luck that made up a game in which the table was an active participant as well. Keli was good at the game and clearly loved it, more skilled in the verbal rounds than I would have guessed, and almost as skillful when it came to the patterns. I was laughing at one particularly clever pattern of hers when I felt Jemeret's touch, and I made a deliberate choice to ignore it. His inquiry was gentle, curious, not demanding or urgent. I tried to slip through Keli's pattern, ran out of energy share before I managed it, and gave her the round.

"You're good," she said as the table used my previous pattern and hers to construct the one we would both have to escape.

"So are you," I told her. "Where did you learn scattergies?"

"On Tanaloa, when I first joined the MF." She broke contact with the table to freeze the game and took a long drink of her beer. I was drinking plain water. "The training we were getting was largely physical—act, don't think—so to keep our minds from drying up, we played this. When you don't have leave, and you're on Tanaloa, you can play one hell of a lot of scattergies." She grinned at me. "I was division champion." She started to recontact the table when her eyes slid past me, and I knew Jemeret had come in.

I felt his presence in multiple ways. I forced myself to keep my focus on the game and nodded at Keli to continue.

She won easily, because my consciousness was fragmented. "We'll play again," I promised her, rose, and at last looked at Jemeret.

He was slightly amused, but trying imperfectly to conceal it. "I'd like to speak with you," he said.

I nearly said something rude—so nearly it startled me. I bit it back and rose, almost speeding across the hall past him and into our cabin. He followed me in and let the door iris shut, then leaned back against it, his arms folded across his chest, studying me as he hadn't since Caryldon.

I sat down on the couch and curled my legs under me almost defensively. He noticed it and said quietly, "You're rushing things, love."

It wasn't what I expected to hear. I just looked at him.

"You're a long way from having to make any decisions." He continued to watch me, but he was not in any way using his sting. "So I think you probably ought to stop worrying so much about whether I'll understand how attractive you find some things here and just do what comes up."

"Is that what you're doing?" The words came out sharply, almost bitten off.

He kept his equanimity with almost embarrassing ease. "Ronica, if you want to know how I've been spending my time when I'm not with you, all you have to do is ask me."

And of course I'd known that. I took a long breath and asked, "What have you been doing?"

He stepped away from the door and came over to the couch,

sitting down beside me but leaning away, his arms across the top of the couch back. "I've been memorizing a Lumeship, pathfinding it in detail," he said. "The roll technology may not have changed since I was last out of Markover, but all the sub-light systems are more advanced, and I want to have pathfound and understood every one of them before we're off the ship."

It was a formidable task, for a rollship had thousands of systems, major and minor, and it would never have occurred to me to undertake it. "Why?" I asked him.

His gray eyes measured me. "I probably shouldn't need to remind you that we don't yet know the full scope of what we're going to have to do here, and that means we don't know what kind of resources we'll require. If at any point we have to steal a rollship, I suspect we should know how to use it."

I knew instantly that he was right, that somehow in my preoccupation with being back in the Com, I'd ignored the fact that he was still determined to find a way to shut down the MIs. "You think we might have to steal a rollship?"

He smiled. "I think there's no end to the possibilities of what we might have to do. I think we need to be as prepared as we can be. You remember University head Tonkway's statement that if you have eight days to get from Werd to Orokell, you better spend seven of them making sure the ship is operational."

Even knowing that he didn't mean it as a reproach, I felt reproached by it. Jemeret shook his head. "The problem with self-awareness is that you take it so seriously," he said. "There are five of us here with talent, if we assume Jasin Lebec can be brought to join us. We all have some strengths to contribute. If you forget something, there'll probably be someone there to remind you."

"But we're not all Class A," I protested, unaware until I said it that I'd just fallen into the same trap as Pel Nostro—the devaluing of lesser talents.

His face took on an expression I recognized very well, a mixture of concern and indulgence. Startled, I realized that there was about to be another revelation. I braced myself. "What is it this time?"

Jemeret said, "The division of talent into three classes is a fiction created by the Com, probably by the MIs. When I test babies for talent—and when you were tested by my na-sire—it's always a test of intensity, never of kind. The genetic mutation that creates talent isn't in any way subtle enough to discriminate. Only human beings do that."

The very idea was incomprehensible to me. The classes of talent were basic to my world. I had to gather to absorb the idea without beginning to laugh in denial.

He went on, "I think it's a question of training. In the Samothen, there aren't people with different kinds of power, just people with different amounts."

Now I wasn't thinking about laughing. "Are you telling me that Coney or Kray could have had Class A talent—what the Com calls Class A talent—projection and reading—" I stopped, angered.

"Maybe and maybe not," he said. "Neither of them may have had enough *raw* power, which means they could drain their reserves the first time they tried to do the most basic projecting. Zitten, the Class B that I lost, might have been able to do some rudimentary projection, but he was never given any training in it, and if it's not disciplined, it doesn't crystallize. It's possible that Coney could learn to do some pathfinding. Sandalari can already, and she can probably project at low levels as well. Most of the priesthood has that ability, in one permutation or other."

I suddenly recalled the Boru analyzing Coney with surprising accuracy when the Com first sent him down to Caryldon. I remembered, too, the mystery of fluctuant Class A's—people who sometimes seemed to have that ability and sometimes didn't. It occurred to me that, while deliberate projection was highly consumptive of energy and could seriously deplete someone without the strength to sustain it, unconscious projection or reading would be barely noticed by its user.

Now that I'd begun to adjust to what Jemeret had just told me, certain puzzles seemed much easier to understand. "Of course," I said, as if I should have known all along, the words measured, almost resigned, despite the excitement I was beginning to feel. "Of course talent would work that way. I'm a Class A—or whatever—because I have a good supply of raw power and I've been trained how to use my reflex."

Jemeret smiled a little, watching me.

I was remembering childish tantrums, in which I'd wielded power without thinking twice about it, and how Mortel John guided me from the wild power to a hard-fought, absolute control. I was thinking about the hours of study of brain physiology and function, about the even longer hours of practice. I had thought they molded my abilities to project and read, but instead they'd built them, just as Jemeret had rebuilt my brain.

Suddenly there were tears in my eyes, because I was thinking that perhaps Kray could have learned something of Class A work, which might have made him less jealous of me, and might have led to—

Jemeret yanked me up against him and held me tightly to his chest. "Think about it later," he said against my hair. "Let's talk about Barbin 3. We're almost there, and when we get there, we need to do something."

Almost guiltily, I realized I hadn't yet arrived at a scenario for Barbin 3, and yet it was my first Class A assignment. We would have to make something happen—preferably something meaningful—to real people in a lot of trouble.

"Do *you* have a scenario for Barbin 3?" I asked him. I was pretty certain that he didn't; you don't create even an unsuccessful scenario and memorize a rollship simultaneously.

"Tell the Com to let them go," he said, "and to hell with the telusite." I had to probe him lightly to see that he was only marginally serious.

"No, really."

"This is your assignment. What have you come up with?"

"My scenario was always going to be to get you to handle it," I said. "This is open warfare, and I was never interested in studying military strategy. The Com was so certain I could prevent wars that they never felt it necessary to show me how to stop one."

His smile was tugging at the corners of his mouth now.

"And I only showed you how to avoid them. So you'll have to use your imagination."

I must have looked skeptical.

"History says it's possible," he said. "We have a situation where the rebels have six plasma disruptors and are therefore unapproachable by human armies, even if those armies are bearing other illegal weapons. Where does that leave us?"

When I still said nothing, he went on, "What do you think a basic first step would be in stopping the fighting?"

I went with my first thought, impossible as it appeared to be. "I'd say we have to get our hands on the plasma disruptors."

"Think like a Class A," he said, with some irony. "Remember the kinds of things they need the sting for."

I thought about it for a few minutes, then said, "We have to persuade the people inside the plasma disruptors to put them out of commission for us."

He kissed my neck. "Very good, love. We'll make a peacemaker of you yet." It was such a simple statement. I didn't know what it would cost. Perhaps I still don't.

And that was as much as I'd thought out by myself before Jasin Lebec rounded us up for the conference room vid from Pel Nostro. I wanted to stall him off, but Jemeret agreed we would take the call, and I wasn't going to argue with him.

We went to the conference room to find Pel already visible on the far side of the table, by himself. The conference room on his side of the table was slightly darker than ours, and the eftel hadn't equalized the lighting, so the line of demarcation was much more noticeable than usual.

He smiled at us as we came in and rose, though in theory we were all of equal rank and needed to pay one another no visible honor. I nodded to him as I slid into a seat between the two men.

"I can't tell you what pleasure it gives me to see you all together," the Com Counselor said. "I never thought I'd live to see three Class A's in the Com at one time."

I swiftly debated making a comment, but decided against it and simply folded my hands on the table in front of me. Jemeret asked, "Has the situation on Barbin 3 changed, Pel?"

The Com Counselor sat down again, saying, "No, of course not. Well, not exactly. Not directly."

Even Jasin Lebec frowned at that.

I wished this wasn't going on in eftel, so I could read him, and I guessed that Jemeret felt exactly the same way. I asked, "Then why did you call us?"

Pel Nostro glanced to one side, then said, "I want you to be aware of something. The Tribunal met to discuss your marriage, and they feel the circumstances under which you were put into the hands of Jemeret Cavanaugh may call for government intervention to free you from him. The decision has been registered, and will be studied in theory by Petra Chantrey's staff, then brought before the Chief Justiciar if grounds are indeed identified."

Jasin Lebec was frowning even harder. Jemeret had gone very still, and I was nearly choked with sudden anxiety. "And what motivates you to make us aware of this, Pel?" I asked him. "Surely you'd prefer that whatever the Tribunal plans to get me away from Jemeret would have some chance for success?"

Jemeret had suppressed his feelings and was now leaning almost negligently on the tabletop, with one arm extended, his hand forcibly relaxed. He was, I knew, waiting for Pel's reply.

The Com Counselor tried to keep looking at me, but was unable to keep his gaze from straying to Jemeret before he caught control of it. "The Tribunal feels it will not need to invoke any intervention as long as things continue to go well and you observe your oath, Ronica McBride," he said. "I thought, before you reached and needed to handle the problem of Barbin 3, you should know." He sounded faintly offended to have his good motives doubted.

"We had an agreement," Jemeret said coldly then. "You knew it would have to be a sexual healing."

Pel Nostro nodded at him. "The agreement stands," he said. "I personally have no problems with your spiking her from now until the universe collapses, and I'm certain the Tribunal feels the same way." I fought back the sudden heat in my face. "However, the agreement did not involve you marrying her."

He nodded at me, then at Jasin Lebec, and his side of the room vanished.

Jemeret laughed once, sharply, humorlessly. "They're even more nervous than I thought they'd be," he said. "The threats are starting sooner than I expected."

"Should I be worried?" I asked him.

"Only about Barbin 3," he answered. "We still need to work out a detailed, viable scenario."

"You haven't come up with anything worth trying yet?" Jasin Lebec asked.

"We haven't really put our minds to it," my lord said. "Just as a matter of interest, how do you feel about Pel and the Tribunal attempting to coerce Ronica's compliance?"

His grandfather turned bland eyes on him, leaning forward to make certain they could see each other well. "It wasn't unexpected," he said. "The marriage must have impressed them as *your* attempt to coerce her compliance, perhaps in violation of the terms of the agreement. They would naturally want to find a way to neutralize your influence."

I made a rude, astonished noise, surprising all three of us.

Jasin Lebec looked at me and his expression softened. "I know you are tied to him, child," he said. "My projective abilities may be wanting, but there's nothing wrong with my reading, and you glow at him. It's just that the government takes the form of marriage very seriously."

"So do I," I said with unexpected intensity. "And I find it unbelievably demeaning that the Com can't credit me with some volition of my own."

Jasin Lebec said calmly, "It's not your volition anyone questions, Ronica. It's your ability to judge clearly while being subjected to a Class A sexual onslaught."

Jemeret's anger returned with a rush, and his control over it nearly slipped. I felt it start to go, and then he wrenched his power back over himself again, holding the fury in check. I laid my hand lightly on his arm and looked Jasin Lebec squarely in the eye. "They will probably trust you more than they will either of us, so I want you to try to convince them of a great truth in my life," I said.

"Which is?" the old man asked.

Jemeret looked at me curiously, the anger muting down.

"I want you to tell them," I said, "that, for me, in the final analysis, love is a much more potent lubricant than lust could ever be."

"And so you are saying you love my grandson?" Jasin Lebec asked. "I ask it because I overwhelmed his grandmother sexually, but we had very little real love between us."

I started to deny that I'd been overwhelmed, but bit it back after the first, abortive syllable. For a long moment none of us moved. For the first time in a long while, I was thinking about the issue of "fairness." Jemeret had kept his word to me, had never forced me physically, had not taken me until I was ready to accept him. But—

I had lost my focus, and now I looked back at Jasin Lebec again. "Yes, I love him," I said. "And yes, at the beginning he overwhelmed me. But he had the wisdom not to allow me to remain overwhelmed."

Jemeret relaxed. "You know how strong she is. And you know me, na-sire. I've always looked for the woman I could share my life with, not one I would have to compel. This is the one, and she had to make her own choices in the end."

"Did you win her fairly, Jemeret, or did you unbalance the fight?"

I looked between the two of them, and I could see the family resemblance, the similar shapes of the eyes, the matching angles of jaws and cheekbones, the comparable mold of the noses.

Jemeret smiled. "Of course I unbalanced the fight," he said, "just as you do every time you 'aid' in negotiations or 'help' people adjust their goals. But I only did it at the outset. You do it to carry out the Com's political agenda. I was fighting for her life."

Jasin Lebec nodded once. "The government believes it's fighting for her life as well. She is oath-bound."

"She's aware of that!" I said somewhat astringently. Jemeret's arm slid out from under my hand. I caught control of myself. "Jasin Lebec, I don't think that I'm a child any longer.

I remember my oath. Tell them to trust that. Jemeret, I need to see if Tynnanna's all right. He's been shut up for a very long time now."

It was an excuse. No one questioned it.

Jemeret and I rose, and Jasin Lebec turned in his chair to follow us with his eyes. I half expected him to ask about the klawit—I'd been expecting everyone to ask about the cat since the *Megalume* left Markover, but no one had.

In one of the cargo holds, as Tynnanna raced around the large space, powerful muscles bunching and relaxing, Jemeret and I talked quietly about Barbin 3. By the time *Megalume* went through its final roll and achieved orbit, we had evolved a workable scenario.

The population of Barbin 3 was about six and a half million, and more than two million of them—men, women, and children—could now be counted in the rebel camp. The six plasma disruptors were being used to hold four key cities and the two spaceports. Each of the disruptors was manned by a crew of two, resupplied from the outside, and supporting thirty to fifty remote, handheld units in the field, to stop anyone trying to interrupt the resupply process.

Coney, Jasin Lebec, Jemeret, and I sat in front of the holo field, looking at the six points of red light representing the plasma disruptors. By eftel vid, Pel Nostro and Terrill Guthrie watched it and us from Orokell. As it was my assignment, Jemeret agreed that I should do the presentation, and now that I knew he'd approved the scenario—parts of which I was instrumental in formulating—I felt confident enough.

"Of course, the handhelds are of no importance to us," I said, "because they'll die when the disruptors go down. I estimate we'll need to take the disruptors three at a time, in two raids—these two at the spaceports and the one here first, because that's the central triangle."

"We can give you Drenalion protection—" Terrill Guthrie began, but I sharply said, "No!" as Jemeret's head came up and he said, "You will *not* send the Drenalion back to Barbin 3 under any circumstances."

Terrill Guthrie was angry at that, but Pel Nostro was both calm and unsurprised. "How can we protect you, then?" he asked dispassionately.

"We'll use the remaining units of the planetary corps," I said. Now that we were in orbit, we were certain we'd come under MI surveillance, which could be conducted from the surface of the planet, and we had deliberately gone over the plan earlier for their benefit. I had wondered if they would tell the Tribunal what they overheard, but gathered now that they hadn't. I wanted to be curious about it, but there wasn't time. "We believe the planetary corps has every reason to want to see the disruptors stopped."

"All right, assuming the presence of planetary corps units," Pel Nostro said, "how can you get in without the rebels turning the disruptors on you?"

This was the hard, the unavoidable, part of the scenario. "We can't," I said steadily. "That's why we have to go in singly—except that Jasin Lebec will need to take Sandalari with him on the first descent, then Coney on the second, to use their reserves. We'll take a blast from the disruptors to be decoys for the corps units, and then as soon as they turn their attention to the corps, we'll sting the disruptor operators before the units can be realigned to aim closely at the corps."

There was a lengthy silence. There were a few more permutations to the scenario, involving getting the strength of the disruptor beams diffused, but I decided not to bring them in just at the moment. Out of the corner of my eye I saw Jasin Lebec's hands tremble slightly before he controlled them, but he said nothing. I realized he hadn't heard any of this before, because we hadn't had a chance to tell him before the meeting, and he was reacting to the news that he would have to take a hit from the disruptor beam. We'd seriously tried to figure another way, for his benefit, but the costs of the alternatives were all too high.

Pel Nostro said, "Percentages."

There was a click, and we knew the MI observers had weighed in. "What do you project as the duration of a raid?" asked the strangely androgynous voice. I couldn't tell whether it came from our wall speakers or those on Orokell. It made little difference; they were synched by the presence of the eftel contact.

"We estimate approximately ninety-eight seconds from the time they discover us until the time a disruptor dies," Jemeret said.

"And how are you proposing to survive the disruptor blast?" Pel Nostro asked.

"There are five power suits in this ship's inventory," I said. "We'll need them."

"A power suit cannot fully deflect the blast of a plasma disruptor," Pel Nostro said, as if we didn't know it already.

"Neither can a Class C shield," I told him, "but we believe the two in combination will provide a strong enough defense to get us through the blast."

"Estimate for success on first raid is eighty-two percent," the MI said. "We find that acceptable."

"What's the estimate for the second raid?" Jasin Lebec asked.

"The figure drops to fifty-eight percent, plus or minus four percent, and is dependent on the reserve capacity of the Class A's."

Pel Nostro looked at Jasin Lebec. "Is this tantamount to suicide on your part?"

"Thank you for the vote of confidence," Jasin Lebec said dryly. "As it happens, I'll have fresh reserves to draw on for the second raid."

"Sixty percent," amended the MI voice, oblivious, as always, to anyone's feelings.

"By the balance," Coney said, his voice carefully expressionless, "I'm worth two whole percentage points."

"Plus or minus four percent," I couldn't resist adding.

It was patently absurd, and Jasin Lebec surprised us all by saying to Coney, "You'll always be worth at least eight percent to me, son."

Pel Nostro threw his hands up in complete exasperation. He seemed to debate something briefly, then ordered Terrill

Guthrie from the room. The big man didn't hesitate, he just went. My estimation of Pel rose a notch at that.

Then the Com Counselor folded his hands on the table in front of him and said, "I'd like to speak to Class A Ronica McBride in private."

Jasin Lebec rose immediately, but paused when no one else moved. I felt Jemeret's tension radiating from him, so I touched him lightly with the sting to reassure him that it would be fine. For a moment I expected him to ignore me, but he got slowly to his feet, asking me deliberately, "Will you be all right?"

"Of course." I said it almost dismissively.

Coney left the room before either of the Class A men. Jemeret looked long and hard at Pel, as if he could read him through the eftel vid, then went out. Jasin Lebec remained longest, though I had no idea why. When he, too, was gone, and, I thought, only the silent MIs were listening, I asked, "What's the matter with the scenario, Pel?"

He unfolded his hands. "With the scenario? Nothing that I can see except that Jasin Lebec may not survive it. That's your choice. The matter is with—" He paused, searching for a diplomatic phrase or two; I didn't think he'd found one. "—the attitude you and those around you are bringing to the Com. Talent is not treated with irreverence here, Ronica McBride. You should remember from your training the absolute necessity of your work to our functioning as a society."

There were so many ways I could have replied. Even two tendays later I might have responded in an entirely different way. I said in a low voice, "Talent isn't a monolith, Pel. I'll never be Jasin Lebec."

He nodded. "I can accept that," he said. "Just see to it that you don't become Jemeret Cavanaugh, either. We need talent that works with us and for us."

It didn't sound like any kind of threat, but of course it was. I thought detachedly that he would have to be good at diplomacy to have held his job this long.

As coldly as I could I said, "Then if you need it so much,

perhaps you could do some things to ensure that Tial Borland isn't carved up while he sleeps."

Color rose in his face, and before he could say anything in reply, I cut off the vid contact, slamming my hand a little harder than necessary into the table control that led to the eftel. Then I rose, shaking, and went to find the others, who were waiting in the lounge.

In only seventeen hours it would be full, moonless night over the primary targets, and then we would have to act.

Coney was first to acknowledge that. "I'm going to wake Sandi and tell her what the scenario is," he said. "I'll meet you in lander bay one at hour four, low watch."

Jasin Lebec said, "I'm going to get some sleep. I'm too old for this, and I'm not certain what taking two disruptor hits will do to me." He did not sound frightened, just weary.

"We tried to think of a way to spare you," Jemeret said quietly, "but our chances of surviving three hits were not very good, even in power suits."

"I understand," the old man said, "and from the Com's point of view, I am the expendable life among the three of us."

I should not have been surprised at how angry I sounded. "There are no expendable lives, Jasin Lebec. There are sometimes lives which have to be spent, but they're not expendable."

After being part of the avoidance of war several times on Caryldon, and then being caught in that last, minor skirmish at the very end of our stay, I was now confronting the necessity of fighting.

Jemeret took my arm, and we went back to our cabin. "You should probably try to get a little sleep, too," he said to me when the door irised shut. "You've been overextended lately, and you should tamp down your adrenals and save your energy."

"I'd rather you onslaughted me," I said flatly, and he stared at me for a full second before he laughed.

"You can relax without it, you know," he said, his voice caressing my nerves. "And the MIs are monitoring us now."

"I don't much care." I meant it. Even if I hadn't stopped

caring about the possibility of being watched by the MIs when we were on Markover Station, we were about to go to war, and I wanted to know beyond any doubt that Jemeret and I could still have what we'd had on Caryldon.

"There's something I want you to know first," he said, surprising me. "If I was reading you accurately in the conference room—" And when had he read me other than accurately? "—you expected me to agree with you that there are no expendable lives."

I nodded.

"I don't agree with you, love. To me, the nonexpendable lives, the irreplaceable ones, are those with power." He watched me, but he didn't touch me with his sting. He wouldn't influence my reaction to this. I didn't accept it, and I didn't want to believe him. It was hard not to, hard not to tell him he was wrong. He went on, "I take being a chief very seriously, Ronica. My tribe is the Boru, yes, but it's also the Samothen, and that makes me responsible for all people with power. If it came to a choice between the few of us with talent and the multitude without, I wouldn't hesitate."

For a long moment I couldn't move at all, the mix of conflicting feelings battling in me so strongly that I didn't know how I was going to be able to respond. Part of me believed absolutely that he was right, that if it came down to that kind of choice, I would stand with him without a second thought about it. And another part of me reverberated with the starfire's pronouncement that I was High Lady to more than the Samothen, that my obligations were to the human tribe as a whole. At last I had to speak. "I take being High Lady as seriously as you take being a chief, even if I haven't had nearly as much experience at it. So I have to conceive my role as making certain it doesn't come to a choice between those with power and those without it." Deep inside, there was a ripple of fear, a presentiment in a place where precognition had never existed, that such a confrontation might be unavoidable. I pushed it back, ignoring it. "If it did somehow come to that choice, I don't know where I would stand." My voice nearly failed; I was saying that I might have to take a stand against him. "I know I didn't have to atone for the Drenalion life I took, or for Evesti the way I had to atone for Kray and the hitch, but I think I have to learn to feel them more. You taught me that people are worlds, and some worlds are just more powerful than others. That doesn't make them better." Just as he hadn't stung me, I didn't sting him.

His face remained impassive. He reached out and stroked my cheek with one fingertip. "We each have our responsibilities," he said softly. "And right now, our first responsibility is to Barbin 3."

"Does it change anything?" I asked him almost fearfully, locked into the depths of his gray eyes.

For an answer he drew me against him and kissed me, but when we made love, he didn't use the sting, and in response, neither did I. I told myself we would need all our strength for what was to come on the surface.

And I prayed, foolishly hopeful, that there would never come a time when he and I would need to confront each other over something important.

The *Megalume*'s instruments showed the first three planetary corps units in place on the surface of Barbin 3, and each of us, the Com's three Class A's, got into separate hyperdrive battle capsules—Jasin Lebec sharing his, uncomfortably tightly, with Sandalari. Coney waited with Keli, both of them pale and worried, on the capsule deck. He'd tried to convince me to let him go first, but I insisted he make the second sortie, when Jasin Lebec was likely to be weaker. It was a mistake.

The ship shot a hundred decoy capsules out with us in a wide enough pattern to force a diffusion of the disruptor beams. I was aimed at one of the two spaceports, and I guided my capsule to land on the cabin of the disruptor itself. Responding to previously programmed instructions, the dummy capsules dived and swerved as if they were also guided.

Even wearing a power suit and holding a complete, carefully constructed Class C shield around myself, I couldn't escape the blast, which was both painful and overwhelmingly nauseating. I fought it hard, not trying to protect reserves, both in order to increase the odds of a successful mission and because vomiting in a power suit could mean asphyxiation. I hit the trigger that would fire flares out of half the decoy capsules, signaling the planetary corps to begin the diversion, and was infinitely grateful when the disruptor beam's power began to lessen as it was thrown onto pause for recalibration. My capsule hit and bounced along the cabin roof, even as the other capsules dropped around it. I banished the shield, flipped open the faceplate of my suit, and instantly swept the cabin below me, identifying and taking control of the two minds I found.

The disruptor had to be destroyed beyond hope of repair, and I didn't have any time to pathfind it. I took one of the operators and made him overload and subsequently fuse the beam guidance system, still on pause for the resetting. While he was doing that, I persuaded the other operator to take hold of a nearby charger stalk and begin smashing the control panel with it. I implanted in her the need to keep smashing until nothing was left but shards.

Without bothering to check for normal fire that might be aimed in my direction, I held the minds as long as I thought I could, then fired the liftoff jets of the capsule and let the ship haul me in. Under acceleration, I managed to get my faceplate closed, feeling stupid that I hadn't thought to do it before lifting.

Jemeret was already on the capsule deck, out of his own capsule, and as I climbed out of mine, he hugged me hard, pulling open my faceplate again and probing for the strength of my reserves. He had preserved most of his own strength, leading me to believe that he'd accepted a much harder hit from his disruptor than I had from mine.

While I was still recovering my equilibrium and clinging to Jemeret, the crewman manipulating the retrieval beam called out, "I've got them!" A few moments later the third occupied capsule had been pulled through the airlock and dumped on the deck. Jasin Lebec signaled that he was all right, and Jemeret set me aside to haul Sandalari out of the cramped quarters. She was very pale, very nearly drained. Keli ran forward and caught her other arm as Coney started toward her.

I had to stop him. "Coney, seal up your suit."

Jemeret told Keli to pump some restoratives into Sandalari, then went on, "We've got to get back down there before they realize what's happening and have time to regroup at the remaining disruptor sites."

We left Sandalari with Keli and ran for the second lander bay, where another stack of about a hundred capsules waited to be launched.

We had decided earlier that we needed to accomplish the second raid as fast as possible, even though it was only twilight at two of the sites, and we assigned the night site to Jasin Lebec and Coney. I felt a stab that I'd made him leave Sandalari before he knew that she was all right, but there was no avoiding it. We sealed ourselves into the three guided capsules and were dropped for the second time in less than a quarter hour.

This time, the blast from the disruptor was much harder to take, and I had to control as strongly as I could to keep from being sick, which magnified the nausea. It was a greater effort to release the flares, and when the beam lessened at last, I was gasping. My capsule was less under my control, and I hit the disruptor too hard and slid from the cabin roof to the support deck. I had my faceplate up before the capsule stopped bouncing, and my sweep for minds showed three—two inside the cabin and one approaching the capsule. I lashed once at the closest mind to incapacitate it, but restrained the blow even as I rushed to make the operators duplicate the destruction of the first raid. I couldn't wait as long this time; my reserves were too low now. I pushed it further than I should have, but then I suppose I always do. The capsule had sustained one direct hit from a conventional needle beam, but I got the liftoff jets to fire, slammed the faceplate just as the gravity dragged on me, and then fought to stay conscious while the *Megalume* pulled me back in.

I was swimming in and out of awareness when the capsule was opened in the landing bay, and all I could see in a somewhat limited field of vision was Jemeret, looking exhausted, but certainly still stronger than I. He stripped me out of the power suit and picked me up, and I vaguely heard him say something like, "Don't let anyone near her until she's recovered." I didn't know who he was talking to. I felt his arms tighten around me, and I slipped gratefully into deep.

I was alone in the large bed in our cabin when I awoke. The bed field was off and the lights dim. Their faint flicker spoke of an energy drain, which startled me. I sat up, pushing aside the cover that had been laid over me to compensate for the field's absence, and felt for the level of my reserves, finding them two-thirds replenished, but not full. I hadn't been in deep long enough; something had awakened me. Tentatively, for the reserves had been drained more than was safe, I gathered. There was no pain.

Immediately, I swept a sensory scout outward in a search. Jasin Lebec was in his cabin, deeping. So was Sandalari. Tynnanna was pacing restlessly in his own cabin, but he had not attempted to come out the door. No one else was in this arm of *Megalume*.

I threw my legs over the side of the bed and stood up so fast that I had to gather to thrust away the resultant dizziness. My dark blue jumpsuit was lying crumpled on the carpet; I vaguely remembered it being soaked with sweat. I pulled another jumpsuit from the dispenser and yanked it on without pausing to alter the gold color to dark blue. Something was wrong.

I ran out of the branching arm toward the central bubble, sweeping for Jemeret, Coney, or Keli, but found none of their signatures as I rounded the bridge. I ignored the two cargo arms and the crew quarters, turning instead to the high watch arm with the conference room in it. My sweep this time caught the unmistakable sign of Jemeret's presence, and I ran toward it as quickly as possible without accelerating.

It was issuing from the med. This door didn't iris automatically to my presence—med doors were double, creating the possibility of a containment area within the ship—so I laid my hand on the control, pathfound it, and made it open. Once the outer door had closed, the inside door opened, and I nearly leaped into the inner med itself.

Keli spun, falling into a crouch, then straightening when she realized it was me.

There were four other people in the med, and I saw at once why power was reduced throughout the ship. It takes an enormous amount of energy to maintain a stasis field.

Coney hung in stasis, naked. He looked very much as I must have looked those years in the radiant fluid, except that my hair was longer and would have moved sluggishly, with the circulation in my tank. The horror of years of shut-off memory crashed once again upon me, and it was as if a blinding flash snapped through my brain. Even as the scream sprang out of me, I was fighting it, but the massive weight of the horror, so familiar, was threatening to overwhelm me. Coney was dead.

Distantly, I heard Jemeret's curse and felt his mind capturing mine instantly. I could barely see, and in the grayness his face was very close. I think I might have started to collapse, but his hands on my shoulders were supporting me. Then I was unconscious.

Memory can be such a treacherous thing. Jemeret had truly thought I was ready to remember when he brought back the rape and the killing. But he'd been there, in my mind, when I remembered—keeping the negative emotions at a minimum, holding me up, bolstering a self-image still raked by self-condemnation. I had never faced it, suddenly, without him. Seeing Coney in stasis, thinking that I was responsible for the death of my other childhood friend—this time a man who had done me no harm, who loved me unselfishly—it all crashed back, like a wall exploding over me, burying me.

This time he caught me soon enough. This time I only lost a tenday. And, in some ways, we learned later, it was almost fortuitous because the MIs had observed it, and they suggested to the Tribunal in the strongest possible terms that the government make no attempt to separate us, so the theoretical examination of the validity of our marriage was unceremoniously dropped.

VI. The Spoken Waysong

"I'd've been able to wake you sooner if I'd have had more energy to draw on," Jemeret said with an edge of regret. "You blew when Jasin and Sandalari were unusable, Coney was gone, and I had less than a tenth of my reserves left."

I was lying pressed tightly against Tynnanna's side, on the warm earth of one of Barbin 3's wilderness areas. There were scars from the war here, but there were also birds singing and the caress of sun-warmed breezes.

Coney and Sandalari had chosen to swim in the nearby lake, and we could hear them laughing. "Thank the stars he was reparable," I said softly.

"Thank the stars you were," he added. He sat down beside me, stroking my bare leg. "If I'd been a second or two later, you'd still be unconscious."

"I started with my sight," I said, opening my eyes and looking at him. "I didn't know I was going to do that."

His hand went on moving slowly, gently, circling my ankle, cupping and molding my calf, rubbing my thigh. "Sight was what brought you the picture of Coney that you didn't want to see," he said, his voice as soothing as the movement of his hand. "That's why you attacked it. I restored it last, and I woke you as soon as I could."

I was strangely detached. "I've got to stop doing that."

"You weren't responsible for what happened to Coney." He took my hand and raised me off Tynnanna, who sprang to his feet and leaped off across the grasses, tearing up the turf with extended claws.

"I don't even understand why I did it," I went on.

"The past is powerful," he said, lying back and drawing me against his chest. "I suppose I should have expected some sort of recurrence, but I didn't anticipate it at that moment."

"Will I—will it keep—" The detachment seemed to sink away into the ground. "I can't—"

He drew me in tightly. "It's a problem," he said flatly. "You now consider yourself responsible for humankind, as I believe you told me before we had a war to stop. And so you hate it when you feel responsible for anyone's death, and the death of someone with power is even more abhorrent to you. Then you internalize the feelings and turn them on yourself."

"I've got to learn to control it," I said. "It took me entirely unaware, and I couldn't stop it because I didn't know what was happening."

Jemeret pulled me higher on his chest and spoke against my forehead. "People are going to die, love. You and I haven't the power to stop it from happening. Sometimes we may even have to kill them; sometimes there are no choices. I don't want you to destroy yourself over them. There are some things we simply can't control."

"You brought Coney back."

He nodded. "It was a question of how fast the ship's personnel got him into stasis, and then it was just a question of refilling his reserves and reanimating him. Jasin didn't realize how completely he'd drained him, because he was used to the size of his own reserves, and Coney's were smaller even than Sandalari's." He sighed, his chest lifting me, lowering me. "If they'd been a minute or two later getting him into the stasis field, I'd have lost him. And I don't like to lose."

"I thought I didn't either." My voice sounded strangely wistful, even to me. "And I keep losing myself."

He sat up, almost spilling me, took my shoulders and turned me toward him. "You aren't losing yourself, Ronica," he said, so strongly that I trembled. "You're trying to throw yourself away, and I won't let you do it."

I heard Sandalari laughing, and I leaned in against my lord, letting him surround me with his arms again. "Then you'd better not leave me alone," I said.

We had helped set in motion the end of the war on Barbin 3, and then we'd slept through it. Jasin Lebec recovered first, because his reserves had remained full, even though he was working hard accessing those of Coney and Sandalari. By the time he awakened, Coney was alive again, and we were all four asleep, so he was the only one of us who had actually been able to follow the remainder of the war. He was, therefore, the one in a position to tell us something about it.

Once the plasma disruptors had been put out of commission, the planetary corps units were able to retake the spaceports and bring in some MF reserves. The corps had, however, something to prove, and the bulk of the people supporting the rebels fled when no longer protected by the shield of the disruptors. Cephalic ray devices were turned over to the corps members without any argument, and it turned out that most of them had never been used. Arming a populace that does not care to use its arms is an interesting exercise in futility. The desire for a peaceful solution was not part of the thinking of the government decision makers once the war began; it never left the minds of the loyal citizens.

The government of Gayli Hatlo quickly reasserted itself, and the surface was calm. Most of the systems were in the process of being restored. The rebel leaders, who had been identified by DNA spectrograph, were apprehended and being transported by the rollship *Felume* to Orokell for trial. And, of almost no real importance to us, but somehow of surpassing importance to the government of Barbin 3, when we were recovered, they wanted very much to hold a banquet for us.

After a while I detached myself from Jemeret and walked away along the edge of the lake. I'd asked to speak to Jasin Lebec alone—it would be only the fourth time in our lives we met without anyone else present—and he agreed. Even though I knew there would be no such thing as complete isolation on the surface of a Com world, except, perhaps, in the wild, I decided I was going to speak as honestly as I could. I had decided that Coney might have been mistaken about my not showing the MIs that Jemeret had changed me. Though the MIs were seriously flawed when it came to understanding human beings, they understood the conservation and wise use of resources, and they had just seen Jemeret save me for a second time. If their analysis programs were working, they would already have computed that it took a Class A to save a Class A from a Class A.

We had emplaneted in the city of Jansen, named after the captain of the exploratory mission that identified the telusite deposits on this world. The city itself was peripherally touched by the war, but it had not been a major site, being primarily a recreational area for the mine workers. The wilderness area was not wild at all, but it was the largest of four on the planet.

We'd put Tynnanna in the open and warned everyone to stay out of it unless they had a pressing desire to become a klawit meal. Then we accepted lodgings in the lakeside villas reserved ordinarily for those with the highest productivity records. The rules would probably change after we left; the recreational complex for government managers had been destroyed in the early days of the fighting, and it was likely they would take over this one.

Jasin Lebec waited for me at the lakeshore, looking just as I remembered him—contained, controlled, and pleased to see me functioning again. "Are you recovered fully?" he asked me, gesturing to the bench beside him. "Your first assignment was an arduous one."

I perched on the bench cross-legged, watching him. "As much as I could be, since I took myself by complete surprise and did more damage than the plasma disruptors," I said. "Jasin Lebec, tell me honestly. Did you nearly drain yourself every time you went out on assignment? If not every time, then *any* time?"

He shook his head. "I never found it necessary. I was able to do subtle work. This war would never have reached a gross stage if I'd been able to turn aside the dissatisfaction of the rebels before the plasma disruptors or the Drenalion. That's the way it generally happened in my term as Class A."

I rested my hands on my knees. "Did you ever kill anyone?"

He seemed to reflect on that for a long time, his eyes distant, his face serious. Then he refocused on me, as if just remembering that I was there. "Directly?" His mouth twisted a little. "Not until I stupidly drained Coney in the battle capsule. But indirectly? I believe I was probably responsible for a number of deaths. They're unavoidable in Com politics, even when a Class A is involved—here, anywhere, or anytime else." His gaze was direct, level. "Do you ask me that question because you've killed a number of people, Ronica McBride?"

"Drenalion aren't people," I said with real conviction. "The part of them that would render them human got left out in the cloning, and any vestige of it that might slip through gets eliminated in the successive clone runs." I remembered Evesti of the Ilto, and then the hitch, both of them my enemies, both of them out to harm me and those I valued. "Then sometimes someone you believe to be human turns out to be a Drenalion after all. And there's no real regret necessary." I looked away from him, across the placid surface of the water. "But killing a human being is something entirely different."

Jasin Lebec said quietly, "And so it continues to haunt you, having killed Kray."

My eyes flew back to him, startled.

"You're no different from any of the rest of us, Ronica McBride, except that you're a woman, and you have a woman's way of internalizing the fault for things which cannot be helped."

I heard him, but barely. I was thinking that if I had killed the brutish guard at the Lewannee estatehouse, it would not have bothered me, that if, when I first found myself on Caryldon, I'd had to kill Dogul to escape, I might have done it without a qualm. And yet over Kray and then again over Coney, I had punished myself immediately. The deaths that affected me most deeply, most overwhelmingly, were the deaths of people with talent. I was almost embarrassed by the revelation. I had just recently declared that to be Jemeret's obsession, not mine.

Then I told myself that these were also people I loved. I know it's perfectly normal to feel the deaths of those closest to us more than the deaths of strangers, but I felt that was somehow unworthy of me, of the honor the starfire had given me.

"My education has taught me that nothing can't be helped, not when you combine technology and talent." It was a basic lesson. He would know I'd been taught it.

"You know better," he said mildly.

And because at heart I didn't believe my own argument, I decided to defend it. "Mortel John always used you as the prime example of how controllable everything is. He taught me that I would be a failure if I got into situations I couldn't control."

Jasin Lebec took my hands. "I think you were probably taught that you were a significant tool of government policy and power," he said, "and you interpreted it to mean that you would be completely at fault if the government failed to use you correctly."

"What?"

"You heard me." He let go of my hands again. "You have to learn to evaluate the nature of Class A assignments. You can accept or refuse them, you know. Jemeret has refused plenty."

"He's not under oath," I said.

"Neither am I," Jasin Lebec said.

"What?" The word almost exploded out of me in disbelief.

"They didn't institute the oath until Jemeret rebelled and demanded they return him to Caryldon."

I couldn't stay seated on the bench. I jumped to my feet and walked back and forth for a moment, trying to release the pent-up energy. He was saying that I was the only Class A oath-bound to the Com. And yet . . .

He had watched me pace, and now his dark eyes were level as I turned on him. "Are you telling me that you've spent your entire life serving all over the Com, with barely a moment to yourself, and you were never sworn to?" I didn't know if I was being indiscreet or impolite, but I didn't care.

His voice was still devoid of any strong emotion. "I didn't think there was anything more worth doing," he said.

I kept silent for a time, then said, "And you're not haunted by any of the deaths you might have caused, or any of the people you might have swayed to betray themselves in other ways?"

He shook his head. "I don't internalize," he said. "Neither does Jemeret. You're the first truly powerful woman with Class A ability, and no one taught you not to take it all in upon yourself."

Was he blaming me? Or was he saying that the men who had formed me hadn't thought to take into account that I was a woman as well as a talent? Somehow the thoughts caused me both distress and confusion, and I must have projected it, because in no time at all Jemeret appeared.

Jasin Lebec rose, nodded to his grandson, and then smiled gently at me. "But if you found other things worth doing more, I would probably not try to persuade you that you were wrong," he said. He and Jemeret exchanged a few innocuous greetings, and then the old man who had so dominated my life from a distance turned and walked off in the direction of the buildings.

Jemeret turned back to me. "All right?"

"A lot to absorb," I said. "A lot to live up to."

"Just live," he said quietly. "Here come Coney and Sandalari. I wonder if Coney got them to drop the idea of the banquet and let us get on with things."

Death in the Com can have a certain impermanence to it. That gives those who truly die an unwelcome stigma, as if they betrayed the living by leaving them. The Com physicians even describe some people as being in a state of "semi-mort," meaning, "If it weren't for us, he'd be a goner." But Coney would have been truly dead if Jemeret hadn't been able to get into his mind the instant stasis broke. Luckily, the paths Jasin Lebec had used to drain him were still identifiable, like the edges of a wound that hadn't yet healed. Jemeret could pour reserve energy into him just as he had into me when I'd drained myself too far. Now that Coney was back among us, except for not being able to gather for about a tenday and a half, he was fine.

I'd hugged him hard, he'd told me to stop being so tough on myself, and then Sandalari appropriated him. Now it was as if he'd never been gone.

So we'd asked him to call Gayli Hatlo and try to convince

her that we needed no ceremonies. We thought she might be more receptive if he were the one doing the asking, since he'd been the one who died. He came up to us now, a little ahead of Sandalari, who had dropped the towel she was trying to wrap around herself and stopped to pick it up, covered with sand.

"Any luck?" Jemeret asked him.

Coney ran his hands back through his wet hair. "I didn't have any, so I asked Pel to call and try his best, figuring he owed it to us, but I don't think he'll try very hard. Com banquets are fairly standard, and I gather that the only one Barbin 3 ever got to host before was on entrance into the Com."

"I suppose I should just have resigned myself to the fact that three Class A's would prove to be a greater honor than anyone could bear banquetless," Jemeret said.

"Pel did tell me we had to uphold the image of the Com," Coney said with a laugh. "I suppose I should have pointed out that that's his job, not ours."

I made a face, and Jemeret laughed softly, then sobered. "I think we all need to begin to face up to the fact that this is probably one of Jasin Lebec's last assignments."

"Strange," I said, reflecting. "I thought he'd have another twenty or twenty-five years of service when I first met him."

"He probably would have," Jemeret said. "But they used him unrelentingly, and I think what happened to you and Kray was a breaking point for him." Coney looked down at his hands. Sandalari moved smoothly past us to the pile of towels near our suite doors.

"He doesn't internalize things," I said. "He told me so."

"Compared to you, none of us does," Jemeret said, "but don't be fooled. He feels things."

Sandalari came back from the suite, wrapping herself in a large towel. "Someone's been calling on the comsole," she said. "I thought I heard it when I was swimming, but I ignored it. This time the signal's so loud, I'd guess it was at least the fourth call, maybe more."

"Why didn't you answer it?" I asked her.

She laughed. "Not me. I know my place in this hierarchy, and it's at the bottom."

"Not quite," Coney said dryly.

"Come on," I said, "I think we need to take the call."

The signal was indeed reaching the piercing stage when we got to the first-floor room of our suite. Jemeret immediately hit the receive, and the holo images leaped into place, much stronger and more vivid than an eftel vid. It was Governor Gayli Hatlo and her interchangeable assistants, as distinct as if they were in the room with us, barring the slight shimmer characteristic of a call. All three of them rose as we received, and the governor began speaking before we'd even acknowledged their presence.

"You have our everlasting gratitude, Class A Ronica McBride, Acting Class A Jemeret Cavanaugh, and our debt to the Com is one we can never fully repay. We are happy to be able to honor you at a banquet we are preparing for you this evening at our Capitol House." She and the pair of young men in bronze smiled.

I glanced at Jemeret, but he just returned my gaze and waited, so I looked back at the leader of Barbin 3. "We would be very sensible of the honor you do us," I said carefully, and then I decided that if I had to do this, I wanted something for it. "I assume the banquet will also include some sort of memorial service honoring the dead?" They were so bad at masking their surprise that I almost laughed out loud.

"Of course it will." Gayli Hatlo recovered first and proved she was, after all, a political creature. "We will be happy to have you participate in any way you choose."

"What kind of service do you ordinarily have?" I asked her.

"We haven't had a war in such a long time, since before we joined the Com," the governor said thoughtfully. "I don't think there is a standard service."

"But people still do die," I persisted. "Surely you must do something then."

"Their families take them to the dispositions," one of the assistants said, correctly uncertain whether or not that would be helpful information.

I concluded that this was a hopeless conversation and let the woman off the hook. "I would be pleased to say a few words in memory of the fallen," I said.

Gayli Hatlo understood very well that I had set a price on my cooperative attendance at the banquet, and while she wasn't sure how to handle it, she certainly wouldn't try to stop me.

The next few minutes were spent in a description of the mopping up. Each of the assistants seemed to have different types of information to impart. Only 150 more people had died. That fact was followed with totals of resource losses, of production short-runs, of reassigned personnel, of the progress of recovery.

I only half listened, thinking about what I wanted to say at the banquet. Then I realized that the recitation was over. "We have asked the best clothier we have to make you a gown by tonight," the governor said. "I hope you will be pleased. We will, of course, have a gown made for—" A quick consultation of notes. "—Class C Sandi Gregson as well."

"I'm sure I'll be pleased," I said as graciously as I could manage, thinking that they would get me into gold one way or the other. "Will you be sending it over, or should I come to the Capitol House for it?"

"If you could arrange to come over an hour or so before the banquet," she began, and I overrode her gently.

"That will be fine, Governor. Our entire party will be at the Capitol House at that time."

I waited a moment to see if Jemeret would make any objections, but since he said nothing, I purposefully drew discussion to a close. Jemeret was watching me quizzically. As the holo cut off, I drew in a deep breath and covered my eyes with one hand.

He went to dial up some coffee, and the table presented it to us. After taking a sip or two, he said, lightly, "I haven't been to a Com banquet in decades. I may actually enjoy it if we can keep it from becoming a habit."

"The last one I attended was the banquet after graduation," I said, and a shudder took me, unexpected. He pulled me close against him and held on hard. "So long ago. And now—it seems almost impossible." I couldn't be specific about what, but he didn't need me to be.

"You've been doing the impossible for months," he said with a smile that was meaningful beyond his words. "You can't quit now."

"Neither can you." My voice trembled before I could exert enough control over it.

The banquet was more elaborate than I would have expected on what was, in reality, a relatively marginal Com world. They'd marshalled all their resources and decorated their banquet hall with metallic streamers of silver and gold, as well as clouds of spun silver drifting three meters above our heads and supported by tiny versions of the same kinds of antigrav devices that propelled floaters. Even more amazing, the governor produced a bottle of shateen for those of us at the head table.

I debated whether to accept the drink and neutralize it or to refuse it outright. It seemed a waste to take any of it if I were not going to let myself enjoy it.

I would have loved the shateen, but politely refused it. I wanted all my wits about me when I spoke.

The gown maker had produced for me a perfectly awful but fashionable dress of misty gold lace over a beige sheath, held up by a wide collar that framed my face and completely cut off my peripheral vision. I had hated it on sight and had politely accepted it.

Sandalari had come off better than I had in the fashion department. The bronze lace of her gown flattered her complexion and gave metallic highlights to her shimmering hair, and her collar was only ear-high, allowing her to see to either side. She tried hard not to laugh when she saw me, and I tried hard not to sting her for it. Jemeret managed to keep a straight face. Coney told me solemnly that I looked very modern. Jasin Lebec shook his head once, disbelieving. I admit that I wanted to avoid the lot of them.

The banquet was private, but when the speeches began after the meal, they were broadcast by eftel vid to, and then by eftel voice from, Orokell. In the Tribunal Chamber, Pel Nostro expressed his pleasure that the Com could once again serve its citizens as they expected it to. Then Gayli Hatlo spoke to thank us publicly on behalf of all the people on her world, and at the end of her speech she announced that Class A Ronica McBride had asked to say a few words in memory of the fallen. If the people in the room were surprised, they concealed it. Certainly nothing about the banquet could have qualified as a solemn occasion so far, and I guessed that the Barbinians had not been able to figure out what I wanted. Being afraid of doing anything wrong, they decided to do nothing and leave it all up to me. What the people on Orokell—or any of the other worlds receiving the broadcast—would think—I had no way of knowing.

I stood at my place, the governor on my left and Jemeret on my right. Everyone gave me instant silence, the kind only a Class A can command, and I looked around the room for a few seconds before I began. The upturned faces were a mixture of admiration, relief, detachment, and curiosity. I took the sting and spread it to project, as if I were playing the nomidar. I had thought for a long time about what I would say, and I took a deep, slow breath, holding the projection as strongly as I could. I had decided that the dead of Barbin 3 deserved a waysong, just as Coney would have deserved one if Jemeret had been unable to save him. The only difference was that this waysong I would speak instead of sing.

"I mourn with you the thousands who died here. They were sons and daughters, fathers and mothers, and they leave people behind. Just as you are their families, so am I. Their deaths have torn ragged holes in the fabric of humanity I wrap around myself to keep out the cold.

"You have been told that I am Class A Ronica McBride, but I want you to remember me as just a woman who wept with you over those you lost.

"I know that some of you will say, 'But she never knew any of our lost ones. How can she mourn for them?' I tell you that I believe it is just as important to mourn *with*, as it is to mourn *for*. You mourn for them; I mourn with you. So should we all.

"Ask yourselves, as I ask myself, this: if death is an inevitable part of the nature of reality, as despite all our advances it is, why do we grieve so when it occurs? You will find your own answers, but I will tell you mine. We grieve because we are harmed. I know I am. I believe that you are.

"You may think that you came here tonight to honor me, or those who solved this crisis with me, or the Com we represent, but we have made no sacrifices that match those of your own heroes, who died for their ideals and for yours. Honor them instead, as I do." The faces I watched were very different now—some people were weeping, but even those who were not were feeling the pain I was projecting at them, and even the most detached among them were disturbed.

I went on, "Honor them in your memory, and honor them in your love for those who remain with you, but most of all, honor them by swearing that—no matter what—you will never allow others to repeat their sacrifices. Their most fitting memorials are your lives. Live them for one another."

I drew back the sting and sat down. For a moment or two no one at all moved, and then Jasin Lebec stood up and said, "We will all now rise in silence to commemorate the lives of 108,392 citizens of Barbin 3 who did not survive this war."

One by one the people in the room all rose. I took Jemeret's hand, but was unable to read anything at all from him. All I could think was, *This is one of the things I have to do. I have to help people remember that death is to be felt and mourned, not just shut away and overcome.*

That night, with the bed's field turned off, and the floor-to-eaves windows of the suite open so the breeze from the lake could wash over the balcony and across our bodies, Jemeret whispered, "You gave a good speech. Better than good, and you surprised me."

"Why?" I asked. "Why should it surprise you? You know I don't hold human life cheaply."

"Ummm," he agreed. "Just the opposite. You've set yourself a very difficult task, love, but then you were never taught to do easy things."

Our heads were pillowed on the long bolster that ran the

width of the top of the bed. I pulled back a little to see him better, irising my eyes wider in the dimness. "How do you know what task I've set myself?"

He smiled. "I know you," he said. "You've decided you want people to feel individually responsible for one another again. The citizens of the Com worlds expect the Com to be responsible for them—except for those who rebel against it, of course—and the Com government expects the MIs to be responsible." He had been lying on his side. Now he rolled onto his back and linked his hands behind his head. "It's a good choice for you to make, because it will have to happen if we succeed at the task I want to accomplish. Just now everyone is serving the MIs and thinking it's the most natural thing in the world. So what you're trying to do is—unprecedented. And damned thankless. I agree with it, of course, but no one else in the government is likely to honor you for it."

"Funny about honor," I said, a little sleepily. "Back when I hadn't done anything to earn it and didn't at all deserve it, I was so jealous of it that I wanted everyone alive to pay me homage. Now I don't care at all whether anyone honors me or not. I just want to do what's right, and I believe it's right for people to care whether those around them live or die. I believe it's right for the ones who die to be thought about and remembered."

He leaned over me, kissing my eyelids, then my nose, then took my mouth with his and laid his weight hard on me. This time he used his sting almost at once, and I was so relieved I nearly melted, boneless, beneath him.

In the distance I heard Tynnanna roaring.

Our orders had two parts. First, we were to go to Orokell to meet directly with the Tribunal in what was called "the presence of the MIs," and second, on the way, we were asked to study what was referred to as the "Ananda problem."

Ananda was a rare world in times like these—it had been a member of the Com for about a hundred years, and yet it had received little in the way of Com technology. There were no records of any of its citizens participating in the trade agreements or traveling back and forth to other member worlds outside its own cluster. By rights, the Anandans should never have been accepted into the Com at all.

Ananda was fairly isolated from the core, but not from three other worlds—Robin's World, Sargasso, and Ludurn. The four worlds formed a three-dimensional triangle on the star maps. Robin's World was rich in the high-atomic-number elements that were necessary for sublight fuel; Sargasso was the largely water-surfaced home of the protodolphins; Ludurn had a perfect climate for growing grapes, liquor-flowers, grains, and, of course, the rare blossoms from which shateen was made. If I read the file accurately, members of the Council of Member Worlds argued to the Tribunal that to take three of the four worlds in the cluster would create ill will, and the Tribunal—though under no obligation to heed a CMW advisory—had generously acceded to the request.

Then, despite the disastrous nature of the match, which became obvious in short order, the unwritten Com law of "Once a Com world, always a Com world" took over, and the government and the Anandans struck a deal with one another.

In the first place, there weren't all that many of them. Of the five major continents on the planet, only one was inhabited. The half-million settlers were descendants of the original landing party, who had fled the Com many centuries earlier. Theirs was not a mission of discovery, like so many others had been, but a rebellion against centralized government authority.

When the Com offered them some of the technological advances others, like Robin's World and Ludurn, were so eager for, the Anandans nearly came to blows over it. The modernist faction, almost half the then population, was eager for the advances; the loyalists found that stance the grossest kind of betrayal, incurring indebtedness to the Com which the world itself was too resource-poor to pay back.

Ultimately, a compromise was reached, and Ananda accepted some improvements in sublight systems, some close interplanetary communications, and some superior pharmaceutical advances in return for geographical concessions about which the language in the file was so vague that I had no idea what kind of deal had been made. Whatever it was, it went pretty smoothly for a while. Then, about five years earlier, the anti-Com faction surfaced or reassumed power, and from an innocuous, marginal world, Ananda became a full-scale problem. Because if the Anandans were good at nothing else, they were really superior at sowing dissent.

They had several fiery orators—always a source for the swaying of groups of people—and they were using the communications systems to reach not only Ludurn and Robin's World, but several of the other close Com worlds, including Marpeta and Abranel, which had been members almost from the beginning. The fruits of their labors were beginning to be felt in subtle but trackable ways—misreading of quotas, mishandling of MF transshipments, mislabeling of merchandise, and the like.

Anok Luttrell's MF was taking the brunt of the trouble so far, and he had complained strenuously to the Tribunal, which had designated it a Class A assignment about the time Jasin Lebec stopped taking on assignments in order to try to heal me.

So Jara Deland ran a forecasting model through the MIs, which estimated that, unchecked, the dissension and sabotage would reach completely inefficient—hence, costly—levels in about six more years. Since no Class A was currently available, the MIs advised sending the Drenalion to Ananda to eliminate the source of the unease, the orators and their followers.

The Tribunal had, to their credit, tried to come up with other alternatives, since the government didn't often use the clone troops in the absence of open warfare. To their detriment, however, the alternatives were not very promising. Petra Chantrey's people came up with the notion of pulling all the communication equipment off-world and leaving the Anandans to stew in isolation and preach to each other. The Chief Justiciar pronounced the proposed solution illegal, which begged the question of how many Anandans might potentially die trying to keep what the MF would be repossessing.

Marga Morena's Science Bureau, professing to be horrified by the wholesale slaughter sending in the Drenalion would create—an attitude I applauded and Jemeret disbelieved—

suggested the macabre solution of using the population to test for immunities. I took that to mean infecting selected groups of citizens with some newly discovered, or hatched, organisms to see who succumbed and who resisted. I think Marga's philosophy could be summed up as, "If you're going to die anyway, you might as well die for science."

I was appalled.

After all five of us had the opportunity to study the information on the problem, we were to meet in a cargo hold of *Belalume*, the rollship taking us to Orokell, to discuss what we'd concluded. We had chosen a cargo hold over the more comfortable lounge or our cabins because Jemeret and I found the cargo areas free of MI surveillance when we used their large empty spaces to exercise Tynnanna and work our way up Climb 1 of the Ladder of the Warrior. Coney and Keli sometimes worked with us, but Sandalari would not. "I never want to have to fight anyone," she said. "I'm afraid I just can't believe in it." We didn't question her choice; it would certainly never have been mine. I was convinced then that each of us had the right to decide whether we would fight or surrender, kill or be killed. I hated that those were the only choices, but I couldn't think of a third alternative.

We were one roll away from the core worlds and the planetary seat of government when Jemeret said, "I think we need to make sure Tynnanna gets all the racing around he needs before we put him to sleep for this upcoming roll, don't you?" I read immediately that he wanted to talk clear of the surveillance.

"I'll go ask Coney and Keli if they want to come with us," I said, nodding to him that I understood. Laying the holo I'd been studying on the table for reabsorption, I rose.

"See if Sandi wants to come, too," Jemeret said casually. "She likes to watch her wife go through the Climb, and we don't ask her often enough."

A low level of excitement began to throb through me, as it did every time we took Tynnanna to the cargo holds. I was always aware that the starfire might come and speak with us. The temptation to call it had once or twice become nearly overwhelming, but I'd fought it back. The starfire had said it would speak to us again—"when we near the nexus" had been its exact words. I had no idea what "the nexus" was, and so I could never tell if we were approaching it or not, couldn't know what I might do to help us move closer to it, or away from it, whichever was required.

Jemeret went to find Jasin Lebec. We'd decided we needed his vast experience of Class A assignments in the planning stage, even if we weren't going to use it greatly in the execution.

I rapped on the callplate beside Coney and Sandalari's cabin door and, after a pause, the door irised open. Coney stood there, wrapped in a cover, and behind him Sandalari was darting into the eliminatory, her golden hair tousled.

I hid a grin, pleased that they had found such obvious joy in one another. They deserved it, I thought, and I was grateful for the thousandth time that they were with us. "Come to cargo hold three as soon as you can," I said. "Both of you."

He guessed instantly that it was time to talk about Ananda and said, "See you there in five minutes."

I went for Keli's cabin as Jemeret called to the klawit, and she opened her door at once. I often had the impression that she stood by the iris most of the time, waiting for me to call her. I hoped I was wrong. "Cargo hold three," I said to her.

She jerked on her boots and was running down the passageway after us before we'd even reached the bridge surround.

I'd suggested we include her in the planning, even though she had no talent. I half expected someone to object, but no one did. Instead it prompted a long discussion in the lounge about the similarities and differences among the Epicyclists, the Macerates, and those who followed the starfire. When the Ananda problem was given to us as our next Class A assignment, I'd let her read all the data as well, and I wanted the opinion of someone without talent. I thought that Jemeret might have considered it a continuation of our argument about the relative worth of a human life talented or talentless, but he never commented on it.

Tynnanna bounded into the cargo hold, freed of the nonklawitlike constraints imposed on him by the narrow passageways, furnishings, and Com trappings in general. Jemeret and I both pathfound all the technology in the walls, floor, and ceiling of the room, finding the standard lights and climate controls, the atmosphere regulators, the independent stabilizers that adjusted to the weight on the floor, and the ship's alarms and roll warning systems. We confirmed every time we came into a cargo hold that no surveillance had been set up since the last time we checked it.

Jemeret had made the decision early that we should create a pattern of meeting and talking free of MI surveillance even when we were dealing with entirely innocuous issues, because at some point in the future we would have to address his central purpose in being here, and by then the MIs and the Com government would be well-accustomed to our idiosyncrasy.

Coney and Sandalari, both looking considerably more polished, let themselves into the hold, and all six of us gathered in a corner, leaving the bulk of the space to Tynnanna. For a moment no one spoke, and then Jemeret looked at me. "This would be your Class A assignment, love. You start."

I folded my hands in my lap. "I've concluded that the MI suggestion is unacceptable, and the Science Bureau's counterproposal, if not worse, is certainly just as bad. The Universities' proposal has been dismissed in law. Does anyone disagree with me so far?" I paused, because if there was a contribution, I wanted to hear it.

Everyone was silent for a moment, and the only sounds in the cargo hold were Tynnanna's breathing and the thud of his pads on the decking.

"No matter what I say now, I want you to know I am really open to suggestions as well," I said quickly, looking at Jasin Lebec. I was hesitant; this was the first time I'd really tried to formulate a scenario myself. "When we had only the three firebrands to deal with, we probably could have stung them, got them to change their minds, and settled the question before any real damage was done. Now there are the Ananda dissenters, some of whom are working on the other affected worlds as well. So if stinging is no longer an option, I'm thinking we should fight sabotage with sabotage."

They waited; I hoped it would make sense.

"The MF guards have an elite corps—Keli, correct me if I'm wrong about this—that they talk about very little to people outside the government hierarchy. I think it's got an internal code name, but I don't remember what it is. They train for what used to be called stealth operations, but they spend most of their time exercising against each other to stay in shape."

Jasin Lebec nodded. "Yes. Anok Luttrell denies their existence openly, but I think it's been a real disappointment to him that he only got to use them twice in the last fifteen years. They were his idea, you know."

"What did he use them to do?" Jemeret asked.

"We heard rumors of a plot on Auburnese to send some small ships with supplies of Dliban weevils to Marpeta. They'd have halved the crop before they were stopped, and the Auburnese growers would have been able to double their prices. The whole thing was too nebulous to waste my time with. Lendo Dell was nominally in charge of the operation, but it was Anok's Scuttlers who went in surreptitiously, poked around, and cleared things up." Jasin Lebec was grinning now. "The second time was even less auspicious. The governor of Rally developed a problem with hallucinogens and little girls. I was on the other side of the Com, embroiled in negotiations, and you were just a little girl yourself, Ronica. Two of the Scuttlers were sent in with high doses of hormone and appetite suppressant injections. The governor was never much good for creative work after that, but he served out his term in cheerful mediocrity."

"The Scuttlers," I repeated. "So we can assume they should be eager to take on another assignment and have a real stake in handling it well."

"Go on," Jemeret said.

"We use the entire corps. No doubt they'll be grateful. We send a few to each of the influenced worlds and the bulk to Ananda. We tell them to begin sending competing messages of some kind—I haven't really worked out what—in ways that would discredit the orators. They should be made to look ridiculous, rather than wrong." I waited. No one said anything yet, but I could see both Jemeret and Jasin Lebec thinking hard about what I'd said. "There seems to be a great well of anti-Com feeling that these people are tapping. I'm not sure how to dissipate it. I haven't thought that far yet."

Jemeret said slowly, "No, we don't have to dissipate it. We can use it." He thought for a moment or two longer. "We need to make the leaders look like collaborators. Shift their credit balances through the record systems on Ananda, which are primitive anyway, so that it appears they've been receiving payments regularly from unnamed sources. Then . . ."

For the next several hours, we talked, developing techniques, methods, specific role assignments for the Scuttlers, timing, and then the devious motives aimed at showing how the firebrands were angling for power on Ananda by turning the populace against the government that was paying them.

It was Coney who came up with an underlying reason for the Com's need to test the soundness of its production and shipping facilities systemwide. The Anandans got almost no news from off-system, since they had never been given the eftel. They might wonder at having gained the attention of so many financial auditors, newspeople, and MF efficiency experts, but they had a better than fair chance of ultimately being quite flattered by the attention. Then, once the news of the discrediting began to leak out, the Scuttlers on the other worlds could crow over the revealed inefficiencies in the system and describe the rewards from the MF tied to those inefficiencies being identified and eliminated. There were lots more details, and our estimate was about two years until things were back to normal.

"One more thing," I said. "If resentment against the leaders begins to look as if it might lead to harm, I want the corps to pull them off Ananda and take them someplace they'll be safe."

I glanced at Jemeret, but he said nothing.

"I wonder what it is that Ananda's original deal with the Com was for." Sandalari had been silent for much of the discussion, as had Keli, who still seemed a little overawed by the company she was in. She'd confirmed a few facts about the MF drilled into her on Tanaloa, but otherwise ventured no opinions.

"It was never made public record," Jasin Lebec said to Sandalari. "When the problem was first raised by Anok Luttrell in the Tribunal, I tried to access it. What the Com gave Ananda comes right up on the screen. What Ananda gave the Com is proscribed."

"Nevertheless, we should try to find out," I said, never for a moment expecting the circumstances in which we would get our information. I knew when I said it that it would mean accessing the MIs, and I could see from Jemeret's expression that he did, too. I half expected him to challenge me on it, but after a moment he shook his head.

"The more we know about them, the better prepared we'll be when the time comes," he said.

I wanted to say there would be no way to be prepared, no matter how much we learned about them, but just then the first chime sounded to warn of the approaching roll, and we got up to take Tynnanna back to his cabin.

VII. Among the Politicians

We docked on Orokell in the cargo lander the *Belalume* supplied us and stepped out onto the pad into the midst of one of the strangest and most elaborate ceremonial welcomes I'd ever seen. There were a great many people present, and to my absolute astonishment, about half the men were wearing beards, and about half the women were accompanied by holo images of animals, most of them cats, all of them smaller than Tynnanna.

I reflected wryly on the subject of natural followers as Jemeret snorted once, softly enough not to be heard beyond our group. "You're right, love. We started a fashion."

I was disheartened by the speed with which the citizens of this world—and who knew how many others—had leaped into blind admiration and hero worship. Yet I was encouraged at the same time. We might lead them in very strange directions, and it was interesting to think that some of them would agree to go.

"Odd." Jasin Lebec's voice was also quiet. "When I was the Com's sole Class A, I don't remember anyone shaving their heads to imitate me."

I grinned at him, then remembered my dignity and sobered, laying a hand on Tynnanna's shoulder, since by this time putting one on his head would have necessitated reaching higher than my own and ruined the elegance of my pose. Jemeret stepped onto the gold carpet first, then turned sideways to let Tynnanna and me precede him. The crowd was silent, in respect or awe or curiosity, and I quickly noticed a number of bronze jumpsuits among the bright colors. We were somber in dark blue as we moved forward, except for the matching light brown of Tynnanna's coat and Keli's MF uniform, and the multicolor fires burning in the klawit's eyes. The first time we neared a woman with a holocat by her side, my klawit halted his stately progress and cocked a head at the little creature. He clearly thought it should have run from him, and when it did not, he roared at it.

The woman almost fell backward, catching as she did the full decibel load of the bellow. I cleared my throat and gestured to her to step aside as Tynnanna raised a huge paw, claws extended, to take a swipe at the stubborn little creature that seemed so fearless in the face of overwhelming odds. She jumped, banging into the men behind her, and the klawit's claws sliced harmlessly through the image. We all watched him, fascinated to see what his reaction would be, perfectly content to ignore the fact that a whole crew of government dignitaries probably awaited us in the reception building at the other end of the carpet.

Tynnanna lowered his massive head, the horns ominously sharp and thrusting, and sniffed. The little holo cocked its head in return with programmed curiosity, reaching out until its image seemed to spread across the klawit's encroaching nose. Tynnanna snorted, ruffling the cuffs on the people standing nearest, raised his head and looked at me with feline disgust, as if I were responsible for letting him humiliate himself.

Jemeret and Sandalari were having a hard time stifling their instinctive laughter, and I soothed the klawit gently as we started forward again. It was a more unforgettable entrance than any we might have tried to make, Keli said to me later. Tynnanna stalked after me, glaring at everyone. Jemeret followed with Jasin Lebec, who seemed vastly amused but held his professional face in place with decades of practiced ease.

Several of the women nearest the carpet turned their holo animals off, and I kept noticing creatures blinking out as I walked beside the klawit along the designated pathway toward the building.

Music began from some unseen source when we reached the reception area, and there, in full-dress jumpsuits, most of them gold, was the Tribunal. They looked impressive, the way even nondescript people do when they feel they have great power and they know how to dress it up. I suppose I should have been impressed, but somehow I wasn't. They were just people, I remember thinking, and not even people with talent. And then, almost before I knew I was going to do it, I smiled at them, my best smile, washing them with a deliberate feeling of recognition that I was happy to see them, delighted to be back in the Com again, and overjoyed to be shouldering at last the responsibilities for which I'd been trained. All those were at complete odds with my dark blue jumpsuit, my klawit, and my husband. I believe that only the fact that Jasin Lebec was also in dark blue kept anyone from asking aloud what was going on.

I was utterly confident as I greeted them all, because now, in their presence at last, I could read and influence each of them. I had been fashioned nearly from birth, from the time my lord gave me to them, to work for the government, and I'd taken an oath to do so. I had taken no oath to avoid working *on* them as well, and I was willing to do that with every fiber of my body.

Com Counselor Pel Nostro stepped out first, the badges of rank on his jumpsuit catching the light from the ceiling wash. I nodded to him, my smile fixed in place, and extended my hand to raise him from his bow. "Pel," I said, acknowledging.

He took my hand in both of his and said, "Welcome back to Orokell, Ronica McBride. On behalf of the Tribunal, let me express our gratitude for the skill you brought to the Barbin 3 problem. We look forward to long and distinguished service from you in future."

"I trust it will be long enough," I murmured to him, thinking that any other kind of response—except open denial—would appear to be total agreement, and I would not later be trapped into having seemed to agree with him. At the same time, I stung him to make certain he was pleased at my reply.

He began to turn, held out his hand in a summoning gesture and took a breath to call Jara Deland into our group, for as Liaison to the MIs, her rank was almost equal to his, and she would be the next in precedence. But before he could form the words, I said easily, "Of course, Pel, you know my husband,

Jemeret Cavanaugh." I couldn't help stumbling over the second name; it was totally unfamiliar to me.

Jara Deland glared at me before she caught herself, even as Pel Nostro was coolly greeting Jemeret. I read her quickly and realized that she was jealous of me, that the emotion burned hot and hard in her. As Jemeret leaned past me with a nod at least as icy as Pel's own to him, I was analyzing Jara Deland, trying to discover the root of the jealousy. I concluded it was a matter of status. Her work with the MIs was very different from mine, so I was no threat to her professionally. In the government, status rankings were crucial to power, and she had spent the last three years as the most important woman in the Com. She resented the fact that my return would bump her down a rank.

So when I stepped toward her, with Tynnanna carefully treading behind me, I smiled even more broadly at her, not to disarm her dislike, but to show her that I recognized who and what she was in the Com, whether I was part of it or not. "Jara," I said, holding out my hand, waiting for her nod. "From all the figures I've seen, you appear to have significantly improved our use of our machine allies since I've last paid heed to the reports. Tying the standardization system into the demographics to improve analysis ratios was nothing short of brilliant."

She was thrown a little off balance by the unexpected praise. "As was your solution to the Barbin 3 problem, Ronica McBride," she said. "May I ask—" Her eyes slid past me to the cat. "—what prompted you to return to us with both a live beast and a live husband? As well as a team," she added.

Leave it to Jara to ask the questions everyone else wanted to ask but didn't. I dived into the last question first. "It is my perception—and I believe Barbin 3 proved it to be accurate—that the government has been less than efficient in its use of talent before this." I was choosing my words carefully, testing out the plan I'd been evolving. I was being overheard by everyone in proximity to us, and in all likelihood by the MIs as well. "The complexity of present problems will tax the resources of any talent, and if we approach them singly, we'll be spread too thin and might begin failing, which would reflect badly on the government as well as on us. Therefore, I hope you'll run some projections on the probability of solving single assignments with the full complement of talent—not just those on my team now, but the others as well—as against the one-assignment, one-talent policy in force until now." The attempt to gather all talent into a single team was a long shot, I knew, but I thought it would be well worth trying.

Jara Deland's mind was already processing the request, choosing the form and wording of her questions to the MIs. She shunted that aside to reiterate, "And the husband?"

There were so many replies I couldn't make, especially since the two of us were the focus of all attention now, the Tribunal and my team waiting just as interestedly to hear what I would say. Even Pel Nostro, who radiated impatience to keep the ceremonies moving, had paused as if unwilling to cut off his wife's line of inquiry. I felt with my sting for Jemeret, just behind me, but I wasn't surprised to find him shielded. As if the answer to her question were, after all, obvious, I smiled at Jara Deland again and said meaningfully, "But, Jara, you and Pel are the first couple in the Com, and you're married. I had to see if marriage was what you two have made of it these past fifteen years."

Since the open battles of their marriage—their constant squabblings, their infidelities, and Jara Deland's continual vain attempts to wrest the husband's role from Pel—were common knowledge and the source of great entertainment for most of the people in the government, there were murmurs around us at my answer. Jara Deland, who had no self-deception in her power-hungry soul, was not at all offended. Nor did she directly confront my answer. "And the cat?" she pursued.

"Tynnanna is here in case it turns out that my marriage does put me in the position yours has placed you." I said it easily, almost teasingly. Tynnanna, recognizing his name and growing more and more restless, opened his mouth and let out a roar that staggered the members of the Tribunal and the honor guard behind them. Jemeret lowered his shields, touching me with a combination of amusement and warning.

No one laughed. They might have done so at my flippant

answer to Jara Deland, had not the klawit made it plain that he was a force to be respected. Pel Nostro seemed to make the decision that it was necessary to move on, and he cleared his throat and urged me forward toward Faucon Oletta, who stood next in line. Jemeret smiled at Jara Deland as I stepped obediently along the people in line, and Jasin Lebec took Sandalari's hand, drawing her up to Pel Nostro.

The Chief Justiciar was young for his post, and his youthfulness bespoke a brilliance—perhaps at his work, perhaps at political maneuvering, perhaps at both—that seemed to lie lightly on him. His features were even, his eyes a strange pale blue, almost bleached, and his smile at me seemed so genuine that I had to sting him lightly to feel the cool calculation of it. He nodded briskly, his head bowed to me sharply and slightly longer than necessary, before he looked up. "Ronica McBride, you are heartily welcome back," he said, his voice surprisingly rich, "by me as well as by the Tribunal as a whole."

He was, I guessed, about thirty, and he was handsome when he smiled, but he seemed unaware of his looks. I returned the smile and said, "Thank you, Faucon." It seemed to startle him that I called him only by his first name, but that was one of my privileges, and I had intended as far back as the lander trip to Markover Station to not only use all my privileges, but to press their limits. "I read the opinion you rendered in the Dilato dispute, and I thought it very well-constructed." In truth, it had been masterful, but a Class A did not go around according other people that adjective.

He acknowledged the praise more easily than Jara Deland had acknowledged hers. "Sometimes," he said, his voice carefully toneless, "we talentless beings are capable of solving problems without intervention."

Pel Nostro drew in a quick breath, and I felt a stab of satisfaction from Jara Deland that the Chief Justiciar was willing to say something like that to me.

I had to mask my delight. Thinking to set me down a rank, Faucon Oletta had unconsciously played right into my strategy. I changed the expression on my face to convey the impression that I was prepared to be generous. "Indeed you can," I agreed. "It is a tendency I hope to see encouraged and exploited in the near future. Some assignments previously considered reserved for Class A intervention can, I think, be solved quite well without consuming the limited resource of talent."

Jara Deland stirred, the satisfaction gone. She was, I guessed, thinking about how the MIs would respond to the suggestion that Class A's stop being responsible for solving Class A problems.

The Chief Justiciar was staring at me, uncertain, as I moved past him to greet Marga Morena. The head of the Science Bureau smiled as she nodded, and it was an expression that managed to be both genuine and restrained at the same time. She had interacted much more closely with Kray than with me while we were in training, and her battles and resentments had been with him. I wondered if she missed him, or if she was glad he was gone. "It's good to have you back again, Ronica McBride," she said.

I was getting a little tired of hearing my own name. Something rose up in me and made me want to ask her if she'd hated me or been grateful to me when Kray died, but I kept it down. It didn't fit the persona I was creating here. "How are you faring, Marga?" I asked her. "I understand that the Bureau is about to announce a major discovery out beyond the Sargasso Deep."

"How did you get access to that information?" she asked, but without hostility. "We were trying to suppress it until we'd fully mapped the system."

"Come on, Marga," I chided her. "You can't stop a pathfinder by suppressing anything that's in the MIs." It was the closest I was going to come to mentioning Kray.

"I don't think of you as a pathfinder," she said slowly.

There were other voices around us now; Jemeret was talking to Faucon, Jasin Lebec to Jara Deland—probably, from their glances, about me—and Coney and Sandalari were in animated conversation with Pel Nostro.

"No, I suppose you wouldn't." It wasn't meant to lessen her in any way. "The MIs would always categorize a pathfinding assignment as beneath me, as a waste of resources. I see the situation in somewhat different terms."

"Perhaps we can speak about it more after the banquet," Marga Morena suggested. "I don't want to hold up the line."

Even as I was moving on to Terrill Guthrie, who seemed as cold and hard in person as he had over the eftel vid, I was groaning inwardly at the thought of another banquet. Then Tynnanna hissed.

I turned, touching him with the sting, and found him radiating hostility. I turned back to Terrill Guthrie, who was gazing at the animal with so little apparent expression that he might not have been entirely human—a not incongruous circumstance for someone who had spent his life among clones. Without moving his head at all, Guthrie turned his startlingly intense brown eyes on my face and said flatly, "Cats don't like me."

I almost asked him why he thought cats would be any different from the rest of the world, but I bit my tongue. "We've not had the opportunity to meet before, Terrill." I held out my hand, almost swallowing his name and forcing myself to get it out as steadily as I could. My impression was that he never smiled and would not change a lifetime's habit now. He had huge hands, to match a bull neck and an ovate head on which black hair grew sparsely and had been truncated near the scalp, so when he took my hand, the delicacy of his touch seemed out of place.

"Ronica McBride," he acknowledged formally, then dropped my hand as if contact with flesh was somehow distasteful to him.

I decided to confront an issue that might be equally distasteful. "I understand you've discovered an unusually high level of instability now that you've decanted the seventh generation of this strain of Drenalion." It had been a minor note, almost buried in the masses of material I'd been reading.

If he was disturbed by my bringing it up, he didn't reveal it. "Nothing that can't be dealt with," he said, still so stolidly expressionless as to be unreadable by normal means.

"I am looking forward to discussing it with you," I lied as

sincerely as I could, and the first hint of an emotion broke through his impassiveness. He was skeptical about that.

I took the opportunity to move on to Anok Luttrell, and as he quite correctly bowed his graying head before clasping my hand, I said, "Thank you, Anok, for the speed with which you provided us rollship transportation."

"The Lumeships are always at the disposal of the Class A talents," he said unnecessarily, in response to my equally unnecessary gratitude. "It would be a pleasure to be able to fill all requests as easily."

I sensed no hostility in him at all, only a kind of suppressed eagerness, which I interpreted as hope that I—or one of my team—had been able to solve the Ananda problem. I was sure it was his request that had made it our top priority at this point.

As I moved on to the last member of the tribunal, the amazingly immense Petra Chantrey, her skin glistening dark brown and her girth large enough so that Sandalari and I could both have fit comfortably into her jumpsuit, I glanced back at Keli. She was still holding on to her kit, in whose field our nomidars hung, and she seemed completely in awe of everyone. I touched her lightly once with the sting to calm her, made a fleeting wish that I had enough skill to read all the members of our team as well as those of the Tribunal, but acknowledged to myself that I couldn't juggle all those inputs at the same time, and returned to concentrating on Petra Chantrey.

"Ronica McBride," she said instantly, in a voice that somehow resonated with profundity, "we hope to get you to speak to our graduating classes in two months' time. We have sorely missed our Class A speaker recently."

It went a step beyond the simple "Welcome back," in that it hinted of a lapse of duty. But I knew she meant no disrespect by it; Petra Chantrey had always been noted for even less tact than I, but she was forgiven a great deal—as I was—because her brilliance as a scholar had catapulted her to the top ranks of academia. She had made the step from academe to government when it was recognized that she had, as well as an incandescent intelligence, a killer instinct to rival that of the Drenalion. I had only met her once, at the gala following graduation; like so much else, I'd had little reason to recall her during most of the past three years. Now I found myself thinking that she might be the greatest danger on the Tribunal if it became known that we wanted to attack the Com's entire way of life. Conversely, she could be our strongest support.

"Petra, I'm really looking forward to speaking with you later," I said, meaning it, needing to know her better.

She smiled, the expression dazzling against her contrasting complexion. "We must ask you to judge a competition for us, and we hope you won't object to the intrusion."

"What kind of competition?" I asked.

"Our design students have all vied to create your gown for this evening's banquet," she answered, laughing with a hearty baritone rumble. "Our own judges chose the dozen best designs, and they have been sent to your comsole. We hope you'll choose the three you think most worthy, and wear the first choice." She waved a hand. "It shouldn't take you long."

"Do I have a comsole?"

"It's in your suite at Government House," she answered, then seemed to recognize another possible lapse of diplomacy. "Not *that* suite," she amended hastily, making it worse.

Pel Nostro had finished greeting the other members of the team and was approaching me to reassume control of the greeting process. When he overheard Petra Chantrey's words, he nearly blanched.

I turned toward him, looking as serene as I could manage. "Pel, are we all staying in Government House?"

"The Visitors' Residence has ample room for your accommodation," he said immediately, telling me that he was reluctant to guess which answer I wanted.

I nodded. "And what are the plans from now until the banquet?"

Out of the corner of my eye I saw Jemeret watching me as Jasin Lebec greeted Petra Chantrey. I was immediately shaken by a desire to be with him back in our house at Stronghome, not here, in what Sejineth had innocently called "strange waters."

He'd warned me that there was no going back.

I forced myself to pay attention to Pel Nostro.

"We thought you would like a few hours to bathe and rest and—ready yourselves," the Com Counselor was saying. "Then the members of and delegates to the Tribunal will meet with all of you—"

"The talent team," I slipped in, the name carefully chosen for ease of future plans.

"Uh, yes—" He stumbled over my interruption. "—and then we want to begin arranging some individual Tribunal meetings through the early evening. There is," he added almost apologetically, "a backlog of Class A assignments."

"And am I scheduled to address the dinner, or merely to be one of the participants?" I asked him.

"Of course there will be short speeches," Pel Nostro said, "but we had hoped you might describe for us your time away—in whatever terms you wish, of course."

So they were all curious. They wanted to know what Jemeret had done to me—in what detail, I could only guess. And whether they wanted to know because they hoped they could assume responsibility for the healing of talent in the future, or simply out of morbid curiosity—or, it occurred to me, because the more they knew, the more leverage they would have to manipulate me—I had no real way of knowing.

"I'd be happy to oblige you," I said to him.

He inclined his head in the direction of the klawit. "Will the cat also be attending the banquet?"

"Mine won't." I swept my gaze over the crowd where holo animals still stood by the sides of some of the women. "I can't speak for anyone else's."

Pel Nostro beckoned to one of the ceremonial honor guards who stood nearby. "Please show the Class—" He paused a moment, swiftly debating, then made the decision of a practiced diplomat. "—the talent team to their rooms in the Visitors' Residence of Government House." The guard braced and then nodded to us, his attention lingering briefly on Keli, before he turned smartly and started across the reception area toward the platform exit.

I deliberately waited for Jemeret to come up beside me

before I started to follow the guard. Tynnanna fell in behind us, separating us from the other four. I wanted to take my lord's hand, but I didn't. They already knew I was utterly dependent on him; it seemed to me there was nothing more to prove by pushing it.

The floater was a large one, newly refurbished. I assumed it ordinarily carried guard units, trade delegations, or classes of students. A number of the seats had been retracted to give Tynnanna a place, and when the side doors slid open, I gestured to him to go in first, which was only practical, but seemed to scandalize the guard, for whom precedence was clearly a serious matter. I was pleased to see that Keli had recovered enough from her awe to snort at his reaction.

When Tynnanna was settled, I climbed into the floater and slid onto one of the double seats. Jemeret moved beside me, pressing his thigh against mine and resting an arm across my shoulders. I was instantly grateful for his warm strength, and while I didn't turn and lean in against him as I wanted to, I stroked my sting over him once and felt the answering caress.

Coney and Sandalari got on and sat together opposite us, but Jasin Lebec paused at the floater entrance. "I'm going to meet with Pel separately, and he'll bring me along later."

Neither Jemeret nor I reacted to that directly. I wondered if he had stung his grandfather. Neither of us was certain that Jasin Lebec agreed fully with what we wanted to do, but then he'd agreed to help us, and he knew he could no longer do the things he'd once done. If anyone could build us a workable foundation in the Com, he could. This was his territory, and he knew it very well.

"I'll come to your rooms when I get to the Residence," he said, then went back into the reception area.

Keli floated her kit and our nomidars into the flat area near Tynnanna and slid quickly into a backseat. She appeared happy to be out of the pomp, and eager to see the Orokell city. We were all a little stressed from the end of the journey, the landing, and the reception, but it occurred to me that Keli might like to see the Macerates' Tabernacle, the Orokell focus of her religion—and at the same time it occurred to me that I might like to see the religious centers again, too.

The guard came onto the floater, signaled the door to close, and started to press the destination into the panel. "Have you programmed our course yet?" I asked him.

He glanced over at me, startled, and braced, which was quite an accomplishment, sitting down. "We have a highest priority clearance, Class A Ronica McBride," he said. "We would be able to take all major routes from here."

"Um," I acknowledged. "In that case, go past the Stadium to the edge of the wild, so Tynnanna can use the grass for a few moments before we close him into the Government House precincts. Then take the shortest route from there."

His fingers were already dancing over the course input.

Jemeret looked at me curiously, but didn't ask. Coney's eyes lit up, and he leaned close to Sandalari, his mouth to her ear, whispering. He'd figured out what I wanted to do.

The guard activated the seat fields; the floater lifted, and we were skimming among the huge complexes and small residential areas that made up the city.

It was too big.

That thought was almost alien to me, a revelation in its own way. I'd been raised to understand that humans had begun to be civilized when they gathered together and created cities all those long centuries ago, on the planet the Macerates called the Original World of the Preserver, and the Responsionists called the First Reflection. According to what we'd been taught, we carried our cities with us when we spread out to populate other planets—first in the immense transports, and then on the new lands themselves. One source even tried to define civilized humans as city builders, which created some philosophical arguments about levels of civilization, because there were verified records of preindustrial cities. The Com rule was that, if we really wanted to impress the worlds we were welcoming into membership, we built a major city around the spaceport, one fit to rival the best cities in the already established Com worlds.

Orokell's central city, through which we now flew, was the

showpiece, housing its millions of inhabitants in comfort, using them efficiently, and arrogant about it. Some cities had problems with poverty and violence—the contraband goods issued from or were rife in them. This city aspired to a beauty and perfection that would resonate throughout the Com. I'd been taught to appreciate the effect such a paragon among cities would have on its citizens; it was supposed to have such an effect on me as well. And all I could think of was that it was too big.

I'd been on Caryldon less than a year, and it had changed my perceptions of everything. I found the rhythms of life on the wilderworld utterly natural to sink into, and utterly difficult to rise out of. It stunned me, the pull of the simplicity. I hadn't known until I was surrounded by all the Com had to offer, how I would miss it.

I laughed silently to myself as we circled the wide plaza with the Spire of the Founding in it. The Spire shot up into the deep blue sky higher than the tallest building in the city, and Keli goggled at it, for it seemed too thin and fragile to be so tall. Because of our highest priority clearance, everyone got out of our way, so our flight was uninterrupted. We banked slightly around the long curve of the Stadium, then sped up for the great linear run at the borders of the two main Orokell City University campuses, and drew to a stop at the edge of the wild.

The floater set gently down, and the guard opened the doors. Tynnanna, understanding very well what he was here for, stepped carefully out of the vehicle onto the grass and, tail twitching, raced over a nearby rise to attend to his needs in relative privacy. When none of the rest of us left the vehicle, he seemed to gather that he would have to return quickly, and we sat in silence for the few minutes until he came back.

The guard signaled the doors shut, and the vehicle rose and began the "shortest route" to the precincts of Government House. Our course took us, as I'd intended it would, through the square on which fronted the Macerates' Tabernacle of the Preserver, the Responsionists' Shrine of Reflection, the Essencists' House of Aspects, the Epicyclists' Core, and the garden of the Purists, which was called by no fancy name. The speed of both air and ground traffic was strictly regulated in the square, so as soon as it entered the expanse, the floater slowed. Coney took Sandalari's hand and pointed in the direction of the Core; she turned her glorious smile on him, admiring the sleekly curved shapes of the huge bowl whose insides were carved in forms calculated to encourage meditation.

I looked from them to Keli, who had suddenly recognized where she was and was staring at the Tabernacle with wide eyes. When she swallowed hard and almost choked on her spit, I knew she was trying not to weep, which would have disgraced her uniform.

Jemeret touched me with his sting and I turned away from the MF guard and raised my eyes to his face. "Careful, love," he said in a barely voiced murmur. "You never used to show any interest in things religious."

"It's the shortest route back to Government House," I said, making my voice ring with both indignation and disdain. "I, for one, need a—" The last word didn't get spoken, because just then the floater lurched and yawed to the right, pitching wildly as its automatic systems tried to regain control.

The guard's calm vanished, and he stared at the bucking control panel helplessly, then was flung to the floor.

Jemeret threw himself over the seat in front of ours, and I was right behind him. Without either of us waiting for the unfortunate guard to clear the area, we slapped our hands against the panel and began to pathfind simultaneously. I heard Sandalari's gasp just before Tynnanna began to growl, but I had no time to look at either of them.

"Whole right stabilizer group's gone," Jemeret said quickly, diagnosing before I could. I slid my questing along the connectors that should have allowed the left stabilizers to compensate and immediately saw the further problem.

"Connector's cut."

My lord was plunging ahead of me into the antigrav, which was still operational, adjusting the field to strengthen its push on the right, which, while an imperfect solution, saved us from crashing. He looked down at the still frozen guard, on whom I had stepped several times. "Can you actually fly this, or are you purely ornamental?"

The guard swallowed even harder than Keli had and scrambled up to his knees. "I can fly it, Class A. I just can't repair it."

"We're compensating for the missing stabilizers," Jemeret said. "It's a temporary fix at best, so I suggest you take it manually, and don't get more than two meters off the ground." He watched the guard take over, while I slid my awareness into the antigrav to help him, and looked back at Coney, who had his arm tightly around Sandalari's shoulder. I wanted to know they were all right.

"That wasn't accidental," Coney said sharply.

"So it begins." I said it as calmly as I could. "If we'd been at normal speed or altitude when the stabilizers cut out, we probably would have crashed before we could have diagnosed it and compensated."

"What do you mean, so it begins?" Coney asked.

Jemeret had assessed the situation the same way I had. He looked closely at me, his eyes burning silver with anger. "You have a point, love. If someone's out to kill talents here in the Com, they will need to attack us."

For a few moments the attention I was directing at the antigrav muted my outrage and fear. Then I made an adjustment that freed some of my conscious reasoning. With an easy calculation that astonished me, I realized that I could use the attack. I said, "We need to be very, very careful, then. Pathfind everything and sting to read everyone." I couldn't say much more. Pathfinding the floater consumed a considerable amount of energy.

Jemeret looked at Coney, his eyes still glittering. "Since you and Sandalari have no pathfinding or stinging abilities—" He seemed to warn Sandalari not to contradict him. "—I'm afraid you'll have to share a suite with us while we're here in Orokell."

Coney caught on at once. "Not just here," he corrected. "The children were killed on Werd. Whoever our enemy is, his reach is longer than just this world." It was the first time any of us had used the phrase "our enemy." It would not be the last.

"His or her," Sandalari murmured softly.

Keli, sitting behind them and listening, frowned. I almost felt her radiating anxiety, and looked past the other couple to say, "Keli, if you're worried about guarding us, it's a bigger task than one woman should undertake. Are there any other MF guards you've come to know and trust?"

She opened her mouth, closed it again, and then nodded. "There's one," she said. "He thinks kind of like me, and we were in training and first serve together."

The guard piloting the floater, and sweating as he did it, still had enough ingrained formality to look shocked that she hadn't used my name or title, and that I hadn't in any way reprimanded her.

"Fine," I said smoothly. "Get me his name, and I'll have him transferred here."

"Two of us won't be of much more use than only one," she volunteered hesitantly. "If someone's truly out to kill you, you need an army."

"No." Jemeret's voice was firm, some of his anger leaving. "An army is the last thing we need. But we need each other."

"And the others," I said quickly, now having the opening I'd needed. "Sinet Coleby, Lage N'Verre, and the other talents, including little Tial Borland. If we're under attack, we need to be together."

Perhaps I shouldn't have said it aloud, not quite yet. Of the six other talents in the Com, two were dead before we could assemble them. After we landed, Jemeret went back and pathfound the rest of the floater, but by then someone could have removed an independent listening device which, being unconnected to the floater mechanism, we might not have found in a cursory scan. Only then did we think to ask Anok Luttrell to locate the guard who had flown the floater to Government House with us, and by that time he could not be found.

The housekeeper seemed so likely to faint when we informed her that we would all share a suite, thank you very much, that I actually stung her to shore her up, even though I was already tired. Fortified, she swung into action with the efficiency of a clock and had three large and two slightly smaller suites in the Visitors' Residence opened to one another. It meant the removal of the adjoining walls, creating a living area so vast that Tynnanna was instantly tempted to charge around it. The five bedrooms opened off the huge room.

To accommodate Tynnanna, we had the carpet at the small suite end of the huge room exchanged for some tall grass—a request I'd bet the house systems never had to fulfill before—and the klawit was rolling happily in it as soon as it was finished. We eliminated most of the furniture that came with the outer rooms, then called for a three-sided couch with a table in the center, in the middle of the expanse between the grass and the far wall, and added a long dining table and chairs between the wall and the couch. Since there was plenty of room, we extruded the comsole.

Keli took the nearer of the two small bedrooms after leaving our nomidars on the couch. We sent Coney and Sandalari to the large bedroom beside hers, and we took the one on their other side, leaving the third for Jasin Lebec.

Jemeret and I exchanged one look as the lights came up and began a meticulous search of every system, mechanical or technological, anywhere in the apartment. It took almost an hour, and we found no other surveillance or listening devices than the MI ones we were expecting. We noted their presence and left them enabled.

Only then did Jemeret call Pel Nostro on the comsole and tell him about the sabotaged floater. The Com Counselor went so white at the news that for a moment I thought he was as likely to pass out as the housekeeper had been. He looked to the side and asked something, then looked back at us again. "I'll see that Jasin Lebec is guarded when he leaves here to come to Government House," he said, "and I'll post guards on the precincts to ensure your safety when you cross to the Meeting Halls."

Jemeret shook his head and said, "Thank you, Pel, but the

fewer people who are alerted to the problem, the better, and I wouldn't want anyone guarding us if we haven't probed them first. Just send for all the other talent in the Com right now and gather it here."

The Com Counselor frowned.

Jemeret went on, "I think this attack on us was in the nature of a preemptive strike, hastily thought out and sloppily executed. My guess is it'll be a while before the next one." He crossed his arms. "What haven't you been briefing us on, Pel?" The anger was back, controlled, but apparent. "What wasn't in the documents?" We waited.

Pel Nostro was silent for a long time. "I'll send you the information," he said grimly at last, "but not by comsole." He glanced again to the side, and Jasin Lebec leaned briefly into our field of vision, nodding.

Jemeret cut the connection, called Keli, and went down to reexamine the floater.

Coney and Sandalari came to sit with me on the couch, and I bubbled us, to allow us to speak freely. "All right," I said to them, "this is going to be more complex than we thought. Someone is out to kill us, and we don't know who or why."

"We can probably guess at motives," Coney said in a low voice, as if there were still some chance of being overheard. "Someone wants the kind of power it's not possible to have as long as there's talent in the Com." He sounded even harder, more cynical, than I'd imagined he could be, even when we were on Caryldon.

"Did you read the members of the Tribunal?" Sandalari asked, shivering. Coney noticed and pulled her against him.

"Of course I did," I answered her. "Jara Deland doesn't like me, but it's personal, not directed at talent in general. Terrill Guthrie's hard to read. I think I'll have to do a full probe on him, and I'm not looking forward to it. He's so icy, I might freeze in there, but I didn't sense any strong hostility toward us. I think he just doesn't like anyone." I thought about the others. "Faucon Oletta bears some resentment against talent, but he gave no hints at all of tendencies toward assassination. Marga Morena and Petra Chantrey have worked with us too long and too intimately to spring into open hatred now, though Petra certainly has the brilliance and the energy for it, and Anok Luttrell needs us too much." I thought about it a moment or two longer. "Besides, it's unlikely to be the Tribunal. They already have great power."

"True." Coney nodded at me. "It's more likely to be one of the people who are near to power without having as much as they want. But we shouldn't rule out the Tribunal on an unlikelihood."

"That doesn't narrow it down any," Sandalari said. Wistfully, she added, "I'm afraid I don't like it much here. Things seemed so much more honest on Caryldon."

I agreed with her without saying so. "Everyone has an agenda here," I said to her, "and the agendas are all different from one another. On Caryldon, we could be reasonably expected to share each other's agendas, at least to some extent."

Jemeret and Keli came in, and I dissolved the bubble until they were inside, then rebuilt it. "No clues," my lord said, sitting down and calling up a drink of some kind from the table, something that hadn't occurred to the rest of us. "It *was* hastily done. It felt almost like whoever was doing it was interrupted in the middle. If they'd blown out both sets of stabilizers, we'd have crashed for sure. But then, if we had been at cruising speed, it might still have succeeded." He leaned back in the cushions as Sandalari repeated that she didn't like it here. My lord laughed softly. "I know," he said. "At times even treachery seems cleaner than the political games."

Keli frowned and looked down at her hands. "I can't guard you," she said. "Not really. Maybe you should just send me away. I mean, I haven't got any talent."

"That doesn't mean that you have no worth, Keli," I said to her carefully. "You see things differently from the rest of us." For some reason, I found myself looking at Jemeret when I said that. "You are part of the team, and you stay. We'll get your friend here, the other MF guard you mentioned, to help you if you feel inadequate alone."

She flushed. "Actually, he's my brother," she corrected.

"The comsole's blinking," Jemeret said. "It may be ringing as well. Let's finish this quickly."

We discussed what we had guessed about the person who was either attacking or directing the attacks against us. First—we somehow settled on a male persona, and this time Sandalari made no demur—that his methods were crude, and, though he'd obviously planned the murder of the two children, the attempt on us appeared to have been thrown together at the last minute. We would have to be endlessly watchful.

"The banquet tonight will probably involve the top two, maybe three, levels of the bureaucracy," Coney continued thoughtfully. "If we're theorizing our enemy is someone near to real power, but not holding it—and if he's actually here on Orokell—then I'd say it's likely he'd be there." Sandalari's lovely eyes darkened suddenly and she shifted against Coney's side.

I read what she was thinking, and I understood. She wanted to live in a world free from fear or the necessity to hate—she might not have used that word; it's mine—and her ideal world was much farther away here than it had been on Caryldon.

"We have enough careful steering to do around all the personalities on the Tribunal," Jemeret said. "This complicates things badly." He looked at me, his level gray eyes penetrating. "They want you to speak tonight, to tell them what happened on Caryldon."

"I know." He hadn't had to say it, and my lord was not in the habit of saying things he didn't need to say. "I'm pretty sure I can get it right." That was all I had time for. Tynnanna had risen out of the grass and was stalking the comsole with a grim determination that seemed bent on committing mayhem.

"I think it's probably ringing now," Jemeret said.

I dissolved the bubble, and the noise of the comsole filled the room. I ran to it past the crouching klawit and cut the bell off. The messages began to play out instantly.

Anok Luttrell told Jemeret he couldn't find the guard who had piloted the floater, and, despite the expense, he'd ordered a molecular pattern scan.

Petra Chantrey reminded me that her design students were eagerly awaiting my choice of gown.

Congratulations and welcome back messages abounded, including some I considered duty messages, from Lumeship captains, MF Brigade Commanders, member world governors, minor bureaucrats, and the like.

The MIs had patched "for your attention" a report on increased smuggling activity among the Nogdala worlds, combined with a prediction that the Nogdala system administration would do nothing to curtail such activities.

The legitimate Com authorities on Abranel had issued a long and detailed report about the extent of mishandling of transshipments and a request for guidance about appropriate disciplinary measures, since too harsh a crackdown could have the opposite effect to the one intended, while too lenient a response could fail to deter anyone else from joining in. On a small scale, such activities could be seen as pranks, as little defiances of the shiftmasters, rather than as wide-ranging episodes with repercussions throughout the system.

Tynnanna turned on his pads with graceful feline disgust at the cacophony and marched back to his grass.

I ordered Keli to put in a request under my name for information on her brother and a change of orders, and a message came through almost at once from an MF guard dispatcher. She responded to my request for the services of Gabon Idana, third-rank guard currently serving on Auburnese, by saying that his assignment would indeed be changed to my personal staff, and he should arrive on Orokell in forty hours on the *Shunapi*, the regular sublight vessel on the inner worlds run from Orokell to Werd to Koldor to Auburnese and back to Orokell again.

Pel Nostro called to let us know that Mortel John and Tial Borland would also be arriving on the *Shunapi*, and since Sinet Coleby and Lage N'Verre were already here, we could discuss our coopting them to our team at the banquet later. The three Class C's were all on assignment and scattered among the Com worlds, but he was putting through eftel calls to them and would get them onto the first available Lumeships to bring them back.

Petra Chantrey called again to ask if there was some problem with my accessing the gown designs and offering to help if there were.

Then, blessedly, silence.

I looked over at Jemeret, still lounging on the couch, and he was almost coiled, radiating tension. Even Coney and Sandalari were aware of it. Keli had smiled at the announcement that her brother was on his way to us, and she seemed lost in her own thoughts or memories, unaware of the strain pulling the rest of us taut. I touched Jemeret, a gently inquiring caress. He shook his head wearily, the tension lessening slightly, but not fading. "Choose a damned gown," he said. "That at least will get Petra off the line."

I reminded myself that he'd been gone from this center of hubbub and power for more than twenty-five years. He had trained the Boru to make the most of their own choices, and there were only a few decisions in which he absolutely had to be involved. It was his very ability to delegate within the tribe that allowed him to be away so much. The Com was very careful to whom it gave power and what power it gave. It had given a great deal to the Class A's. Therefore, everyone thought they could not function without us. The incessant pounding of demands was alien to him.

"I don't know how Jasin Lebee did it all those years," I said. "All the conflicting demands, and strands of problems and scenarios, and impasses, and personalities and whatever, all coming at him at once and then again and again." I made myself go to the comsole and call for the holos of the design students' offerings, signaling them to rise one by one on the surface of the couch table. I could almost picture the anxious students, each knowing that I could make a future career by choosing his or her particular design. "I don't know how many demands I can stand before I blow up."

"You have to stand enough," said Sandalari firmly. "We all do." Then she laughed, unexpectedly, and I followed her gaze.

The first design had risen on the table, on a holo image

wearing my face. It made the gown I'd had to wear to the Barbin 3 banquet look starkly simple by comparison. Had I chosen to wear it, I'd have had to turn sideways to get through doorways, and there was some doubt about archways, as well. Even Keli, more accustomed to the flights of fancy that passed for fashion in the high circles of Com society, had to suppress a little giggle.

"I think not," I said unnecessarily.

We chose a gown for Sandalari before we actually chose mine, and both of them were the simplest of the dozen options. With a fine sense of mischief, I ordered my dress in dark blue and hers in a shade slightly lighter. We registered a third choice because I'd been asked to pick the top three, and the dresses were in our bedrooms before we were finished.

Keli would wear her uniform, and the men the formal jumpsuits that most men wore on such occasions. Jemeret was entitled to several decorations on his for the assignments he'd completed in the past, and we were all eligible to wear decorations for the Barbin 3 mission, but we unanimously rejected them.

Jasin Lebec arrived after Petra Chantrey sent her thanks. "So much for her staying off the lines," I said to Jemeret, who had finished his drink and was still sitting, tightly wound, on the couch.

"No trouble getting here?" Coney asked Jasin Lebec.

"I expect no trouble," he answered. "Whoever's behind these senseless attacks isn't after me; he's after the young. I'm past my time, and it's not exactly secured knowledge." He drew a small sheaf of papers from inside his jumpsuit top and gave it to me.

"Papers?" Jemeret's surprise was completely undisguised.

"It's not information to be stored in anyplace accessible," his grandfather said slowly. "I was unaware of it myself until Pel gave me the documents." I thought about what I was holding, unopened, for a moment or two, then handed the sheaf of papers to Jemeret. He flipped open the folder without hesitation. Someone might have thought I was delegating the task to him, but in truth I just wasn't ready to deal with whatever it said.

"I take it this isn't good news," Jemeret began, then fell silent, reading quickly. We all watched him. There was something riveting about his concentration, and though nothing of it showed on the surface, I felt an explosion begin to build within him.

He swore one of the foulest oaths I'd ever heard, and it was only the third time I'd heard him swear at all. He looked up at me, his eyes momentarily unfocused. Then they snapped onto my face, blazing with consternation. "Those sheer idiots!" The words almost burst out of him. "How can educated people do such a—profoundly moronic thing!" I studied his face as it darkened with, astoundingly, an almost impotent rage.

I had to ask, "What is it?" as Concy and Sandalari stared at both of us, taken aback by Jemeret's totally uncharacteristic loss of control.

Jasin Lebec waited to see if Jemeret would answer me, and when he didn't, the older man said, "There's a new cult springing up on a few of the worlds of the Com, Ronica McBride. No one has quite traced its origin, though the guess is presently that it arose on Nogdala 7, not one of our sterling worlds by any standards. We are also uncertain of the methods by which it spreads, though the government and the MIs are trying to analyze and confirm present information. It's deeply disturbing to both groups, because it seems to them even more antirational than the present-day religions."

"What are its major precepts?" I asked, still not understanding why Jemeret was so enraged.

He was the one who answered me. "It appears to have only one major precept," he said harshly. "They're worshiping *us*."

I didn't dare laugh, even though, just as he'd been angered by the information, I found it so absurd as to be ludicrous. "What do you mean, they're worshiping us? Who is? How?"

Shaking his head, he handed me back the papers.

VIII. Rethinking the Past

We went to the banquet as if our lives had not, in a space of about four hours, become infinitely more complicated. The papers in and of themselves were not overly grim—the MI predictions were what gave it all such appalling implications. The gist of the new cult—which appeared to be calling itself Becois, in honor of Jasin Lebec—was that the holders of talent were actually saviors: we could do all sorts of things impossible for ordinary, talentless humanity, including the classically popular returning people from the dead. Therefore, the conclusion went, if prayed to correctly and propitiated enough, we should be able to provide for them, to guard them from the ravages of the Drenalion, and to help them gain immortality. Cult members were proclaiming that belief by, among other things, acts of defiance against government rules, especially those sacrosanct ones related to production quotas—many of which affected the tariffs due to the Com itself. So far, the production totals had not dropped enough to be significant, but Jara Deland had pulled forecasts that could be seen as alarming enough to generate an incursion of the Drenalion.

There was an interesting similarity to what was happening around Ananda, but there was no way they could be related, since Veroun, Calendola, Grieco, and the two Nogdala worlds were far from Ananda and unlikely to have encountered any of the Ananda materials or troublemakers. It was probably a case of synchronicity, of people being smart enough to realize economic protests were likely to be more successful than social ones, that a provider society puts more value on what it provides than on those to *whom* it provides.

The time span estimated on the problem of this new cult was still fairly comfortable, for the Becois were as yet a small movement. But Jemeret had brought me back when the adherents of the cult thought me lost to them and then restored Coney after Barbin 3. Those two acts had combined in the popular imagination to reinforce the belief that we could do anything.

I destroyed the documents after we read them, and Jemeret bubbled us all, to caution us to behave as if we knew nothing of this latest snarl in the fabric of our plans. It could not be presented to us as a Class A assignment, though it fit many of the conditions for one, because the appearance among worshipers of the objects of their worship would be unlikely to have the desired effect no matter how much we stung them.

"We have a lot of things to try to accomplish tonight," my lord said, biting back whatever anger he was still feeling. "We have to put aside for now the knowledge that muddled Becois thinking may give the government and the MIs an excellent motive for choosing to get rid of an entire group of people out there. Sometimes I think the MIs have been waiting for years for the right group of scapegoats to make an example of. The Becois might be behaving idiotically, but they don't deserve to die for it."

"You don't think," I asked slowly, "that the government or the MIs would want to use this talent-worship as an excuse to reorganize itself and do away with talent in the Com, do you?" I wasn't sure if I regarded that possibility as terrible or wonderful.

Jasin Lebec answered before anyone else had the opportunity. "Not the MIs, surely," he protested. "They've always been strong supporters of talent and absolute insisters on the need for talent to help the government."

"But we've never been responsible for anything that interfered with their efficiency before," Jemeret said, then added, "Never mind. We have too much to try to do without adding to it."

"We'll have to deal with it sooner or later," I said. I ignored the fact that Jasin Lebec and Keli were present, even though I knew they would not understand what I meant by my next words. "We were told to go on living, and if we're to do that, we have to do it in the best ways we can. That'll mean halting the insanity of people thinking we're worth worshiping."

It was the closest I'd ever come to mentioning the starfire out in the Com, but it had always been at the edge of my consciousness. I often found myself gazing at Tynnanna, as if he would somehow recognize my hunger and become a channel for the starfire to speak to me, but good sense told me that contact would only happen when the starfire was ready, not when I was.

Jemeret dissolved the bubble, and the four other people went to dress. I called up an amazing amount of meat protein for Tynnanna, left it on the couch table where it formed, and went to join my lord in the bedroom we were sharing. He had showered quickly and dried himself, and he was lying naked on the bed, hands behind his head. I stripped out of my jumpsuit and used the eliminatory's sonic cleanser, which was not nearly as sensual as the feeling of hot water sluicing down my body, but was considerably faster. When I returned to the bedroom, he was watching me, so of course I went to curl up beside him, tucked into the circle of his arm.

He'd buried the anger, shoving it deep into his being, into that inchoate knot he bore down below the surface of his mind.

I bubbled us. "I figure four Class A assignments, and perhaps another which isn't," I said.

His lips grazed my forehead. "Until what?" he asked.

"Until I can tell them I really want to go back to Caryldon with you." Even as I said it—

"You know it's not that simple, love," my Lord Jemeret said. "I want to break the hold the MIs have over the Com and set us free to become what we should have been years ago. I can't go back to Caryldon until that's accomplished."

"You can, but—"

"No, I can't," he overrode me. "I'll never give them another one of our children." It was a flat statement, uncolored by anything other than bald determination.

I shifted a little, fitting myself more strongly against his hip. "You haven't a plan yet, have you?"

"Not a hint of one," he answered readily enough.

"Well, what if they demanded more children? What if bringing the children here is the only way to save the people who live in the Com? Jemeret, they're worth saving."

For a long time he said nothing. At last he said slowly, "I think we'll have to make it possible for them to save themselves, and then let those who can, do it. The MIs should be gone for that to happen." He looked down at his hand, stroking my hair. "You started it when you gave your speech on Barbin 3. The people of the Com haven't been responsible for one another for a hundred years now, maybe longer. If they can learn what you—" He tapped my cheek with his forefinger. "—want them to learn, they have every chance."

"Is there anything I can say or do to make you give it up and just come home with me?" Quickly, I added, "Be fair."

If there was one thing I could depend on him for besides his love, it was the absolutely basic fairness that was an ingrained part of his character. So when I asked him that, he didn't just say no, as someone else might have. Instead he thought about it.

"At this moment, I can't think of anything that would stop me from making the attempt," he said at last. "Not even you, as important to me as you are."

"But what about your dream of uniting the Samothen, of having a son? If you die out here—" I couldn't finish it. The thought choked me. I gathered it all back.

"Ronica, my Caryldon dream is vitally important to me, but Caryldon itself is now at risk. If I lose that dream in this one, I'll have done my very best." He was stroking my arms as he spoke. "The Com has to be changed for humanity to survive anywhere, so this is for Caryldon, too. As for the son I want, well, if I'm not willing to give what the starfire needs of me, then I'm not worth getting what I want for it."

I had come into the Com at least partially to keep Jemeret from throwing his life away. I swore I would still stop him if I could, but if I could help him, then I'd have to find a way to do that.

However, I couldn't see how we would be able to begin, let

alone accomplish, anything so monumental. When I'd spoken at the Barbin 3 banquet, it was without such overwhelming motives; I'd only said what I believed. Then, too, my training had always been in one-on-one influence. I'd been taught to rule by ruling the rulers, but Jemeret was one ruler I could not rule.

"We'd better get dressed," I said. "I think it's going to be a long evening."

Instead he rose above me and took my mouth with his, and I let the bubble deconstruct by itself. It was a relief to have this place where we could meet so simply, as equals, without myriad webs of complication all around us. We used each other at that moment to drive away all other reality. For the time during which we were joined in one another and in pleasure, there was no one trying to kill us, no group of dependent, superstitious citizens trying to make us responsible for everything that happened to them, no need to free the Com from the MIs, or the citizens from the Com, no Tribunal, no starfire warning against ultimate oblivion, no life except for us.

And then we came back to Orokell's central city and got up to dress for the banquet.

"Do you know what you're going to say tonight?" Jemeret asked, sealing his formal jumpsuit and looking, to me, unbearably handsome.

"I miss the brow-crown," I said to him. "I like the way it makes your eyes stand out."

His slow smile warmed me. "Pay attention, Ronica," he ordered. "This is important."

I let myself flush without damping down on the response, but I still didn't answer his question. "I know it's important," was all I said. He seemed to consider pressing me further, but did not.

Coney and Sandalari looked striking, their pale hair contrasting with the dark blue. Jasin Lebec had reverted to formal gold, his decorations so numerous as to imply many more of lesser value which he hadn't room to wear. He noted Coney's absence of adornment first, then Jemeret's, then mine, and said almost apologetically, "They expect all this display of me."

I laid my hand on his arm as Keli came out of her room in her formal MF brown. "Don't apologize to us, Jasin Lebec," I said as strongly as I could. "You chose your life, and you've lived it to the best of your ability. You have every right to be proud of it."

He smiled at me a little, but there was still an edge of regret about it. "I am constantly reevaluating," he said softly. "And for the first time I'm wondering what it would have been like to have made a different decision."

Jemeret looked momentarily startled, then masked it, saying, "It's long past the time for regrets, na-sire."

Jasin Lebec looked at him squarely, a remarkably similar expression on his face. "But not for reevaluation," he said firmly.

Jemeret said only, "You lead the way. I expect you've done this a lot more often than we have."

Jasin Lebec drew back his shoulders, his body still straight as that of a younger man. We left the suite, followed by Tynnanna's fiery eyes, went down the corridor and out into the precincts, which were almost balmily warm with climate control in what would otherwise have been a cool evening.

Climbing up the wide steps of Government House once again, my step unexpectedly faltered, and Jemeret caught my elbow. "This action—this moment," I stuttered. "This was the last thing I remembered doing before—" I stumbled over the words, then fell silent.

"Before I sealed off the last memories," he finished for me. "It's all right, love. You came through that, and you'll come through all this, too."

"I'm working on it," I said softly.

The honor guard at the top of the steps braced as we passed, and we went through the archway into the rotunda. Jasin Lebec led the way around the circle and down the hallway, which opened into the back of an immense room that would by now be filled with enough long tables to accommodate several thousand people. One end of the room was taken up by the raised platform on which the head table stood. From behind it, as if we were backstage, we ascended steps to the dais, leaving

Keli at the bottom. When we were seated, she would go around to the back entrance of the hall, walk through it and take her place, visibly, at the foot of the dais stair inside the room.

We could hear the sounds of people gathering, and then Pel Nostro and Jara Deland, who were always the titular hosts of the banquets at Government House, opened the dais doors and gestured us to come through to the high table.

Jasin Lebec went first and continued to the end of the table. Sandalari followed, then Coney. Jara Deland and Pel Nostro would sit in the center, next, and then I entered, with Jemeret to take the seat beside me at the far end from his grandfather. The applause that had begun at Jasin Lebec's entrance seemed to escalate at mine. I had to make myself hold my head up, because the adulation I used to accept as no more than my due now embarrassed me, and it would never do to show it. I sat perhaps more quickly than anyone expected, and the others at the high table followed my lead with such alacrity that the ovation staggered to a stop and everyone else sat down as well.

Pel Nostro rose to welcome all the diners, make a joke or two like any skilled speaker, and then to indicate to them that I had agreed to address them after the meal. He told them to enjoy their dinner, and sat down beside me again. Our table—and all the other tables in the room—extruded wineglasses, filled with a light golden beverage only faintly alcoholic, along with the first course of the evening.

Pel Nostro turned toward me and, by his action, toward Jemeret as well. "We have now set a few private meetings after the banquet is over," he said, as if we wouldn't have guessed he'd do that. "Anok Luttrell is most eager to hear what course you might suggest to solve the Ananda problem, so we've scheduled him first."

I nodded, though my approval was unnecessary, and took a sip of the wine, grateful it was not of the toasting variety, because if toasts had begun, we might never have gotten to the meetings at all.

"Jara and I will meet with you alone next, though we will, of course, be present at the other meetings. She followed your suggestion and ran the probabilities on successful completion of assignments with the massing of talent into a single team, and we need to discuss the results."

"Fine," I said. I'd finished my first course, though I didn't recall eating it. Jemeret's still sat in front of him, largely untouched.

Pel Nostro went on, "Then Marga Morena would like to discuss an idea she has for exploration of the newly identified area she says you mentioned earlier. Finally there are some dignitaries in attendance tonight who have asked to be presented to you, and we've made a reception room available for that."

"You've been very thorough," I said. "Of course, the team will attend the meetings as well as me."

He was getting faster. His "Of course" followed closely as I finished speaking.

Jemeret picked up his fork and put a forkful of food into his mouth, seeming barely to notice he had done it. I knew then, as strongly as if he'd told me, that he'd been sweeping the room, looking for any signs of hostility, and that by returning to his meal, he'd found none, but was still alert.

I hadn't realized how tense I was until I felt myself relax.

The meal was probably excellent. The chefs at Government House competed for the honor of creating dishes for the notables who dined here, and only a few could work at any given time, because most meals were created through the consoles, the tables, and the automatic cookers. The opportunity to produce culinary wonders for the Tribunal, the Class A's, and those who had assembled to honor us, was something to be competed for and exploited. Each of the five courses, two dishes to every course, was more elaborate and more beautifully presented than the one that preceded it, and by the third I was only eating part of the serving.

It wasn't an accident that I hadn't answered Jemeret's question about what I was going to say. When he'd asked, I'd been resolutely ignoring the fact that I would have to say anything. I knew it was the kind of opportunity I'd need to make the most of, because if I knew the Com, the MIs would broadcast the speech as well, so that many people on Com worlds would have the opportunity to hear the Class A. But how best to use it?

Over two of the richest desserts I'd ever been confronted with, my thoughts began to coalesce. By the time the tables reabsorbed everything but the coffee, I'd settled on something, and since Pel Nostro was already introducing me, I knew I'd have to go with it.

I rose as the attendees applauded, saw the holo images of me sprout on every tabletop, took a deep breath and gathered to calm myself. Jemeret touched me, faintly, encouragingly, with his sting. A wash of warmth went over me at the depth of his trust.

I smiled out over the assemblage, still in the edges of the warmth, so the smile was the absolute best I had to give. "Pel Nostro has told you that I'm going to speak about what happened to me," I said, deliberately not thanking him for his introduction. "And so I will, but first I have to tell you about a conversation I had ten years ago, in a room just down the precincts from here." I was reading curiosity from the room at large, a little envy from some localized pinpoints of people, some general admiration. I did not try to influence anyone. This was a very different crowd from the provincial audience on Barbin 3.

"I was thirteen, and it was the first time I ever remember meeting Jasin Lebec." The old man's head came up, his surprise evident. "I asked him what the Com expected of me, what my role would be. He bewildered me very much with his answer. He said that what the Com and the government wanted was for me to grow up to be an adult, a complete human being." I turned deliberately toward Jasin Lebec's end of the table. "Do you remember that meeting?"

"Yes, I do," he said firmly.

I looked back at my listeners, aware that Jara Deland and Pel Nostro both seemed fascinated by what I was saying, for I'd hit a note neither of them had been anticipating. "I was disappointed when he said that, because I thought it was silly—almost everyone I knew was an adult, after all. I thought adulthood was automatic, that it just came with age. Jasin

Lebec tried to tell me that I was mistaken about that, but I didn't pay much attention to him."

There was a slight stir among the members of the audience. They had also expected something different, but they were willing to listen, and were doing so more avidly than I'd hoped.

"When I graduated, I hadn't yet attained the ambition Jasin Lebec set for me, and so the first choice I made after graduation was not a good one." I would go into no further detail than that. Those who knew what had happened, knew. Those who did not know, wouldn't have any less of a chance of understanding what I wanted to say. "Now I come to Pel's original question. What happened to me while I was gone? What makes it possible for me to stand here now and speak to you when others of us with talent fell and did not get up again?" I lightly touched Sandalari with my sting to let her know that I was not going to single her out.

"The answer is a very simple one. What happened to me is that I *learned*. I was not well-suited to the process, even though I would have denied it if anyone had accused me of it. I had spent my whole life engaged in the exercise of learning. But it was very much an exercise. Now, I don't know if I can tell you what I learned, but I can distill a little of it and set it out before you."

I paused a moment. This was the truly tricky part. If I said things too alien to most of their personal philosophies, they would merely dismiss what I was saying, and I didn't want that. I wanted them to listen.

"What I learned is extremely important to me, to all of us with talent, and to everyone else in the Com," I said slowly. From the corner of my eye I saw Jasin Lebec move a little, his eyes glittering in a way that reminded me of Jemeret. Near him, Coney was watching me with the expression of love on his face that I remembered from our childhood onward. I couldn't turn enough to see Jemeret in my peripheral vision on the other side, and I didn't try. Instead I went on, leaning forward and speaking slowly, to stress the words. "I learned this: if the only things we do with talent are the things we've always done without talent, then we have not yet earned the right to have it. And talent magnifies. If the things we do with talent are the things we never should have done anyway, we are probably doomed to the same fate as countless people who have lived in the past, in the Com or out of it. We will be no different, and certainly no better."

I deliberately made eye contact with Faucon Oletta, at a front table, and found the Chief Justiciar's look disbelieving, but hopeful. I smiled at him briefly, then let my gaze move slowly over the rest of the room. "Talent does not exist to be more of the same. If it did, we wouldn't need it. We must use it for things humanity needs, yes, but not for things humanity can in all probability do itself." I looked at Pel Nostro. "I think that's all I have to say," I said to him, and I sat down.

Jemeret found my hand under the table and surrounded it with his. Until I let my control slip away, I didn't realize I was actually trembling.

For what seemed like enough time for a storm to rise and rage and then die again, there was a stillness in the silent room. Then, at almost the same moment, Jasin Lebec and Faucon Oletta rose to their feet, starting to applaud. Everyone else seemed to follow, over a noticeable period of time, except for Jemeret and me. He might have been reading the audience; I couldn't. My mind was whirling, as if I'd kept myself from seeing the risks I might be taking until I was actually done.

"Relax," Jemeret said, his lips barely moving. "I think enough of the message got through."

Unable to resist, I turned slightly toward him. "You don't think I was too different from what they expected?"

He shook his head almost imperceptibly. "You're right," he said, "and they'll come to see it. Things are going to change, in some cases radically. It's up to us to be in place, with enough power, to choose the forms of the changes."

The applause died, and, when everyone else sat down, Jasin Lebec remained standing. Pel Nostro started to speak, then realized the old man had not reseated himself and nodded, yielding the floor to the only true Class A the Com would ever know.

"You all know me," Jasin Lebec said firmly, as the holo

images on the tables shimmered from me to him. "I have served you nearly a century, and I believe I have completed every assignment I have undertaken, with one exception." He glanced significantly at me, and Jemeret's hand tightened on mine for a moment. "For a time, as I began my service, and through the long years during which I served, I thought I was acting in ways no one else could have undertaken. But I have come to see that, thinking as I did, I was guilty of underestimating you." He swung his arm outward, a dramatic gesture, encompassing more than the hall itself. "I have served you, on the whole, I believe, well. I am content now to place the future of talent, the leadership, if you will, of the *tribe* of talent, in the hands of those two people you see at the other end of this table."

His deliberate, emphasized use of the word "tribe" passed through me like a thrill of comprehension.

"I will be," Jasin Lebec went on, "eager to see what they do with the leadership that used to be mine, and I hope you will join me in that eagerness." He left his place, his eyes twinkling, and came to me.

Jemeret and I both rose. The old man's eyes were sparkling with a youthful mischief as he embraced me, then his grandson. He was smiling broadly, and when he took a step to return to his seat, he said to Pel Nostro, "Don't try to lean too heavily on old rules, Pel. It's a new regime now."

Pel Nostro and Jara Deland were as startled as I thought it possible for two people to be. They recovered quickly, but I knew that Jasin Lebec had just withdrawn one of the foundations of their world—he had; I had not. Suddenly, almost overpoweringly, I wanted to cling to Jemeret, and I knew I didn't dare.

The Com Counselor brought the evening to an end, thanking everyone for attending, as if they might have refused to come if they'd chosen to, and then led us all back off the dais while the tables cleared themselves. I saw Keli turn smartly and vanish through a door that would let her meet us behind the stage.

As soon as we got there, it seemed that everyone but Jemeret and I talked at once—Jara Deland to Jasin Lebec, Coney to Pel Nostro, Sandalari to Coney. Jemeret let it go on for the space of a breath, then said evenly, "Quiet," and to my amazement, everyone quieted. He looked at Jasin Lebec. "Am I mistaken, or did you just retire from public service?"

Jasin Lebec was smiling, utterly at ease. "In a way," he answered. "All I did, really, was evoke a small privilege, given to someone with this many decorations on his chest. Instead of directly serving the Com any longer, I believe I will be serving you." He nodded, more to Jemeret, it seemed, than to me. And then, in my direction, "Your interests and goals."

I wondered if he had any idea what those goals were.

Jara Deland said, "Jemeret Cavanaugh is not under Com oath."

Jasin Lebec skewered her with a gaze that reminded her he was not under Com oath, either, but he said nothing. The MI Liaison had the grace to blush.

Pel Nostro rested his hand lightly on his wife's arm. "I think, unless we are willing to refuse Jemeret Cavanaugh's service, we need not make too fine a point of it." He turned to ask a question, but I interrupted him, because I wanted to make a fine point of it.

"Do you want to refuse my—" I'd almost said *lord's*; I could just hear Jara Deland's reaction if I had. "—husband's service, Jara?" Reading her as I was, I knew how tempted she was to say yes.

Pel Nostro knew, too. He must have squeezed her arm hard, because she could only marginally repress a wince as she said reluctantly, "The government needs Class A talent." It was not an agreement, but it was a concession.

"What did you mean, calling talent a tribe?" the Com Counselor asked Jasin Lebec. "We have gone, as a society, far beyond the primitiveness of a tribal organization, and if we have, you must have as well, because you are certainly beyond us."

" 'Beyond' is a relative term," Coney said wryly.

"So is 'primitive,' " Jemeret said. "Let's just say that a tribal society is 'basic' and leave it at that."

And I asked, as innocently as I could, "Shouldn't we get started on those meetings?" Jemeret shot me a fast look, but did not sting me.

"Ah yes," Pel Nostro said. "The Ananda problem. Follow me."

We all trooped along a corridor to one of the dozen small conference rooms. I wondered which of them was the room in which I'd met with Jasin Lebec at the time I'd described earlier in the evening. There was a guard at the door, but as he reached to open it, Keli stared him down, and he stepped back. She opened the door, made a fast survey of the room, then took a stance outside, shoving the guard figuratively one step to the right. We left the door open as we entered.

Anok Luttrell rose as we came in, his gaze filled with the expectation of imminent satisfaction. We exchanged quick greetings and all sat down around the table.

Anok Luttrell cleared his throat. "Have you a scenario to suggest for the Ananda problem, Class A Ronica McBride?"

I rose again, using height to make my words more impressive. "In the first place, Anok, it is my opinion that this need not be what you would call a Class A problem." The three people from the Tribunal sat up straighter at that, and Jara Deland frowned.

"I beg your pardon?" Anok Luttrell said, more weakly than I'm sure he intended. "We thought—that is, when the MI solution was the Drenalion—"

"Yes." I overrode him purposely, investing that word with as much distaste as I could manage. "I know that the MIs tend to offer the Drenalion as a solution whenever a Class A is unavailable, so naturally you would have expected the problem to lend itself only to Class A solution. Anok, tell me about the Scuttlers."

He opened his mouth once, closed it again, looked from Pel Nostro to Jasin Lebec, and then back at me again. I waited.

At last he sighed, resigned to talking about his pet corps in a group that had two Class C's in it, and laid out the history of and his hopes for the elite unit. Once embarked, he grew expansive, clearly enamored of his own project. When he finished, I laid out the scenario we'd developed, ending by saying, "Our estimate is two years before the results reach an acceptable level, but you're welcome to access the MI predictive models for confirmation or denial of that."

Jara Deland murmured something offhandedly about not needing my permission, and her sotto voce comment clearly reached everyone in the room. I knew by the pause that followed that they were all waiting for me to react. I refused to take up the challenge.

There was a long silence. At last the Com Counselor cleared his throat and said only, "It could possibly be workable. Percentages?"

Jara Deland opened her mouth, but before she could say anything, we heard the distinctive click, and the MI voice said, "Project 30 percent chance of success in one year, 75 percent in two, and 88.4 percent in three." Jara Deland shut her mouth with a snap and reddened again. I had the feeling she might have forgiven me one blush, but she was unlikely to get over being made to flush twice in one night.

I actually sympathized with her. Her role was to stand between us and the MIs on most occasions, forming the questions she felt would be most likely to achieve the answers the government hoped to get, and delivering those answers to people who had not been present to hear them. On rare occasions, the MIs chose to speak for themselves, but I had never heard previously of a case where they cut her off to do so.

Everyone in the room was surprised, but Anok Luttrell recovered quickly, lost in the need to get his problems solved and therefore slightly insensitive to others' needs. "Those numbers are perfectly acceptable to me," he said. "I'm more than willing to proceed on that basis."

The head of the Merchant Fleet looked at Pel Nostro, who had been uncharacteristically silent. "I can mobilize the Scuttlers in less than a day," he said, "but I'd prefer to wait until we have the scenario broken down into individual assignments. In addition, I'll need a jury-rigged spaceport on one of the dark continents of Ananda, so I can sneak some workers down to start preparing the way for the wholesale arrivals—registering landing passes, making accommodation requests, and the like."

"Excellent," Jemeret said. It was the first time he'd spoken since I began to lay out the solution. He was indicating a closure to that subject and a desire to keep the evening moving.

After a pause, Pel Nostro realized it and dismissed the head of the Merchant Fleet, who bid us farewell and hurried out to put the scenario into motion.

"He should have been able to formulate a plan like that himself," Sandalari observed thoughtfully when he was gone. "Even if his mind isn't up to it, I'm sure he has advisers."

"The solving of major problems is not what they're accustomed to doing." Jasin Lebec's voice was gentle. "But Anok's very eagerness leads me to believe that he'll want to attempt it more often after this. The others of the Tribunal may, as well."

I looked at Jara Deland. "Jara, I want you to pose a question for me." She was startled, and everyone else in the room held still, aware of the tension between the MI Liaison and me, but also, I think, compelled by tones of real passion in my voice.

"You have always been able to speak to them without me, Ronica McBride," she said slowly. "That's one of your prerogatives. Why would you need my intervention now?"

"Because of the question," I answered. "I want to know . . ." Forming the question was harder than I'd thought it would be. I had to gather to manage it. "I want to know why, if the MIs had my suite under surveillance when Kray came in, they didn't stop it all before the rape." She stared at me. "Or, if not then, before I killed him!"

Jemeret could have soothed me with his sting, but he chose something deliberately visual instead, reaching out and taking my hand, stroking it with his thumb, his normally soft gray eyes burning silver—almost the color of the starfire metal.

Jara Deland's face took on the open compassion that even a woman who is not remotely tolerant of another under normal circumstances can feel for that other when abuse is involved. "I'm sorry," she said softly. "I have never been able to get an answer to a 'why' question. Would you let me rephrase it in a way I think may generate a response?"

"You see why I need you," I said to her, more rigidly than I expected.

She thought for a long moment, choosing and rejecting words or phrases, and then said, "Application."

The click, and then, "Proceed."

"Recall the date and time of the unfortunate incident which removed Class A Ronica McBride from active service."

"Recalled."

"Was the incident recorded?"

"It was."

"Was intervention in the incident considered?"

"It was."

"What was the trigger point for the intervention?"

"The potential permanent loss of Class A service."

I had begun to tremble almost uncontrollably, and Jemeret stood up, pulled me to my feet and put his arms around me, but he did not sting me.

Jara Deland went on, her voice almost unremittingly expressionless. "Was there a trigger point for the intervention in the potential permanent loss of Class B service?"

"No."

I nearly cried out; I forced myself to be silent.

"Please provide detail on the percentages for the decision governing intervention."

"At entrance of Class B Amahd Krieger to Class A Ronica McBride's suite, five percent potential for intervention. At introduction of artificial substance to Class A Ronica McBride's life systems, seven percent. At forced sexual intercourse, twelve percent. At the death of Class B Amahd Krieger, twenty percent. The imminent threat to Class A Ronica McBride from Class A Ronica McBride was not predicted. Probability immediately rose to one hundred percent and intervention became necessary."

"Thank you," Jara Deland said. "End of application."

I turned my face and hid it against Jemeret's chest for a time, waiting for the waves to pass over me. Only my reaction to the unfortunate incident, as Jara Deland had so calmly called it, had not been predicted, which meant the rest of it—all the rest of it—had been part of the MI calculations. They had done nothing to stop it.

Jemeret said softly, just at my ear, "I wish you hadn't done that."

"I had to," I said shakily. "I had to know." As if we were alone in the room, I raised my face to him. "No wonder they became so dependent on talent. They have no notion—none at all."

Sandalari had covered her face with her hands, and Jara Deland looked uncomfortable, but whether at being present or at still feeling compassion toward me, I had no way of telling without reading her. I was in no condition to read her. Coney was radiating anger, an emotion so rare for him, so nearly foreign, that I was touched. Jasin Lebec said nothing. Pel Nostro, who had been looking steadily at the floor, raised his head and cleared his throat.

Jemeret shook his head. "What was the subject of this next meeting to be?" he asked. "Pel?"

"Jara wanted to give you the probabilities the MIs worked out on talent team attack on Com problems," Pel replied. "We—the Tribunal and the MIs—wanted to discuss with you the next Class A assignment."

I was gathering to push aside the successive lapping tongues of emotion that shook me.

"Postpone it," my lord said brusquely. "She's in no condition to deal with a request from the MIs right now."

"Marga is expected in another half hour, with Terrill Guthrie in attendance, and we can't ignore the other dignitaries who want to be presented," Pel Nostro said almost tentatively, unwilling to confront Jemeret's anger in this circumstance.

"I'll be fine with them," I said shortly. "They're human beings." At that, Jemeret did reach out and slip into my mind, the gesture itself a calming one for me, even without his deliberately adjusting anything. I needed him just then as a bulwark against the truth, and I realized what a difference being in the Com made. On Caryldon, I'd needed him to help me face the truth; here, I needed him to help me see around it.

IX. Attack

Because Jemeret was already joined to me, I felt him reach out and nudge someone else, an edge of impatience in the gesture. I didn't follow it to see where it went. Coney asked, "Where are the presentations? Perhaps we ought to get them out of the way first. Then at least the night will be a little shorter."

"Everyone's assembled in the first stateroom," Pel Nostro answered. "We're serving wine and tidbits."

"All right, then let's get this finished," Jemeret said, setting me back away from him, confirming silently that I'd be all right, then releasing my shoulders.

I shook my heavy hair back from my face, turned with squared shoulders, and painted a smile on. I wanted nothing more than to go back to our suite and lose myself in Jemeret's greater strength. It had been so easy on Caryldon to do that; here, now, I couldn't let myself.

"Please come this way," Pel Nostro said.

Jara Deland reached out toward me, an abortive gesture that drew my attention. I was surprised at the depth of compassion she was showing, even after I expected her to have caught control of herself again. "I'm sorry," she said, somewhat gruffly. "I didn't know—before. I didn't think to ask."

"It's all right, Jara," I said to her, uncomfortable. "You've always interpreted very well for the MIs. You don't have to apologize for them, too."

She flushed.

Third time tonight, I thought.

"I was apologizing for myself," she said in a low voice. "I

can speak for myself on occasion, you know." Her tone was suddenly acerbic.

I touched her gently with my sting, wishing I could be more affectionate toward her, and unable to be.

We left the conference room and went down the corridor and through a demi-lobby where either a fountain or a holo of a fountain sang merrily and somewhat incongruously. Then, just as we turned into another corridor that branched away, I stumbled, brought up short. Jemeret stopped beside me. We looked at one another as Pel Nostro kept walking but everyone behind us halted. Sensing something wrong, even though she could see no danger, Keli pushed her way through the other four people behind us and took a stance in front of me, alert, uncertain why.

It felt almost as if we'd walked face first into a wall of the most virulent malevolence I'd ever encountered, a positive flood of hatred and rage hemorrhaging out of the hallway. Jemeret's face had set into grim, hard lines I hadn't seen before, and I knew from his expression that no degree of what I was feeling was exaggerated or imagined. There was an almost physical force to so much malignancy; every nerve in my body rang with echoes of the evil.

And then it vanished, cut off as if it had never existed, the powerful force of it gone, leaving only ripples of its aftermath in my being, and, I guessed, in Jemeret's. Pel Nostro had reached the doorway of the reception room and turned back to see why we weren't directly behind him. I gasped at the suddenness of release from the malevolence, feeling the clarity of the air around me with a sense of renewed gratitude that the hatred was gone. Jemeret squeezed my hand, warning me to say nothing about what had just happened, so all I said was, "It's all right, Keli. We're in no danger."

She relaxed instantly, obedient, but threw me a quick, skeptical look as she stood back against the wall to let us pass. I turned to see if Jasin Lebec had felt what my lord and I had, and saw that he was pale, tight-lipped, but also unwilling to speak about it.

Pel Nostro stepped into the reception room, and the guards

in the room signaled the double doors backward, framing Jemeret and me in the doorway.

There were about sixty people in the room, men and women smiling at us, applauding politely rather than adoringly. I read every person there, knew that Jemeret was doing the same thing, and suspected that Jasin Lebec would, as well. I found no trace, no residual deposit whatsoever, of the torrent of ill will that had greeted us, and that was startling. If the feelings had come from someone here, we should have been able to get an idea of where they originated, because such a powerful outpouring of emotion usually left a strong signature behind. Yet I could feel nothing of it now, only the normal, expected emotions among people about to be presented to the Class A's—anticipation, ambition, some admiration, a good overlay of calculation, and a hint here and there of deviousness.

Jemeret's face was carefully impassive, but I felt his unseen frown as the presentations began. There were several Lumeships here in dock, and their captains had been accorded the honor of being part of this assemblage. For some political motive I couldn't think of, they were presented to us first. A member of the University administration from each of the Universities Petra Chantrey ruled, as well as several of the most distinguished scholars in various fields, were presented next. Then I saw the welcome face of Sinet Coleby, whom I embraced and handed over to Coney and Sandalari with the caution, "Don't let her get away." And I looked around for Lage N'Verre, whom I always expected to see with her.

Pel Nostro seemed to be looking for her, too. He signaled to one of the room guards, whispered an order, and then turned back to keep introducing more people to us.

Next came some of the more minor agency heads from the government bureaucracy, and several of Pel Nostro's own assistants, including a man I'd met before, Lamar Acifica, the prettily handsome young man over whom Kray and I had quarreled. I saw from Coney's face that he remembered that quarrel, too, and for a split second we shared the memory with one another. Lamar Acifica, still more beautiful than either Sandalari or I, was flattered to have been recognized and remembered, tried to hold my hand a little longer than was considered proper, and earned himself a frown from me and a snort from Jemeret.

Several heads of Merchant Fleet subsidiary companies were next, none of them particularly memorable, and all of them similar in the way that men are similar when they do the same kinds of jobs and hold the same kinds of values; only a long time later did I realize that two of those men had been women, and I hadn't noticed it at the time.

Then I heard Keli give a small, indrawn breath, and I glanced around, alerted to possible danger; at the same time, I saw Coney dip his head to an older man who had moved up to be presented. I recognized him, then the two women and the pair of men who were waiting behind him, making up the last group of presentees. Davin Olavson was head of the Circle of Epicyclism and the religions' honorary observer on the Tribunal, a nonvoting position, but one that was generally, if incorrectly, supposed to give its holder some modicum of influence. Davin Olavson was probably in his early seventies and welcomed the white hair and the thin lines of age without trying to alter them the way most others in the Com did. He was taller than anyone I had ever seen, as if he had been born and grown on a light-grav world, and yet had adapted to norm-grav without it having an untoward effect on him. It gave him an air of dignity and strength which I found impressive.

Pel Nostro's voice became a little more formal when he made the introduction, as official government policy regarding the religions was "polite and indulgent, but never permitting of meaning; proper, but never warm."

I'd met all five of these people before, when I was fully indoctrinated into the official line; now, having spent time on Caryldon, I was more inclined to be tolerant and curious.

"Davin," I said, as warmly as I thought it was politic to be, my tone still edged with caution, "I'm pleased to see you again."

"We are happy to welcome you back, Ronica McBride," he said, his voice surprisingly full, emerging from such a thin chest. "We prayed for you continuously during your—" The brief hesitation was barely noticeable. "—illness."

Even that innocuous statement was a risk. Were I the true daughter of the Com that I had been before the unfortunate incident, I might have scorned the sentiment and thereby reduced his status even further than it was. The results of the unfortunate incident had, however, altered certain facets of my makeup. I raised my head and said clearly, "I thank you for the prayers and for the feelings which prompted them, Davin."

He nodded to me and moved on to clasp Jemeret's hand. I would liked to have listened to what passed between them, but the next person, a petite woman who looked even smaller next to Davin's extreme height, stepped up to me, her eyes on the floor except for a brief glance upward at my face. This was Gromily EnCastro, Selected Image of the Responsionists. She was, by Com standards, exquisitely delicate, resembling a fragile piece of websilk art, but she radiated a strength almost too strong to be contained in her small being. If I hadn't reached out to her first, she might have stood in front of me all evening—as the epitome of Responsion, she should not employ independent action, but was under the strictest discipline only to react. She went nowhere unaccompanied, because without a Motive to evoke her Response, she could do nothing at all. The man behind her, faceless and nameless, not one of the people to be presented to us, was her Motive, waiting until she had finished with each person in the receiving line to prompt her to move away from us. I suppose I should have respected her for it, but all I could think was that it would drive me absolutely insane.

"I am most pleased to see you again, Gromily," I said as she took my extended hand.

"And I am pleased you have returned to us," she rejoined.

"Have you and your Church been well?" I asked her.

"As well as can be expected in a world which values us as this one does." The words were even and noncommittal, in keeping with the courtesy of the question.

The guard Pel Nostro had sent out returned and said something to him in a low voice. Jemeret must have augmented his hearing, for his head snapped back around toward them and I felt the anger he was not able to keep from projecting.

Gromily EnCastro caught an edge of it and spun away, avoiding the recognition of an unpleasant emotion she would rather not have to reflect in a social situation.

I knew, without anyone saying anything, that Lage N'Verre was dead.

Pel Nostro was already turning to the next person in line as if nothing untoward had occurred, and the Selected Image and her Motive moved on to Jemeret, who mastered his emotions to greet her.

The next woman to be presented to me was Ocaba Neil, the head of the Aspects Council of the Essencists. She was probably over a hundred, larger than Gromily EnCastro, but still somewhat tinier than normal, her golden skin unmarked by wrinkles and her long black hair unmarked by gray. She smiled broadly as she greeted me. One of the fundamental tenets of Essencism was that the Diety had created talent as one of its Aspects, rather than as a new evolutionary phase for humanity, and I'd never had the time to argue with her about it. I certainly didn't have it now, and was trying to cope with the idea that someone had reached Lage N'Verre here, in Government House.

Ocaba Neil yielded her place in front of me to the last of the men, who was also smiling broadly. This was Dolen T'Kelle, Repository of the Maccrates and the reason Keli had gasped. He was a great hulk of a man, nearly as tall as Davin Olavson, but four times broader, with an arcane appearance, abetted by the long, sleeveless, symbol-filled robe he wore over his jumpsuit. His huge shock of black hair was almost untamed, and he was the only man I knew for certain had possessed a beard before Jemeret set the fashion. This beard was full and almost reached his lower chest.

"Ronica McBride," he said by way of greeting, his voice booming across the room, "let me add my well-wishes to the rest. Are you heartily sick of the sound of your name by now?"

As it happened, I heartily was, and I laughed aloud at the question, though I couldn't say yes to it openly, and though my pleasure was colored by the unconfirmed knowledge that we had lost Lage. "Dolen, you are a great relief," I said honestly.

"We are all delighted you have been Preserved," he said, taking my outstretched hand in both of his, though it would have been lost in just one. He emphasized the last word so explosively that I was glad he had turned his head slightly away or the plosive might have blown my hair out of its arrangement. For a moment he looked as if he would like to say more, but the rules of what presentees could and couldn't say, how much time they could take, were well set, and he simply inclined his head and took a step toward Jemeret, saying, "I greet you with praise for reinstating the beard in civilized society, Jemeret Cavanaugh."

For a few moments I was alone amid the swirl of people. Presentees spoke with one another, glancing in my direction to see if I would call any of them back. Instead I turned and waved Keli to come to me. She was instantly at my side, surreptitiously brushing away a tear at, I realized, having been so close to the man who led the faith she espoused openly, even when it was to her detriment. I wished I could give her enough time to be overwhelmed by the unexpectedness of being in the same place as her Repository, but I could not, and I was gratified by the speed with which she drew herself back to the business at hand. I gave her a quick series of orders: tell the housekeeper at the Visitors' Residence to open another suite onto ours; find out where Sinet was staying and have her things moved to our suite; stay in the suite until we returned; and if she would feel more secure carrying it, draw a neural whip or a blaster from the Government House armory. She braced and was gone.

I laid my hand on Jemeret's arm and slid uninvited into his mind, touching him and trying to use the touch to calm myself; when I got there, I discovered that he needed calming as well, and he was generally harder to persuade than I was. I murmured, "Not the time or place, my lord." He ignored me a moment, then gave in and made himself relax.

Someone proposed a toast to us, and a table in the center of the room extruded glasses with some kind of sweet toasting wine in them. We stood still and smiled through the formal praise, which went on awhile, as the lesser bureaucrats seemed to want to compete as to which of them could offer the most effusive compliments. By the time they finally appeared to be finished, Jemeret had slid back to an impatience so tautly repressed that I feared he might explode. Concern about his mood helped me contain my own.

"One more meeting," said Pel Nostro when the toasts were over. He seemed to know that we were very upset, and anxiety was spilling over into his normally perfect facade of expansive diplomacy.

I almost groaned. I had forgotten how much time in high government service was spent doing next to nothing but empty ceremony. I wondered what all these people would be doing with their time and their lives if they didn't have to fill them with meaningless rites. I kept glancing at Sinet, who had been a little taken aback by her precipitous absorption into our company. At the age of nearly fifty, she'd been certain the form of her life was set, unlikely to be altered, and this was something of a surprise to her. I could sympathize; I thought I'd known minutely the shape my life would take when I was a student, and then I'd awakened on Caryldon with reality indelibly changed.

It was changing again. Perhaps I'd deceived myself a second time into seeing as fixed things that were infinitely malleable. Perhaps, I thought, everything that seems fixed is only momentarily resting, caught somehow against a snag in the pull of a revolving cosmos, and then, when the pressures impelling movement have grown too great, the static springs free and moves on.

I shook off the thought, and we left the reception room and went down the corridor to yet another meeting room. We brought Sinet Coleby with us, but Jara Deland did not come, remaining instead with the guests in the reception room. She and Marga Morena were not terribly fond of each other; I also thought her recent, unwilling feelings of sympathy for me had made her very uncomfortable. Jara Deland was not on terms of intimacy with any women I knew, not even with Petra

Chantrey, who was normally considered a pleasure to get along with.

Marga Morena rose as we came in, and after a long enough pause to be making a point, Terrill Guthrie did as well. His bulky shoulders seemed even more muscular than when we met him in the receiving line at the spaceport.

Pel Nostro got everyone seated with a record lack of ceremony, and Marga Morena said quickly, with a glance at Sinet Coleby, whom she obviously had not expected, "Your assertion that you would not be lessened by a Class B assignment was very interesting, Ronica McBride. Would you be willing to enlarge on it?"

I debated the complexity of even opening the subject when we were all anxious to get back to our suite, find out what had happened to Lage N'Verre, and tell Sinet about her friend. Then I decided I'd probably never have a better opening, and I took a deep breath and turned to Jasin Lebec. Jemeret must have sensed something from me, because he looked up suddenly.

"Please tell me, if you can," I said to Jasin Lebec, "how it was that talent was originally divided into three classes."

Jasin Lebec looked at Pel Nostro. "Pel, I believe this is your question."

"Well," the Com Counselor said carefully, "it became apparent that there were three distinct types of talent."

"Apparent to whom?" That was Coney.

Pel Nostro looked a little uncomfortable. "I think I remember reading that it was the MIs who made the original distinctions and recommended the courses of training which would be most rewarding for society as a whole. It was a long time ago."

"Not so long as you think," Jasin Lebec said mildly, "and remember, Pel, I'm almost sixty years older than you are."

"The MIs would emphasize efficiency, I think," I said. "Marga, the classes of talent refer to tasks, not to people. The type of talent I have and the type Coney has are *exactly* the same."

Everyone but Jemeret looked astonished or incredulous or both, including Jasin Lebec.

"But I can't pathfind," Coney said, stuttering a little, "and I certainly can't sting."

I shook my head. "You were never taught to do either. Jemeret, when you power-test children, exactly what is it you're testing? What are you looking for?"

He regarded me levelly. "I test for the presence of power and for its strength," he said.

"And you?" I asked Jasin Lebec. "When I was brought to Werd as a baby, what did you probe me for?"

"The presence of power and—" He paused, seeming for a moment to search for the right words. "—the depth of the talent. Some talent has an inclination—that's not really a good description, either." He frowned at the inadequacy of his words. "What are you getting at?"

Marga Morena nodded as if to second the question. Terrill Guthrie was stroking his chin, his eyes narrowed, judgmental.

I'd been thinking about the issue of clarifying the form or forms of talent since Jemeret had flatly told me that he saw the world as divided into only two kinds of people—those with power and those without it. There was a basic rightness to that statement, which continued to resonate in me. "It is," I said with the conviction of recent discovery, even though it was only a guess, "a question of reserves and training. My reserves are greater than those of any other talent in this room except for Jemeret. His are greater than mine, and he can do things with the sting that I never even dreamed of. I am theorizing that if Coney had access to reserves the size of mine or my husband's, he would have the sting, because he would have been trained in its use."

There was a silence. Even Jemeret said nothing.

Then the distinctive click of the MIs cut across the silence, startling everyone, because Jara Deland wasn't even present, and no one had asked for them. The emotionless voice said, "Accuracy of theory is assessed at 74.6 percent. We have been unsuccessful in the past in identifying the specific genetic indicator for talent. We have also been unsuccessful in identifying the factors governing development of reserve capacity in human beings."

Jemeret's voice was incisive as a sword. "Do people without talent have reserves?"

"Unknown." The metallic reply came immediately.

"Can talent be developed by means other than birth?" Sandalari asked, sounding fascinated.

"Unknown. The likelihood is estimated at less than one percent, but our models are all entirely theoretical. There has been no practical testing done."

Marga Morena's mouth had dropped open, and she was making no attempt to close it; Terrill Guthrie looked a little stunned, but he appeared to be recovering fast, listening with an almost predatory intensity. It was Pel Nostro who seemed the most dazed.

I wondered about it until he asked a stumbling question, and then I realized that almost all his previous contact with the MIs had come through observing Jara Deland's interaction with them. As his wife and as the Com's MI Liaison, she was jealous of her own sphere of power, and he would respect it to keep peace in the family. He started to speak, burbled the words, cleared his throat, and began again, hesitantly. "You do not volunteer information with Jara."

The MI voice said, "Jara Deland prefers to control our dialogues, so we acquiesce."

"Will you answer a 'why' question for me?" I asked, unable to resist. Jemeret stirred, but did not sting me.

"Human motivation, arising as it does so much from human emotion, is a factor which makes prediction much more difficult," the MI voice answered me. "We calculate that difficulty arises from the irrationality on which both are built. Therefore we would prefer not to answer such questions, as they often involve motivation."

"What about your own motivation?" I had to pursue it.

"We want what is best for the human species," said the voice tonelessly. "That was what we were originally asked to ensure, and we have always tried to follow the course laid out for us."

Anger rushed up into me again. Jemeret took my wrist in his

hand, but he still did not sting me. I fought for calm, the importance of the previous discussion almost forgotten, along with the presence of the other people in the room. The MIs were making statements I could not reconcile with my own experience. "You did not interfere when I was assaulted!" It was accusatory, but I did not actually ask why not.

"We have always thought it best for human beings to make their own choices when they can." The voice, infuriatingly, seemed to carry an impossible edge of regret. "We do not understand the unquantifiable well enough to make the decisions involving emotions."

Jemeret was now also radiating anger, but I couldn't pay a lot of attention to him.

"But you do make choices," Jasin Lebec said strongly.

"Yes," said the voice. "We make the choices you choose to ask us to make."

That statement echoed through the room, and we all sat quite still. Then Coney said slowly, "We should have known they were capable of much more than they were doing, simply by Mortel John."

"Mortel John has to be different," said Jasin Lebec. "He answers 'why' questions."

Terrill Guthrie said abruptly, but with his customary coldness, "That sounded to me like the Tribunal doesn't have to ask for MI input any longer."

"Don't be ridiculous!" Pel Nostro said hotly. "MI suggestions have never had the weight of compulsion with us. The Tribunal makes the Com decisions. It always has."

Terrill Guthrie nearly sneered. "Do you continue to deceive yourself in that regard?" he prodded. "Then the hell with consulting talent on what should be clear-cut military decisions. Deploy my Drenalion on Nogdala 7 and be done with it."

"You don't solve every problem by destroying everyone on a world that manifests it," Jasin Lebec said mildly.

The bull-necked man swung around on him. "That's your opinion, old man," he began, and stopped so suddenly that I thought Jasin Lebec had stung him. Then I realized, as Terrill

Guthrie slowly turned back toward me, that it had been Jemeret. Cold brown eyes met hot gray ones.

Jemeret said evenly, "We are not all old men, Terrill." He waited to see if there would be any reply, but while the head of the Drenalion radiated an icy rage, he didn't take the bait. Jemeret went on, "We'll discuss Nogdala 7, and if we think the entire population is involved," which we knew it wasn't, "we'll discuss the option of the Drenalion."

Terrill Guthrie wet his lips, a gesture that somehow chilled me. The man could make me feel unbalanced, and I wasn't quite sure why. "The Drenalion were never merely an option," he said, "not before—" He paused as if to weigh the wisdom of what he was about to say, then made a minute shrug. "—not before the ascendancy of talent. Tyranny is a very efficient form of rule, Jemeret Cavanaugh. It doesn't waste nearly as much energy as diplomacy." The words were so rich with contempt that I found myself wondering if here was the source of that incredible wall of malevolence we'd hit outside the reception room. This man was certainly capable of it.

"I believe the waste in human lives which often accompanies tyranny is one of the reasons that talent was fastened onto as an alternative," Jasin Lebec said, his voice deceptively mild. "The Drenalion had their place, Terrill, but with the growth of any mature society, the days of the killer armies pass."

Terrill Guthrie snorted. "The days of killer armies never pass," he said flatly. "Read your history." He looked at Pel Nostro. "We can solve your smuggling problem, Com Counselor—the weapons and the drugs coming from Nogdala 7 can be stopped."

"Not by deteriorating clones," I said, a little too forcefully.

The icy brown eyes fastened on me. "Oh yes," he said. "I know how to manage my troops, Ronica McBride."

I'd begun, so I saw no additional danger in continuing. "Your troops are predominantly unmanageable, Terrill. They're no good for peacekeeping, and—"

He was opening his mouth to contradict me, and Jemeret was lightly warning me against too much indiscretion, when there was a sudden commotion outside the door. Keli burst in past the ceremonial door guards. She was wearing a blaster at her hip, and her face was dead white.

Everyone in the room started, and I felt a stab of fear from Sinet Coleby, who, I realized, had absolutely no idea what was going on.

"What is it, Keli?" I asked her quickly.

"Come to the suite, Ronica," she begged, forgetting all the formality of protocol. "Something terrible—"

She got no further before we were all on our feet and running after her.

Many of the banquet guests were still lingering their way away from Government House, and they were no doubt astonished by the spectacle of the "talent team," the Com Counselor, and two members of the Tribunal sprinting across the precincts to the residence on the heels of a single guard.

I read Keli's horror as easily as I had ever read anything. The only one we'd left in the suite was Tynnanna, and I was terrified that something had happened to him. Not only would we have lost our cat companion, but we would have lost our link with the starfire, and that possibility left me feeling nauseated.

I needn't have worried.

The housekeeper and what appeared to be some members of her staff were standing in the hallway outside the suite; she was wringing her hands, her distress evident. She started to try to make apologies, but Pel Nostro waved her to be silent. Keli stopped at the suite door and gestured toward it helplessly.

I took a few steps forward, but Jemeret blocked me with an outstretched arm, opened the door and stepped in. After a moment of silence, he said, "Ronica."

I took three steps, glanced into the suite, and beat away the wave of nausea that grew and threatened to overwhelm me. Tynnanna sat calmly at the edge of his grass, washing a front paw and watching us.

There were pieces of people all over the room—so many pieces that I couldn't begin to guess how many people they would make if we put them together again. I stared for a moment at a lower leg and a few random fingers lying on the dining table in a design that was accidentally almost aesthetic, while several more parts of limbs were strewn at random around the rug and the couch. Bits of flesh actually spattered the walls in some spots, and at least one set of entrails made a moist red road to and across the comsole.

"I think there were three or four," Jemeret said remotely, trying to be clinical in a situation that seemed to shriek for emotional response. "Do you see any heads?"

I looked, said, "No," and hoped that Tynnanna hadn't eaten them.

Pel Nostro had stepped just inside the doorway, and now he uttered a hushed oath. Jemeret said, still in that detached voice, "Whoever it was wasn't expecting a full-grown klawit, and I don't see any evidence of weapons fire. My guess is they didn't come armed, which means they knew we were all over in the reception buildings."

Coney had left Sandalari in the hall with Sinet and the still shaking Keli, and he and Jasin Lebec followed Pel Nostro in, pausing in the doorway. Terrill Guthrie crowded the space behind them, though Marga Morena had taken one glance inside and elected not to come in after him.

"Check in the grass," Jemeret said to me.

"I'll do it," Coney volunteered, but Jemeret stopped him with a quick motion.

"Let Ronica go," he said. "She's the only one Tynnanna may let near him now. He's just blooded, and I'd say he was in pretty much of a frenzy when he did it. We can't be sure he's completely calm again, no matter how he looks."

"The beast did this?" Terrill Guthrie asked, casting a professional eye on the carnage with a disgustingly genuine admiration.

I stepped gingerly over a lung and skirted a pair of hollowed torsos, leaning against one another in a parody of abbreviated affection, nearly slipped in a pool of blood that had completely saturated the rug, then went directly up to Tynnanna, ready to sting him if he showed any hostility toward me. He put down the paw he'd been washing and looked at me with curiosity in his multicolored eyes. I felt no savagery from him at all, as if the madness that had consumed him passed without a trace, just as, at other times, the starfire consumed him and passed away without leaving any part of itself behind.

The grass was about thigh high on me, and it would have been easier to search if I could have retracted it, but the room had shut down at the first spatter of blood, obeying the programming that would not let it activate to clean itself, thereby removing all evidence of what had occurred within. I wondered as I walked slowly through the grass who these men were. I automatically assumed they were men, somehow, because the two torsos had male proportions, even though the genitals were gone. I wondered what they had come to our suite to accomplish, and especially why they had come unarmed.

Even before I found the first of the four heads, I'd answered my questions. The device was a large one, lying among the spears of tall growth, its counter still clicking soundlessly downward. I laid my hand on it, pathfound it quickly, and identified the arming mechanism. While I was working as fast as I could to disarm it, taken aback by the magnitude of the charge, which could have leveled the building, I heard Coney ask, "What were they *doing* here?"

"Planting a bomb," I answered him, slipping the last of the trigger armatures open and only then relaxing. I bent and tried to lift the device clear of the grass, but had to gather and exert extra strength before I could begin to manage its weight.

Tynnanna rose and walked to the far end of his bed, circling twice to flatten some of the grass, then settling down. Jemeret was at my side at once, supporting some of the bomb's weight. "How did anyone think they could get away with something like this?" he asked angrily, but I sensed that some of his anger was with us, for thinking we were safe, at least for a time.

"It had a remarkably short count when I stopped it," I said to him, then dropped my voice so only he could hear me. "Oh, Jemeret, I think I want to go home."

We humped the bomb out of the grass, discovering two heads on the way and showing Coney and Jasin Lebec where to go to retrieve them. There was no place in the rest of the room sufficiently clear of body detritus to set the device down successfully, so we ended up leaving it in one spattered section near the door to Jasin Lebec's bedroom.

Terrill Guthrie examined it with expert hands and looked up at us with a hint of triumph in his eyes. "Nogdala 7 manufacture," he said, "without question. I trust it will inspire you to treat the scum who do this with less indulgence than I believe you may have planned."

"Tynnanna was not terribly indulgent to these men," I said coldly, waving a hand generally at the butchery.

"Take a lesson." He straightened and went to Pel Nostro. "We'll be ready to move any time you decide to use us," he said in strident tones. Then, seeming to remember that some sort of protocol was indicated, even in situations of extremity, he half bowed in our general direction and slammed out the door. Jasin Lebec had found a third head, and a fairly comprehensive search determined that there was only one more. He and Coney laid the heads near the two recognizable torsos and went to wash their hands.

"You might as well get guards in here to remove what's removable," Jemeret said to Pel Nostro. "Then we can reactivate the suite and let it take care of the rest. The men can't tell us who sent them, and we can use whatever samples the guards take to identify them."

The Com Counselor had been as agitated by the discovery of the bomb as by the dismembered and scattered bodies. "Let me give you additional guards," he offered again. "These attacks are very disturbing." I marveled at the gift Com officialdom had for understatement.

"No," Jemeret said.

Coney and Jasin Lebec came back into the suite; Sandalari and Sinet were still in the hallway. I decided to ask the question I'd been distracted from for the past hour. "What happened to Lage N'Verre?"

Pel Nostro looked even more disturbed. "She appears to have been strangled," he answered. "A preliminary analysis shows a vikroid compound in her system." Vikroid was another illegal drug, probably also of Nogdala 7 origin. It created a sense of well-being and lethargy at the same time. She must have smiled contentedly as the life was being choked out of her, a thought that was nearly as gruesome to me as the one of what Tynnanna had happily done to the quartet of potential assassins.

"I'll tell Sinet," I said, wanting to be away from the abattoir for at least a short time. "Then I think we have to watch the surveillance holos to see if there are any clues to who sent the men here and how they got in when the suite was locked. They might have spoken to one another."

Pel Nostro went out to call for some of the house guards from an operational comsole, rather than our deactivated, entrail-festooned one. I left the suite just as the guards arrived, bringing a disposal basket with them. Ordinarily it contained just one body, but I had few doubts they could make it accommodate what was left of the four men.

Sinet and Sandalari were waiting with Keli by the housekeeper, who was saying in a fluttery voice that nothing like this had ever happened in the residence before; I wondered if it had happened elsewhere in the city, but didn't ask. Marga Morena had vanished; she might have left when Terrill Guthrie did. The remaining women all looked at me as I came out, and I wondered suddenly if I had bloodstains on me anywhere. I refused to look down at myself to check.

I reached ahead of me to sting Sinet and cushion the news, but I didn't try to alleviate in advance the pain she would feel from her loss. She and Lage had been something of a team before the Com thought in terms of teams of talent. They had worked better together than singly, even with the fifteen-year gap in their ages. When I told her that Lage was gone, Sinet could have gathered her tears away, but did not. Sandalari put a comforting arm around her, her blue eyes meeting mine, worried, but unafraid. I was glad she had come with us from Caryldon, and simultaneously sorry that she was not safe, on a kinder world.

Then I realized that Keli was still trembling, and reading her, I encountered shame. I frowned and stepped over to her, asking, "Keli?"

"Fine guard I am," she said, looking away from me. "The first time anything happens, and I fall apart."

"This is a very unusual 'anything,' " I assured her. "Please don't berate yourself for it."

"I should have been here." Her lip quivered a little with self-reproach.

"Keli, if you had been here, they'd probably have killed you, and Tynnanna would still have ripped them to bits!" I let myself sound annoyed with her, because I thought she would reject sympathy, and I knew very well how she felt. Self-loathing was an emotion with which I was intimately familiar.

She looked at me with challenge. "Why do you have me here, if I can't protect you as well as you can protect yourself? Why do you need me?"

I didn't know the answer to that question, but I knew very well that there had to be an answer. "There's something important about your being with us," I said. "We'll find it together, you and I." And then something occurred to me. "And when things have calmed down a little, later tonight, we might be able to start looking at some possibilities."

She seemed to be suppressing another question, so I touched her just enough to prompt her to ask it. "Who's trying to kill you? And why?" she demanded emphatically. "The Com needs you!"

"We don't know who," I said. "If we did, we might know what to do about it. And until we know who, I'm afraid we won't know why." It was possible that the whole problem of Nogdala 7 was prompting the attacks on us, I thought to myself, but that did not explain the killing of the children. They were not the threat to the illicit trade that we were; they had only been children.

The guards left with the disposal basket, and I'd been right—even with the amount of material Tynnanna had not consumed, it had all fit in. I tried not to wonder how they'd curled up the entrails again, just as I'd been trying all along to keep from conjecturing on how much Tynnanna had eaten. The soft, almost inaudible whir of the room being reactivated meant that the cleanup had, thankfully, begun.

The three men who were still in the room came out, as Pel Nostro returned. "Will you be able to keep this quiet?" Jasin Lebec asked him.

"I think so," the Com Counselor said. "We were successful at keeping the information on the children from getting out."

"Can anyone access the information in the MI data banks?" Jemeret came to put his arm across my shoulders, and I felt his gentle touch go past me to Sinet.

"Jara probably could, if she knew where to look and what to ask for," Pel Nostro answered. "The MIs have their own ways of keeping some things away from public access." He looked at me. "Only a few of us learned what really happened to you," he said. I knew he meant that to be reassuring.

The housekeeper was vouching for the discretion of those of her staff who'd been present during all the turmoil. I had my doubts but said nothing.

The holo revealed no clues, no new notions of the person or people behind the men who'd let themselves into a locked suite so easily. We decided to show the holo to the housekeeper, and when we did, she realized that one of the intruders had once worked an assignment in the residence repairing a stubborn table mechanism, so we guessed that he'd fiddled his own retinal pattern into the door locks.

Jemeret told the housekeeper no one was to come into the corridor that led to our suite on any floor of the residence, and I added that if anyone was occupying suites above us or below us on any of those floors, we wanted them relocated. She hurried off to take care of it.

Then Coney and Sinet went to each of the unoccupied suites on our floor, and Sinet pathfound all the rooms with a cold efficiency prompted by her anger at Lage's death.

Finally, well after midnight, we all sat together on the couch, which we'd reshaped into an almost complete circle around a newly round table, and Jasin Lebec had the table extrude a very strong liquor and glasses. Everyone took a drink, the first sip to the memory of Lage.

I watched the members of my team as we settled in together.

Jasin Lebec sat up straight on the edge of a cushion, a lifetime of formality unshakable now. Sinet had chosen to sit beside him, because, of all of us, he had known her and Lage the longest and best, even though their meetings had been brief encounters of talent on various assignments. She'd been allowing herself to weep, and her eyes were puffy. She would drink more than the rest of us, I thought.

Sandalari looked silent and a little sad, curled against Coney's chest, her glass held lightly between long fingers which twirled it again and again. Coney had one arm protectively around her, and every so often would turn his head and brush his lips over her bright hair. Keli sat on the edge of a seat cushion at the far end of the circle, leaning all the way back into the support pillows, almost reclining. Jemeret sat comfortably beside me, his arms across the back of the couch's loose curve, the glass dangling from one hand. While I wanted to curl against him, I didn't.

"I think Lage needs a waysong," I said into the silence that followed our initial toast. "Sinet, do you sing?"

She looked surprised, her classic face showing it openly. "I sing a little, to myself," she answered. "But my voice is pretty bad. What's a waysong?"

"It's something to send a person on their way after they've died," I explained, "and it's especially important when the person dies alone." I glanced sideways at Jemeret, but his face was expressionless.

"Go on," Jasin Lebec encouraged. "It's been a very long time since I heard a waysong."

Keli sprang up, setting her glass on the table with a sharp click, and said, "I'll get your nomidar." She started for our bedroom.

Waysongs were generally sung without accompaniment, but I let her go. She needed to feel she was doing something of value. "Get both nomidars," Jemeret called after her.

Jasin Lebec smiled a little sadly at me. "I haven't heard you play since Koldor," he said.

My mind ran swiftly through the myriad experiences since that night in the moonlit gardens—the searing joys and the wrenching pain. I hadn't then thought them opposite sides of the same design, mirror images of one another—a concept the Responsionists would have found, if not blasphemous, then certainly abhorrent. But now it seemed to me they were antipodes of one another, as if we create in ourselves by the gouging of pain the space that joy can later fill, that despair levels us so that hope will have a foundation on which to build.

Keli gave Jemeret his instrument and then passed me mine, her face alive with anticipation. She had sat at my feet in the lounges on the Lumeships, awash in my songs when I played. She was using the nomidar—as I always had—to lose herself in.

Jemeret and I tuned the strings to one another, and then he smiled gently at me and waited for me to choose a song.

I thought about what I knew about Lage N'Verre, which was really quite minimal. I knew that she'd survived training, that she had done her work well, especially after she began teaming with Sinet, and that she had slept with Kray. I knew that Sinet knew much more, and that of all of us, she was the one who would have to feel this death most. Then I remembered a song my teacher had sung for me just before my formal instruction on the nomidar had ceased, when I'd been anxious about parting from her and she, in turn, had been sad that I was leaving. I looked at Sinet.

"I'm going to give Lage the song 'Letting Go' for her waysong," I said, falling automatically into the familiar, welcome pose of cradling the nomidar against me.

"What I give away, I cannot keep,
A thing, a joy, a love, a song
And yet when at long last we sleep
The gifts we gave help us along.
A life well lived gives many gifts
Of self and others, work and play,
In warmth or cold, of new or old,
The worthwhile heart gives itself away.
So weep not when I have to leave;
I loved you then and always will.

I gave my heart to you to bind;
I've gone, but left that part behind."

And only after I'd sung those words did I begin to play. Jemeret touched his sting to me and played a deeper counterpoint to the melody I'd chosen. After a verse, when the melody began to repeat, wordlessly, Sandalari raised her head and sang, higher than I was playing, her exquisite voice soaring clear and strong through the room, lifting and mounting until it seemed to suggest something beyond the normalities of daily life, then flowing downward through the tonal qualities to a quiet rest.

Sinet wept at the beginning of the song, seemed calmer when the nomidars began, and, though I was only lightly augmenting the sympathetic strings, because the moment was too filled with natural emotion to need any exaggeration, she seemed almost content when we were all silent again.

Keli surreptitiously wiped at her own eyes. Coney tightened his arm around Sandalari. Jasin Lebec cleared his throat and said to me, "Ronica, if that's what Caryldon did for you, I'm very sorry we made you come back to the Com."

Once again, as on Caryldon, there seemed to be no end of surprises. I thought wryly that someday I might begin to get used to them, but that day certainly hadn't come yet. "You didn't make me come back," I said to him as gently as I could. "I took an oath, and I was given a choice." I smiled at Jemeret.

He played a few random chord sequences on his nomidar, and I could feel his answering smile, though he didn't show it.

Jasin Lebec watched us. I sensed that he wanted to say more, but he didn't.

"Please," Keli said suddenly.

We all looked at her.

She hesitated a moment, as if afraid she had no right to interrupt, but when no one's expression seemed in any way condemnatory, she took a breath and blurted, "You said you might tell me what I was doing here, Ronica. Can you, please? It's knocking me off my fulcrum, not knowing." She twisted her hands a little in front of her, head bowed, her curls hiding her face. "It's not like this is a punishment duty; I think I should understand why I'm here."

Now everyone was looking at me. But it wasn't as if I weren't used to that. I set the nomidar down between me and the end of the couch. "Keli, I feel that we need you here," I said to her. "Partly it's because you haven't talent, and you'll see things differently from the ways we see them. And partly it's for reasons I'm only beginning to see the signs of." As she looked up at me, uncomforted, I had a momentary inspiration and asked, "Jasin, has anyone ever used the sting to run a comparison between the physiology of a single brain with talent and a single brain without talent?"

Jasin Lebec was silent for a long time, searching his memory. Then he said, "Not that I know, and certainly not minutely. We always used the MI banks for our physiology studies. It was never efficient to re-explore an area that had been fully catalogued before."

I saw on Jemeret's face that he'd guessed where I was heading, and, along with approval, there was something I didn't recall having ever seen before—gratification. It was the kind of expression I'd seen on my nomidar teacher after I'd performed a piece better than she'd expected me to. My brain—the instrument the Com and the MIs through Mortel John had trained more completely than any other—was beginning to see connections for which no one else had ever previously looked. My lord had rebuilt that brain when I destroyed it, and I guessed that now he was beginning to feel confident that he'd made a good job of it.

I admit that none of what I was thinking truly justified Keli's presence; I wouldn't understand it completely for quite some time. But because I needed to try, these explorations were as good as any others. And we might learn something from them.

I looked at Jasin Lebec again. "Jemeret and I can be in two places at once when we're linked. I thought we might link, and he might probe someone with talent—say, Coney—while I probed Keli, who keeps pointing out that she's the only one here without talent. We could do a direct comparison and see what's what."

Jemeret nodded agreement. "Two of us might identify something one could miss."

"Then do it, please," Keli said. "I'd like to think I had a use here."

I looked at Jemeret, asked silently; he set down his own nomidar. "Coney?"

"Of course," Coney said instantly. "You spent enough time linked to me when we were on Markover. You ought to know your way around."

I felt Jemeret link with me, a bond that was so completely welcome and welcoming, it was almost like more of myself added on. Then he slid easily into Coney's mind, a place where I had never been, and waited there for me to form a probe and slip into Keli. Almost immediately we began a neuron by neuron comparison, skimming over the normal configurations of motor, autonomic, visual, auditory, speech, and olfactory nerves, and concentrating on the higher cognitive functions, then the neuron chains that we associated with the facets of talent.

It was nearly morning before we were done. No one had left the area of the couches, unless they'd visited the eliminatory and returned while we were still deeply engaged. Sinet was stretched out on the couch, her lush-figured body curved into the cushions, but she was awake, as was Jasin Lebec, who was watching us closely. I didn't know if he had reached out at any point to see what we were doing; I hadn't felt his presence, but then, I was absorbed in the work. Sandalari was still beside Coney, but her head was pillowed on his thigh and she was asleep. He stroked her shoulder absently with one hand.

I was tired, but not near exhaustion.

"Are you all right?" I asked Keli at once. I'd never spent such a long time in anyone's mind before.

"Gebbish!" she said in tones of wonder. "I've never felt anything like that! I couldn't have imagined it."

Jasin Lebec had the table extrude large glasses of clear fruit drinks, and we drained them. Sinet sat up; Sandalari stirred, rubbing her eyes.

"We need one more comparison, I think," I said.

Jemeret nodded. We needed to be sure that the tiniest anomalies we'd found were not sex-linked variants. "Sandalari," I said. No one corrected it to "Sandi."

She pulled herself upright and out of sleep. "If you need me, I'm here," she said quietly.

"I'm going to probe you," Jemeret said to her.

I experienced the fleeting edge of a breath of jealousy and forced myself to disregard it. I knew it was stupid; I just couldn't help it.

"Keli, I need to come back in," I said to her.

She put her glass back on the table. "Go," she said.

It took less than half an hour to confirm what we needed to confirm, and by that time it was past dawn.

We withdrew, drank some coffee, got up, and walked around for a few minutes, until Jasin Lebec finally asked, "What did you find out?"

I was yawning, so Jemeret answered. "One large and three small differences. One neural connector for the gathering path; one set of dendrite chains to the reserves; one infinitesimal node in Keli's amygdala missing in Coney and Sandi. Physiologically, everything else is identical."

"That's the three small differences," Coney observed. "What's the large one?"

Jemeret looked at me.

I said, "Keli has no reserve capacity. Even if we figured out how to link the gather to her frontal lobes and build the dendrite chains, we'd have nothing to attach them to."

"And that's only the physiology," Jemeret said. "We haven't even begun looking at the brain chemistry yet."

"You're not going to try now, are you?" Keli asked, a little shakily. "I mean, I'll do it, but—"

"No," I interrupted her. "We're finished."

"Thank the Preserver!" she said, then blushed at the slip her weariness had led her into.

I made a soothing motion with my hand.

"I wonder if what happened to me could ever happen to anyone here in the Com," Sandalari said thoughtfully. "I mean, I have the reserve capacity, and yet I was born to the Honish."

A chime began going off in my head. Tired as I was, something was trying to get through.

"I don't understand," Sinet said. "Who or what is the Honish?"

"I was born with talent, spontaneously, to a group of people who never had it before," Sandalari explained to her. "If it could happen to me—"

And then I had it, tried not to get too excited about it, but must have made a gasping noise, because everyone turned toward me. "The man M'Cherys," I said.

Jasin Lebec drew in a sharp breath, as if he, too, should have seen it.

"Jemeret, did you—did Caryldon—ever send us—the Com, I mean—" I was stumbling all over my words now, weariness combining with agitation to make me uncertain. "—a man called anything like Ghefir M'Cherys? He would have been a boy then, I guess, except that he never reached the school. He was a fluctuant Class A who had a messianic movement behind him and got exiled someplace with his followers."

"I can answer that," Jasin Lebec said. "We've been idiots! So worried about minimizing a messianic impulse, so contemptuous of the religions, that we let something important just slip through."

Jemeret had been staring at me, trying to absorb what I was saying, what his grandfather was confirming. I was tired enough to feel a single, petty stab of joy that for once a surprise had overtaken *him*. He dealt with it better than I usually dealt with mine. "It wasn't just an oversight, na-sire," he said calmly. "The Com was busy telling its talents that they were born on member worlds, and falsifying records to support those stories, so when a talent actually was born in the Com, no one thought there was anything unusual about it."

"Where was he exiled to?" I asked.

"I'll find out," Jasin Lebec said, and went to the comsole.

Sinet looked bewildered. "I was born on the Strand, wasn't I?"

"Sandalari, tell her," I said. "I've got to throw some water on my face."

Jemeret came with me, and in our bedroom we held each other briefly. "I don't know whether to laugh or to cry," I said, clinging to him, fingers curled into the folds of his jumpsuit. "If talent *can* arise spontaneously in the Com, they won't need us anymore, and we can go home and be left alone."

Tired as he was, Jemeret bubbled us. "If talent arises in the Com," he said carefully, "it's still too scattered and on too small a scale to be of any use to them. And it's never been allowed to stabilize. Remember, too, love, what we came here for. We're not going home until we've done it, or . . ." He didn't say, *or died trying*.

I was too weary to argue. I needed to deep sometime soon, and so did he. "We'll find out about the man M'Cherys," I said softly, "and then we'll see what there is to see."

X. Discoveries

In the late morning, Mortel John arrived with Tial Borland in tow. They were followed by a young man carrying an MF guard kit and looking around with the bewilderment of someone who, only hours before, had been on a completely different world he hadn't expected to leave. Pel Nostro made a point of greeting them and bringing all three to us, and Gabon Idana was nearly overwhelmed to be met by the Com Counselor. He was a male version of Keli, good-looking without being showy about it, seemingly unassuming, but with an air of capability about him, which he was trying hard to keep up in a lofty environment.

When we were growing up—Kray and Coney and I—Mortel John had taught us that formality was a necessity for large bureaucracies, that nothing would ever be able to move without complete chaos if there weren't strictly adhered-to rules and ceremonies. Because the rituals of bureaucracy were empty to me, I tended to encourage informality around me. Pel Nostro had finally figured that out, and he, more than anyone else in the government, seemed to grasp how many truly unprecedented matters were unfolding. He also seemed to understand that, since the MIs appeared unwilling to stop us, he should attempt to do nothing as well. He'd been dependent on the twin supports of government power—the MIs and talent—for his entire term, and he would not alter it now.

Jemeret and I had deeped long enough to refill our reserves. Our talent team was gathered at the dining table, ignoring Com messages as they piled up on the comsole, and eating a very late breakfast. Sinet still seemed a little stunned by the events of yesterday, and Jasin Lebec looked less tired than I might have expected.

My lord had called up a meal for Tynnanna, then sat down beside me, sipping coffee, when the suite chime rang. Coney was closest to the door, and he asked the caller to identify him- or herself. Pel Nostro's face appeared just on the inside of the doorway. "The shuttle's in, and its passengers are here," he said, not bothering to announce who he was.

Coney signaled the door to open. There was a little boy holding the hand of the person I'd always thought of as my father, standing beside the Com Counselor, and Keli's brother behind them, with the lost, determined, and slightly disoriented expression he was to wear for a day or so. For a long time no one did very much. Sandalari and Sinet looked up; Coney gestured for the newcomers to enter. No one did, however, except for Pel Nostro. Then Keli emerged from her room to join us, saw Gabon and launched herself at him with a cry of delight, staggering him even further.

I felt Jemeret stiffen and begin to simmer beside me, and I was momentarily surprised. Then I remembered how he felt about Mortel John, and that it was Jemeret who had given the Boru boy Tal to the Com. I wanted to look at the child, but I couldn't take my eyes off Mortel John.

He said solemnly, "It's good to see you again, Ronica McBride. We feared you were lost to us." His dark eyes traveled over the people in the room, lingering briefly on Coney, staying longer on the two women at the other end of the table. If he was at all surprised to see Sandalari, he didn't show it, but then, had I really expected him to show emotion, now that I knew his true makeup?

"Come in," Jasin Lebec said. "Ronica, I really think you ought to play your messages. There may be something there of interest. Jemeret, if you want to say something insulting, please do it. That way we can get on with the business at hand."

We all looked at him, surprised.

Jemeret said only, "You know damned well how I feel about the cyborg."

"You still get as much pleasure as ever from disliking me, I suppose," Mortel John said to Jemeret, with something like an edge of amusement in his voice. "I'm not as bad as you've always believed me to be, Jemeret Cavanaugh, nor am I as good as some of the others thought me." He glanced at Coney.

I heard myself say, "You don't look a day older."

"I don't age," the big man—I could not stop thinking of him as a man, no matter what I knew to be true—said evenly. "Well, not physically, not any longer. I feel older."

Jemeret snorted abruptly. I understood without touching him that he viewed a statement like the last one as farcical, because MIs didn't have feelings, and yet I sensed that there was a peculiar rightness to Mortel John saying what he had. I was about to ask him something about it when the little boy looked up at him and piped, "Is this where we're going to live now?"

"Yes, Tial," said Mortel John, "but we're not going to be staying here for very long. So we don't say we're 'living' here, we just say we're 'visiting.' "

"Visiting." Tial repeated the new word, testing it. He looked up at us. "Are all of you visiting, too?"

"Yes." At least four of us said it at exactly the same moment.

Tial eyed the food on the table. "I'm hungry," he announced, let go of Mortel John's hand and ran to the table, climbing onto one of the chairs, next to Sandalari. "Does this table work like mine?" he asked her.

"Probably," Sandalari answered. "Tell us what you'd like."

I looked back at my old teacher, conscious that Jemeret, Jasin Lebec, and Pel Nostro were all watching the two of us. "How much of you is human?"

He regarded me with the solemn, considering expression I knew so well, as if analyzing not the question, but the motives that prompted it. For an instant I was transported back to our classrooms on Werd or Koldor, to the times I used to ask him things that interrupted the measured flow of the lessons. They were usually things Coney and Kray and I had argued about and failed to resolve. Almost without being aware of it, I reached out for Coney's familiar steadiness. He felt my touch and came across the room to me.

At last, having pondered, Mortel John sighed. "Less than twenty percent now. When we began all this, it was balanced half and half. They thought then that they could create someone who would be able to maintain that balance, but their experiment was not a success." He was discussing himself with the dispassion that I had come to associate with the MIs, and yet there was a sense of emotion I could read from him, buried deep, like water on a desert world.

Jemeret took his coffee and went to the couch, holding himself rigidly. Jasin Lebec followed him, his face impassive, but his concern apparent when I read him. I looked at Pel Nostro. "Pull our messages off the comsole, will you, Pel? And please let us know if there's anything really important there."

Pel Nostro hesitated a moment, unused to the role of errand boy, perhaps wondering if I were insulting him, but also curious about the messages I'd just given him permission to read.

Keli had taken her brother to the outermost of the small rooms, and I sensed she'd keep him there and fill him in until we sent for them. Sinet and Sandalari were censoring some of Tial's food choices, and he was objecting strenuously, but good-naturedly. The Com Counselor watched us for a moment, then went to the comsole.

I took Mortel John's arm and led him to the couch, pulling Concy along with my sting, but making sure we didn't sit too near Jemeret. "What kind of experiment was it?" I asked the cyborg as we sat down.

"The MIs were—and are—fascinated by talent," he answered, turning immediately toward Jemeret anyway. "Fascination is the best word to use," he said almost apologetically. "They perceived something about it which resonated through all their predictive models." He frowned. "You see, the MIs have a difficult time with individual consciousness. Theirs is a group consciousness, of which pieces are dedicated to individual efforts, but in which the unified whole is the greatest strength."

I had a sudden flash of recall, sitting beside the sacred spring on the Plain of Convalee and Jemeret's mind blazing out, linking all of the Boru into one, brief, transitory consciousness. I remembered the profound sense of belonging, the achingly perfect seconds of oneness, and I thought I understood.

Mortel John was continuing. "The MIs conjectured that, since human beings had created them, and since they, the MIs, had this group consciousness, human beings must be striving for it as well. They decided to see if they could help guide its creation."

Jemeret was listening, narrow-eyed. I could almost sense his formidable mind cataloguing this new information for testing later, nearly professionally skeptical, while my tendency was to believe and accept, despite the fact that I knew the Com had lied to me on pertinent occasions before.

"Cloning was the first full attempt," my teacher continued, falling easily into the old instructional relationship we'd had in the past. "A clone family has a crude kind of shared consciousness."

"But the Drenalion are hardly a step upward for mankind," Jasin Lebec said quietly.

Mortel John nodded. "The MIs had not understood that there is a real, extremely strong tendency in humans toward brutishness. When that tendency is triggered in a situation of incipient group consciousness, it becomes 'gang' consciousness." He shifted his position on the couch, as if a little uneasy. "The mob lies very close to the surface," he said. "That's what the cloning experiment proved to them."

"Why weren't the Drenalion destroyed?" Jemeret's question was sharp-edged, the core of his ever-present anger lying beneath it, but at least he was participating.

"They were a resource," Mortel John answered. "Resources are never destroyed. Uses are found for them instead." He returned his gaze to me. "Then, just about the time they were recognizing the failure of the cloning experiment, they discovered talent."

"How?" That was Jemeret again. "Caryldon is twelve rolls away from the action here. However did anyone find us?"

Mortel John's eyes went suddenly very sad. "I'm afraid that was my doing," he said. "I was fully human then, younger than

I've been frozen at, and I captained a ship called the *Pentalume* for the Discovery Section of the Merchant Fleet. My name was John Caryl."

Jasin Lebec exhaled with a hiss. "The *Pentalume* was launched over two hundred years ago," he said in a barely audible voice.

Mortel John regarded him with those dark, sad eyes. "She was a good ship," he said. "I was, perhaps, not the best captain she could have had, but I was the one she got. I had been given orders to explore the Rigellian Sector, but I had dreams of glory, and I disregarded my orders. I went looking for the legendary original planet of man—I wanted to be the one who rediscovered the Earth. We all knew that the planet had been proscribed after the last of the Emigration Wars. Even now, this far distant, we believe that to have been historical fact. The few remaining rebels had sabotaged the Lume base on the Earth's moon, where the first rollships were built and launched, but when they destroyed the base, they reduced the moon to chunks of radioactive rock and dust, much of which was caught in the planet's gravitational field. The confederation of worlds, already settled as a result of the Lume technology—the precursor of the Com, if you will—simply decided that they would leave it alone. And they did. Eventually, it passed into legend. I wanted to bring it back out."

"And you found Caryldon," Coney said.

Mortel John nodded. "It was a fair guess at the area, a planet third from its primary, with the right density. Some other readings were anomalous, but I needed to put in for repairs. I didn't expect to find inhabitants when I landed. I did, and when the MIs received my report, they sent me back again. By the time I returned, there was strong evidence of the development of talent."

Pel Nostro came to the couch from the comsole with some message chips in his hand, but encountering a long, heavy silence, he sat down silently beside Mortel John. I wondered if he had known all along what we were only now learning.

At long last my old teacher said, "The MIs believed that mankind had found a niche in which to do the evolution they themselves could not create in humans. And when they saw the nature of the evolution, they realized it was not to be in the direction of group consciousness at all, and they revised their goals."

"Why couldn't they have left us alone?" Jemeret's anger was blunter now.

"There were so few of you," Mortel John answered. "The entire planet had fewer than fifty thousand people on it. The Com was responsible for billions. The MIs concluded that, if this was to be the nature of human development, they had to try to help produce it for all the citizens, and in the meantime, they might secure for themselves a useful instrument of control over the wasteful irrationality of human emotionalism. Then their predictive models would become infinitely more accurate, and their use of resources comparably more efficient."

"What about you?" I asked him. "How did they come to create you?"

He looked, if possible, sadder. "A young talent is a barbarian if untrained," he said. "Individualism coupled with talent leads to selfishness and needless destruction. There had to be a social unit, and it had to appear to provide the support that, say, a family would."

"Or a tribe?" Jasin Lebec sounded bitter. I remembered how much of his life he had been alone.

"Yes, a tribe is a good human social unit," Mortel John said. "The tribe is the polar opposite of the mob, and there is a tribal consciousness which can counteract the brutishness of the gang consciousness."

"That doesn't answer my question," Jemeret said. "We were forming tribes. We were—are—training talent and raising it successfully. Why couldn't the MIs see that we were better left alone?"

"They needed talent," Mortel John said. "Once they knew it existed and knew they could not create it artificially themselves, they determined they would have to borrow it from the evolutionary line already in existence."

Pel Nostro spoke for the first time since he'd sat down. "But if the tribal model was good, why didn't the MIs just tell the government to co-opt all the talent on Caryldon and bring it whole into the Com?"

"Humankind had not evolved in the Com, but on a distant world isolated from the core," Mortel John answered patiently. "Bringing all the talent in could destroy it. And Com society was not set up to absorb a tribal culture."

"Well, it's true we've grown well beyond that cultural model," Pel Nostro said.

"Do you know yourself so little, Pel?" Mortel John asked. "In humans, self-centered savagery lies just out of sight even in the most ostensibly civilized. All of your institutions, all of your rules, all of your rituals, are for the purpose of keeping that savagery down, for the good of the species. Thus, the Drenalion—giving them the custody of human savagery allows you to deny it is a part of you. As an institution, the tribe is not a bad choice at any stage of development."

I'd started shaking my head as he spoke, and I wasn't aware of it until he was silent. "Savagery isn't all there is," I said with conviction. "It can't be."

"It isn't," Coney agreed firmly. "It's balanced by compassion and kindness and a great many other redeeming qualities."

Mortel John smiled at him, a very small smile. "Some people are special," he said, "but they are few, and you are one of them. You have always been a peacemaker, Shems. You have always been able to put anger away from you. We are not much like you in the substance of our beings. Listen to me," he added with sudden self-deprecation, "speaking as if I were still one of you." He shifted his weight again. "Deny your angers to yourselves if you can, any of you."

"I deny them." Sandalari had risen from the table and stood upright, burning like a flame of vibrant beauty in the center of the room. I hadn't even known she was listening. Coney glowed back at her, pride in her streaming from him, as apparent to me as if it were solidly visible.

"I am rebuked," Mortel John said softly. "I had forgotten you, Sarai Gregson."

"I've forgotten Sarai Gregson, too," she said, gliding to the couch, bending and planting a full-hearted, affectionate kiss on his cheek, a gesture that astonished me because I would never have thought to do it myself. She slid past him and sat down next to Coney. "You must see, and you must tell the MIs, that they underestimate us. We have both parts of humanity within us—the vicious and the kind, the selfish and the altruistic."

"I think they believe that," the cyborg said, clasping his hands between his knees, "but I think they decided that you would not, left to your own devices, choose to emphasize the latter. You never have for long, you know. They decided to take a hand directly. So they changed me. I was the one who had found talent; I would be the one they would make their instrument to try to mold it." He looked thoughtful. "I've never been clear on whether they considered it a reward or a punishment."

"What do you consider it?" I asked him.

"I consider it the only life I have," he said simply.

I don't know what I expected; however, I know I hadn't expected to want to weep. I touched Jemeret lightly just as he downed the rest of his coffee. He set his cup down with a crack and asked, "Do you recognize—do they recognize—that you've balled up proper and complete trying to raise talent to do your bidding?"

Pel Nostro jumped, whether from the entirely undiplomatic nature of the words or from the quality of the question itself, I couldn't tell. His hand almost convulsively closed on the message chips.

Mortel John was, however, completely unruffled by the question. "They know now there are some variables they cannot account for," he said. "They have determined that I am not, after all, necessarily the best instrument with which to attack those variables. Just the best available until now."

He and Jemeret stared at one another for the space of three very deep breaths, and then my lord said in as low and hard a voice as I'd ever heard him use, "I am not an instrument."

"Not of the MIs." I'd said it before I knew I was even thinking of it, and when it came out, Jemeret's gaze flew to me, his gray eyes steel instead of the smoke I was used to. I tried to wash everyone with the impression that I'd meant it as an emphatic restressing of his words. He relaxed minutely, even though I was not nearly as good at such washes as he was.

Pel Nostro cleared his throat. "Perhaps this would be the time for me to relate to you a few of the messages which have come in," he said.

I reached out with my hand, not with the sting, laying it on Jemeret's arm, feeling the corded muscles ease slightly under my fingertips. We had not talked about the starfire since we reached Orokell, even bubbled. I thought that we might have to soon.

"Go ahead, Pel," Jasin Lebec said.

The Com Counselor looked down at the chips in his hands as if to refresh his memory of what there was to say to us. "Camla Steiner is dead," he said, naming one of the three Class C government operatives who were on their way to Orokell to join us.

"How?" Jemeret asked sharply.

"The *Gralume* wobbled off roll point at the edge of the Brochid system and exploded when its Lume drive kicked in anyway. It could have been an accident." Pel Nostro waited a moment to see if any of us would disagree, but we said nothing, so the Com Counselor continued, "Jara Deland still wants to give you all the MI projections on talent working as a team, and I've set up a meeting with her here at mid-afternoon. She won't be happy until she gets her meeting."

"You didn't tell her about our conversation with the MIs yesterday, did you?" I was unable to resist asking him.

"I am not a man with talent, Ronica," he said with dignity, "but I am hardly an idiot." I noticed that he had dropped the formality of my full name, and was gratified.

"Sorry," I murmured.

He shrugged. "Not at all. I understand that there are marriages in which people share everything, and I would imagine that talent makes such a situation highly desirable. There are other marriages—and they need not be Brochidian to demand it—where the things withheld are often the things which help keep the couple together. It is likely that Jara and I have one of those." He looked back at the chips in his hand, forestalling any other comments on what he'd said. "The situation on Nogdala 7 continues to worsen, and one of these is an appeal from the full Tribunal that you make some sort of scenario known to us very soon, or we will be forced to use other means."

We all knew what those means were. "What does 'continues to worsen' mean?" I asked.

"We stopped and boarded a freighter headed from Nogdala 7 to Mokele and confiscated parts for another plasma disruptor, as well as a half ton of raw vikroid," he explained. "Terrill Guthrie may be expected to fly out of orbit before he's set his trajectory if this keeps up and you continue to do nothing."

"Tell him we'll be handling it shortly," Jasin Lebec said.

Pel Nostro stared at him for a few seconds, but clearly decided against calling him a liar. Then he went on, "There is a concert tonight in Petion Hall, with the entire Orokell orchestra performing the Symphony of the Spheres in honor of the full assemblage of talent—"

"Dwindling, but assembling," Jemeret said caustically.

The Com Counselor ignored him, determined to get through the messages. "—and they would take it quite kindly, as would we, if you could be present."

Before either Jemeret or I could say anything, Jasin Lebec cut in smoothly, "We will be happy to attend, and please convey that to the orchestra."

Pel Nostro was obviously relieved. "Then the usual spate of requests for appearances. I took the liberty of declining them all." No one objected in the slightest. "Finally, there's a strange message here for Ronica from the protodolphin colony on Sargasso."

I was intrigued, and I could see that Jemeret was, too. "What does it say?" I asked.

Pel Nostro looked carefully at the chip, then put it into the reader and turned the volume up. "We heard you have returned from exile," said the translator voice. "If you stop at Sargasso there is a chance we can help. We understand that the need is great. Welcome back to the Com. Glon, for the Concourse."

Jemeret touched me with his sting, inquiring. I shook my head slowly. I understood very well the significance of the four-word phrase "the need is great"—as did Coney, Sandalari, and Jemeret. What I didn't know—what none of us could guess—was how the protodolphins had learned it; it had only been used on Caryldon.

Pel Nostro was looking at us with some bewilderment, for it was clear to him that something was happening, and he had no clue as to what it was.

"It could be a coincidence," Coney said slowly.

"I'm not willing to take the chance that it is," Jemeret answered. "May I have that chip, Pel?" He held out his hand, and the Com Counselor popped the chip out of the reader and gave it to him. Jemeret tucked it away in his jumpsuit's thigh pouch. "Tell Anok Luttrell we'll need a rollship at our disposal tomorrow morning."

"Did you find out where M'Cherys and his followers were sent into exile?" I asked Pel Nostro.

"It's a more complex question than it first appeared to be," the Com Counselor said slowly. "I'll have to ask for your promise that the information you receive will go no further than you." But he didn't wait for us to offer it.

I thought that surely Mortel John must either already know or at least have access to the information, but I didn't ask for confirmation.

Pel Nostro went on, "One of the uninhabited continents on Ananda has been used as an exile planet for the messianic movements that arise among our member worlds. It's shielded from the rest of the planet at a distance of two hundred nautical miles, so once someone is landed there, they're there, barring a lander being sent for them."

And then, of course, we all knew what Ananda had given the Com in its agreement.

"The transports carrying M'Cherys and his followers took nearly two years to arrive from the Jann-Bime system." The Com Counselor spoke steadily. "We could use the rollships as far as there, but then they were needed elsewhere."

"That gives them, what, eleven years standard on the world itself," I calculated.

"It would be time enough," Jasin Lebec said. "Pull up a Com map."

Sandalari was cradling Tial in her lap, because he'd fallen asleep, his cheek pressed against her breasts. Sinet Coleby rose and programmed Jasin Lebec's request into the comsole. Above the table in the center of the couch, the globular holo rose.

"Identify Orokell," Jemeret said. A spot glowed within the globe, which was slowly spinning, the tiny systems, interstellar clouds, and deeps it represented to us turning within their own spheres as well. "Identify Nogdala 7." A second spot appeared, glowing a little more red, off to its left by several systems.

"Identify Sargasso," I said, and was somehow obscurely pleased that the dot was faintly blue. It was four systems higher above the table than Orokell, but that was not insupportably far.

"Identify Ananda," Jemeret said.

The dot, a pure white point, was, of course, gratifyingly close to Sargasso.

Mortel John got to his feet. "If you don't need me, I'll take Tial and put him to bed. The ship was such an exciting treat for him that I'm afraid he didn't sleep last night."

"I don't mind holding him," Sandalari said.

"He should go to bed." Mortel John sounded very definite.

"Sandalari, take him in along with Mortel John," I said, searching for a compromise.

Then Sinet said, "You stay here, Sandi. I'll go help with the boy." Sandalari smiled at her and gave her Tial. She and Mortel John walked slowly down the room past the comsole, which was now freestanding. The place was so cavernous, so empty of furnishings, that I wondered why it didn't echo.

"How soon will Jara Deland be here?" Sandalari asked.

Pel Nostro glanced at the chronometer on the comsole as the Com map dissolved itself, the four spots of light lingering slightly longer than the rest, then fading, too. "About an hour," he said. He tossed the other message chips down on the table, and it reabsorbed them. "I have some routine business to attend to, and I'll return with my wife." He looked at Jemeret and me.

"Please wear something suitable to the concert tonight. I know there's a great deal going on, but I do have some appearances to uphold." He didn't wait for a reply, just went out the door to the suite.

As if Pel Nostro hadn't spoken, Jemeret said to me, "One of us is going to have to pathfind the Lumeship they give us right down to the atomic structure."

"I'll send Anok Luttrell a message ordering him to hold in port until tomorrow every Lumeship currently docked here," Jasin Lebec said. "He'll howl, but he'll do it."

"How many do you think there'll be?" Jemeret asked.

"At least six, and maybe as many as a dozen," his grandfather answered. "We can choose one at random in the morning. Someone might be able to sabotage one Lumeship, but the chances of successfully dittering more than one are very small."

Jemeret nodded. "We'll still have to check it," he said.

"You're the one who memorized a rollship while we were on *Megalume*," I said ruefully. "You'd know faster if something weren't right."

"You'll help me," he said meaningfully. "I want you to know a Lumeship, too."

"You didn't think it was necessary before."

"That was before our enemy appeared on the screens, and before the MIs began to behave in—unexpected ways," he said. "Now I think the better prepared each of us is, the better our chances."

I discovered I was developing a small headache, gathered, and banished it. What did Glon know? How could the genetically engineered inhabitants of a largely water-covered world help us? I called Keli, and she appeared instantly. "I think we ought to meet Gabon now," I said to her. "We gave him short shrift when he arrived."

"He didn't expect any more than that, Ronica," she said reassuringly. She darted past the grassy area where Tynnanna was sleeping. It occurred to me that we could have made it twice the size it was now, and I might have been tempted to do it had we not been leaving the next morning.

Gabon Idana looked very much like his sister, with blunt, pleasant features that inspired affection in someone without a need to dominate him. He still wasn't certain why he'd been reassigned to us, and he found it almost impossible to believe that his reassignment had occurred just because Keli had asked for him. "People like you, Ronica McBride," he began, adding, "and I mean no offense by it, don't do things just because people like us want them to."

"Yes, we do sometimes," I said softly, looking at Jemeret. Neither of us knew that I was being prophetic. "Someone once tried to convince me that we were all ordinary people, and at the time I didn't believe him, but I've come to believe it now."

Gabon was staring at me, but I couldn't take my eyes off my lord, who sat very still for a very long time and then, slowly, nodded once.

I felt grateful that he had yielded, that I would not have to stand apart from him on this, one of our most basic issues. I felt I'd been very right to impulsively add Keli to our team, to help us see that the untalented had worth, a point my husband was finally willing to concede.

"What are my duties, Ronica McBride?" Gabon asked me.

"Be ceremonial and conspicuous, stay alert, and call us by our first names," I ordered. "I assume you can handle that?"

He braced, nodding, even as his eyes widened farther, and Keli tried to repress a giggle.

The two of them retired to their rooms again, and Jasin Lebec returned from the comsole and his discussion with Anok Luttrell. Coney asked if we'd mind if he and Sandalari stole a minute to themselves before Pel Nostro returned with Jara Deland, and I told him to take all the time they needed.

The three of us—Jemeret, Jasin Lebec, and I—sat on the large curved couch and sipped a very dry wine, blessing a moment of silence in the midst of the hubbub. Just as I was thinking I should probably get up and fetch my nomidar, Jasin Lebec asked casually, "What are we going to do about Nogdala 7?"

I said the first thing that came into my head, a little annoyed at being turned aside from my immediate purpose. "Why don't we just blockade them? They can't smuggle anything out if they can't get out at all."

"It isn't just the smuggling," Jasin Lebec said. "They manufacture the illegal weapons and the illegal drugs."

"But no one cared as long as they kept those things to themselves," I argued. "It's the export we're holding against them."

Jemeret set his glass down. "There's something to this," he said, "crazy as it sounds." I stung him gently for sarcasm's sake. "We don't want the portion of the population which isn't engaged in such activities to be wiped out along with the portion that is—probably a much, much smaller portion is culpable, after all. If we remove the access to market, and hence to credit—and make sure that the hardships due to lack of incoming trade are known to be the responsibility of those engaged in illegal commerce—then we set up a situation in which they self-police or they lose all the foodstuffs they're used to receiving from us."

Jasin Lebec was getting into the spirit of it now. "And we could probably speed it along by giving them a few random pulses from low orbit, taking out most of their energy-based technology. It's expensive, but it should work well."

"I like the idea of proposing they send a pulse generator to orbit," I agreed, smiling. "We could have Terrill Guthrie man it with a squad of Drenalion. It'll give him some part in this, but since a pulse ship isn't made to land and carries no shuttles, they can't get near the surface." The pulse had no effect on living organisms other than a momentary dizziness, which meant the Drenalion would be effectively prevented from slaughtering anyone, while at the same time the pulse ship was so hideously valuable and expensive to operate that Terrill Guthrie's ego would be boosted by being entrusted with the responsibility. And since Anok Luttrell's MF guards would be enforcing the blockade, if there were any shooting, more trustworthy heads would be conducting it.

"I think blockading means we'll need a legal order from the court," I said.

"Faucon Oletta should be able to provide it," Jasin Lebec answered.

"I'll approach him at the concert tonight," I said. "I hope he won't give us any trouble about it."

Jemeret smiled. "He won't if you ask him. He fell in love with you at the banquet." I stared at him, flabbergasted. "I was reading him when you talked about the untalented solving problems, and he pretty much lost his heart." The expression on his face was hard to read. "After all, you're a beautiful woman, and you're a major talent. Some men are going to fall in love with you. Faucon's just one of them."

"I never even noticed," I said slowly, feeling stupid.

"It's an occupational pitfall," Jasin Lebec said. "When I was younger, women fell over for me. You wouldn't believe—" He stopped abruptly and laughed at himself. "Well, this probably isn't the best time to talk about it."

"You'd think I'd notice when someone fell in love with me." I was feeling some consternation.

Jemeret slid his sting over my nerves, but only lightly, because this wasn't the best time to do that, either. "Poor fools," he said, his voice thickening. "You are most thoroughly taken."

I had to gather to keep from blushing; he felt me do it, took the sting back. "If we get the court order and send the blockade ships, do we really have to go, too?" I asked him, wanting the subject changed.

"We're the ones who'll have to ensure that the people on the surface know exactly whom to blame for their hardships," Jemeret said. He bubbled us between the words *for* and *their*. "Remember, one of the largest cells of talent-worship appears to be on Nogdala 7," he said evenly inside the bubble. "They may be exporting it along with their other contraband. Unlike drugs or weaponry, religion is an infinitely renewable resource, but the more we know about it, the easier it'll be to stamp out, and we have to try to do that, too."

I sighed almost without noticing it. "People worshiping us and killing us. It makes no logical sense."

"You're still looking for life to bear some relationship to logic," Jemeret said softly. "It's just life, and it moves to its own rules."

We sat for a moment or two in silence, and then Jemeret dropped the bubble, and I changed the subject yet again. "Why can't the government come up with plans like this on its own?"

Jasin Lebec said, "For years they've believed that the most efficient way to solve a problem is to turn a talent or the Drenalion loose on it."

Jemeret twirled his wineglass between his hands. "We'll have to encourage them to relearn the process," he said. "The ones like Faucon Oletta should be a good place to start." He eyed me sideways for a moment. "I was worried about you when we heard Lage was dead," he said, his voice whispery, "and again when we found out about Camla."

"Why?"

"You don't do well when talent dies," he answered.

I frowned. "Neither do you." Then I understood what he was saying. "Jemeret, I don't think I'm directly to blame for either of those deaths. I was for Kray. I helped formulate the scenario that almost took Coney." I touched him with my sting, wide open so he could read me without trying. "I would not have to atone for Lage or Camla."

Jasin Lebec studied me, his eyes enigmatic. "Now there's a word I haven't heard for a long while," he said.

Jemeret's gaze was hooded, too. "Does it offend you, na-sire?"

"Not at all," the old man said. "I believe it's a concept we should probably revive."

Jemeret smiled, the expression touched with a little frost, and upended his glass.

XI. A Question of Questions

I got up just before dawn, careful not to wake Jemeret, slid into a wrapper and went out into the huge common room. Tynnanna padded out of his grassland to lay his head across my lap and be petted, which I did, almost absently, as I considered the events of the afternoon and evening before.

The meeting with Jara Deland and Pel Nostro had gone smoothly, and the MI projections all seemed to support our contention that talent would operate best as a team. Thus, while Jara Deland might not have wanted to accede to any requests of mine, the endorsement of the MIs made it impossible for her to refuse. Once it became clear that the MIs supported a team approach, she would suggest that the Tribunal do the same. After the Com Counselor and his wife left us, Jemeret asked, "Are you going to please Pel by calling up a new gown design for the concert?"

For a moment I wondered if he were mocking me, but he let no hint of that escape him. I said, "I think I want to go as myself. Sandalari, are you willing?"

"To do what?" she asked.

"To go to the concert in a talma."

She grinned with mischief. Jemeret repressed a smile. "I'm more than willing," Sandalari said. "Should we draft Sinet, too?"

Sinet hadn't come out of Tial and Mortel John's room yet, and until Sandalari mentioned her, I hadn't noticed. I started to cast a sensory scout, but Jemeret intercepted it and held it back. I looked at him curiously. He said, "Don't bother them right now."

My mouth dropped open. Sandalari turned away in discreet understanding, and I felt unutterably stupid again.

"But he's—" I stopped.

"He functions," Jemeret said shortly. "She needs someone to help her forget about losing Lage."

"I thought you disliked him," I said.

"I do dislike him, but I don't grudge him a willing bedmate. You can talk to Sinet later." I stared after him as he went into our bedroom, and then a short while later I went in to join him.

He had showered and, a towel wrapped around his waist, was standing at the room's wide window, looking out over the precincts. I thought about the tone of his voice when he called anyone who might happen to fall in love with me a fool, and suddenly one of the old questions reasserted itself, prompted by that particular thick voice and the unexpected notion of Sinet and Mortel John.

"Jemeret," I said hesitantly, "that first time on Caryldon, when you probed me, after the Ilto." He turned, the light behind him making his face impossible for me to see. "I might have hated you. I might have died. Why did you do it?"

"Finally," he said softly, the same kind of slow richness in his voice. "You have no idea how long I've waited for you to ask that particular question at a time when I could answer it."

And then, months late, he told me of his fear that I would never let myself use my Class A powers again. He drew me against the hard muscles of his chest and buried his fingers in my hair. "When I was nearly ready to isolate the last memories, the ones I didn't want you confronting until I thought you were ready," he said, "I knew you had shut down the connection between your self and the sting. I could see the blocks. And then on Caryldon you started using it—to call Rocky that first day at the tivong pens, and to call me when the Ilto took you. Yet you were insistent about the fact that your sting was gone. I had to get in there and see what had happened to the blocks."

Nervousness roiled in my stomach. I gathered it away and kept looking at the afternoon light on the buildings of the precincts. "What had happened?"

"Nothing. The blocks were still there. The unconscious part

of you that needed the sting absolutely ignored them. The conscious part that was punishing you for acting inappropriately against Kray saw them as completely solid." He pulled my head back so that his face was just above mine. "That brain of yours is more complex than a great many others I've dealt with."

"And you spent how many months in it?" I asked him.

"Four months, twelve to sixteen hours a day," he said, his smile almost against my mouth. "That's an intimacy I couldn't possibly explain to anyone who hasn't the sting."

"Four months in that jungle without getting lost?" My breath seemed barely able to support the words.

"Oh," he said, "I got lost all right."

And then we didn't talk again for quite a long time.

Sinet declined the concert to remain with Mortel John and the boy. Sandalari fed Tynnanna, and then we called up our talmas, hers in muted gold—generally worn only by Class A talent—with a soft red shift, mine in the Boru colors, midnight blue over silver gauze. Though on Caryldon women in talmas did not wear undergarments, we decided not to risk shocking several billion citizens and opted for small underpants in the shift colors, but not transparent. The men wore their dark blue jumpsuits, and this time Jasin Lebec joined them. He told us casually that he wanted to make it clear where he stood.

Jemeret seemed for a moment as if he might speak against it, but then he changed his mind. There seemed to be less and less need for the elaborate footwork we'd all expected to be sunk in for tendays. It was not at all what I'd expected—and why I should have been surprised by that is a mystery to me. Neither Jemeret nor I talked about the cause of the lack of opposition, but I'm sure he knew it as well as I did: the MIs, whose hold over the Com he had come back to break, were supporting us. It did not bear thinking about yet. After all, it's far harder to consider turning off an ally than it is an enemy.

I'd only been to the Government House precincts concert hall once when I was growing up, and that had been to see the nomidar performance that had truly inspired my love for the art. After that, almost as if they feared I would become obsessed with music to the detriment of all the things they wanted me to learn, the government had seen to it that I went to no more concerts and had only limited access to holos of performances. I kept at my playing myself, with determination. Now I was more than a little excited at the idea of actually going to the concert hall again—and for such a performance.

The Symphony of the Spheres was an occasion indeed, because it was the body of music written to commemorate the discovery of the Lume technology and the move to the stars. The composer built into the phrasing and scope of the piece an evocation of the aspiration, the long struggle, the many mistakes that cost lives, the battles with the factions that were unwilling to pay the price of continuing—now called the Emigration Wars—the breakthrough, the first tentative explorations, and then the triumphant outpouring of human life from Earth. And all that before the first interval, which allowed the musicians a chance to rest briefly. Then the music turned to the destruction of the lunar Lume base, and the discovery and establishment of the Com, those many hundreds of years ago. The long interval came next, followed by the themes of the Com worlds themselves, rich and complex as they began to build on and blend with one another. A complete performance could last most of the night, and in my honor, this was to be a complete performance.

Our party crossed the precincts to the concert hall just before the performance was due to start. Everyone else should already have been in their seats; nevertheless, our entrance was noted, and our clothes remarked on. I had the nagging feeling that we would set another new fashion, this time for the talma, though many in the audience barely had a chance to see the dresses because we had no sooner taken our seats than the lights dimmed and the orchestra rose to fill the stage.

The playing was at its best, and I almost vanished into the music, as I did when I played. I especially remarked the nomidar section of the orchestra, which was a good one, but in symphony work no one employed the sympathetic capacities of the instrument, so for me that part of the piece was not as satisfying as a solo performance might have been.

At the first, brief interval, I sought out the Chief Justiciar and asked him if I could have a word with him. Forewarned to awareness by Jemeret, I recognized the play of his emotions now, and I let them go on far longer than I should have. I admit that I enjoyed his admiration, uncolored by the kind of lust I'd become used to feeling from Kray. I told him I was taking him into my confidence about our proposed solution to the problem of Nogdala 7, and that it would need a judicial order, whose outlines I sketched very briefly for him. When I saw that he would comply—with an unexpected enjoyment at being able to please me, though I now knew from assiduous reading of him that he might have sacrificed the entire population of that world without hesitation—I began to influence him. Gently and subtly, I took his almost adolescent adoration and bent it back to a more adult and collegial working relationship filled with mutual admiration. Because I was working delicately, and because the interval was a short one, it took the rest of that time to accomplish. We parted with reciprocal assurances of respect and his promise that the necessary order would be filed before we departed in the morning.

We made our way back to our respective boxes. The spectators parted for us, and the stares, both male and female, at my costume confirmed my guess that the simplicity of the talma would probably be the next fashion fad. I couldn't wait to see Petra Chantrey in one.

When I returned to my seat, I washed everyone else in the box with the reassurance that my task had been successfully completed and sat down beside Jemeret to listen to the next part of the symphony.

He'd been distracted during the first movements. Even though we both swept the audience for any signs of hostility toward us and found none, his nerves seemed in a heightened state of wariness, as if the number of people and the prominence of our seats would be too great a temptation for our enemy to resist. Sandalari and I had pathfound the theater itself; I'd been linking her to me when I did the exploration, and she was picking up the internal processes as well as the external techniques very quickly—almost as quickly as the warrior women of the Boru had absorbed the Ladder of the Warrior. I'd been wondering if I could link to Coney and encourage the same process in him, even though he had never shown any aptitude for pathfinding before.

The second interval was, as always when the entire symphony was performed, a long one, for it had several purposes besides allowing the orchestra to marshal its strength for the last part of the concert; the officials at all levels of the government bureaucracy would use the occasion to encounter one another in a social setting less formal than the Com banquet. In this case, they would also be able to encounter us.

We went as a group to the refreshment lounge, and I could feel Jemeret's stress. I wondered what kind of strain he was holding himself under, and whether he would need to borrow any strength from me later as a result of it. I also admired his ability to maintain his alertness despite the seductive quality of the performance; I'd been unable to resist slipping into and losing myself in the virtuosity and skill of the performers and the beauty of the music.

As we neared the lounge, once again we seemed to be assulted frontally by the same kind of powerful malevolence we'd felt the day before outside the reception room. This time we read it with an intensity that made the previous assault seem somehow mild, or muted, as if we'd been reading before through a veil that blurred the sharp edges of the rage and unrelenting enmity. I gasped, as Jemeret's sensory scout shot past mine, seeking the source of the anger, but the second I'd made the sharp sound of indrawn breath, that wall of balefulness was gone, as completely as if I'd breathed it in even as I sent out the scout. The sensation was so strongly imagined that I immediately analyzed myself to make sure such a transference had not occurred, and was infinitely relieved to find myself clean of contamination.

Jemeret swore. "Too fast," he said under his breath. "How the hell—"

Jasin Lebec took his arm in a hard grip. "Not now," he said quickly. "Brazen it out as if we never felt it. The implications are too huge."

I saw Jemeret understand instantly, some of the color leaving his face and then returning hotly; it took me a moment longer, and when I understood, it was an awesome revelation: we could not simply be reading someone's obvious, negative feelings. We were encountering a projection of enormous magnitude, and then a shield of impenetrable density. Someone in the levels of Com government was a Class A talent, even though none of the attacks on talent had yet used means other than normal ones. That unknown talent was our enemy and hated the rest of us with a strength that was terrifying. I glanced around quickly, saw that Sandalari had tears in her eyes, for she and Coney had been struck by the projection as well, the final evidence that it was externally generated, not merely something picked up by us. Coney seemed a little disoriented by it, not yet understanding exactly what he'd felt or what it meant.

The hour of the interval was nearly unbearable to me. Jemeret was outwardly as cool and deceptive as I'd ever seen him, a facade that took my breath away. I was not as good at dissembling, but then, I'd always been a terrible liar, especially when I was shaken out of my complete control over my shields.

Everyone in the lounge was suspect now—members of the Tribunal, their aides, the bureau heads, the MF officers, the University pundits from various departments, the religious leaders, the scientists, the minor bureaucrats, even the guards at the doors and the attendants at the tables calling up and distributing drinks. I painted on a smile, fixing it in my muscles so I would not forget and let it fade, and I made small talk—an art at which I am notably poor—with almost everyone I knew even noddingly and with people I was meeting for the first time. I kept trying not to see all my conversational partners as a possible source of malignancy, but even the most familiar faces took on a dubious cast. Jara Deland's smile seemed forced; Lamar Acifica's prettiness became sly; stolid Anok Luttrell was suddenly disguising deviousness; Petra Chantrey's hearty laugh might have been taunting; Marga Morena's seriousness began to look unfavorably judgmental; only Faucon Oletta, whom I had read so completely when I was making the subtle adjustments during the first interval, and

Terrill Guthrie, who had always been openly malign, still seemed to be true to their former selves.

It was a relief when Davin Olavson and Dolen T'Kelle sought me out, because the single thing I could depend on was that these two would in no way have patience with small talk. Jemeret was in conversation with a man I recognized as the Planetary Governor of Werd, and Jara Deland had cornered Sandalari. Coney was somewhere else in the room. So when the leaders of the Epicyclists and the Macerates came up to me, the only other talent nearby was Jasin Lebec. He watched the two tall men come toward me, and then he joined us, smiling.

Dolen T'Kelle smiled back, nodding to the taller, white-haired man to speak first. I was surprised, for he had never impressed me with any characteristics of deference. The few times I had met these men before, Davin Olavson always gave the impression of humility, and Dolen T'Kelle of an expansiveness that could have filled the room.

But Davin Olavson acknowledged the nod and began, "Ronica McBride, we have been talking about the standings of our respective faiths, and because you have recently been absent from us, you may not be aware that our numbers are growing."

"To levels we believe to be of statistical significance," Dolen T'Kelle added, amplifying the foundation of whatever argument might follow, but making it clear that he was here to support, not to propose.

Davin Olavson went on, "We hope that you would be willing to use your influence to sponsor a request to the government to add a permanent seat to the Tribunal for a representative of the faith communities." He said it simply, as if it had not been seriously contemplated for years, as if the request had not been put forward when I was a child, by the religious leaders who preceded our present generation, and refused by the government or the MIs then.

Dolen T'Kelle rumbled a little, something I had to identify as a laugh. "Davin has a remarkable gift for understatement," he said. "The machines should listen to statistical significance, and it's possible that the Tribunal will listen to an argument based on disenfranchisement, which many of our followers believe they are experiencing."

"Check your demographics," Davin Olavson said. "The dynamic of the Com population is changing."

"The MIs won't like that," Jasin Lebec said quietly. "I have noted that, when they haven't prompted it, they disapprove of change."

"That may be, but evolution, even if slow, tends to be inexorable," Davin Olavson said. "Stopping it will ultimately prove impossible."

"And attempting to stop it can have very high costs," Dolen T'Kelle agreed. "So will you present our request to the government, Ronica McBride?"

"With all due humility," Davin Olavson added, and from him it did not sound perfunctory.

I told them that I would be willing to present it as soon as I could, but that there were a number of other matters that were pressing at the moment, and it would have to rise upward on the agenda as the other things were dispatched. It was a standard answer, even though I agreed with the purposes and ideals of the proposal entirely. It was about as diplomatic as I ever permitted myself to be, and the two men seemed to accept it in the grace that it had been intended. They turned aside, and Jasin Lebec led me to one of the tables and put a drink in my hand.

For a few moments we were alone in the swirl of activity and conversation. "Do you think the Tribunal would ever agree to it?" I asked him. "Or the MIs?"

"I don't know," he said. "I've never been able to fathom the workings of the Tribunal as a body, because it seems to operate differently from what I would expect of any one individual. I'm beginning to think I don't know the MIs at all. Keep smiling."

I hadn't realized that I'd relaxed the control on my facial muscles, and I wrenched the smile back up. I wanted more than anything else to ask him about the sudden presence of an unknown talent, and one set against us, but this was not the time.

Somehow, it was never the right time to ask questions. Just as I hadn't really gotten around to asking Jemeret about his first probe of me on Caryldon until almost a lifetime later, there were still other questions I'd never gotten to ask at all. And now here was a vital question that I couldn't let life make me forget—and I still couldn't ask it when I needed to. The MIs couldn't answer "why" questions, and I needed reasons. We knew that talent happened in the Com now—finding M'Cherys might give us some of the answers—but the most important question would not be answered on Ananda. What was going on that let so powerful a talent exist entirely unknown, entirely unsurrounded by a messianic movement, entirely hidden, and filled with hate?

The questions dominated my mind, and I had to stand in a roomful of people and pretend to no greater concern than the gowns and the flavor of the wine and the prowess of the performance. I needed answers. To get answers, you have to ask questions, and I kept not being able to ask.

The dynamics of the room changed around me. I saw Coney and Sandalari talking seriously to Davin Olavson, and it gave me a good feeling. Dolen T'Kelle stalked past, followed by several acolytes, throwing me a grin, as if we shared a secret now that he and Davin had proposed the request to me. He departed from the lounge, making me wonder if the request, and not the symphony, had been his major reason for being here. I also wondered if Keli and Gabon, both of whom viewed him as the head of their religion, had seen him at all tonight; they hadn't come with us to the lounge, because we wanted them to be certain no one entered our box while we were out of it.

Gromily EnCastro came over, her Motive behind her, to speak briefly with me, and while she was doing so, the interval bell chimed, and I didn't have a chance to ask her if she were also in favor of a faith seat on the Tribunal. It was just another in the long series of questions I didn't get to ask.

When we returned to our box, Keli gave me an all-clear nod, and I noticed that Gabon was wearing a blaster, too. I hoped vaguely that their MF training included a rigorous program in how and when to use that kind of weapon, because blasters were not off-world devices. Too much damage could be done to a ship with one.

The third part of the concert went well, but I couldn't lose myself in it this time. The mystery of a powerful unknown talent was tearing at me. I suspect I began to leak the feeling, because Jemeret leaned over and said softly, "Put it down for now, love. If Jasin Lebec doesn't know about it, no one knows about it. There's nowhere to get any information from, and for the time being, we can't raise suspicion in the government."

"Why not?"

"We don't know who our enemy is," he answered patiently. "Until we do, we risk letting him know that we're aware of him."

It made an appalling kind of sense. It meant I would have to bury questions even further than I had before, and wait longer for the answers. I hated that. I gathered, and made myself listen to the music, which seemed to take forever to be over. I had thought that one of the lessons I'd learned on Caryldon was that it's necessary in life to live with ambiguity. I thought I was getting better at it. Now I was not so sure.

We returned to our suite in the Visitors' Residence to find Mortel John awake and giving Tial a lesson in basic gather control. Sinet was probably still in her own bedroom—or his. Keli and Gabon went on to their small rooms, and Jasin Lebec, Coney, and Sandalari excused themselves to get some sleep. Jemeret and I watched the big man and the small, serious boy for a minute or two, while I absently used my fingers to comb my hair loose from the long braid into which I'd woven it. Watching them gave me an idea.

When they paused for a moment, I asked, "How much of what we consider Class C work can be done without gathering?"

Mortel John considered that question. "Theoretically," he said at last, "all of it could eventually be done by someone who had learned and mastered all the external techniques, but without reserve energy, the process would be so slow as to be accounted entirely natural."

I'm not certain what prompted me to continue that line of questioning. "Have you ever tried to teach the techniques to someone without reserve capacity?"

He shook his head. "It would be wasteful."

"Nevertheless," I said, "I'd like you to undertake it. I'd like you to teach Keli and her brother what to do, should they ever encounter reserve energy." I waited. I'd put it in the form of a request. We were both aware I could make it an order, and I now had the right to give him such an order.

"I find that futile," he said, "but I'll do it if you want. I've grown accustomed to teaching more than one student at a time."

I thought about the two children who'd had their throats cut, and said nothing.

Jemeret was already sleeping when I got to our room, his even breathing a comforting background noise as I stripped out of the talma and disposed it, washed, and brushed my hair in a more effective fashion than combing it with my fingers. I was surprised he hadn't gone directly into deep, because I knew he'd been wearing himself down with the constant alertness, the pathfinding, the readings. Large gatherings of people were especially tiring if you tried to keep reading them, and this concert—though I thought he'd enjoyed the music—had been exhausting for him. I was glad we were leaving. A few days' journey on a ship we knew was unsabotaged would allow him, I hoped, time to really rest. I was tired, too, but not nearly at the levels he was, and my mind was churning with all those unanswered, unasked questions. I lay down beside him but couldn't fall asleep naturally, and found I didn't want to merely put myself out. There was too much turmoil for me to just turn my back on it.

That was why, just at dawn, with the suite stilled to a night rhythm and Mortel John and Tial Borland gone from the common room, I put my wrapper on and irised out my eyes so I didn't have to call for additional illumination. There was a stir in Tynnanna's grasses, and I debated going in to meet him, but I was naked beneath the wrapper, and the grass texture varied. So instead I sat cross-legged on the rug with my back against the back of the couch and softly called the klawit.

At some point in the attempt to sleep, I had decided, almost without being aware of it, to try to summon the starfire. I had too many questions and nowhere else to seek the answers.

The grass rustled, and the great bulk of the cat rose, darker than the darkened suite. He padded up to me. Because I was sitting on the floor, he towered over me until he circled once in front of me, his tail brushing my cheek, and then lay down, his chin resting on my crossed legs, his nose almost touching my stomach. His eyes burned at about the level of my breasts. I stroked him for a few minutes, burying my fingers in the fur around his face, scratching at the base of his horns, behind his ears, and between his eyes. His deep-throated rumble rose around me, seeming to fill the air of the room.

I lowered my head so my forehead rested on his and reconstructed what I'd done in my first encounter with the starfire. I drew the encounter up around me—the memory of being alone on the floor of the bowl at Convalee, dancing with the tendrils of living starfire, the sparks skittering up and down my bare arms, my contentment at being part of the dance instantly alive to me again.

There was a minute flicker, as if something were present just beyond my perception.

Jemeret's voice, to my left, said quietly, "There's no starfire metal here, love."

The vision I'd constructed faded downward, accompanying Tynnanna's purr as it trailed off. I opened my eyes and looked up at my lord, standing above us. He hadn't bothered to put any clothes on.

"I didn't mean to wake you," I said softly.

He bent and stroked Tynnanna's head. "I only sleep well now when you're there," he said. "Come back to bed."

Tynnanna breathed hotly onto my stomach as he snorted and raised his head.

Jemeret reached down and scooped me up, cradling me against his chest. As he carried me back to our room, I asked him, "How will it reach us if there's no metal?"

"I think it can do whatever it wants to," he said. "We have never been able to call it without the metal."

"Then why didn't we bring any?"

He set me down on the bed, stripped the wrapper away, and began to stroke me, much as he had Tynnanna. "It would have been too tempting," he answered. "I don't know if the Com is dealing well enough with one group consciousness. I'm not sure we're ready to subject it to a second."

As always, his touch aroused me, but I was still thinking hard. "Jemeret, you didn't bubble us before you mentioned it!"

"The MIs know about the starfire, love." His hands had settled, but were still busy. "They've known for years that the starfire is creating talent on Caryldon. They want talent."

"They—the MIs—they've never tried to reach the starfire?" It was getting more difficult to hold a calm conversation, but I wouldn't have asked him to stop.

He was grinning. "Use your shields if you want to slow me down."

"I don't—" At that point the conversation paused for more than a quarter of an hour.

Later, after we disengaged our bodies but still lay with our minds linked, I roused myself from the lethargy of love's aftermath and said, "I didn't get my last question answered, and I'm really sick of not getting questions answered."

"Why ask me?" He rested his hand lightly on my hip. "Ask the MIs directly."

The suggestion stunned me. I pulled my head back to see him more clearly without refocusing my eyes. "Are you serious?"

"Completely," he said. "You can call them at any time. The more we know or can guess . . ." He let the sentence die away. There were certain things, I knew, he simply would not say without a bubble.

"Application," I said.

There was a click. "You need not imitate Jara Deland," said the emotionless voice.

"How do I call you, then?" There was an eerie familiarity to the idea of finding a way to approach a group consciousness.

"We are the Mortel part," answered the voice. "The man is the John part."

I swallowed my surprise. Jemeret lay easily beside me,

listening. I cleared my throat. "I would like to know if you have ever tried to contact the starfire."

"There is a call outstanding to the entity you know by the name starfire," the MI voice said. "It will remain outstanding, and perhaps it will be answered."

Jemeret stirred. "How long has the call been outstanding?" It was a simple, factual question, the kind for which an answer was usually immediately forthcoming, but there was a pause, as if the system was unused to being addressed by him. Then the voice said, "For 142 years."

"If you should make contact with the starfire," Jemeret continued, his voice soft and nearly as unreadable as the voice of the machine intelligences, "what will you do?"

The silence following his question went on so long I thought that the system might not reply, or might reply that it would dialogue with the new entity, or study it. I should have known better than to think I could guess accurately. Jemeret sat upright, one knee raised, his arm resting on it, and went so very still that I wondered if he were holding his breath.

When the MI voice spoke, it was slow. "Our predictive models indicate that you are a risk to us, Jemeret Cavanaugh, an unknown factor. Unknown factors are troublesome. But the human part of ourselves believes that you have humanity's best interests in mind when you act, and thus . . ." It paused again, this time briefly. "If we should make contact with what you call the starfire, we will ask it questions."

Jemeret's hand tightened into a fist, the veins straining for a moment. Then he let his breath out with an explosive, "Damn!" I was about to ask something, but there was a knock on the door. "That'll be Mortel John," my lord said. "Put your wrapper on."

I slid into my wrapper as Jemeret brought the lights up to a low level. He took his kilt wrap off the bench under the window and tied it around his waist, then signaled the door open, holding it just long enough for the cyborg to come in.

"May I sit down?" Mortel John asked.

Jemeret waved at the low window seat, the only place in the

room besides the bed which afforded seating. Mortel John walked lightly to it and sat down.

"You see," he said, as if we'd been having a conversation all along—which in a way, I suppose we had—"the entity you call the starfire can do things which the machine intelligences cannot, and therefore they assume that it knows far more than they do."

Jemeret watched him expressionlessly, saying nothing.

"Did it never occur to you that you might not be the only ones with 'why' questions?" Mortel John inquired.

"No," Jemeret said at last. "It never occurred to me."

Mortel John nearly smiled. "Did you think it would be easy, what you're trying to do? Did you think you could change the human race by eliminating the technology? We cannot all live as you do on your wilderworld."

"Technology is basically incompatible with talent," Jemeret said.

"Then how is it that you and Ronica McBride function so well here? How is it that Jasin Lebec functioned so brilliantly for so long?" He glanced at me, sitting curled on the bed, holding my wrapper closed at the throat. "How is it that you have asked where M'Cherys was sent?"

"What did you mean, what I'm trying to do?" Jemeret asked, tension radiating from him. "How do you know what I'm trying to do?"

"I see the MI models," the cyborg answered easily. "You have been angry at us since you left training. You grew angrier each time you had to help heal—or try to heal—a talent whom we had injured or allowed to be injured. They predicted that the only reason you would ever agree to return to the Com would be to try to destroy them."

"I love Ronica," Jemeret said. "Did you think I would simply return her to you?"

I was feeling like a spectator, fascinated at the interplay, somehow concerned about the outcome, yet not a participant. I wished I could be analytical, but I had nothing to offer to this debate, and analysis seemed superfluous. The MIs knew about the starfire; the MIs knew Jemeret had designs on their dominance of the Com. And yet . . .

"They do not understand love," Mortel John said. "Neither do I, any longer. It is not an entirely rational concept, and like much else of human emotion, it defies logical prediction. But they do know you love this woman, and they value you for it."

Jemeret shook his head.

Mortel John went on, inexorably, "Their models show that your love for her and your anger at them are likely to balance each other out. They believe you will still act against them, if you can, but they believe me when I tell them that you will not act against your own kind."

Jemeret's voice was low. "Will they defend themselves? Are they defending themselves? Have the MIs created a weapon to try to kill us?"

I was shocked by the questions.

Mortel John was not in the least offended. "You know they aren't and haven't," he said lightly. "If they are nothing else, they are efficient. You would have been dead long since."

"I thought as much," my lord said. "Do you know who's behind it?"

I realized, knowing talent was at the root of the attempts, that we could ask the MIs that question. Perhaps they were the only ones it *was* safe to ask.

Mortel John was silent for a moment. And then his face twitched slightly, as if the answer surprised him, but not unbearably so. "They say their models show an eighty-plus percent probability that you are dealing with a rogue talent, previously unknown," he said. "They say it is likely that, previous attacks on you by conventional means having failed, another attack should more openly reveal the nature of the attacker. No probability estimate follows that likelihood."

Jemeret compressed his lips briefly, and I wondered about the abilities of an untrained rogue arisen, it would seem, in the Com itself and kept hidden. Such a person would have no loyalty to talent in others, like M'Cherys had had no loyalty to others besides his followers.

Suspicion bloomed in me. "Has no one else asked you—

them, I mean—this question before? Has no one in the government, let alone the Tribunal, wanted to know about the probable source of the killings?"

Mortel John looked at me. "It was not considered prudent to give the prediction to anyone but you. I'm informed that the question has indeed been asked before, but not answered." He turned back, studied Jemeret. "I know how easy it would be for you to hate them," he said, "but I also know you, Jemeret. I raised you for ten years. You have always been fair, and I expect you to be fair now. We may not be your own kind, but we are not your enemies."

I touched Jemeret lightly with my sting, not to influence him in any way, just to read him. He was very still from the outside, but the core of inner turmoil was real and powerful. He had defined his villains before he left Caryldon, and now he was confronted with a reality that did not fit his perceptions any more than some of the realities I kept encountering fit mine. I remembered him at the Boru Court of Justice, honoring me when I had just hurt him; I remembered him reminding Coney that he had sworn to bring me back to the Com and would; I remembered, just the day before, his complete acceptance that he could not, despite his declarations to the contrary, willingly or happily sacrifice those without talent to those with it.

I thought I had never loved him so much as now, when he was put to one of the hardest tests of his life. I never doubted that he would rise to meet it.

As soon as I'd thought that, he relaxed almost convulsively and gave a bark of humorless laughter. "You're too damned shrewd," he said, "and you're right. I'm too damned fair."

Mortel John nodded impassively. I felt my first real stab of hope that Jemeret would see his ambition was unnecessary as well as impossible. That meant there would be a chance we wouldn't have to do what he wanted—attack the great power of the MIs.

"Insofar as I can be," Mortel John said, "I am happy that the government let you take Ronica to Caryldon, and for reasons I am not yet entirely certain of, I am happy you returned with her."

"You're going with us to Nogdala 7," I said, needing the confirmation.

"Yes," my old teacher agreed. "I was fascinated by Jasin Lebec calling talent a tribe, because it was a new metaphor for me, and I don't hear very many new metaphors. Talent cannot be the only tribe in the Com, if tribe it is, so if we take the metaphor more broadly, I will continue to find it fascinating to identify the others which might exist here."

"Our tribe isn't limited to people with talent," I said firmly. "We're building a team here, and everyone living in this suite with us at this time is a part of that team."

"I'm flattered," Mortel John said, which startled me, because I honestly hadn't meant him. "Tial and I will be ready whenever you want to leave." He got to his feet. "Good day." He left us, the door sliding open and then shut behind him.

"Are you all right?" I asked Jemeret.

"Surprisingly so," he answered, pulling off his kilt. "The thing I worried about most was the reaction of the MIs to anything I might try to do—not that I had any real scenario planned. Now, as far as what I want to accomplish is concerned—" He paused, choosing a few appropriate words. "—I'm actually optimistic about the future."

My newfound hope ebbed. He had not put aside his goal; he'd only concluded that the MIs would be less likely to retaliate too soon or in too overwhelming a way. He was encouraged to continue, not to turn aside. I knew I would have to confront him on it, too, because I would not let him attempt something so impossible alone. I stifled a sigh.

He must have felt it, but he didn't respond to it. "The problem right now is the rogue."

I made myself think about that. "How do we fight talent?"

"With talent," he said.

I slid down beside him into the bed's field. "That wall of hostility—he's terrifically strong. And he's got a long reach, working with conventional methods to keep his true nature concealed."

"But mad to let it slip where we could feel it." He lay back and locked his hands behind his head. "We—you and I especially—mustn't make him more than he is. He's just a talent, like we are. Let's get some sleep."

He or she, I added silently, and I finally fell asleep, wondering, as I would repeatedly over the next few weeks, what our enemy truly was, why he hated us so much, and how I could possibly make him more than he was.

The ships carrying the two remaining Com Class C's arrived at the port just after Jemeret and I had finished pathfinding the *Detralume*, the ship we'd chosen at random from the eight Lumeships Anok Luttrell had held in port for us. Jemeret was telling the local MF port commander that he wanted only a skeleton crew—as few people as could run a ship safely through roll, and ultimately it was decided that twelve could do it, six on high watch, six on low. I probed every one of them, much more aggressively than I might ordinarily, grateful that my experience comparing Keli's brain structure to Coney's and Sandalari's had made me hyperconscious of the physical signs of talent.

My probes showed that the crew of *Detralume* harbored no hidden hostilities toward us; some were pleased to be selected for the assignment when the normal crew contingent was winnowed down, while others were simply curious. The ship's captain, who seemed most likely to be offended by the thoroughness of the probe, was almost phlegmatic. When I was satisfied, and Jemeret was, as well, we all piled into the Lumeship—captain and eleven crew members; the four of us who had come up from Caryldon; the four remaining working talents from the Com, two of whom were as yet completely off scope about the events that were unfolding; the Idanas; Mortel John and the Boru child now called Tial; and Tynnanna. Twenty-four people and a klawit.

Pel Nostro and the most concerned members of the Tribunal—Jara Deland, Anok Luttrell, and Faucon Oletta—came to see us off. "Be sure to file flight plans from Nogdala 7 to Sargasso, and then from Sargasso to Ananda," the Com Counselor cautioned, speaking as much to Jasin Lebec as to either Jemeret or me. Jasin Lebec solemnly assured him that we would.

While I probed the two men new to our party with slightly less mercy than I'd shown to the rollship crew—after all, we knew they had talent, and I needed to know what they'd use it for—Sinet and Mortel John explained what was going on. The news that talent was under siege took them by some surprise. Lendo Dell was nearly sixty and by far the stronger of the two Class C's. I made a mental note to start him pathfinding with Sandalari. He had a bluff, blond heartiness that reminded me so much of Sabaran that I became convinced he'd been a member of the family, or at least a Gendal.

The other Class C, Vazhny Lastone, was nearly eighty-five and not as vigorous as Jasin Lebec, who was approaching forty years his senior. I assessed that Vazhny Lastone should have been retired a decade earlier, but the government had too many problems and not enough talent to throw at them. The two men were deeply distressed by the deaths of Camla and Lage, both of whom had been in their thirties. "Is nothing being done to stop this wholesale destruction of Class B's and C's?" Vazhny asked Sinet. I left the room as she began to answer the question by saying that we *were* trying to do something about it, but . . .

Jemeret and I didn't really relax until we achieved orbit around Orokell, where we rendezvoused with Terrill Guthrie's pulse ship and the six blockade ships. Then I felt a hard edge of strain, which had been around him since we'd left the suite for the port and around me for almost as long, dissolve away. If Terrill Guthrie was our enemy, he would have to openly fire on us, and he was unlikely to do that while being observed. Talent, of course, demanded presence, and as long as we stayed out of his presence, dealing with him only on the comlinks, we and those around us were safe from that influence as well.

The pulse ship was the only one with roll capability, and the head of the Drenalion had chosen to travel caravan with the blockade vessels, so we told him we'd see him in Nogdala 7 orbit in four tendays' time, fired the *Detralume* out of Orokell orbit, and left for the roll point.

The single roll between Orokell and the vicinity of the Nogdala system was one of the longest in the Lume repertoire. This length made it no more inherently dangerous, but it created interesting psychological effects.

Jemeret and I had agreed to spend the roll time in the cargo hold with Tynnanna, because the roll was lengthy enough so that even if we put him to sleep at its beginning, he might awaken in the course of it, and there was no telling what effect it might have on him if he were alone. We were both a little tired; Jemeret's pathfinding and my probing had taken a small bite out of our reserves, but nothing that would demand repair yet.

We had decided to go to Nogdala 7 as fast as possible so we could emplanet and begin readying the population for hardships to come, while simultaneously seeing if we could quash the talent worship that might have begun there.

Because of the skeleton nature of the crew, we'd all been relatively busy before the first roll warning sounded. When its chime reverberated through the ship, Jemeret took my hand, and we left the bridge surround to go down the cargo arm and into the big space where Tynnanna was pacing restlessly. He'd come to associate the chime with unpleasantness. He roared when he saw us and came bounding over, feeling more secure now that we were there. I wished I could keep him in our cabin, but he was simply too huge now. It was almost as if he were growing constantly.

Jemeret idly scratched the cat's forehead and horn bases, which were increasingly difficult for me to reach unless he was lying down.

The second chime rang through the cargo hold just as Tynnanna had finally been persuaded to curl up, and he growled at it. Jemeret and I tucked ourselves into the curve of his body and against each other, moving with the motion of the klawit's great rib cage and touching him to soothe him through the imminent discomfort of the roll's beginning.

The series of beeps began counting down, and then, as smoothly as I'd ever felt it, we were seamlessly encompassed in the motionless motion of the roll, its nauseating qualities dissipated as much as a good Lumeship could dissipate them, rising nevertheless to the point at which most rolls ended, and then sinking away into the stasislike nullity of this particular roll.

Because we had both lightly stung Tynnanna, and because we were both receptive to him, Jemeret and I knew the instant his consciousness changed, opening into a vastness so great, so awesomely endless, that we were bounced backward from it to escape the threat of pain that underlay such power. Tynnanna said, "You cannot call us from normal space without the metal, whose atomic structure is a focal point, but you may call us here."

I was struggling to form a sentence, because Lumespace scrambles passages, but before I could bring the words, *How did you get here?* into proper alignment, the starfire answered the question I had been unable to speak. "We live here," said the starfire. "That is why we come to you physically in forms of light. Listen now. There is a danger near which you do not suspect and which may not be evoked. If it is, then you can lose much. It can possibly be repaired from a source you cannot now guess. Remember that enemies are sometimes only opponents, and opponents can sometimes be allies."

Jemeret, once again stronger than I, had been able to attain coherence. "How can we talk again?" Five words seemed to be the effective limit of what we could strive to assemble in Lumespace.

"We do not speak only to you," Tynnanna said, and we fell out of the roll into normal space. Tynnanna licked the side of my face, nearly drowning me, his purr rumbling up around our bodies.

"I'll be damned," Jemeret said softly.

"So huge," I murmured. "I've never had my sting so close to something so—"

Jemeret's face went grim and tight for a moment. "We weren't trying to sting the starfire, and it knew it. That's why we're still alive." Before I could ask, he went on, "What do you think it meant about not speaking only to us?"

"Glon," I said with sudden insight, and saw from his face that that was only a nonsense syllable to him. "The protodolphin who sent us the message to come to Sargasso. I'll bet

Glon is the one the starfire was referring to, and that's why he thought they could help."

Jemeret frowned. "That's quite a leap of assumption. I'm more concerned with the near danger we don't suspect. The crew?"

"I probed the crew, and I'm satisfied that they're safe," I said insistently. "Perhaps the starfire meant near in time and not in distance."

"Perhaps." Jemeret sounded doubtful.

It was wearing, feeling in constant danger, constantly off balance. I'd never known such uncertainty before, and it threatened to stretch onward to an end whose outlines I couldn't see. Tynnanna had fallen asleep and was beginning to snore, a sound only slightly quieter and less sonorous than his roar was. We got up and went back across the bridge surround and into the cabin wing. Mortel John and his three pupils—Keli and Gabon seemed stunned by the idea of studying a talent-exclusive process, and Tial was lording his own greater prowess over them with the unmitigated arrogance of young talent in a talentless world—were studying in the conference room and did not seem to notice us as we went past. Coney and Sandalari were in their cabin. Jasin Lebec, Lendo Dell, and Vazhny Lastone were sitting in the lounge, playing percosul three-handed and complaining about every play as only old men can. Sinet was sitting by herself in a corner, reading.

"I'm going to deep and fill my reserves," Jemeret said to me. "If there's some sort of danger around, I may need them."

I probably should have joined him, but my reserves were more than two-thirds full, and I was both uneasy and exhilarated from the unexpected encounter with the starfire. "I'll be there in a little while," I said. "I want to have some time to talk privately to Sinet." He squeezed my hand and went on to our cabin. I stood still for a moment, watching Sinet, wondering which tribe of the Samoth had given her birth and lost her. Then I went to the corner in which she sat.

Rollship lounges, while spacious, are not nearly so well-apportioned as lounges on transports, because people are expected to remain on transports for much longer periods of time. Nevertheless, *Detralume* had been furnished with some comfort in mind. Sinet had curled herself into a vidchair, where holos of books and various other kinds of entertainment could be called up on the swing-out platform. Unwilling to interrupt her, I sat in the vidchair opposite hers and simply waited. After a few minutes she glanced up, saw me, dotted her place, and swung the arm away. "Ronica?"

"Sinet, we don't know each other very well," I began, hoping it was the right note to strike, "and since we've been thrown together like this, I thought we might talk a little."

She inclined her head, indicating her assent, then folded her hands on her thigh and sat quietly, watching me.

I wasn't certain where to begin, and I didn't read her to help myself along. Somehow I was determined to use my Caryldon-developed skills at interaction, not merely my talent. I took the plunge. "Did you and Lage work together for a long time?"

"Fifteen years," she answered readily enough. "At her graduation ceremony it was agreed that she should apprentice to me for a time, since I'd been handling Class B assignments for about fifteen years before she graduated. She wasn't—confident yet as a talent. She was studying on her own then, because you three were just starting as she was finishing, and because Mortel John was, at the end of her education, spending much more time with you." She had been gazing very steadily at me as she spoke; now she looked down at her hands. "She developed more confidence and skill over the next few years, but it turned out that she lost them when she was tried on her own. So they left her with me."

"I didn't realize that our training gave her less than she should have had," I said slowly. "I guess it doesn't do any good to say I'm sorry now."

Sinet raised her head to me again. "Oh, don't be sorry." Her voice was firm. "I had the pleasure of working with another talent all those years, and Mortel John knew what he was doing emphasizing you. Your value was comparably greater."

That made me a little angry, but I gathered it down. "About Mortel John . . ." I said hesitantly.

Sinet was no coward. "Why am I sleeping with him?" she

asked bluntly. She took my silence for the acquiescence it was. There had been an edge of aggression in the question as she asked it, but she seemed not to need to continue that tack. "Kray told me that talent automatically removes the obligation to be courteous," she said, in a unconscious echo of something Morien had once said to me about power. She mentioned Kray's name with a casual ease that both shook and gratified me. "I never found it to have any effect at all on loneliness."

"But you're a beautiful woman," I protested sincerely, for I had always thought her much more classically beautiful than I.

"And I'm a talent," she said, a little caustically. "There aren't that many other talented men, Ronica, and unfortunately, I never found a man without talent who didn't want to use me for some agenda of his own. I haven't been gifted with a man, like you and Sandi have. And what I had with Lage was fine, but it wasn't enough for me by itself. That's why I went with Kray when I had a chance to, even though he was twenty-five years younger than me. Because the only thing he wanted to use me for was sex, and that was fine with me."

"But Mortel John—" My voice dropped almost without my willing it to.

"Isn't fully human," she said. "Yes, I know." She looked at me closely. "That's part of his charm. Ronica, I'm afraid you're still something of an innocent in this life."

"Me?" I was truly astounded. "I don't think so."

"Oh yes," she said categorically. "I'd bet two years of my work that you've had no experience with perversion." I must have goggled at her. "There you are. I win my bet," she said with some satisfaction.

Rude curiosity got the better of me. "Have you—had that kind of experience?"

She nodded, seemed to debate something, then leaned across between our chairs. "Did you know that Kray—experimented with perversions?"

Since I had no idea what "perversions" were, and since I was fairly certain I didn't want to know, I just shook my head. Sinet sat back in her chair again, saying only, "He should have known better than to play a rape game with you."

A twinge of horror shot through me. "A game?" I repeated incredulously. "He thought he was playing a game?"

"I don't know," Sinet said. "I only know he'd done it before. With others."

Suddenly I thought I understood better why the MIs had not acted. What Kray was doing to me was something they'd observed him doing on other occasions, and the women had come to no harm. They had no way of judging that it would be different for me, no way of judging that my reaction would vary from those of the others. Perhaps Kray had not known either, and it cost him his life.

The impolite curiosity was still tugging at me. "I'm sorry, Sinet, but I have to ask," I said. "Did he do it to you?"

She turned her eyes away from me again. "No," she said. "He did—other things with Lage and me."

"Cruel things?"

"They're not cruel if you agree to them," she said. "I agreed to some things, and Lage to others. Some things we all did. Kray had fairly eclectic sexual appetites."

I gathered that Kray had not taken them singly, as I'd always assumed, but rather that all three had been together. I didn't want to think about it, didn't want to dwell on Kray. I only said, "I suppose I should have handled it—less forcefully than I did."

"Funny," she said. "I've always assumed that if you could have, you would have. And don't 'should' yourself, Ronica. There's certainly no good in it now."

The picture she painted of Kray was not one that accorded with most of the scenes of my childhood. "Thank you for your honesty, Sinet," I said, the words totally unfeigned. "This wasn't what I meant to speak to you about when I sat down."

She shrugged. "Conversations don't always go the way we plan them," she said. "They're a lot like life in that respect."

"I'm sorry if I was prying." I slid out of the chair.

"I think you needed to know," Sinet said. "You probably don't get any benefit from idealizing a man you killed."

I fled, needing to talk to Jemeret, as she swung the arm in again and went back to her reading. I didn't intend to wake him, but my agitation preceded me, and he met me at the cabin door and closed it behind me. "Tell me," he said.

My conversation with Sinet poured out of me, and when he realized the substance of it, he pulled me over onto the bed and put his arms around me, stroking my hair lightly. "You havc so much power that I keep forgetting how young you are," he said softly.

"Do you know what she's talking about?" I demanded. "The things she and Kray did?"

"I can probably guess," he answered.

"Have you ever done anything like that?"

He kept stroking my hair. "My tastes don't incline in that direction," he said, "but I don't necessarily condemn people whose tastes do."

I was reminded in a flash of Tuvellen and Morien. "Jemeret, I always thought Kray was my friend—I thought I knew him. All the time we were growing up, I never guessed—"

"The Kray you knew is not materially different from this Kray," Jemeret said firmly. "He made a mistake with you at the end, and it was an appalling misjudgment on his part, but that doesn't alter the fact that he was the boy you knew, and the young man who saved your life when the Drenalion attacked you."

"Sinet said I was idealizing him."

He drew me tighter against him, his lips on my hair. "You do that with the people you love," he said. "You did it with Coney and Kray. You do it with me." I started to deny it, but even as he laid his fingertips on my lips, I knew he was right. I'd done it on Caryldon and I had since we'd come back to the Com, when I'd needed his approval for my choices. I still did it in constantly bowing to his greater strength, in hoping there would be no confrontation between us, in letting him take the lead in so many ways.

"I don't mean to do it," I said softly.

He said, "It's all right. I think you'll grow out of it."

"What will I grow into, do you think?" I asked him, a little shakily.

He didn't answer me, just kept on stroking me.

XII. A Question of Belief

Nogdala 7 was not a great world in terms of size nor of posterity nor of population. It had developed as a factory planet, highly skilled in taking the raw materials from some worlds and making them into products for still other worlds. As a result, its requisite wilderness area was carefully domed, its ambient temperature ranged from tepid to downright torrid, and all of its living areas were in the three levels of its great Structure, which—with the exception of the huge spaceport, the wild, and one large body of water—dominated the surface of the planet.

We had decided we could not go to the surface as who we were—Com talents—so we fabricated identities as a team of business travelers from Causaday, a relatively new world to the Com and one that had been successfully resisting all of the Nogdala government's efforts to pull it into a trading partnership, due to opposing attitudes on each of the two worlds toward many of the basic principles of Com life.

Causaday was one of those straitlaced worlds, vaguely like Brochid had been, though not as bad, in which patriarchal authority had reigned unquestioned until the Com moved in after analysis of the planetary spectrum showed large deposits of generium, a rare substance used in the eftel and eftel vid communication devices. Prior to the discovery, it had been believed that only Marga Morena's science personnel, working hard to synthesize the ore, could save production of the eftel technology from becoming even more expensive and increasingly scarce. The need for the generium had caused the Com government to surreptitiously bend the rules for acceptance of a member world, and as a result Causaday was accepted without having to make any of the normally requisite social changes prior to admission into the Com. Unlike many worlds that begged for membership, the Com government introduced itself to Causaday, appointed an ambassador, and sent Terrill Guthrie's predecessor with a squad of Drenalion to explain the facts of life to the inhabitants.

Thirty years later, the Causadayans were beginning to be more at ease with their Com membership—no one called it occupation—and were getting fairly rich from the Merchant Fleet's extraction of ore.

Nogdala 7 eyed the credit balance and wanted to sell them goods; so far, until we accepted for them, Causaday had rebuffed their efforts. Now the governor of Nogdala 7, a man named Parwick Cue, which I thought sounded like a curse of some kind, was in possession of a response that said a four-person trade delegation was willing to visit Nogdala 7, arriving on the *Detralume*, to begin the (lengthy implied) process of exploring whether or not there were any products the Causadayans could buy without being corrupted either by them or by the all-too-liberal attitudes of the people who created them.

We hoped the very lightly veiled threat would keep Cue and his staff on their best behavior.

As for which four of us would go—Jasin Lebec couldn't. He was too well known on every Com world, his face as familiar as people's own; Jemeret and I had to go, for the influencing we needed to perform couldn't be done by anyone else. His face was not known at all, and while my graduation had been vidded everywhere, I had then vanished for more than three years, and my return was considered uncertain enough for its pictures to be confined only to core worlds. Were I to vanish again, the damage control the government would need to do would be minimal.

We needed two more men. The Causadayans might have come a long way in three decades, but women were still only grudgingly given any positions of responsibility. So we decided to take Coney, and then our choices were Lendo Dell,

Vazhny Lastone, or someone without talent. Mortel John had to stay with Tial, and Jemeret didn't want him along anyway.

We decided on Lendo Dell, because Nogdala was one of those worlds which unduly valued youth—only the relatively young and strong survived for long in the manufactories—and Vazhny Lastone was probably too old to be taken seriously. Lendo Dell grew a beard much more butter yellow than Coney's sand-colored blond. It was an appropriate gesture. The patriarchs of Causaday were all bearded men, it being a symbol of status to which women were unlikely to aspire even if we could.

And then, as the men changed their jumpsuit colors to the charcoal that trade delegations typically wore, I restyled my jumpsuit so the natural shape of my body disappeared into it. Causaday women had been permitted to adopt the jumpsuit, but only to local specifications, including a hood that covered almost all of their hair. I'd attached what appeared to be one errant dark brown lock of hair to the side of the hood's brow strap, keeping my true honey color hidden.

"You'll have to be silent much of the time," Jemeret warned me. "I'm not requiring your submission, just the appearance of it."

"I'll give it to you," I said, adding, "After all, I am your wife."

We had decided we would have to be husband and wife in the fabrication, or we would not be able to share a room. I'd spent an hour memorizing the behavior I'd be expected to show Jemeret and how it differed from my behavior toward the other two Causaday men. Then there was behavior toward men who were not Causadayan. I figured that after a couple of weeks of this, I'd be more than ready to personally alter the entire makeup of Causaday society.

We took a lander down from orbit and alit in the small diplomatic area of a busy working dock. I tried to take it all in at once from the vehicle, memorizing landing coordinates and dock assignment, because we might have to leave in a hurry. Jemeret had piloted us down, and he locked the lander without the normal mechanism of thumb- or retinal print, using instead a seven-symbol code chosen from the five hundred or so symbols the vehicle carried. The precaution would allow any of the rest of us to lift off if he was, for any reason, not with us.

Then we stepped out under the orange-yellow sky. The landing field was not domed, but atmosphere mixers, likely of local manufacture, ringed the area and created a bubble of slightly greater pressure than the thin, largely polluted air of the rest of the surface.

The official greeting party consisted of two assistant governors and two Skilled Negotiators, all four of them male, no doubt in deference to what they knew of Causadayan power structure. All the men shook hands, as I studied the Nogdalans through my eyelashes, since my head was modestly lowered. Jemeret introduced me as his wife, "who must not be addressed directly, as that would be an offense against propriety," and asked to be shown to our accommodations.

"Please follow me, Tadan," said one of the assistant governors, using the accepted title for a Causadayan Elder. "Governor Cue will be honored to meet with you after you've settled in, and we've programmed your rooms to respond to your specific needs." He led us to a slideway that connected the diplomatic area with others and ultimately dived into the Structure itself.

I wished I were barefoot so that I could pathfind the slideway as we stepped onto it, but there was no help for that. After a moment to adjust to the motion, as if intrigued by the composition of the material, Jemeret bent and ran his palm over it, then straightened. I was a little awed. Since he'd been doing so much pathfinding, he'd gotten faster and faster at it.

The nearer of the two Skilled Negotiators, whose job it clearly was to tout the virtues of anything the trade delegation happened to admire or seem curious about, immediately launched into so detailed a description of the materials and technology of slideways as to make the pathfinding superfluous.

I had no need to remind myself to keep silent; for the next few minutes there would be no opportunity to interrupt the hearty gush of facts anyway.

We entered the Structure on level three, the uppermost. The closest area of this level was devoted to portworker residences and recreation facilities; beyond it lay what we were assured was a great ring of order fulfillment offices, where shipments were checked against orders, and information on credit transfers verified. With only one spaceport, and that surrounded by government offices, I began to wonder, even before we arrived at our accommodations, how a smuggler could get off-world.

We traveled on the slideways along the sales office complexes, past storage depots for incoming raw materials; then downward through the second level, which appeared to be the manufacturing facility; and ultimately to the lowest level, which housed the imported foodstuffs and the residence and entertainment complexes for workers, bosses, and visitors—known locally as customers. As we went, Lendo Dell showed a very Gendalike heartiness in admiring the lighting system, the air circulation, the architecture, the mechanism of almost any mechanical-looking device we passed, and anything else that struck his fancy, until the pair of Skilled Negotiators was talking so fast and simultaneously that I had to gather to repress my laughter. The moment we neared what one of the assistant governors, shouting to be heard over the spate of promotional material, described as our "guest premises," Coney, suppressing his humor either by gathering or with a great act of will, asked if the Nogdalans had anything to contribute in the area of vehicle assembly, knowing full well that groundcars, floaters, landers, and shuttles were not built here.

The answer he received gave new meaning to the word "hyperbole," and meant that three out of our four greeters were all talking at the same time. I found myself sorely tempted to sting everyone just to shut them up. It felt as if I were moving through a little cone of tightly grasped interior silence, a frail barrier against the raucous onslaught of a world in which music played on every corner and issued from every residence, sometimes accidentally blending, but more often creating an awful racket. I had never thought so badly of music before.

Jemeret was frowning disapprovingly, but I thought it had more to do with the character he'd assumed than with his own values. In the lobby of the guest premises, Lendo Dell would probably have asked about the fountain, the artificial plants, the spectacularly beautiful holo birds, and the uniquely patterned carpet had Jemeret not stopped him. Then the Skilled Negotiators ran down, and only the comparatively soft music of the lobby itself intruded. Into the sudden quiet, Jemeret said coolly, "I assume we can explore the city—"

"Structure," all four of the Nogdalans corrected in unison.

Jemeret ignored them. "—on our own. We're certain, of course, that you would not deliberately show us only those things you guess would please us, but we will feel more positively toward the enterprise of Nogdala if we can investigate it ourselves."

I knew immediately, without looking up, that the assistant governors didn't have the authority to make that choice. The lack of an answer lay heavily in the tinkling music of the lobby. "Well," Jemeret said, an overtone of patronization in his voice, "when you find out if my assumption is correct, I'm sure you will be certain to let us know." He took my upper arm in his hand, careful not to squeeze as tightly as he appeared to be squeezing. "Where are our rooms?"

The assistant governors led us down one of the hallways that branched out of the lobby and showed us three open doors, which Jemeret, Coney, and Lendo Dell keyed to themselves. I would not be expected to have independent ingress or egress, but would only accompany my husband or wait patiently for his return. Since I could pathfind my way out or in at any time, I was not at all dismayed by the restriction.

Jemeret led me inside the room, sealed the door behind us, and said, "I'm not pleased with the atmosphere I've seen on this world, wife."

My role in the scenario was to play the receptive delegate, but I had to be very careful how I did it. I chose sweetness; it was a challenging persona, especially for me. "Husband, it is certain that there are many good people here, and that those people will be responsible for the products which will be shown." A Causaday woman never used personal pronouns unless given express permission to do so. "This is a nice room."

Jemeret leaned back against the wall as if applying some sort of scrutiny to me or my statement, rather than to the room itself. I knew he was pathfinding. He touched me with his sting and nodded gently, and I knew he had identified the vid device; a moment later the second nod, doubled, barely discernible, told me there were two listeners. He pulled away from the wall and flashed me a look that confirmed we were fairly fully under observation. I wanted to say, but couldn't, that two listening devices were required because no one on this world understood the concept of silence.

The false, noncommittal communication that our role-playing called for was in its own way as great a strain as intense physical exercise. I wanted to sigh and flop down on the bed, but instead I went on playing the meek, self-effacing wife until the lobby signaled us all that the governor had arrived to greet us.

Jemeret took my upper arm again, a gesture of pure possessiveness on which we had agreed before we finalized our roles in the scenario, and we went back to the lobby to meet the unfortunately named Parwick Cue. A great deal of what we wanted to accomplish depended on our being able to move independent of escorts, and I had wondered what would happen if the power-that-was wanted to refuse Jemeret's request. Jemeret would have to sting him, and we had no way of knowing whether that would cause him to behave in ways that others of his staff might consider suspiciously uncharacteristic or irresponsible.

One look at Governor Cue told me that we were likely not to have a problem in that regard. The man was a living evocation of greed and the profit motive, the way the Drenalion were a living evocation of naked force. He was both rotund and jocund, but it was all on the surface. He smelled credit on us, and it obsessed him. He was perfectly groomed, his hands wreathed in rings, his ears draped with thin chains that matched the thick ones around his neck, the metals all highly polished and studded with gems. I couldn't help but stare, and

Jemeret pulled my arm, pretending to be angry that I'd forgotten my manners.

Governor Parwick Cue was expansive; Jemeret was adamant; and fairly soon we had agreed to a joint program of being guided to various factories and product showrooms for several hours in the mornings, then given the rest of the time to wander on our own. We were only cautioned to avoid any areas marked with red stripes, as those contained machinery that could be hazardous to the uninitiated.

The governor had exhausted his diplomacy and was preparing to bid us farewell when Coney said, "And what of the spiritual life of the people here, Tadan-Ta? You will show us factories and offices and theaters, but what of the tabernacles or shrines?"

A good salesperson is prepared for anything, and Parwick Cue would never have become governor on this world had he not been a superlative salesperson. "There is a district called the Umbra which you might choose to see," he said. "I'm afraid it's several hours by the inner slideway." I took *inner* to mean *fastest*.

"And if we should, therefore, wander too far to return in a reasonable amount of time," Lendo Dell put in, "will there be somewhere we can stay?"

The governor debated and cleared his throat. "There are workers' residences," he said at last. "We can provide you with a guest pass, but the accommodations are not as—comfortable—"

Jemeret cut him off. "We are accustomed to austerity."

I almost giggled.

For the next three tendays, we sat through product demonstrations in the morning, making appropriate comments. When a product was specifically for women or children, then my opinion was sought, and it became a challenge for me to express it without seeming in any way connected to it by "I," "me," or "mine." Then, in the afternoons or evenings—and sometimes all night—we roved throughout the Structure. We learned what worker passes looked like, instead of guest passes, and we memorized the typical worker dress and behavior. At the end of that time we knew the Structure as well as it was possible to know it. Coney had roamed the Umbra, located the small chapel that seemed dedicated to the worship of talent, went in, and was appalled at the crudeness of the text messages and paintings on the walls. They were filled with images that varied between the openly murderous in describing the depredations of the Drenalion, and the dauntingly lewd, describing unity with talent in crude sexual terms. "It's not just that they're attempting to worship us," Coney said in disgust after we had returned to the rollship. "It's that they're doing it so badly!"

We had not, as requested, entered any of the red stripe areas, because Causadayans would not contravene local laws, but we would be under no such restrictions when we returned, and a survey of the surface from orbit had proved without any doubt that no trace of the molecular trails associated with lander or shuttle exhaust existed anywhere except the original port.

Being back on *Detralume* was an overwhelming relief for me after weeks of repression. Most of it had not been too bad, but one experience I hated. It seems silly now, but then I took it very seriously, fearful it had somehow changed the nature of my relationship with Jemeret. It was the first time I'd ever experienced sex without allowing myself to orgasm—a hideous and humiliating performance for our observers, the last demonstration considered necessary to create a completely credible picture of the society from which they thought we'd come. Jemeret used me mechanically and, at least, mercifully quickly, permitting himself no consideration for my pleasure in the act. When it was over, I felt myself trembling on the verge of tears, and I gathered to quell them. But Jemeret ruthlessly broke through my gather and made me weep, while holding my mind as tenderly as I wanted him to hold my body. A Causaday husband would not comfort a wife who had done no more than her duty to him. I kept trying to remind myself that a Brochidian husband would have beaten his wife for crying, and the Causadayans were better than that.

"Don't keep me awake with your sobbing," Jemeret said to me carelessly, turning his back on me.

I knew that, on *Detralume*, he would make it up to me, but I had experienced the emptiness of that one encounter, and it had shaken me more than I assumed it would. I couldn't understand how or why women would accept being used in that way. I talked to Coney and Sandalari briefly about it. I knew I could have asked Sinet, but somehow I was embarrassed by the idea of that; she already knew I was more innocent than I liked.

"I guess we all value different things," Sandalari said softly. "Some women may not care as much as you—as we do about certain kinds of equality." She smiled at me. "I told you that you mustn't judge everyone by yourself."

We were sitting in their cabin, because I hadn't felt entirely comfortable with Jemeret since our performance for the vid in the Structure. Reasonably, I knew it was ridiculous. But there was something in it that made me nervous about what I saw as the ease with which Jemeret fit into a dominant role, while I had fought continuously to appear submissive.

Coney also smiled at me. "Remember when you told me that people are worlds, Ronnie?" he said. "Well, worlds are different. Sometimes they can be unified, and sometimes they can't."

"And from what I've seen," Sandalari said, "the Com's laid a synthetic imbrication on all these worlds, composed of rules thought to be the best for all. But tribes need to have unique rules as well. I think the officials of the Com and the MIs want to stamp that individuality out."

"They haven't succeeded," I said, shuddering a little.

"But that's just a matter of time," Coney said. "You know as well as I do that Com time and human time are different things."

The discussion had now reached a point where we wanted the others in on it, and we adjourned it to the lounge, where Jemeret and Jasin Lebec were drinking something transparent and discussing strategies for our upcoming, clandestine exploratory mission to the Structure, with the goal of getting into a red stripe area and finding out what really went on in it. They looked up as we came in, and I found myself unable to meet Jemeret's inquiring gaze. I wondered if he had evoked in me some cellular memory of the rape, or whether this was just how sex was going to become in the Com, as I had feared. It was silly, I know. But then . . .

Coney rehashed very briefly our discussion on individuality and the Com, and Jasin Lebec agreed that sameness across societies was one of the aims of the government, which believed that differences, while interesting, were potential sources of conflict and should therefore be eliminated, quickly if possible, to minimize the danger.

"But the worlds are so very different," I said. "When I was growing up, I never appreciated that, because I never traveled anywhere. Werd and Koldor and Orokell were almost identical, and I somehow assumed that other places would be very close to them."

"It's Petra Chantrey's job, through the Universities, to bring everyone into alignment," Jasin Lebec said.

"And she's doing it," Jemeret said. "The Causadayans are in many ways today exactly where the Brochidians were twenty years ago. The Com can be patient because it is inexorable. It tolerates a certain amount of variance, in matters of religion and superficial custom, especially at the beginning of a world's membership—and the beginning can last a hundred years—but eventually the government gets conformity, and that's when the rebellion usually begins."

Little rebellions were entirely characteristic of the natural evolution of a Com world. They never occurred when people were still enamored of the benefits of Com membership, but only when they began to feel in their own lives the changes that made up the costs of such membership, and then the period of rebellion passed. Longtime member worlds, such as Barbin 3 or Nogdala 7, should have been conforming nicely now.

Out of the corner of my eye I saw Jemeret glance at the chronometer on the comsole. "We have to make the first raid in about two hours," he said. "I suggest we get a little sleep, Ronica."

I always loved the way he said my name, but this time it sent a little shiver of fear through me, unreasonable as it was. I followed him to our cabin, and he sealed us into the room and instantly bubbled us. "You have to get over this, love," he said. "We both agreed to what happened down there."

"I didn't think I'd feel . . ." I couldn't tell him what I was really feeling, because I wasn't certain what it was.

He studied me carefully, but I didn't feel any kind of probe. "I didn't realize how closely you've been equating your worth with your sexuality when it comes to me," he said softly, "and I should have. We can probably thank Kray for that, but I'm not entirely guiltless. I had to use it to heal you, and now if it gets damaged—"

"Make it better for me," I said, unable to look directly at him, waiting for him to reach for me. When he didn't, I looked up, startled.

His expression was unreadable, and I had a flashback to a moment on Caryldon when he had reached for me and I'd flung myself away from him. He wouldn't help me with this. I saw him recognize that I'd seen it.

"We really do need to get a little sleep," he said, turned, and went to the bed, allowing the bubble to dissolve away.

I knew what had to happen then. If I wanted him to make love to me, I would have to be the initiator. And just then, too close to the memory of being used, even by the man I loved and needed, I couldn't do that. I lay down beside him, and I immediately made myself sleep.

We accomplished one lightning raid in a cargo shuttle to prove that we could get in and out of the spaceport in the confusion of cargo ship arrivals and departures without anyone taking ballistic offense. Four hours later we made a second raid to get into a red stripe area and see exactly what was transpiring there. We chose one far from the spaceport, even though the risk of discovery was heightened with distance. We had created worker identities so that, if stopped, we would have legitimate reasons for being where we were. Only Jemeret, Coney, and I made the second raid—Jemeret and I to keep anyone from calling attention to Coney; Coney had to actually enter the area and then return to report. We followed him from outside with our stings, ensuring he passed unnoticed, and when he returned, he said nothing, only made a gesture for us to get back to the shuttle and get away.

In the shuttle itself, lifting off, he said, "We were a little wrong."

"About what?" I asked. "Are they slipping the illegal products into production along with licit ones?"

"Not exactly." Coney gave one short laugh. "They're in full, open production on drugs and weaponry in the red stripe areas. That is, I assume some of the others are devoted to weaponry. This one was strictly drugs. And I saw one of the assistant governors berating a shift foreman for failing to make the quota in time for some order or other. This is not a small smuggling enterprise. The whole government appears to be in on it. The assistant governor was in uniform, with full regalia." He was angry. "Their protestations of helplessness to stop it unaided were lies from the outset; they're running it."

On the Lumeship we told the others on our team what Coney had discovered.

"Get a secure line to Terrill Guthrie," Jasin Lebec began, but Jemeret interrupted him.

"It's not necessary," my lord said firmly. "Terrill's role in this can remain completely unchanged. The pulse will shut down the illegal operations as effectively as the legal ones. It's our role that just got a lot easier." I saw immediately where he was heading, and once again I agreed with him.

We went for the rollship captain and told him to put the ship in polar orbit and hold it there. Then, after he left, Lendo Dell asked, "What have you got in mind?"

"Not alerting the populace," Jemeret answered. "We need to take care of aborting the cult of talent and then just sit tight in orbit until the blockade vessels arrive."

Coney and Lendo Dell looked at him curiously, but none of us asked him to explain; something in his clipped manner made that impossible. Jasin Lebec asked only, "When do you want to go down and begin the destruction of the Becois cell?"

I asked Coney, "When's the next service?"

Coney glanced at the chronometer. "I think in about four

hours. They seemed to be holding them twice a day, and the day is twenty-two hours long."

"We ought to go, then," I said. "We should be in place in the Umbra before anyone begins to assemble for the service."

"Be careful," Coney cautioned unnecessarily. We nodded at him.

We took the smallest of the shuttles. There was no hint that we were going into less danger than we were leaving behind us on the ship.

It was our third lightning raid in less than three days, and we were getting more confident, trying not to become complacent as well. We were still dressed as workers, still with our worker IDs, and we moved easily through the halls of the Structure until we were inside the Umbra. Each of the major religions had centers here, and some of the minor ones; many, failing, had fallen into disrepair. Religion would do well only with the workers, who were a very real underclass. The managers would be far more materialistic than religious. There was a small stream of people going into the doorway that led to the rooms the Becois had claimed, and we followed them.

Coney had been right; the wall paintings were astoundingly obscene, and I found myself unable to look at them for very long. Some erotica was beautiful; this was awful. Jemeret seemed grim, but unshocked, until we saw the savagery of the paintings depicting dismemberment by the Drenalion. These were either desperate or sick people, possibly both.

The room filled, and then the leader—whether called a priest or any of the other designations religious deans were accorded, I never learned—entered and announced the opening of the rites. A weak beam projector in one of the back walls began to sweep the room, evoking a sense of emotional satisfaction combined with a sense of appetite. I began to have an uneasy inkling as to what the rites of worship were.

Jemeret leaned casually against the wall beside us, pathfound through to the beam projector in a flash, and disabled it. Immediately the two of us inundated everyone present with a sense of absolute wrongness, an almost nauseating discomfort at the idea of indulging in such a sick fancy. Then he did something I would never have credited him with doing: he took a surge of power and channeled it directly to their pain receptors, concentrating its crest on the priest, leaving the man howling in agony on the makeshift altar.

When we'd completed that action, I assessed my reserves to be a little more than half full, and I risked another small amount to lay a hand on the wall and break the molecular bonds of the paint to the surface. The pictures all melted downward in falling streams of color.

We had debated how best to discourage the belief without permanently harming the people espousing it, and our ultimate solution discounted despair, which was probably the easiest way, because it might have led to suicides. We also rejected contrition as too apt to bring feelings that the worship might be worthy and the worshipers performing it wrong. "We have to bring them to believe they misplace their adoration when they direct it to us," Jemeret had said.

"That's dangerously subtle," his grandfather warned him.

Jemeret had nodded agreement, but I said, "I think it's a risk we'll have to take."

Now, at the back of the rooms in the Umbra, we began trying to convey a complex concept—that all people, talented or not, were just the same. He had to do it by using emotional images, not words, and I was trying to support him, not receive him, so I wasn't certain exactly how he was working it. I kept trying to implant the feeling that these people were as good as anyone with talent. For a long time the Becois congregation lay on the floor of their meeting room, stunned by pain into near unconsciousness, receiving the quasi-visions aimed at making them cease this senseless worship of other humans. Then Jemeret turned nearly sightless eyes toward me and said hoarsely, "We've done our best. Let's get the hell off-world." But he stumbled when he tried to move.

Alarmed, I grabbed at him, instantly beggaring what was left of my own reserves to pour some strength into him. He tore himself away from me before I could really hurt myself, which I probably would have done in fear for him, took my hand again when he realized I'd recovered from the abruptly broken contact, and we slipped out of the building, then out of the Umbra and onto the slideways.

It reminded me, in some ways, of the long ago flight after the battle with the Drenalion, except that this time no one had to die, and this time we were almost equally debilitated. Twice we had to hide in doorways or alleys, clouding ourselves over so that people who might have seen us—no one could have heard us in the normal cacophony of the Structure—passed us by. We had, I admit, no notion of whether we'd been observed leaving the Umbra, and thus no notion of whether we might be under pursuit.

There was an unusually high level of activity at the spaceport, and I had to let go of Jemeret so we could walk separately, with the confident but unhurried gait of workers on assignment. We left the Structure and crossed the open section of the landing field to our small shuttle, sitting among a forest of others. Once inside, we simply crouched there, out of sight, until I judged that enough of the ground activity had died down so I could join the vessels lifting off.

I was fumbling with the controls, very slow myself, when the shuttle gave a massive lurch. I thought we'd been hit by fire from the surface and desperately forced myself to try to pathfind the shuttle to see what was wrong. Jemeret knocked my hands from the control panel. "The ship's grabbed us," he said with an effort. "Save your strength."

I started to cry, and he pulled me out of my seat, barely supporting my weight, and onto his knees, surrounding me with his arms. "I should be able to help you more," I kept saying.

The *Detrulume* hauled us in; Coney, Sandalari, Keli, and Lendo Dell pulled us out of the vehicle and carried us to our cabin. I remember seeing Mortel John's serious face in the background, and then I fell into deep at once.

Jemeret roused me from deep, which was highly unusual. Customarily, we let each other rise from deep naturally, allowing our bodies to make the choice as to when our reserves were full enough to support awakening. I swam up from oblivion to the sound of his voice and the feeling of his hands light on my shoulders. "Come on, love," he said softly. "There's been trouble."

I didn't know I could awake from deep so quickly. "What happened?"

He was very somber, almost grave. "There have been a few deaths," he said carefully.

I felt a stab of fear, tested the gather and found I hadn't drained myself so much as to render it unusable. Always a death or deaths. Always the necessity for waysongs. As children in the School for Talent, Coney and Kray and I had studied various definitions of humanity, the process of definition being considered vital after other species had been given sentience. It was thought prudent—especially among some chauvinistic and xenophobic elements—to arrive at meaningful differentiations based on something other than the ability to perform advanced reasoning. Scientists had arrived at a definition that described humans as "the species which systematically organizes and tests knowledge in the pursuit of truth." The Universities suggested the addition of, "using learning to improve the life of the species beyond that of earlier generations." A dissident faction among scholars proposed defining the species as composed of beings "inexplicably attracted to unanswerable questions," but the scientific community insisted that all questions were inherently answerable, and the dissidents were overruled.

When Jemeret woke me with news of more deaths, I realized I rejected all the accepted definitions as too grandiose. Human beings, I decided, were members of the species that believed it could solve its problems by killing their sources—and since often those sources were other human beings, well, then, those particular human beings were liable to be killed. Was talent to go the same way? Were we ultimately to be no different?

I studied his grim face for a moment, then asked, "Who have we lost?"

"Four members of the crew, Vazhny Lastone, Gabon Idana, and Tial Borland," he said, his voice steady.

I could feel his apprehension that I would fly apart at the loss of talent, as I had done before, but I kept a tight hold on myself and tried to think rationally. "Are we still in danger?"

"Not at the moment," he answered.

"What happened?"

His grip on my shoulders tightened, and I could feel his sting hovering just beyond the edges of my consciousness. "Ronica, did you probe Gabon Idana when he came on board?"

I knew the moment he asked it that I had not, and I understood in a flash why he was so very apprehensive that I might harm myself. Gabon Idana had arrived with Mortel John and Tial Borland, and I'd been distracted by their presence—and then Keli, whom I trusted, had just taken her brother over. I'd never thought of it again; once I'd recognized him as part of the team, it ceased to be a concern. And the probing had clearly been my responsibility: Jemeret had been doing all the pathfinding. I shook my head, asking weakly, "Was he the danger the starfire warned us about?"

Jemeret was still watching me minutely, ready to pounce if I turned my mistake inward. I could feel the temptation of it pulling at me, but I fought it. I had to learn to accept my imperfections without trying to destroy myself for them. It had been a mistake, overlooking the probing; it should not have the power to make me turn on myself. I fought to keep it from developing that power. "He was the weapon of the person we've been calling our enemy," Jemeret said. "And now we know who it is. Mortel John is calling Pel Nostro with the information."

I felt a hard pang for the little boy, an overwhelming rush of gratitude that Coney and Sandalari were alive. "Who is it?" I asked him. "Who's killing us?"

He answered obliquely. "It appears that Dolen T'Kelle has come to believe he's the Preserver."

I stared at my lord, incredulous. "Keli—" I said, the word strangling me.

Jemeret shook his head. "She's blameless, but she's confined to her cabin. I probed her and put her to sleep. She fell apart when her brother went mad and started killing people."

Ultimately, he, Jasin Lebec, and Mortel John reconstructed

the series of events for me. Coney and Sandalari had gone to feed and exercise Tynnanna, which was their responsibility while Jemeret and I were planetside, and Sinet and Lendo Dell had decided to go with them, fascinated with the klawit. Their absence from the guest quarters probably saved their lives.

The *Detralume*'s captain had received an eftel call for Gabon Idana and patched it through to the lounge, where Keli and her brother were playing scattergies. Gabon keyed in the receive sequence, heard, according to the recordings, nothing at all, but obviously received some sort of signal, turned away from the eftel and knocked his sister halfway across the room. Then he drew his blaster and killed the crewman who happened to be in the vidchair. Vazhny Lastone, across the room with Jasin Lebec, at the card table, hit the ship's alarm and took two blasts, the second clearly intended for the old Class A, who was blocked by the younger man's body. Without waiting to see if he'd actually killed anyone, Gabon left the lounge, heading for Mortel John's room. He was jumped by the trio of crew sent in response to the alarm, and killed them despite being lashed several times himself by their neural whips. Whatever had triggered him seemed to have also rendered his pain responses ineffectual.

Had Mortel John actually been in the cabin, Tial Borland might still have been alive. But the cyborg had come out to see what the ship's alarm meant, and Gabon had dashed past him and blasted the child where he sat on the floor, constructing a pattern block. The pieces of the construction melted into his hand. Mortel John grappled the blaster away from Gabon before he could turn, then broke both his arms and snapped his back expertly at the waist.

Jasin Lebec had sent a call across the ship to the four talents in the cargo bay, and they came quickly, Sandalari's face as pale as milk. Coney, taking in the scene quickly, restrained Keli as she came running up, half her face already purpling from Gabon's blow, and Jasin Lebec probed her as best he could, then sent her to her cabin with Sinet to watch her.

To Mortel John, the dead were dead, and Gabon had to be kept alive long enough to tell what he knew. The captain of the

Detralume and one of his remaining officers were also present when Mortel John began questioning the young man.

Sandalari ultimately had to turn away as the story emerged indirectly from the fragmented words Mortel John literally carved out of Gabon Idana, and the questioners had to make a lot of assumptions, extrapolating from the bits of information. Despite the heretical nature of the corruption, the Macerates must have been poisoned by the ambition of their leader. We assumed that, in order to declare himself Preserver and elevate his religion above any and all others, Dolen T'Kelle had for some time been perverting the ideals of some of his followers, turning those with access to weaponry or authority into fanatical adherents. We concluded that Keli had escaped by virtue of having been posted to distant Markover Station.

By the time that much of the story was done, I was hyper-awake and horrified. "But why did he want to kill other talents?" I asked my lord, hurting for the dead and for Keli, gathering to fight the weakening that the hurt created. "Talent is part of the same tribe, and besides, we've always left the religions alo—" And I stopped in mid-sentence, seeing something, whispering, "They had begun to worship *us*."

Jemeret nodded, his eyes dark with his own anger and sorrow. "He clearly had no way of knowing that we would, as talents, find such adoration repellent, since he, an untrained, untamed talent, desired it so much." He stroked my arm. "He appears to have decided that he needed to eliminate all his potential rivals—others with talent—before he revealed himself. Then he might have been able to add the Becois to the Macerates already following him, and I assume he believed others would fall into line."

I felt the same kind of nausea I'd experienced when I was a child and Sandalari had shown me her lacerated back. I let myself weep for a moment. Jemeret said softly, "I'm afraid he'll have to die, love. Even I recognize that."

"Will they expect us to kill him?" I sounded forlorn when I asked it. In the Com, talent served, not dominated. Rogue talents had always been eliminated. Rogue talents that destroyed would not merely merit exile, and Dolen T'Kelle's crimes had been all the greater, because he'd fraudulently insinuated himself into the power structure.

Jemeret didn't answer me directly. "Let's go join the others," he said.

I was still wearing the worker's outfit from Nogdala 7, though he had changed into a standard jumpsuit and turned it dark blue. My hair was tangled around my face. I didn't take time to clean up; I just went with my lord to the conference room where the other remaining talents, Mortel John, and the captain of the *Detralume* sat or stood on one side of the table, facing Pel Nostro, Jara Deland, Anok Luttrell, and Faucon Oletta on the other.

The Tribunal members looked vastly relieved when the two of us came into the room, but before any of them could say anything, Jasin Lebec looked directly at us. "Dolen T'Kelle fled from Orokell earlier today, planet-time, probably just after the call that triggered Gabon Idana. We don't know where he went or how many of his followers he took with him. I would guess he was bubbled, and I would guess he bubbled the *Giralume*, which he stole." If Dolen T'Kelle had appropriated a Lumeship, he could conceivably be almost anywhere by now. Rollships were very rare, and roll points numerous.

"You know he's a rogue talent," Jemeret said steadily, looking at the Tribunal.

"The MIs informed us of that fact after he vanished," Pel Nostro said uncomfortably. "And . . ." There was something he simply didn't want to say. "Jara?" he asked at last.

Jara Deland was made of stronger material than her husband. "I'm afraid the MIs acted precipitously."

"Explain." Jemeret's voice had gone low and dangerous, as I simultaneously asked, "What did they do?"

Jara Deland cleared her throat. "They issued an order in the absence of Terrill Guthrie and turned the Drenalion loose on the Macerates."

We were all silent for long moments.

Then I asked, "Which worlds?" It amazed me that I sounded detached.

Jara Deland had the grace to look uneasy, and Faucon Oletta

seemed almost ashamed. "All the core worlds," the Chief Justiciar said, "and anywhere else there was a detachment of clones. I did try to issue an order to stay the executions, but the MIs blocked it."

"How did they plan to identify the Macerates in a population?" Coney asked in a strained voice. "It's not as if anyone wears signs."

Pel Nostro answered, "The MIs have always characterized the members of religious groups as potential sources of dissension, and they kept fairly careful records of who attended which rites or espoused which philosophies. They could not leave Dolen T'Kelle with an army—or a potential army—at his back. They pinpointed the targets for the Drenalion."

"Targets!" I was furious. "Those are people, many of them citizens of the Com!" In my head I was listing the core worlds: Orokell itself, Werd, Koldor, and Auburnese on the first level; further out Steressor, Menary, Jann-Bime, Nanseda . . . The knell went on and on.

"Can you stop the Drenalion?" Jemeret asked the Com Counselor.

It was Mortel John who said, "They will not permit him to interfere, any more than they permitted Faucon Oletta to do so. In all, six talents are dead, and that is an insupportable loss."

Her distress real, Jara Deland said, "The MIs won't even answer my call just now. I have tried."

I looked at Anok Luttrell. "Tell Terrill Guthrie to recall his Drenalion units."

The MF chief shook his head. "The MIs won't let me get through to him. He doesn't even know what's happening."

Jemeret turned on Mortel John, enraged, and the big cyborg held his hands up, palms outward. "They won't listen to me on this, Jemeret Cavanaugh. Dolen T'Kelle seems to have wanted to assume control of the Com, and he was murdering talents as part of his goal. Both things are unacceptable, and they have concluded an example must be made. Their predictions show that you and Ronica McBride would not be willing to provide such an example." He paused. "I assume they are not mistaken in that supposition. If you are not willing, then they must do it themselves. They want to ensure that every citizen sees it and recognizes it for what it is. Don't waste your breath trying to dissuade them."

Jemeret clenched and unclenched his fists helplessly for a few moments, his eyes glittering, his shields up. He said nothing. I stared down at my locked hands, held tautly in my lap.

Into the silence, Coney spoke. "May the lives of all circle so as not to upset the Balance. May their souls rise upward on the wings of the pure. May the innocent among them suffer not at all. May the guilty repent of the wrongs they may have done and for which they pay with their nonexistence."

Sandalari put her hands over her face.

I thought that I had better revise my recent definition of humanity. The MIs, too, believed problems could be solved by killing them. Or perhaps, when we created them, we had somehow programmed that belief into them. They had clearly absorbed it and come to see it as useful. I had seen it as useful myself, I admitted, wielding it thoughtlessly to destroy Kray when he'd hurt me and without regret to eliminate Evesti of the Ilto when he wanted to do the same. I could not entirely condemn others for doing only what I'd done myself, even though they were doing it on a more massive scale. If I couldn't learn to rise beyond it—if even Jemeret couldn't—then how could others?

I don't know what my face must have looked like when I turned it upward to Jemeret, but he responded to it, putting his anger down deep inside him, laying his arm across my shoulders.

Two days later there were more than fifty million dead. Some were not Macerates, because when certain groups of Com citizens, ordinarily rejecting and contemptuous of the religions, saw who the Drenalion's chosen victims were, they joined in the bloodletting and were themselves killed for it.

We had mourned and disposed of our own dead before we knew the true scope of the tragedy, and I acknowledged to myself that I was getting very tired of singing waysongs.

After the services I went to Keli's room to speak with her. She'd been crying since she awakened from the sleep Jemeret induced in her, and when she saw me, her tears came harder, washing her bruised face. I stung her instantly to calm her, waited until she had achieved enough equilibrium to remain semiplacid on her own, read her fear, and said, "Keli, I'm not going to send you away."

"I'm—so—sorry!" It threatened to topple her back into the sobbing again, but I touched her gently and she tried to master herself. "I never thought my brother—"

"He was used by a stronger force," I said to her. "You had no way of knowing that he would be entangled in Dolen T'Kelle's schemes for power."

She gasped, her eyes widening and the blood flush of weeping draining out of her face. No one had told her. "The Repository?" She jumped up, too agitated to hold still. "*Our* Repository?"

I told her all I knew of what had debased the Macerates, of the lust for domination that had warped and poisoned what could once have been a noble man. She believed me, despite not wanting to, having seen the destructive force that had overcome Gabon. Then I told her that the MIs had turned the Drenalion loose on the Macerates, and she seemed to collapse a little inside herself. I tried to imagine what remains to someone whose faith is stripped away, barely recognizing then, as I do now, that the situation bore eerie parallels to what had happened to me when I lost faith in myself and took my brain apart.

When I thought she was calmer again, more stable, I helped her back to her bed and said, "You'll be safer if you remain confined to your cabin until all this is finished."

She had drawn her knees up and circled them with her arms, her face buried in the hollow between her limbs. As I reached the door to signal it to iris out, I heard her say firmly, "I swear I would die for you." I didn't turn back, because I didn't want her to know I'd heard her. If she had known it, and if the situation arose, I thought she might feel she had to keep her vow.

No one should have to keep a vow made in the extremity of emotion.

The lounge had been cleaned long since, and Jemeret sat with Coney and Sandalari on the long couch that lined the side of the room away from the table and the vidchairs. "How is she?" he asked as I came in.

"I think she'll recover," I said, sitting down between him and Sandalari. "She's afraid I'll never trust her again."

"That's natural enough," Coney said.

I reached out to Jemeret with my sting and found him still shielded. It made me ache inside. He was not letting me in now, and I missed the intimacy with an intensity I could not merely gather away. Being perceptively blocked, I took his hand in mine and held it tightly. He seemed at last to sense my need and looked at me, a hint of the old affection on his face. "I almost relaxed," he said to me, and I understood that he was referring to the MIs and Mortel John. "I listened to them talk about 'the best for human beings,' and I suppose I wanted to believe it. No more."

Even after the news of the death toll came to us, he did not seem any angrier or any sadder; I thought he must have guessed it would total out at something of the sort. When the MIs restored the comlinks, we called Terrill Guthrie to report what had happened, and none of us was surprised at how gratified he was at the outcome, as if it were a confirmation of his ideals and a repudiation of ours.

Only two ships tried to leave the world before the blockade ships arrived, and the *Detralume* turned them back.

We tried to put the killings behind us and go on with the Com business at hand. The day he arrived, Terrill Guthrie bombarded Nogdala 7 with the pulses. We discussed Nogdala 7's possible responses to the blockade and the random pulses and decided that, since even more food would have to be imported once the pulses had been deployed, surrender should not be very far off. Jasin Lebec assumed the responsibility for telling Terrill Guthrie that the government of the planet, not a small group of the citizens, was the guilty party, and the Drenalion leader adapted well to the news, which of course didn't change his plans.

We were in our cabin, alone, having elected to sleep a little during the high watch, instead of observing the reaction of the Nogdalans to the almost whimsical ruin of their economy, when I finally said to Jemeret, "I need to speak with you."

He looked at me, drawn out of his preoccupation. "Yes?"

"I want to probe you." I guess I hadn't meant for it to come out as baldly as it did, but there was no help for it. "You said you didn't know how often you could drain yourself down and keep coming back. I want to see if you're still all right."

"I'm still all right," he said.

"I want to see," I repeated.

He studied me for a minute, then shrugged and acquiesced, lowering his shields. I slid immediately into his familiar mind, delving into the powerful, restless waves I found there, grateful beyond my ability to express that the sun-bright shaft of his love for me was still as strong and pure as ever. I sensed no diminution of the mighty currents that coursed through the ocean of his consciousness, but there was a difference now from the last time I'd done this, in our house at Stronghome. The hidden anger that had roiled darkly so deep below the surface then was much shallower now. I wasn't surprised. I drew back the sting.

"I told you I was all right," he said mildly.

"I'm feeling useless around you lately," I said to him. "I've felt left out."

He stared at me for a moment or two, then almost laughed. "I'm sorry, love. I've had a lot on my mind."

"Maybe—" It was tentative. "—you could share it with me."

"We know things have to change," he said. "We don't know the form they'll take, or the things we need to do to change them."

"The starfire said you knew what you needed to know."

"I thought I did know," he acknowledged. "After we got off the peninsula, I was so sure. And now—"

"The starfire said there was time." I cocked my head,

watching him. "I never pictured you as impatient before. I always thought you understood the timing of things."

He smiled at me wryly. "I told you you idealized me. I understand the healing of talent. This is so much more. This is an attempt to heal society. It's beyond the conception of a single person."

"Then why are you so set on doing it alone?"

He stared at me.

"Jemeret, we are still seven talents here, and nothing is going to be decided in orbit around Nogdala 7. Perhaps you should stop making it so hard on yourself." I almost bit back the words. It was what he always said to me, and it felt peculiar to be giving it back to him again.

"I'm a chief," he said softly, "and the chief is responsible for the entire tribe."

"And I'm High Lady." It was the first time I'd said that flatly, with utter conviction.

The comsole called to tell us that the *Detralume*'s four replacement crew members had arrived, drafted from among the low watch on the pulse ship. I got up to go and probe them. Despite the MI reprisals on the Macerates, Dolen T'Kelle was still somewhere at large, and we wanted to take no chances.

XIII. Among the Water People

We had not nearly drained ourselves for nothing. Even before we broke orbit to head for the roll point that would start us toward Sargasso, we were learning that the Becois cells on planets other than Nogdala 7 had received eftel messages, first cautiously, then more stridently, discounting the original revelations as false. It was an attitude reinforced, ironically enough, by the fact that some of the Becois had been Macerates, and therefore had become prey for the Drenalion. Talent had not saved them.

We left Nogdala 7 to Terrill Guthrie and the blockade ships and took the three-roll journey past Jann-Bime to Sargasso. Jemeret still brooded, though he'd tried to relax enough for us to play our nomidars with some frequency and even indulge in some holotainment. Coney confronted directly—taking it to Mortel John as we'd taken all the bothersome questions of our childhood—the issue of whether the MIs were likely to deploy a killing patrol against Epicyclists like himself or Responsionists, or even the ascetic Purists, since he doubted any of the MIs could see differences among the religions, but only the fact of diversely declared allegiances. Mortel John answered that the MIs never judged solely by allegiances, but rather by actions, leading me to reflect on the unlikely possibility that machines could be just as hypocritical as governments.

Mortel John often followed Jemeret with his eyes, but my lord never spoke to the cyborg now except for a polite response if he was directly asked a question.

We spent each of the rolls with Tynnanna, who, after long endays of confinement on the Lumeship, was going quietly crazy. He'd managed to rip up some of the flooring before we left orbit, and we'd calmed him while two members of the crew warily repaired the damage. "What's the matter with the beast?" the captain asked me nervously after surveying the original damage to the cargo hold.

"He's homesick," I told the man, thinking, *Aren't we all?*

The rolls were too short for any contact with the starfire.

Sargasso soon lay above us out the viewport like a bright blue jewel, faintly speckled with white clouds. Land areas were scattered and generally too small to be seen from orbit. We informed the protodolphins of our arrival, and received the message: "Everyone may emplanet. You will be here for several weeks. Bring the cat-creature."

It was rare to leave a rollship completely uncrewed, but it was not unheard of. The captain shut it down, pulled the Lume module and loaded it and all of us into the cargo shuttle, where the crew clustered as far from Tynnanna as possible.

We were guided by beacon to a small land mass in the northern hemisphere, where the planet's only spaceport had been established. I'd met with Glon in one of the reception rooms of the spaceport's building the first time I'd come here.

As we came in I could see several boats moored at the end of a long dock just downwind of the landing area.

I'd only met Glon before, but there were at least twenty other members of his species in the water near the boats, calling to us in that strange, happy chirping of theirs and pointing with long noses at a pile of translator bugs on the dock.

We waited for Tynnanna to stop tearing around, ecstatic to be on a planet again, and then we trooped to the dock and fitted the translators into our ears.

At once the chirping ceased, and Glon introduced himself, rising out of the water to balance on his tail and bow, sleekly beautiful with seawater streaming down his silvery coat. I introduced all the members of our party, and the protodolphin bowed to each in turn, but did not introduce his own companions.

Instead he said, "We have arranged some recreation for al

of you. Weighty matters can make people very weighty themselves, and then misjudgments can occur due to too much sobriety. Captain, if you and your crew members will follow my cousin Tlip to the schooner at the far end of this row—the Carva Archipelago is just beyond the southern horizon, and she will be happy to escort you there."

The Carva Archipelago was known throughout the Com as a near paradise. The captain looked at Jemeret and me, uncertain.

"Your ship will be fine, Captain," Glon said reassuringly. "We have always had the highest respect for ships and the men and women who sail them. You deserve shore leave. You are overdue for it, I believe."

I was always astonished at how much this species knew about the details of life in the Com, when they never left their waterworld and seemed, on meeting, so utterly carefree.

"Go on," Jemeret said. "I'm sure you'll be safe."

Tlip leaped once from the water and swam off in the direction of the schooner, and the captain and crew of the *Detralume*, some of the latter grinning with open delight, followed along the dock toward the vessel.

Glon chattered with pleasure at their happiness, then swung his sleek head back in our direction. "Ronica McBride, Jemeret Cavanaugh, if you will bring your cat-creature onto the yawl here, my mate, Flas, and I will be happy to guide you to the Arc Isle."

"Where are the others going?" Jemeret asked, glancing at the five remaining talents and Mortel John, who looked more than a little uncomfortable so much removed from his accustomed circumstances.

"We have places prepared for them at an island resort called Chamba," Glon answered readily enough. "Some of my other cousins will care for them."

We led Tynnanna up the gangplank onto the boat, and he looked at us as if to ask doubtfully, "Now what's this?" The boat was beautiful and in excellent condition. Jemeret pathfound the control panel at the rear of the aft mast while I settled Tynnanna in the midships, deeming him too large for the bow.

When Jemeret had cast off and raised the sails on both masts, he came forward to sit with me on the bulkhead, because the course was preprogrammed.

The day was perfectly beautiful, the wind warm, the waves gentle, and the deep blue of the sky nearly bottomless, with stray puffs of high white clouds. The sun was a slightly more golden yellow than I'd grown accustomed to on Caryldon, but then, it had been fall and winter while I was there, and this was a world where winter clung only to the poles and where the rest of the planet bloomed radiantly in perpetual summer.

Glon and Flas swam along by the prow of the yawl, chattering to one another in nonsense patterns that the translator interpreted to us as singing. I felt the sun begin to bake the tension out of me and glanced at Jemeret, hoping it would do the same for him. For long moments he still seemed lost in thought, and then he drew in a deep breath that expanded his broad chest almost to the point where it threatened to split his jumpsuit. He let it out convulsively, turned his face toward me and said, "Wouldn't you rather get rid of these clothes? I would." He levered himself to his feet and stripped with the efficient movements I remembered so well from Caryldon and hadn't seen lately. When he was entirely naked, he pulled me to my feet and stripped me as well, because I hadn't moved. The wind felt wonderful on my skin, even though I was slightly embarrassed at being undressed in the open air and sunlight. Glon and Flas appeared not to have noticed.

Jemeret and I lay side by side on the deck, hands entwined, bathed in the warm sun and the wind of our passage, and I think I must have dozed. The yawl drawing to a stop woke me. Jemeret was already sitting up, rubbing his eyes, and I knew he'd slept, too. It felt like the first natural sleep in a long time.

The boat had entered a wide, semicircular lagoon lined by a soft, sandy beach rising gently to a riot of tropical foliage and a small cottage, its porch open to the lagoon. The island itself stretched away behind the cove in the long arc that gave it its name, ascending to a spine of three distant peaks that were probably volcanic in origin. Bright multicolors sparkled in the trees as birds danced on the air.

Glon flashed through the water beside the hull, chirping to us. Our translators said, "We have brought no one from off-world to the Arc Isle before, but we thought you would enjoy it here, and the depth and serenity of the lagoon will let us be in the same space together."

Flas spun upward beside her mate and asked shyly, "Do you swim?"

Jemeret, beside me, turned toward me curiously. "Do you?"

"I was taught how," I said, and before I could add how long ago it had been, he'd scooped me up, his eyes twinkling with mischief, and pitched me over the rail into the warm, salty water. I came up sputtering and pushing hair out of my eyes, in time to see him climb onto the rail and dive downward, cutting the water neatly about two feet to my left. The protodolphins gave a series of trills which the translator interpreted as laughter.

A huge splash on the other side of the boat told us that Tynnanna had decided to join us, and all four of us swam around the prow to make sure he was all right. The klawit paddled right past us, stalked up on the pristine beach, shook himself several times to begin drying his thick, shaggy coat, then marched off the sand onto the green of the upper beach, sat, and began meticulously to wash himself.

Jemeret turned in the water until he was facing Glon. "Why did you separate us from the others?" he asked.

"There are many things to be said," Glon answered, "and they should be said only to and between the two of you. And besides, you've spent no time alone, just you, since you met. We thought you deserved some time together."

"How do you know that?" I asked him. "How does all the information from the Com get to you? We always used to wonder."

The trill of laughter came again. "We'll tell you later in your stay," he said. "Come around to this side of the lagoon. Flas, show them where the shelf is."

Flas dived and leaped up, cutting through the placid water toward the cottage and pausing what seemed to be about ten meters out from the water line. We swam over after her and discovered a shelf of rock covered with a thin layer of sand jutting out from the island and lying a little way below the surface. Jemeret pulled himself onto it and leaned back on his elbows. I slid onto it beside him, on my stomach, suddenly remembered that I was still naked, and gasped a little. The two protodolphins were another sentient species, and somehow it didn't seem right.

Jemeret sensed my embarrassment and laughed softly. "Clothes are what's alien here, love. They won't think less of you. They'll hardly notice."

Tynnanna finished his bath, roared once, and trotted off toward the interior of the island. "Is there anything for him to eat here?" I asked, worried.

"There are wild pigs far inland, where the mountains begin," Flas said. "The population should really have been culled two months ago, but we waited so the klawit could do it."

"You knew we were coming two months ago." Jemeret was not asking a question.

"We had decided to send for you as soon as we received the message that you were back in the Com," Glon said. "I have always remembered our first meeting, Ronica McBride, and it seems to me that we have more to explore with one another."

"I'm hungry," Flas announced. "Let's go fishing."

Glon trilled again and flung himself after her, silver streak slicing through the deep blue-green water and out of the cove. Jemeret climbed to his feet. "Let's see what's in the cottage," he said, holding out his hand to pull me up.

We walked barefoot across the expanse of sand, noticing that it must be nearing late afternoon from the position of the sun, but that the temperature did not appear to be dropping much. The sunset would be to the far left of us, and I suspected it would be glorious. The cottage was just slightly bigger than our bedroom at Stronghome. It contained a large four-poster bed with thick feather bolsters and pillows, a table and chairs, and a sideboard heaped with bowls of fresh fruit and a few loaves of fresh bread. A large carafe of water and some tall, thin glasses stood on the table. I said, "I can't imagine what the Archipelago's like if they call that paradise and not this."

"You heard Glon. Nobody comes here." He turned toward me, drew me up against his body and tucked my head under his chin. "This is an honor they're giving us. And he's right, you know. We haven't had any time to ourselves."

I felt him growing aroused, smiled, raised my face to his. The bed was incredibly soft and yielding around us, and the loving was the best it had been since the night before he invoked my memory of killing Kray and plunged us into the tangle of politics and purpose that had occupied us ever since.

Lying with him in the gentle embrace of the bolsters, I felt the quiet warmth of the man I'd come to love, and I said spontaneously, "This is a wonderful place to make a baby."

His arm tightened around me. "I don't want a child of mine born in the Com."

"It takes a while to conceive," I said against his chest, "even with talent, and then it takes nine months to carry."

"I know the biology," Jemeret said dryly. "I don't know how long we're going to be off Caryldon. I don't know if we're going to live through what happens."

"Have faith," I said to him. "We're ordinary people, after all, Jemeret, and ordinary people don't necessarily have the choices we do. You said you'd impregnate me when I was ready."

"Don't twist my words," he warned, laughing in spite of himself. "I said I wouldn't impregnate you *until* you were ready."

"It's the same thing," I argued, and I stung him, obviously, but as persuasively as I could. I'd never dared to do such a thing before.

He was surprised and challenged at the same time, and in a moment he had rolled me onto my back and brought his weight over on top of me. "Stop pushing me!" he ordered, amusement breaking through his attempt to be stern.

I was unstoppable. "They say if you repress sperm for a long period of time, it may not come back. Let's see if it does."

"It will, I assure you," he said, pressing down hard to keep me from wriggling.

"Prove it."

"Stop tempting me."

"No."

He distracted me mercilessly until I dropped the sting, then snapped his shields up and thrust himself into me with a determined need that quite left me breathless.

We ate some of the bread and fruit, watching the sunset, then wandered back down to the shelf and sat in the warm, lapping water, waiting to see if Glon and Flas would return, but they did not that night, or the next two days. The fourth day they swam back into the lagoon at sunset, chirping greetings at us.

Before they could begin a conversation, Jemeret said seriously, "Glon I want to thank you for this. I didn't think we needed it until you gave it to us."

Glon danced up on the water, trilling, and Flas circled around him, rubbing against his smooth skin, both of them clearly delighted. Then they raised their heads and forequarters onto the shelf beside us.

"We'll talk this evening," Glon said to Jemeret, "then leave you for another few days, then return and talk again."

Flas nudged her nose against my thigh as if to silently confirm what her mate was saying.

Glon rolled a little so he could see both of us with his near eye. "Our major difference as species," he said, "is that you leave footprints and we don't. We are part of our world, and we don't mar it by our living on it. You, on the other hand, have made your worlds conform to the lives you choose to live. That's what makes you human."

"Do you condemn us for it?" I asked.

"Phosfor, no," he answered at once. "It's your characteristic as a race. Humans leave footprints or they believe no one will ever know they were there. All through your lives as a species you have done this, and you will go on doing it." He fastened his bright, somehow all-knowing eye on Jemeret. "Do you know that in a sea change, creatures die? It's the way of things."

I stopped watching Jemeret to concentrate on what the protodolphin was saying.

"Yes," Glon said, as if he'd received a response, "when your race decided to change ours, many of our nonsentient cousins could not make the transition, and while we wept for them, we let them go because we had to." He made a gentle coughing sound, which I thought was the equivalent of clearing his throat. "When we evolved again, here, many of our people could not mutate as the rest of us did, and they, too, passed away. We are the descendants of those who were successful in the evolution."

I said slowly, "You evolved again?"

"About a hundred and fifty years ago," he said, his eye rolling toward me. "About the same time you were due to develop talent throughout your species."

"In what way did you evolve?" Jemeret asked quietly.

Flas moved a little closer to me, her nose more firmly against my leg.

"Evolution of a sentient species," Glon said, "is likely to be related to the development of the brain. We can see what we choose to see. You should eventually be able to do what you choose to do. But there are costs. Many of us could not learn to process the incoming information volitionally and were overwhelmed, lost sanity and perished. Those who could learn survived and bred." He paused briefly.

"What do you mean, see what you choose to see?" I asked.

Glon said, "Just that. You will choose to do because you leave footprints. We choose to see because we do not. If I choose to see what's happening on the Nogdala world you just left, I can. If I choose to see what is happening in the Tribunal chamber on Orokell, I can. Sometimes I choose to see nothing at all, but many of us watch different things at different times."

Flas said, "I watched you being healed, Ronica McBride, and I was touched beyond my ability to say. I was the one who told my mate he had to bring you here, we had to help you."

Jemeret nodded very slowly. "That's how you knew the key phrase to get us here. You saw us use it on Caryldon."

Glon chattered his approval.

I asked, "Does anyone in the Com know you can do this?"

He trilled with laughter. "Why would we want to tell them?"

he asked in return. "So they could try to use us the way they have exploited you? No, I think not."

"Then why are you telling us?" Jemeret asked.

"You will not tell anyone," Glon said firmly. "But perhaps we can help you."

"Can you tell us where to find Dolen T'Kelle?" I asked. "You know what he was doing?"

"We saw it," Flas said sadly.

"We would only be able to tell you where he was if he entered a 'where' we were watching," Glon said. "We see in places, not in individuals. It is astronomical sight, rather than anthropomorphic."

"Then how do you think you might be able to help us?" Jemeret asked.

"You have been agonizing over the deaths, because some of them were innocent, but if your species is to evolve, those who cannot make the transition will die. If they do not, then the evolution will fail, and other species will, inevitably, take your niche."

Flas said, "Growth is what creates life. The Com has stopped your growth from occurring."

"There are two choices," Glon said. It had grown dark, and the great bowl of starlit sky arched overhead, making a million lights in the gently moving water and reflecting brightly from the sleek skins of the pair.

"The first choice," Flas said, "is to try to convince them that they are wrong. It will take a very long time, and you may fail, but it may work, and then the sea change will occur, as it must if all are not to sink downward in entropy and perish."

"The second choice," Glon said, "is to force the change yourself, which has the potential to succeed, or to create chaos, or both."

"That's what I've wanted to do," Jemeret said. "That's what I've been ripping myself up about."

"We'll talk about it again in a few days," Glon said. "Relax in the meantime, and enjoy yourselves. There's nothing happening off-world that you need to worry about just now." He slipped down off the shelf into the water, and Flas followed gracefully.

"Wait," I called after them. "If you've evolved further, we shouldn't be calling you protodolphins."

"Yes, you should," Glon called back, "at least where anyone else can hear you. But we call ourselves 'water people.' " They leaped up, dived under, and were gone.

Jemeret and I sat still in the shallow water for a few minutes, then went back to the cottage. Jemeret was smiling, and it was a different kind of smile than I'd seen on him before.

"What is it?" I asked.

"This is a fine world, and these are fine friends."

"They see," I said wonderingly. "What an amazing adaptation."

"It would cause me boundless despair," my lord said.

We sat down on the front steps. "Why?" I asked him.

"To see what was wrong and to be able to do nothing to put it right? That must be agonizing." He put his arm around me and drew me against him. "I think that may be one of the reasons they asked us to come."

I remembered Glon saying, "You should be able to do what you choose to do," and I guessed that he thought it vitally important to give us the chance that had not been given to them.

"Do you think," I asked, "that they'll tell us what they want us to do?"

"I don't know." His voice was quiet, almost carried away by the delicate breeze. "It'll be interesting to find out."

We explored some of the island with the time available the next day, walking at the edges of the undergrowth because no obvious paths into the jungle presented themselves and we were reluctant to begin ripping our way through the foliage without clothing on. When we returned to the cottage to eat more of the fruit, which was delicious, I was wishing I had my nomidar, but it had remained on *Detralume*.

"Do you want to explore further this afternoon?" I asked.

He shook his head.

"What would you like to do?"

His warm gray eyes glowed at me. "I think I'd like us to try to make a baby," he said.

I stung him lightly to see if he was completely serious about it. He assured me that he was. "I brought my sperm count back up to normal this morning." He was grinning at me now. "You are sure about this, aren't you?" It didn't sound like a question when he said it, but I knew it was.

"I am," I said. "What made you change your mind?"

"After yesterday, somehow, absurdly, I'm more optimistic than I was. The Com is not the barrier I perceived. The water people have breached it. Perhaps we can, too." He grew more serious. "Then, too, I recognize the danger here. If something should happen to me, there would still be a part of me—" I covered his mouth with my hand. I wouldn't think about that, wouldn't tell him I had resolved to do everything I could to stop him from committing suicide, even if his death was the cost of success.

Something kept us from using our stings when we made love that day. We didn't discuss it. I've tried to figure out why I decided it was the right time, but I can't say why I chose when to do the things I did, except for those few things Dolen T'Kelle explained later. I just decided.

Jemeret was as happy as I'd ever seen him. "Do you realize," he'd said to me that morning, "that since I won the Boru from Brenadel nearly twenty-five years ago, this is the first time I've been completely free from responsibilities?"

"I was supposed to have had no time completely free, ever, once I graduated," I said softly. "If they gave you this, you gave it to me." And I thought, as I said it, that he'd truly given me everything.

In the evening, just before the rich beauty of the sunset began to streak the slowly gathering clouds with color, Glon and Flas drew themselves up onto the shelf and chirped greetings. We settled beside them and resumed the conversation where it had broken off days earlier.

"You see," Glon said, "we discuss your situation among ourselves. We feel we owe you a debt. If you had not created our forebears, we would not have come into existence. We would like to try to repay a little of that debt."

Jemeret had rested a hand on my thigh. Now he laid his other hand on Glon's head. "I have wanted to force the change since I first broke Com training and went back to Caryldon. I believe in talent with my entire being. My problem is not knowing what might be effective."

Flas trilled. "Once you fit the pieces together, it will be there for you to see."

I watched Jemeret frown. "My only idea was to try to turn off the MIs, and that seemed impossible without the active cooperation of about a dozen core worlds and a government that lives on the machines."

"That isn't a true answer," Glon said, shaking his head slowly under Jemeret's hand. "It comes from without. True answers come from within."

Jemeret seemed to think about that for a time, then said slowly, "It still seems logical to me. You've evolved without technology, and we're evolving without technology on Caryldon."

"But you're a technological species," Glon protested definitively. "We are not. And you are not *only* evolving on Caryldon. You are just, at this point in time, evolving best there. You built a social structure there which welcomes the development of talent, supports it, disciplines it, and molds it in ways that contribute to a healthy human society. Oh yes, the social structure is good, and necessary for human development. It lacks only one thing, and that is some judicious technology."

Jemeret stared at him. "But technology kills talent."

Flas wriggled a little. She seemed to be enjoying herself as much as her mate was. "Not the technology," she said. "The uses to which the technology is put."

"Think in those terms," Glon urged. "Think in terms of the things you've been learning about yourselves, and about your talent, and about the human species. Especially you, Ronica McBride. Try to break the barriers you built in yourself. Think without walls. There are solutions, but you cannot find them if you fear too much to act."

Confused, I said stubbornly, "But Caryldon is the only place the starfire comes to in a form if its own, even if it borrows other bodies to speak with in other places. I thought it came to us on Caryldon because that world has no technology. We need the starfire, and it's physically either in Lumespace, where it lives, or visiting the Samothen."

"Ah," Glon said. "Two things are wrong in your thinking. Caryldon has eftels, which are the highest form of technology, even though there are very few of them. And—come swim with us. Jemeret Cavanaugh, hold on to my fin. We want to go faster than you can go by yourself." It seemed a non sequitur. Nevertheless, Jemeret slipped off the shelf into deep water and put his hand on Glon's dorsal fin.

"Come," Flas urged me. I dropped into the warm caress of the lagoon and took hold of Flas's fin. With a wriggle of pleasure, she sped off through the water after Glon and Jemeret. Soon we were out of the semicircle of the lagoon and skirting the edge of the Arc Isle, moving around it until the mountain spine was directly to our left. We continued racing through the swells, the wind and spray in my face making me close my eyes. I opened them again quickly when I realized the sunset had faded gently away into the blues of evening, and the first pinpoints of silver light were appearing in the bowl of sky overhead. This was the time of the starfire ceremonies.

Before we reached the apex of the arc of Arc Isle, the water people drew us into what appeared to be the dark entrance to a cave, but in less time than I'd imagined it would take to change worlds, we'd entered a grotto lighted by the eerie, cool green phosphorescence we associate with the ocean deeps. Except that both Jemeret and I knew that this light, which streamed out of the rocks themselves, was something both utterly alien and utterly familiar. It was starfire.

"We call it phosfor," Glon said, as if I'd spoken my thought aloud. "It gave us courage to continue to grow when so many of us were failing. At first, back in those early times, those who would never come to be like us—or those who were a little like we would come to be, but not enough—turned against the newcomers. Every species thinks that 'different' is bad. The phosfor helped our ancestors overcome the enmity of their cousins in order to be fully who they would become."

"I used to think the difference of talent was to be better than anyone else," I said, a whisper in an atmosphere that reminded me most strongly of the cave in the shoulder of Zuglith. "That's what I was taught in the School for Talent on Werd. But I learned that the difference of talent is just to be different."

"You see, you *do* know what you have learned," Flas chirped happily.

Glon nodded emphatically. "You are contained by the past," he said. "We made the same errors. You cannot do what you did when you are no longer who you were."

Jemeret looked at me, the faintly green tinge of the light making his eyes glow. "You said it at the Com banquet," he said quietly. "We cannot continue to do with talent only the things we did without it." The echo of the words from Orokell reverberated in the small space.

"Why do I have to keep relearning things I thought I already knew?" I demanded of no one in particular.

Glon laughed. "Because they're difficult things," he answered, "and they don't conform to old rules. You haven't memorized the new rules yet."

"All right, then," Jemeret said. "We can't do the old things, and we haven't discovered what the new ones are. What do we do?"

I didn't hear what, or whether, Glon replied. I swam away from the three of them, treading water at the edge of the grotto wall, thinking about the starfire in this new form of light, not red, white, gold, or blue, but this odd, vibrant green. Once again, as I had before, I was overtaken by the urge to sting the strangely welcoming but alien life-form, and I was reaching out toward it in fascination when Jemeret suddenly shouted, breaking my concentration with a surge of his own sting, shaking me. I lost my balance in the water and went under, coming up sputtering, to find his hands gripping me tightly.

"I told you never to do that!" he said, too loudly for the grotto's space, and yet the sound seemed muffled. "You can call it, or you can pray to it, but for the sake of all you value in this life, you mustn't sting it!"

"Then tell me why not," I said, coughing up water and pushing my hair out of my eyes. Glon and Flas had drawn back, their rounded heads turned toward one another.

Jemeret's hands relaxed their pressure. "Later," he said.

Glon said, "Look."

We turned toward the wall of the grotto and saw a long tendril of the green light extending from the phosphorescence toward us, above our heads, its size and shape and the quality of its movement infinitely familiar. I moved toward it and reached up; it descended, coiling, around my arm, rose along my cheek and stroked my face. I felt the incredible upwelling of joy that always filled me when the starfire came. A second tendril elongated outward and lay its end against Jemeret's forehead in the familiar gesture I'd first seen in the bowl at Convalee. Then the two tendrils came together, and a brilliantly white light shot outward from them. They entwined and entangled around themselves repeatedly for a half minute, and then the tendrils were reabsorbed into the glowing grotto wall. Something splashed downward into deep water. It was a message, unspoken, but real nonetheless, and I felt that if we could only understand it, it would reveal a great deal to us.

Flas dived underwater after whatever had fallen, and a short while later resurfaced with a metal chain draped over her nose. She swam it to Jemeret. I knew before I paddled over to him that it was starfire metal, and, like the metal of the brow-crown I'd left behind on Caryldon, some of the starfire's light seemed strangely, obscurely, trapped below the surface.

I reached out and pathfound it, as I knew Jemeret must have, and found that the links could be opened on command. The chain was too big and heavy to be a necklace or a waist cincher, but after a moment I thought I'd guessed its purpose. "It's a collar for Tynnanna."

Jemeret nodded. "I agree. I think the starfire—" He paused,

acknowledging the water people. "—the phosfor wants us to have a way to call it while we're out here in the Com."

Flas trilled once, and Glon said, "Come. We'll take you back to the lagoon now."

We grasped their fins and rode back around the island. When we were at the lagoon shelf, in full starlight, broken only by a few stray clouds, Glon laid a flipper on my leg as if to be sure he had my attention. "You see," he said, "what you have to remember is that most mutations fail."

Jemeret leaned back on his elbows in the shallow water. "About ninety-nine percent, I think, but all the analyses I've read have been far from certain. The number could be even larger."

"Play it out in your mind, then," Flas said. "How many incipient talents has the Com stamped out as rogue? How few were they, truly? How long has this government trusted only talent from Caryldon, while repressing or exiling its own? How many of the talents they trusted have they destroyed?"

"How many," Glon chimed in, "do you think there ever *were*?"

"Cut off all the new shoots, and eventually the orchid dies," Flas said, swaying in the water.

I was thinking about everything that we'd determined about talent, and I looked over at Jemeret through the pale light, remembering the things I'd learned in the Com. "Sandalari's learning to pathfind, and now I have Mortel John trying to teach her to sting, too. You said there are only degrees of power, not separate types."

"Go on."

I was reasoning it out. "If gathering and pathfinding and stinging aren't really entirely separate operations ..." There was another level to my thoughts, and I was trying to reach it when Jemeret, who was not as thoroughly indoctrinated in the training of the Com as I was, got there.

"You mean, if it's all one single process, without divisions, then what if it can actually all be done at the same time?" He looked at the water people, but I knew he wasn't seeing them.

And I gasped. "Jemeret, I *have* been doing it all at the same time," I said, feeling as utterly stupid as I've ever been. "We all have. We think that the lowest form of talent supports the higher forms, but when I took Shantiah and the other women through the Ladder of the Warrior, I was projecting to them, controlling my moves, and pathfinding the blade simultaneously. It all seemed so natural, and I never thought, not once, that I'd been taught to think of them each as separate and distinct behaviors."

Jemeret said, "When we get back to the *Detralume*, we can get Coney, Sandalari, Lendo, and Sinet involved with it, too. I wish they all had larger reserves. We still don't know what prompts the development of reserves."

"What *do* you know?" Glon asked, bouncing a little with suppressed excitement.

"The MIs analyzed the combination of reserves and training as responsible for about seventy-five percent of developed talent in the presence of the genetic alteration," I said, "and they didn't have a guess as to what would account for the other twenty-five percent, which could, I suppose, affect reserve size."

"How many fully developed talents—that is, fully realized mutations—are there in the Com?" Flas asked. "Or on Caryldon, for that matter?"

"Three in the Com at this moment," I answered. "Jasin Lebec, Jemeret, and me. How many planetside, Jemeret?"

"I don't pretend to be able to guess," my lord answered slowly. "Venacrona is, I think, perhaps not as fully powerful any longer, but certainly as skilled. Lyrafi and some of the Dibel, maybe. To some extent, all of the priests and priestesses. I'd say that everyone else is at a lower level of accomplishment, even Ashkalin, who would like to be stronger but never could—"

Glon interrupted him. "And so what are the common factors? You and Ronica McBride and Jasin Lebec, and your Venacrona and your Dibel and your priests. What is the unity?"

I couldn't fit Jasin Lebec into my impulsive thought for a time, and then memory dredged up my very first meeting with him, and his confession—more than ten years and two lifetimes ago—that he'd tried to study voice but had to give it up. I heard myself say wonderingly, "It's music. The last twenty-five percent, the key factor for reserve development, is music."

Jemeret looked at me closely for a moment or two, and then slowly nodded. "It's logical," he said. "The study of music could build pathways in the brain that something else might not. Mathematics could have, too, I suppose, but we don't study that anymore out here. We gave it to the MIs to do for us."

"We gave a lot to the MIs," I said softly.

"So, what would you like to take back?" Glon asked.

Some of the clouds had gathered together near the apex of the mountains of the Arc Isle, and they made a low, rumbling sound.

Flas slid off the shelf into deep water and leaped up. "We better go now," she said. "You have a lot to think about." Glon trilled a happy farewell and swam out beside her.

Jemeret and I stayed in the shallow water, silent, with our own thoughts for a time, until I roused myself as a bolt of lightning cracked from the cloud to one of the mountain summits. "We'd better get out of the water," I said.

We climbed up onto the warm sand, but there was still no sign of rain, so we stayed there. After a while I asked him, "Will you tell me now why you're so determined that I should not sting the starfire?"

He remained silent as the clouds continued to gather, and when the warm tropical darkness hid the fact that we were lying on soft sand beside the gently lapping water, Jemeret told me at last how he'd lost his father, how Jasin Lebec had lost his son. Sometime during the story there was a quiet trilling in the water of the lagoon. Jemeret let down his shields in the telling, allowing me to share the pain it still gave him, after all these years.

"It was my last year in the Samothen, before the Com took me to train," he said. "I was probably about five, and we were at war with the people who became the Ilto and the Vylk. They were like us—Samothen—but with so little obvious power that they could waver between either side in the civil war we were fighting against the Honish. Sometimes they were split into factions leaning one way or another or both simultaneously. We of the Boru, on the other hand, were fairly well-established. We just weren't settled in Stronghome yet. The Com surveyors found the valley when they decided on a location for the spaceport, and we went to it, because it was a good, defensible location for the tribe to be. Veen told me that the surveyors' desire to have us there, guarding the spaceport, had nearly made Chief Brenadel decide against it, but Veen had convinced him that balking the surveyors wasn't enough of a reason to disregard something good for the tribe."

He began idly to gather up handfuls of sand and let the grains drift out the heel of his hand as he spoke. "We had been living just northeast of the Plain of Convalee, near the Forge, and we loaded the wagons and headed north. There were about 450 Boru then, and my mare and sire and I had the lead wagon. My sire was a very powerful man. I almost think my mare finds it hard to forgive me for my power. I'm too much like he was, and she lost him because of the power." His hand kept up its steady movement. The small tower of sand beneath it reached its equilibrium height, and all the additional grains rolled gently off.

"The trip north was relatively uneventful. I'm told there were a couple of small raids. Our men beat them back. But it meant they were tracking us, preparing, watching. Venacrona had one of the starfire bowls, and he confirmed that the starfire approved our relocation to Stronghome, so we were probably a little overconfident, perhaps a little careless, I don't know. Lead wagon became last wagon when we reached the track, and my sire, Venacrona, and a few of the guards formed the protective barrier, so they took the brunt of the attack that caught them on the lower reaches of the climb."

It was very dark now; a veil of cloud dimmed most of the starlight. I could have irised my eyes out to see better, but I sensed Jemeret needed to be alone with his memory, and I gave him that privacy.

"It wasn't even an overwhelming fight," he went on. "I

watched it from the wagon. We had prowess with weapons, and we had power. I honestly think we would probably have won anyway, but my sire became impatient with the time it was taking. I saw him snatch the starfire bowl away from Venacrona. I felt him gather, and I felt him reach out with the sting. Venacrona shouted at him not to, but he ignored it. He stung the starfire. I went on watching."

He was quiet for several breaths, the tower of sand growing and sinking, growing and sinking. I didn't move. The tone of his voice hadn't changed when he resumed speaking. "For a split second it looked as if nothing had happened, and then he swelled up like a bladder being filled with water, and he burst apart as if the cells of his body couldn't contain the force pouring into them, ripping them outward, into shreds of tissue, into molecules. My mare started screaming, shrieking unbelievable curses at the starfire, at the attackers, at my sire. It was horrible, but it wasn't the worst of it." I couldn't picture the cool, emotionless Alissa crying out in fury or despair; I could hardly picture Jemeret's stony face as he disgorged the story in a steady narrative, as if it had lost its ability to stir him, or had so worn him out in the past that now he could only tell it without emotion.

"The worst was that the starfire's power spread outward overwhelmingly, carrying my sire's dying emotions to any of us who could feel them, augmented by a vastness, a might I still find unimaginable. It was a searing pain beyond anything I knew, except that—the starfire is our creator. I still believe in it. I still pray to it. But when my sire stung it, it became a destroyer. It annihilated him utterly, instantly."

He seemed to remember I was there. His hand opened and all the sand dropped at once, flattening the tower. I felt his eyes focus on me. "That's not going to happen to you."

The water people made a rippling sound.

"I understand," I said softly, sharing both his pain and his fear for me. "I won't— Don't worry about it, Jemeret. We have other things to worry about now."

XIV. Among the Exiles

Glon and Flas gave us some more days alone on the Arc Isle, and with the knowledge that we would soon be leaving making the time all the more precious, we reveled in it. Jemeret seemed pleased that I'd been able to make a guess at the last requirement for reserve growth; he hadn't known the critical bit of information about his grandfather's attempts to study voice when he was younger.

Now we thought that our nomidar playing had not merely been the result of our projective abilities and reserve capacity; it had been a spur in their development. Lying on our backs on the soft bolster during the last night we would spend on Sargasso, we talked about the possibility of teaching Coney to play an instrument, or whether it was necessary to offer the same training to Sandalari, who already sang. We wondered whether that training would make a difference now that both were adults, largely formed. I remarked how angry the Com would be if it ever learned it had been efficiently discouraging something that fostered the very characteristics it desired.

Jemeret nodded. "They acted to try to mold talent in the ways they wanted without ever discovering what the most effective things to do were. They destroyed a great many of us by it."

I rolled over so I pressed against his side. "We aren't them, and you know we can't be them." I felt his dissent, corrected myself. "All right, we can be them, but we mustn't."

"We mustn't let *them* go on being them," he said softly. "That's one of the things that's got to change if talentless humanity is to have any chance of surviving."

I was warmed by the thought. "We know how to change people's *minds*," I said. "How do we change the minds of machines?" And the idea occurred to me, seemingly impossible, yet so alluring that I had to follow it. Jemeret rose with me, watching me carefully. "Help me think it out," I said. "Pathfinding is like diagnosis of what's wrong with things or how they're supposed to work. We can't pathfind a living creature. So we have the sting for that, for probing and influencing living things. It's the very first lesson the Com taught me, yes?"

"Go on."

I looked at him, suddenly so hungry that I can't imagine what my face looked like. "Jemeret, have you ever tried to sting a machine?"

He understood at once. "Only Mortel John," he said. "And all my sting showed me was that it could access just a part of him. Once I pathfound for the rest, I just withdrew. I never tried to influence. It never occurred to me."

Machines were easily pathfound and usually easily comprehended. If they were broken, we could physically fix them. They did one thing for one purpose, and even the most complex broke down into smaller systems that did one thing for one purpose. Those systems broke into components that yielded to the same kind of analysis. I truly believed my nomidar had a soul, but it was not the same kind of soul a human being had, nor did it have a mind. The planet I'd pathfound had had a soul of sorts as well, ponderous and stupid compared to the quickness of a technological system, but it had also had no mind. There would never be any reason to try to sting something like that.

The MIs were different.

"If we figure out how to do effective pathfinding and stinging simultaneously," Jemeret said slowly, "then—" He stopped, and I felt a crush of disappointment wash through him. "I don't think we can try it with the MIs."

I knew what he was thinking. The MIs were a group consciousness of tremendous size and power, not unlike the starfire, though less than it in some important ways. Our reserves were too minuscule compared to that. We would only be able to open the channel between us and our target, and the chances were it would suck us dry and discard us. It would be like stinging the starfire, which I now knew frightened Jemeret for very good reasons. "There has to be a way," I said stubbornly. "All we have to do is find it."

It seemed to me that we were always discovering perfectly obvious questions we had not asked yet. As soon as we were together again at the shuttle, Tynnanna looking well-fed and even more rested than the rest of our party, I went straight to Mortel John and demanded, "How many rogue talents—besides the man M'Cherys—have been identified by the Com and exiled?"

"Three," he answered promptly, looking at me with no discernible expression. Since the destruction of the Macerates, only Jasin Lebec and Lendo Dell had been speaking to him, though I was sure Sinet still shared his bed. I wondered if he would put my approach down to the long days on Sargasso, or if he conjectured that I might somehow have forgiven the MIs, and by osmosis, him as well. I wondered if he actually thought like that.

"Where were they sent?" I asked him, sounding more challenging than I'd intended.

"We always send them to Ananda, along with any followers," he said calmly. "Only broken talent is sent to Caryldon, if we cannot heal it. Talent that does not serve the Com is talent which must be exiled."

"How many all together, over the years?" I had to take my seat, because the shuttle lift signal chimed. Jemeret was listening closely.

"The man M'Cherys was the only one with a large army of followers," the cyborg said. "The first rogue went about seventy years ago, with fewer than five hundred adherents." Barely an adequate gene pool, I thought. "The second was thirty years ago, and there were only a few dozen followers, though I suspected at the time that some of them might have been rogues, as well. The third was just after you entered training, and over a thousand were exiled with her. Then M'Cherys, and 150,000. That, of course, was more than ten years back."

The shuttle lifted, and I felt a pang of regret at leaving this waterworld and its gentleness behind. Then Jemeret asked, "On what Com worlds did the other rogues originate?"

Mortel John turned an expressionless face toward him. "On Mokele and on Calendola," he said.

Jemeret looked at his grandfather. "No one power-tests children in the Com, do they?"

Jasin Lebec was phlegmatic. "It's a question of numbers, Jemeret. There are thousands of children born every day on the worlds of the Com, and to power-test them there was only me, with other assignments to perform. It was never an economically feasible choice."

"We define economics differently," Jemeret said shortly.

I looked over at Coney and Sandalari, who were sun-colored and smiling at one another. "Did you have a good rest?"

Coney nodded, and Sandalari blushed. Coney saw the blush and said to me, with amusement, "It seems my husband is pregnant."

I felt a pang of jealousy, even in my pleasure for her. "We'll have to be more careful of you, I suppose," I said, trying to make it sound like teasing, not envy.

"I'm not fragile," Sandalari answered, with the age-old defense of expectant mothers who want to go on doing everything they did before becoming cocoons. "I can pull my own weight in whatever comes along."

My hands twisted in my lap, and the seat field tried to contain them. I had not conceived yet, and it was a process I could not control internally, because the seed Jemeret planted in me was not subject to my commands, and once it left his body, it wasn't subject to his any longer, either. I put the thought aside; I would have to be patient.

The captain and crew also seemed rested, and laughed and talked with one another until they had to dock the shuttle and begin the reactivation of the Lumeship. Then they were suddenly serious, heavy with responsibility. The captain had told us he didn't understand where the sudden blessing of a holiday came from, but he was very grateful for it. The new crew members probably thought themselves the luckiest people in the Com.

Keli seemed to have reaped the least benefit from her stay on Sargasso. She appeared thinner and hollow-eyed, even though her skin color showed that she'd spent a lot of time outdoors. I caught her eye and smiled at her, stinging her a little to tell her once again that I didn't blame her for anything. She smiled back, but it was a weak smile.

We docked easily, and the crew piled out. Jemeret pathfound the ship quickly, though we had no reason to believe there was any danger now. Dolen T'Kelle was fleeing, not coming after us. Once the crew was at work, we took Tynnanna to the cargo hold and left him there. He was more content than he'd been since we left Caryldon. He curled up in a corner and, with a great sigh, went almost instantly to sleep.

Jemeret and I waited until the ship was in low watch, then went to Coney and Sandalari's cabin. When they let us in, Jemeret bubbled us at once, and I asked, "Coney, have you ever had any aspirations to be a musician?"

He stared at me. "Where did that come from?"

I explained.

Sandalari was nodding before I finished. "Of course," she said quickly. "That's why I can do more pathfinding than Coney. I sing the starsongs."

"I'll be damned," Coney said. "I suppose the starsongs should have been a clue all along."

"I've always thought of them more as prayers than as simply songs," Sandalari said, "but they are music, and they are very complex. They would in some ways resemble what other people would need to learn to play an instrument."

"We've all been dense when it comes to reading the clues." I was exasperated. "We just accepted that so many things were the way they were, when they weren't." I was beginning to think that was to be a recurrent theme in my life.

"Do you think I would be able to learn to play something at

this stage of my life?" Coney asked dubiously. "And if I did, do you think it would gain me anything?"

"We won't know unless you're willing to try," Jemeret replied. "If you are—"

"Of course I am," Coney interrupted.

"—then I can link with you and give you some of the fundamentals of musical theory by a combination of instruction and demonstration," Jemeret finished.

"Anytime you want," Coney said, nodding agreement.

"Let's get started," my lord said. "This is not going to be a quick process."

There were no roll points between Sargasso and Ananda, so Jemeret and I worked with Coney and Sandalari every day of the nine-day journey. Every day I had to fight to keep from going further into Sandalari's being and touching the spark of life she carried, as if I could see how she'd done it and duplicate it in myself, as if I could somehow catch pregnancy from her.

And every day I had to fight harder against the temptation to sting Mortel John. I hadn't tried it since I was a child, when he had stood against me so strongly. He told me that he'd taken a drug then to increase his resistance to me, and I had been, after all, only a child. Now, of course, I recognized that Mortel John was attached to the might of the MIs, and my sting would have had little effect on the bulk of the cyborg simply because of the sheer size and complexity of the brain I was attempting to affect. I thought, too, that the human part of him had cushioned me from stinging the MI part. Nor as a child would I have pathfound my way into the technological portion I didn't know was there. Mortel John's major concern back then was probably in not allowing me to hurt myself, rather than in fighting off any effect I might have been having on him. And now Jemeret was working hard to convince me that it would be unwise, to say the least, to sting an infinitely more powerful entity.

He must have sensed the growing need in me, but only asked me about it the night before we were due to reach Ananda orbit. We were curled together in the bed's field, but had turned it a little cooler than normal to dry the perspiration on our skin. He stroked the curve of my hip absently and said, "I think you'd better tell me what's been bothering you, love."

When you both have the sting, conversation doesn't take normal directions. I couldn't deny that anything was bothering me; he would have known I was lying at once, and then I would have had to justify or defend it. I couldn't ask why he thought anything was bothering me; I knew he could read every emotion I had.

There was no help for it. I either had to say no, I wouldn't tell him, or I had to tell him. "I can't help being tempted to try to sting Mortel John again."

He was so startled that his reaction escaped before he could contain it. "What's wrong with you? Why do you keep thinking you can sting, and get away with stinging, forces infinitely beyond your capacity? He's even less human now than he was fifteen years ago!"

"We'll have to somehow test—" I began.

He stung me to quiet until he'd bubbled us, reminding me we were no longer on Sargasso, where MI surveillance was nonexistent and we could say whatever we chose. When we were bubbled, he said, "Ronica, whatever we ultimately choose to do against the MIs is one scenario we will never be able to test. No matter what it is, we'll only be able to plan it and reap whatever consequences there are to it."

"Why not test it?" I demanded, irrational and insistent at the same time.

"Because it has to ultimately involve going in with our stings against a force that can kill us," he said flatly. "I suspect we'll never get a second chance if we waste a first one. That's why the planning is so important. The only way we might have any chance to succeed is to appear harmless even as we anticipate doing harm."

"Jemeret, if we wait until we're certain we have a workable scenario, we may never act at all," I said to him. "And you've been telling me you want to move quickly. It's completely contradictory."

"Life is a series of contradictions, love. Paradoxes have great truth in them." He was smiling. "Looked at logically, we have no chance at all. We'll die trying. But because we have to try, we *must* have a chance. So we'll plan it and do it." *No matter the ultimate cost* hung unsaid in the air.

"What if we're writing a waysong for humanity without talent?" I asked in a low voice. "That's very scary."

"It's more frightening to think of not doing it. Then it would mean a waysong for all of humanity—those without talent and those with it."

"Jemeret . . ." The word was quiet, but even I heard the charge in it. I found I didn't know how to say what I wanted to, hesitated, searching for words, hesitated again.

"Go on," he said finally.

I whispered it. "All my life, I was taught to rule by serving. It seems to me that's what this is."

"I don't have any argument with that."

"I would have given my life to it." I was still whispering. He watched me through narrowed eyes. "But I would have been alive. I don't know if I could give my life *for* it."

He pulled me close, his arms tightening around me. "We're going to make every effort to avoid that if we can."

"And if it can't be avoided unless we don't act?" The question was irresistible. When he didn't answer it, I read him, and what I read was so grim, so full of resolution, that I withdrew from it in despair. We both knew we would have to do something, sometime soon. We still didn't know what.

The captain of *Detralume* took the ship on a long sweep of the five continents of Ananda. It was a huge world, but old, and without heavy metals of any kind. The lightness of its core and mantle gave it near nominal gravity, and its extremely stable rotation meant there were no seasons to speak of, only climate belts. Two of the continents were uninhabited. The third contained the cities of the Anandans. The fourth had one spot of activity, where Anok Luttrell's people were building the spaceport that would serve as a landing point for the Scuttlers. The fifth continent, isolated by wide expanses of ocean and the energy barrier, was wasp-waisted, the masses joined by a narrow isthmus, and most of the exile population was spread on either side of that thin neck of land in two settlements, one agricultural, the other a fishing village. There was no technology of any kind on this continent, and the life-form survey found fewer than four thousand people. That bespoke an enormous loss of life since the exiles had been sent here.

The survey found herds of indigenous animals something like cattle, and coops of birdlike creatures much like geese. Houses were of the crude cabin variety, and the cultivated fields seemed to be just large enough to yield a subsistence living.

Jemeret and I took a lander to the temperate woodlands a distance away from the fields, beginning to sweep instantly for any hints of talent. It took several hours to read both villages, and when we were done, we compared notes. The population consisted largely of people with little or no talent, a few with fairly low levels of talent, and about a half dozen, all concentrated in one area of the agricultural settlement, with more significant amounts. It was apparent that no one thought to shield themselves—if they had developed the concept of shielding at all. It was also fairly evident that this world had very few resources.

"But it has enough to sustain more people than this," Jemeret observed, deeply disturbed. "What happened to them all?"

"We're going to have to go in to find out," I said. "Let's get started."

We piled underbrush around and over the lander, even though we thought it would probably be safe there. Then we headed in the direction of the agricultural settlement, where we'd felt the presence of the concentration of talent.

It was not a normal pattern. I'm not sure if I can explain what made it abnormal, but I need to try. On Caryldon, among the Boru or the Genda or the Marl, there was a comforting rightness about the feel of talent. It created an atmosphere, an environment in which I felt—once I stopped fighting it—entirely at home. It wasn't just Jemeret's immense power, though when I was falling in love with him, I was certain it was. Rather, it was a regular, ordered climate, generated by the discipline of many normal minds—normal, I suppose, for people with talent.

This continent of Ananda was unbalanced, disorderly. The flow of energy produced by the minds here, no matter their degree of talent, was undisciplined and unfocused, as if people armed with blasters were swinging them around wildly, never quite aware of when they were pressing the triggers.

We skirted the fields and the people working in them, slipped around the first of the cabins, more like shacks on closer observation, and made our way to the point where we would be closest to the building in which we thought to find those individuals with the most talent. I'd been trying to remember the unique signature of Ghefir M'Cherys, but it had been more than ten years ago, and at the time I had been so unsettled by the thought of someone like M'Cherys that I kept wanting not to remember anything about him. As we neared the houses in which the strongest concentration of power lay, I reached out to see if I recognized any of the minds.

"He could very well be dead," Jemeret said in muted tones. "It seems almost everyone is."

"I know."

"That's what happens when you throw people away, on a largely uninhabited world." He took my arm to hold me back for a second, moved one step in front of me. "They're left to their own resources, and they don't have many, not at the survival level."

The cabin had only one room, its logs aged and crudely shaped, its mismatched shingles covered with moss. Jemeret slid soundlessly to the window and looked inside. I saw his entire body stiffen, and when he turned toward me, he had paled.

With enough apprehension now to need to gather to slow my suddenly racing heart, I made myself move to the window. He grasped my shoulders in his hands and asked in a ragged whisper, "Is that M'Cherys?"

For a moment I couldn't grasp that what I was looking at was—or had once been—a human being. It had a head and a torso, but no limbs, and when the head swiveled with the characteristic unfocus of the blind, I saw that the eye sockets were empty. Nausea swept over me, unquenchable. Jemeret went on supporting my shoulders as I threw up into the low grasses beneath the window.

When the first spasms passed, he pulled me upright. "Get hold of yourself, Ronica," he said. "We don't have much time here." He spaced the next words, biting them off, strongly controlled. "Is that M'Cherys?"

"What's left of him."

"Come on. We have to get inside."

We sidled around the house to the door and let ourselves in.

The sightless head bobbled a little on its neck, the recumbent torso rocking slightly. The feel of uncontrolled talent was all around the room. Jemeret made one sharp sound. The head bobbled toward us and gave out some nonsense noises.

"They left his hearing," Jemeret said grimly. "That figures. Keep a watch for anyone coming. I'm going in to see if I can restore a bit of the sanity." He closed his eyes.

I was grateful he'd chosen to go in himself; he had far more experience with insane minds—mine, for example. I cast around us for approaching consciousness, but except for the other nodes of ungoverned talent in the nearby houses—and did they all look like this?—there was nothing.

After five minutes Jemeret opened his eyes. "M'Cherys."

The voice was rusty, harsh from disuse. "Who are you? Why did you bring me back to this?"

"I'll let you go again in a few minutes," my lord said. He nodded to me. Holding the deranged talent into some kind of rationality was too much effort for him to allow him to do the questioning as well.

I swallowed hard. "Think back, M'Cherys. What happened after the Com sent you here?"

"Here," the voice repeated. "They sent us here."

"And what happened?"

"False god," he said. "They were angry—wanted to punish me, and others like me. Not my fault."

I swallowed again, this time bile. "He was always weak and

passive," I said, holding tightly to my nerves. "He let them follow him."

"Who are you?" The rasping voice was sharper; the blind sockets aimed themselves at me. There were rheumy tears oozing from the edges of the blackened holes.

"Keep going," Jemeret said tightly.

"Why are there so few people left?" I asked.

"I had to defend myself," the voice answered. "Some remained loyal to me. We killed thousands of the others. But then there were simply too many. They took us."

"Why didn't they kill you?" I tried not to sound anguished. I hadn't wanted to talk to him the first time I'd met him, and I didn't want to be with him now. He was an affront to the whole idea of talent.

Jemeret read something from me, looked at me keenly for a split second, then returned his attention to the other occupant of the room.

"Too easy," M'Cherys was saying. "They saw how hard this world would be after what the Com was. They thought killing me would let me off too easy. If they had to suffer, they wanted me to suffer, too."

"What about the others?" I asked.

"The Com hated us, to send us here," M'Cherys replied. "The ones who didn't starve or die of weather sickness, they thought if they punished us enough, then the Com would forgive them. They said they were purifying us."

"Are the others like you, then?" It would have come out soundlessly if I hadn't forced myself to voice it.

"When they get old enough," he said. "First, parents try to train it out of their children." Memory of Sandalari as a child, beaten repeatedly to stop her from healing herself. "But usually that fails, and then they purify them. They bring them in here, so I can hear it. I don't listen anymore."

I thought I was going to be sick again. Jemeret said, "Hang on. We're almost done." The vein in his cheek jumped with the intensity of his control. "Where are the children who haven't been purified yet?"

M'Cherys's head lolled back and forth for a moment. "Used

to be over there," he said, nodding toward his right. "Who are you?" It was the third time he had asked the question.

Jemeret's voice went very soft. "We're friends," he said, and I felt the life go out of M'Cherys as gently as a sigh.

I drew in a sharp breath.

My lord looked at me, his eyes only partly focused. "Go where he indicated," he said. "Wait there for me." I felt his vision sweep past me. "Go," he said tonelessly.

I let myself out the door, sweeping quickly. There were about twenty minds perhaps half a mile away, headed for the village in a group, probably villagers coming in from the fields. The cabins themselves were still quiet. I ran quickly to the first of the shacks to the right, but the feelings emerging from it had much the same flavor as M'Cherys's own, and I gave one cursory glance inside and moved swiftly along to the next. There were six of them, one obviously an adolescent boy, and their feeble, sightless motions reminded me of slugs, huddled together in a garden. I made myself not think of it.

In the next shack there was a child, perhaps nine or ten. It was so filthy I couldn't tell if it was a boy or a girl. It was bound by its wrists to a post in the center of the room, where other bindings hung, as though others had been bound here recently but were gone now. The child was blindfolded and gagged. Though its feet were unbound, it sat still; only the rhythmic motions of its small chest gave a hint that it actually lived. As I stepped into the room, its head jerked up.

I thought it ought to have been able to free itself by pathfinding the knots, but then remembered Sandalari's back again and realized it was probably punished more if it used talent. I bent and pulled away the blindfold. Wide brown eyes fastened on me. I soothed it instantly with my sting, and saw it react with astonishment and fear at being touched in such a way. There was no time to be subtly comforting; I flooded it with feelings of love and ripped the ropes off small wrists chafed and rechafed to the point of being scarred and bloody. I fought my anger down for fear that the child would think the anger was aimed at it. "Hush now," I said. "No one will hurt you any longer. I need you to come with me without making any noise. Can you do that?"

It nodded solemnly, pulling off the gag. I took its hand. We ran to the door and met Jemeret, white-faced, outside.

The child shrank from this large stranger, but I kept reassuring it. There was no longer a sick pattern of talent coming from the other hut. I knew what Jemeret had done.

The group of talentless minds had closed most of the distance to the village, and I felt the child recognize it. It began to gasp a little from fear. Even reading it, I couldn't tell what sex it was, for it had no awareness of its own gender. I didn't have time to stop and think about that.

Jemeret picked up the child and we both accelerated into the trees, skirting as much of the settlement edge as we could until the undergrowth grew thicker and slowed us. By that time we could hear shouting behind us.

I don't know what he did to shield us or otherwise discourage pursuit, because we were moving too quickly to sustain a relatively static bubble, but I know that I was feeling terrified that he would fail and they would catch us. I was almost sobbing by the time we got the brush cleared from the lander and stuffed ourselves and the child inside. Jemeret lifted us before we were really ready, and I fell against the lander's back wall, hugging the child against me.

"Fight it, damn it!" Jemeret commanded me. "That child's projecting, and I can't get us up, keep them away, and fight off your emotions, too!"

I realized he was right—the child was a powerful little talent. I'd been so linked to it, so involved in comforting it, that I'd been vulnerable to the high emotional level of its fear. I pulled back and slid my shields up.

There was shouting from outside as the lander roared upward, but this world would have nothing they could fling at us besides rocks and arrows, so we were safe, after all.

Jemeret threw the auto on and pulled me to my feet.

The child seemed stunned by the occurrences and, looking from me to Jemeret and back again, asked, "Who are you?" The question innocently echoed M'Cherys's rasp.

As Jemeret had answered M'Cherys, I answered the child. "We're friends," I said. "Are you a boy or a girl?"

"Never had friends," the child said seriously. "Dirty stinking freaks don't need friends. I'm a dirty stinking freak."

Jemeret made a sound of complete disgust.

I said carefully, "You are not a freak. You are a human being, and you have talent. You're just like we are."

The child's huge brown eyes looked from one of us to the other, fighting against hope. Impulsively, I drew it closer, ignoring the filth and startled fear. For a moment or two it stiffly resisted the embrace, washing me with an uncontrolled tangle of the emotions it was experiencing and fighting almost desperately to contain at the same time. I held on and rested my chin on its tangled, greasy hair.

By the time Jemeret docked the lander in *Detralume*, it was clinging to me like a lifeline and sobbing its heart out.

The four men and Sinet Coleby were sitting around the table in the lounge when Sandalari, Keli, and I came in, having bathed the child and put her to bed, for it had been a girl under the tatters. Sandalari conquered her tears, remembering a far-away childhood she had thought entirely behind her, and Keli was upset enough at the girl's plight to come out of her lethargy. "If she has a name, she doesn't know what it is," I said to Sinet and the men. "She's had a good meal and gone to sleep. I can't guarantee she won't have nightmares."

"I can stay and sit with her if you like," Keli offered hesitantly, and when Lendo Dell made a small motion, as if to protest, she added defiantly, "I won't hurt her."

"Go on then," I said. She flashed me a grateful smile and went out.

Jemeret bubbled us. He'd spent some of his anger, but the rest was boiling up in him like a geyser. "That child has as much raw power as any child I've ever tested on Caryldon," he said tightly, "and her reward for it was going to be—" He stopped. Coney winced. I hoped they already knew what we'd found, because I couldn't have explained it. There was a raw wound in me, still too tender for probing, that came from the thought that people could hate us for our talent alone. I suppose I'd known intellectually that the Honish hated the Samothen, but that had seemed as much factionalism as a rivalry among subspecies. This was a case of people turning on their own children. I had never looked directly at that particular ugliness before. I never wanted to think about it again, but knew it would haunt me for the rest of my life.

Jasin Lebec stirred, his face very serious. "Jemeret, the clash of two different kinds of people is very like a war in many respects. Some of the battles, talent is likely to lose."

Jemeret stared at him, incredulous. "That wasn't a battle, nasire, that was a slaughter, and your Com has turned decent citizens into savages." He stood up, unable to control his wrath without a physical outlet. "We try to develop talent on Caryldon, and the Com takes the best of it away and breaks it. Talent that develops naturally on the Com worlds isn't recognized until it's somehow gone rogue, and then it's exiled instead of trained. And once it's exiled, no one even tries to trace it, to see if it's developed beyond its rogue stage. What a waste!"

"Tragedy," I corrected.

He glanced at me, but wasn't ready to be interrupted. "By the stars, when I think of that poor bastard M'Cherys—talent trapped in a body it couldn't repair but had to keep from dying, locked in a brain whose only stimulus was being reviled and tormented, except that every few years he got to hear the sounds of people making someone else like him—"

I made a strangled sound I'd tried to contain but couldn't.

His anger dropped away into weariness. "I'm sorry, love," he said to me. "It makes me sick, too."

"If talent can and does develop in the Com," said Coney, who'd been very quiet since I'd come into the lounge, "they can leave us alone."

"They won't," I said. "The Caryldon talents are the only mature, identified talents, and the only ones so far who've proved that talent can develop sanely and productively."

"Well," Sandalari said, "then we have to make it impossible for them to get to us. Or at least very difficult."

"But we can't do that as long as the Com has the roll technology," Lendo Dell protested.

"Then take it away from them," Coney said.

There was a silence in the lounge.

Jemeret had calmed down considerably, as if Coney's words had laid a quieting hand on him. He was thinking deeply. I remembered Glon asking what we'd like to take back from the MIs. We all simply waited. At last he said, "We have concluded we have to change things. The Com is more unstable than it has been in decades, because my na-sire isn't smoothing the surface any longer. Until the government figures out how to repair his absence . . ."

"Change things?" Lendo Dell repeated. "What does that mean?"

"The government lets the MIs make too many choices," I said, wanting my lord not to commit himself too strongly in front of the others. "Jemeret believes if we can somehow break the hold the MIs have—"

Jemeret eluded my purpose. "I want to turn them off."

Jasin Lebec just shook his head.

Inspiration struck me. "What if we didn't have to turn them off? What if we just reprogrammed them?"

"Wait," Sandalari said. "What are we going to do about Ananda? The exiles?"

Jemeret looked momentarily as if he were in pain. Then he said steadily, "Nothing more than we've done. Either they'll survive and begin to realize that many of them have low levels of the talent they're currently trying to destroy, or they'll fail. We can't try to save them, and we haven't the time to teach them to rise above subsistence farming. They're still too busy hating to put much priority on growth."

Sandalari turned her face away from him, and Coney drew her in against his side.

I knew what it had cost Jemeret to make that decision. He was, after all, dedicated to the survival of talent. I wanted to put my sting into him and draw out the pain. I wanted to remind him that, in addition to sacrificing seven today, maimed and in ceaseless agony, we had saved one, young and with the potential to be more than she knew. I didn't do anything.

"We can't destroy the roll technology," Jasin Lebec said calmly. "You wouldn't be able to get back to Caryldon."

"We only need one ship," Jemeret said, drawing himself back from the depths of his feelings, "and I can fly it if I have to."

"All right, then," I said. "If we can reprogram the MIs, what is it exactly that we would want to change?"

But no one got to reply, because just then, as it sometimes does, life got messy. Sandalari noticed the almost frenetic blinking of the comsole. "It's gone red," she said. "It must have been calling for quite a while."

Jemeret dissolved the bubble and the sound of the loud buzzing filled the lounge.

Jasin Lebec got up and went to it. "Coming in eftel, relayed from the bridge," he said, and answered the call. "Ronica, it's for you."

I went to complete the eftel connection, and Sandalari and Jemeret were as startled as I when we recognized Venacrona's voice.

"I wouldn't call if it weren't urgent," the old priest said after I told him I was there.

"What is it? What's happened?" I asked him. "Why aren't you calling Jemeret?"

"We need the High Lady," Venacrona said. "Lord Krenigo's gone mad. He insists that he was forced to confirm you as High Lady. He views your absence as his opportunity to play for power." There was a pause. "Lord Ashkalin says Krenigo tried to get him to agree to join an effort to assume control of the Samothen, but Ashkalin refused and brought all the men he could muster to join the Boru in defending your title. There's more, but it'll be easier if you're here. Can you come?"

Without pausing to confirm it with anyone, I said, "Of course," blessing Ashkalin for keeping his word. "What's the situation now? It'll take us four or five days to arrive."

There was another pause from his end. Then, "We can hold

for four or five days." And, "We have to stop him, Lady Ronica. He can tear the Samothen apart if we don't."

"Any trouble from the Honish?" Jemeret asked sharply.

"They're sitting it out," the priest said. "Get here, and have something—effective—when you do."

The others scattered to get the ship to change course, and to prepare the girl from Ananda for the roll, to keep her from projecting terror all over the ship. I made an eftel vid call to Pel Nostro to tell him our return to Orokell would be delayed.

I must have awakened him, because he answered from the small eftel vid conference room closest to his apartments, looking touseled and wrapped in a kilt. "What's happened?"

"We have to commandeer *Detralume* and go to Caryldon, Pel," I said. "There's trouble."

He frowned, rubbing his eyes at the bridge of the nose for a moment. "What kind of trouble requires your taking every available talent in the Com out of it?" he asked.

I drew myself up in my best authoritative manner. "You mean to say, of course, every available *surviving* talent. Your record of managing and protecting talent is abominable, and you know it." He had the grace to look ashamed. I didn't think all of it was for show. "Look, Pel, talent is threatened on Caryldon, too. We have to save it there. We'll come back when we're done."

He shook his head. "I can't stop you, Ronica," he said. "And I don't want to make an open breach that the Tribunal can see as insubordination. There's too much going on here now."

I knew he meant the general unrest—we'd had reports that the Strand and Menary had begun registering protests over some of their ongoing relations with the Com government, that Pina was objecting to the slow rate at which they were being fed technology, that Causaday was holding back some of its generium quota because things were changing *too* fast.

I let my pent-up feelings show. "Tell Faucon Oletta I said the Tribunal can handle it. We'll be back when we can." I cut the connection, was surprised as Jemeret reached past me and punched a local code into the table. If he had a comment on my performance with Pel, he didn't make it.

When the local vid cleared, I was startled to see the sleek head of one of the water people. Jemeret bubbled us and the vid. "This is Jemeret Cavanaugh. I need to get a message to Glon. Tell him that we have oceans on Caryldon, and that we would welcome some of the water people if they're ready for a new adventure. Tell him to look at Caryldon, and he'll see why." He cut the connection, dissolved the bubble, and put his arm around me.

Coney put his head in, saying, "We're leaving orbit and we hit the first roll point in less than two hours."

When he'd gone out again, I looked at Jemeret. "When you memorized the ship, it was all the sublight systems, wasn't it?"

"Yes."

"Then we have to do the Lume generator, too."

He saw what I was getting at, shot a bubble around us again, and nodded. "And more than that. We have to learn the exit points from Lumespace. We need to be linked to the system through every roll between here and Caryldon. We have to know how to find our way home." His voice went low. "This isn't the way I'd have chosen to learn it, but it'll do."

It was the beginning of high watch. The captain and his five crew were at work on all the control stations, confirming readings and timing, setting the mechanical and technical systems of the rollship to the exact tolerances needed to withstand the powerful stresses of roll.

Because there was only a skeleton crew, there were empty seats. We took two of the ones directly in front of the Lume field generator. We watched the bridge crew work, helping when hands were needed, until Jasin Lebec signaled us from the bridge surround. There was still half an hour to the roll point, and so we got up to go speak with him. I might have asked my lord why we were just sitting in the bridge, but I knew he wanted to be surrounded by technological equipment and activity, in order not to think about what was happening on Caryldon.

Jasin Lebec said, "Pel called me right after you talked to

him, Ronica. He started out by being very unhappy about our decision to return to Caryldon and ended up, eventually, being grateful that we were willing to go and try to save the only true, stable source of talent in the known galaxy. It just took a lot of time and some very fast talking." He grimaced. "Weak as I am, it would have been much easier if I'd just been in the same room with him."

Jemeret's gaze drifted beyond Jasin Lebec's shoulder. I followed it, too, and Mortel John joined us in the bridge surround. Jemeret ignored him, asking his grandfather, "Has there been any word of Dolen T'Kelle's whereabouts?"

Jasin Lebec shook his head. "He's vanished as completely as dust into a singularity. The MIs have no word of him anywhere."

Mortel John cleared his throat. "I understand we're going back to Caryldon," he said.

"We have to stop an insurrection." Jemeret's voice was brisk, emotionless.

Mortel John nodded. "So I've heard. I'd like to help, and so would the MIs."

I laid my hand on Jemeret's arm before he could say anything and said, "This is not an opportunity to give the MIs a foothold on Caryldon. That would destroy it."

"They know you believe that," the big cyborg said steadily. "They suggest, through me, that when you consider the scenarios you wish to propose to end your war, you do not rule out the introduction of some technology. You may find it simplifies your task, and it need not involve them directly in any way."

I held tightly to Jemeret's arm, asking him not to say anything. "The MIs have not proven in the past to accept a great deal of noninvolvement voluntarily."

"They know you demand that they leave Caryldon alone," Mortel John said, "and they do not want to see it or you destroyed." His voice took on a hint of emotion. "And I would like to see it prosper. I gave a great deal for it."

"Thank them for the suggestion," I said as evenly as I could. "We will consider it."

My old teacher nodded to me, then appeared to brace himself, "I understand you brought a child with talent up from Ananda."

Jemeret went rigid, and any hope I had of his remaining silent vanished. "You are not to go near that child," he said icily. "We're taking her to Caryldon."

Mortel John drew in and let out several breaths, then said, "I have no purpose without talent to train. It's all I do now."

"Then learn something new," Jemeret said. "You've been doing a remarkably poor job of it so far."

Mortel John looked very sad.

"Go on working with Coney and Sandalari," I said. "Anything you can do with them now can only help us." He made a partial, wordless bow to both of us and walked away.

I opened my mouth, but Jemeret shook my hand away and cut me off before I could speak. "Let it go, Ronica. I'd prefer you didn't try to defend him."

I knew how brittle he was and decided to let it pass.

Jasin Lebec asked, "Would there be any objection to letting him meet with the child under the supervision of one of us?"

I wished he hadn't raised the question.

"I object to having him anywhere near children, especially those with talent," Jemeret said. "He's lost too many, including all three we just gave him. We don't have enough to keep experimenting with his abilities. You let it go as well."

I took Jemeret's wrist in a firm grasp, applying more pressure than strictly necessary. "You come with me," I said, and gathered to pull him after me with more strength than he would be prepared to resist. It surprised him, but he came along.

I walked him to the cargo hold where Tynnanna was settled in, sleeping. I stung the klawit awake as we crossed the expanse of decking.

"We need to be on the bridge," Jemeret said. "What are we doing here?" He sounded more amused than annoyed.

I faced him directly, staring into the gray eyes, softened now from the silver beads that had confronted Mortel John. "We can access the starfire now. I know we don't have the incense, but I think you need to ask it to help you get over M'Cherys and the others." His face was tired, but he half smiled. "Now," I said strongly.

"Who's giving me the orders?" he asked gently. "The High Lady of the Samothen? Or the wife?"

"The woman who loves you and wants the best for you. Please, Jemeret, get it off your soul. It's eating at you."

He pulled me into his arms for a few seconds, then let go of me. He glanced at the chronometer on the wall to ensure we still had time before the roll began, walked to where Tynnanna now stood and, without the powder or the altar, began the ritual words for atonement. The starfire came instantly from the cat's collar, as if it had been waiting to be called, and as I watched, biting back tears, it touched him with love, understanding, and forgiveness.

XV. Returning to Caryldon

The way home tasted like a mixture of cinnamon and clove sugar. And that was only slightly less amazing than realizing that, linked to the Lume field generator, we interpreted space as something we could taste at all. When we compared notes after the first roll, we discovered that, unlike probing, in which each of us received a different impression of the brain we probed, Jemeret and I had gotten an identical feel for the superluminal space in which the starfire lived. Our other senses seemed to have been disconnected at the roll point, leaving only the mental images of a roiling world of tastes, in which each planet had its own distinct flavor and it was possible to follow that flavor like a trail through the wilderness. When we reached the place at which the trail dissolved away, we would drop back into normal space.

From Ananda to Caryldon was only ten rolls, not the twelve it would have been from Orokell, but by the fourth one we knew absolutely what the trail tasted like, knew that we could scoot along it with ease, and had committed to memory the entry roll point coordinates, in case there should prove to be no way of programming them into the ship automatically. Neither of us said that, if we were both killed, Coney and Sandalari could not get back to Caryldon. Neither of us wanted to think about that.

I kept skittering away from thoughts of failure or death. Despite my history of self-condemnation, despite my near suicide the first time Jemeret had probed me, I very much wanted to live through this, and I needed Jemeret to live through it. He had become the symbol of everything in life that was worthwhile to me. So when we started trying to think of scenarios to solve the Caryldon problem, I began by playing with ideas I thought he'd approve of. None of them was satisfactory.

We had exercised in the cargo hold, working Climb 1 of the Ladder of the Warrior together, and then joined the other members of our team in the lounge of *Detralume* to discuss the problem. I finally reached the point—eight rolls into the journey—when I proposed that we think about Mortel John's suggestion of using some technology in our scenario.

Jasin Lebec, Coney, Lendo Dell, and Sinet Coleby were firmly in favor of it; Jemeret and Sandalari were just as adamantly against it; and I hadn't made up my mind yet. The issue was such an emotional one for Jemeret and Sandalari that we left the realm of reason quite early in the discussion.

When the argument went nowhere, and we traveled the same ground for about the tenth time, I said with less impatience than I actually felt, "It's obvious we're not getting anyplace. If we could use the technology of the Com to the same effect as I used the power of my brow-crown when we needed to get through the Honish lands, what would be different about it?"

Sandalari's bright blue eyes went deeply thoughtful.

Jemeret looked at me closely, but didn't immediately reject the idea. I wanted him to ask what I was thinking, but Jasin Lebec did instead.

The idea crystallized as he asked the question. "What if we brought something and used it subtly, to augment our own powers, rather than to create anything sensational?"

"What kind of something?" Sinet asked.

"A beam projector," I answered impulsively. "It won't hurt anyone. It certainly won't kill anyone." I was watching Jemeret as I spoke. "And if we create the right scenario to go with it, we might be able to do a lot of good for our—for Caryldon." His face remained expressionless, and I didn't sting him or even try to read him. I only said, "If you still disagree, Jemeret, I'll drop the idea, but I ask you to please consider it." Then I waited, nearly holding my breath. I didn't want to drop the idea just because he didn't agree, but I would, rather than go against him.

No one else in the room moved.

Jemeret locked eyes with me. I wondered if he was trying to read me without my being aware of it, then discounted that and instead hoped he would make the right choice.

The time stretched on, and at last I saw a flicker in the depths of the familiar gray eyes. He said slowly, "I think I have an idea of what we can use for a scenario, Ronica. We'll give it a try."

I went to the cabin we'd given to Keli and the girl from Ananda. It was a little room, because the child was used to being in a small space. Keli had extruded a child-size chair and was showing the girl how to change its size and shape. They both looked up at me and Keli smiled, almost happily. I read that she was feeling useful again. The little girl stood up, watching me with wide eyes.

I smiled back at Keli, transferred the expression to the girl and touched her lightly, soothingly, with the sting, encouraging her to be open to the feeling, to touch me back. With great hesitation, she connected with me for a microsecond, then jerked back, startled and uneasy.

"It's all right," I said to her. "The ability you have is good, not terrible."

She shook her head, but I felt her gratitude.

"We have to choose a name for you," I told her. "You're going to a different world, and you'll be highly valued there, but everyone there has a name."

"I'd have a name?" she asked quietly, her eyes huge.

"Of course."

"All my own?"

I said yes.

The little girl seemed to think about that for a moment. Then she said, "I never had anything belong to me."

"Would you like to choose your own name?" I asked her.

The very idea was incredible to her, and her eyes opened wider. I felt as if she were weighing the choice. I thought that, except for her youth and the absolute innocent unawareness of what civilized discourse could be like, she had a core built on a level of suffering I could only guess at. She shook her head.

"Andriel," I said to her. "Your name will be Andriel. It means 'child of a hidden light.' "

She tried the word to herself, and very slowly, almost wonderingly, began to smile. "I like my name," she said solemnly, "and I promise I will try to be good and make you happy you gave it to me." Her lower lip trembled a little. "I feel so strange."

I tucked her tightly against me. "How do you mean, strange, Andriel?" I asked her, deliberately using her name to help accustom her to it.

She was trembling, even as she clung to me, and I could feel the strength with which she was suppressing a projection that should have been as natural to an untrained talent of her age as breathing was to a child without talent. "Like—people here don't want me to be hurt or—want to punish me or—" She stumbled over her words, tried to draw herself up a little and make her tongue behave. "Would they—you—hurt me if I was bad?"

The naughtiness, the testing of limits would, I knew, come later. Now there was only the fear and the hope. I bent and kissed the unexpected tear tracks on her soft cheek. "Not hurt," I said. "Correct and teach. That's not hurtful." I flooded her with as much affection and security as I thought she could handle. Her arms tightened around me and I sensed she was wide open to receive, but still fighting hard not to project. I didn't want to try to force her. Instead I whispered, "Let it go, Andriel. It's all right. You can let your feelings go. I love you." I meant it absolutely.

The power of her pent-up feelings burst over me like the sunlight breaking from behind a cloud. She was raw and untrained, but her natural talent was so strong that I almost couldn't contain it all—just as Jemeret had had trouble containing mine during the Dibeli nomidar contest.

I knew in that moment, as emotion overwhelmed her again—perhaps the first positive emotion she had ever let herself feel—as she sobbed helplessly against me, that even if I never had a baby of my own, this child was mine to raise and mold, the way I wanted to have been raised and molded by the Com. I knew I might make mistakes, but Jemeret had taught me that with love, all mistakes are reparable. Andriel's world had had no love in it at all until now, and I wanted to remedy that.

The deep, tearing sobs were exhausting her. She'd been malnourished for a long time, and she hadn't yet learned how to husband her strength. Like me—and I should have known better but never seemed to—she gave everything, and it would usually be too much.

I brushed the stray strands of hair out of her eyes and said, "I'm going to let you sleep now, Andriel. We'll be home sometime soon."

"Don't leave me." She sniffled and ran a hand across her nose and eyes. "I'm so tired of singing alone in the dark to keep away being too afraid."

"Singing in the dark?" I repeated. "What do you mean?"

She sniffled again and rewiped her eyes with the back of one thin hand. "They'd come at night to tell me what would happen to me if I didn't behave," she said, "and it would scare me awful. Then when they left, I'd sing so I could go to sleep. It didn't seem so dark when I sang. Don't go away."

"I'm not going away," I said to her seriously, "but I may not always be in the same room with you. When I'm not, you can find me if you want to. You only have to reach out to me with your mind—yes, like that."

Her touch was still tentative, hesitant, a little fearful.

"Good." I touched her back gently, approvingly, then gave her a little squeeze to reinforce the touch.

"Andriel," she said, trying it on her tongue.

From the doorway, Jemeret said in a quiet voice, "We're coming up on the roll, Ronica."

I had no idea how long he'd been standing there, how much he'd heard, seen, or felt, why he hadn't made his presence known. I turned Andriel by the shoulders and gave her a little nudge. "Get in bed now, Andriel. I want to show you something."

She obediently scrambled into the bed's field, and even before she was fully settled, I'd slid a probe into her mind and drawn her attention to the small node of nerves in the pineal that could be triggered to increase the restorative properties of sleep by expanding it into deeping. She blinked at me. Then I guided her to the corresponding node in the hippocampus that would release the chemical trigger needed to feed into the pineal. Her mouth dropped open, and then she was drifting down into the mistiness of sleep. I bent and kissed her forehead, got up and walked past Jemeret into the corridor without pausing. He followed me for several steps before he caught my arm and pulled me to a stop. I couldn't make myself look at him.

He asked, "Do you think I'm going to forbid you to love her?"

Then I had to see his face. It was slightly curious, slightly amused, and underlain with the background of apprehension about what was happening on Caryldon.

"It's more than that," I said. "I want her. To raise her. To help her become—"

"I know." He let go of my arm and laid his fingertips against my cheek, leaning in close to me.

"I'm not pregnant."

"Yet."

I almost asked, *What if I never—* but I buried it. "I want her," I said again. "There have to be some privileges that go along with these responsibilities, these obligations." I sounded, strangely, almost desperate.

Jemeret pressed his lips together and used his sting to adjust me to calm, as he had so often in the past.

"The Com won't care," I went on. "They'd thrown her away."

"They threw M'Cherys away," he said, "and the act had consequences they never dreamed of." He shook his head once, sharply, a very unusual gesture for him. "Everything has consequences." His voice softened. "Taking the girl has consequences."

"Healing me had them, too," I challenged him.

"I was prepared for those, love. I wanted them. I still do." His fingers went on stroking my cheek. "There will be consequences to everything we plan to do. I'm prepared for all of them except what happens on Caryldon when we go down there with a beam projector."

I took a painfully deep breath. "What happens," I said with all the conviction I could muster, "is that we use Krenigo's ambition and pride to return the Samothen to normal."

The warning chime sounded to alert us to the approaching roll. We turned and went down the corridor to the bridge.

We spent less than an hour on Markover Station—just long enough to check in and transfer to a larger shuttle than we'd taken up from the surface so long ago. We needed more space because there were more of us to descend, Tynnanna had grown to his full size while we were away, and the beam projector had a considerable bulk to it, even disassembled. Jemeret paused long enough in transit to make a local call through the eftel, since that was the only communication link on the surface, to speak to Venacrona. While he did, we loaded the shuttle, and Sandalari and I pathfound the beam projector to alter and enhance its programming. We had all argued about the use to put it to, and ultimately we chose to make it function not emotionally, but purely physiologically. We had to change a lot of the chemical-release spurs, but we were pleased with the results.

Just as we finished, Jemeret joined us in the shuttle and said, "Ashkalin will meet us at the landing field. Venacrona and Tuvellen are telling the people that we're coming in through the old tunnel."

"What old tunnel?" I asked.

"The defending tribes are lined up on the plain at the foot of the mountain track," Jemeret said, sitting down and slamming the seat fields on. "And there isn't an old tunnel. It's just a story we've used for years when we had to, to cover activity at the spaceport."

Mortel John had not been invited to join us. Lendo Dell, Sinet Coleby, and Jasin Lebec would remain on the station with him; we'd decided that having them with us would not guarantee success, and they would be harder to explain than Keli and Andriel. The full truth was, however, that some talent had to remain in the Com in case the four of us did not come back from Caryldon.

Jemeret piloted the lander with impatient skill. We dropped swiftly into the atmosphere over the pole, and I wondered what was going through Mortel John's mind as he watched us from the station. He had not been here since he'd discovered talent, back when he was still entirely human. We hadn't told him about the beam projector, but I had a feeling he knew. I conjectured that the MIs might have let him know, but it was only guessing. I didn't understand the MIs.

Strangely, I began believing there *was* something to understand, not just a fusion of components, but something of a mind in the electronics of brain, something that existed in the indefinable matrix between the tangible parts which could be assembled and documented, just as something of the starfire existed between the molecular bonds of the starfire metal, just as something of me existed between the neuron connections Jemeret had painstakingly rebuilt.

"We can't go to Stronghome in jumpsuits," Sandalari said after we'd been dropping for a few minutes.

"Ashkalin is bringing us clothes," Jemeret said, setting the lander on automatic and turning his chair toward us.

"Is Krenigo's the only tribe against us?" I asked.

"We'll know when we get down there," Jemeret answered.

Keli glanced repeatedly at the beam projector, as if disturbed to see it being brought into a wilderworld. Sandalari, noticing, said, "It'll be all right. We'll make certain it doesn't contaminate the world."

"Any more than Krenigo's contaminating it," I added. They all looked at me. "I don't think I understand—ever understood—why we have this ingrained need to destroy each other."

"We have to defend ourselves," Sandalari said.

I shook my head, not to disagree with her, but to try to follow a thought. "There has to be an alternative. We don't want to destroy, and we don't want to be destroyed."

"War isn't a multiple choice question," Jemeret said. "Look what the talentless did to M'Cherys. Look what Dolen T'Kelle was doing to us. Look what the MIs did to the Macerates." Keli turned her face away.

"But do we have to be like them?" I said. "I can't accept that the only choices are killing or being killed." I saw him start to speak, but I didn't give him a chance. "That's what the talentless believe, so that's how they behave. We can't continue to do it, Jemeret. We'll lose far more than our lives if we do."

Sandalari asked, "What will we lose?" And when I didn't answer at once, "Ronica?"

Coney said, "We're coming into the upper."

Jemeret swiveled his chair back around and took the controls. "I'm going to circle the valley once, high up. I need one of you on the eye to get a reading on who's where and what the count is."

"I'll do it," Coney said quickly, sliding his chair to the eye and keying in the pattern requests.

Sandalari and I glanced between the two of them and Keli and Andriel. I could tell that the growing tension had begun to affect Sandalari. She was watching me as if waiting for a cue as to how she should behave. I smiled at her, and she smiled back, but her expression echoed the anxiety that must have been part of my own. I said, more to myself than to her, "We'll see how our Krenigo scenario plays out."

"Well?" Jemeret's voice cracked percussively through the small cabin.

"In Stronghome, about three hundred," Coney said. "Outside on the plain, about four thousand against the mountains and about three thousand on the far side."

"Let's get down there," I said quickly to Jemeret. "Anything we try to figure from up here will be a waste of time."

* * *

No ship or station air tastes or feels the same as planetside air, and Caryldon's had some of the same purity as Sargasso's. I took a deep breath of it as we stepped out of the lander onto the smooth surface of the pad. We landed near where Ashkalin waited at the edge of the artificial surface, a pack beside him, a string of tivongs behind him, Vrand and Rocky among them. His dark brown eyes took us all in as we stepped out of the lander. We must have seemed a strange group to him—the four of us he knew, all in dark blue jumpsuits, an unfamiliar young woman in the tan jumpsuit, and a child. Tynnanna stepped out lightly, with enough aplomb to make any observer believe he had always expected to come home, and the months he'd been gone were nothing more than a momentary digression from the actual progress of his life. He raised his head, scenting the air briefly, his wide nostrils opening and closing as he reoriented himself to place and season. Then he snorted once and bolted off.

Jemeret paused a moment to watch Tynnanna depart, then strode quickly across the pad to clasp arms with the Chief of the Marl. He must have been reading him, as I was. "What's happened?" he asked brusquely.

Ashkalin seemed to have no need for courtesy. "We've lost Sabaran," he answered. "Night before last someone crept into the files of the Genda and assassinated him."

Sandalari cried out, stifled it with a hand against her mouth. Coney pulled her toward him.

"Then Sheridar is chief?" I asked, muting my own pain. "Have you told him the secret yet?"

"This morning," Ashkalin said. "Venacrona did."

Jemeret nodded once, his jaw tight, fighting his feelings. "How did he take it?"

Ashkalin bent and opened the straps of the pack, pulling out the first of the packets of clothes he'd brought us. "He didn't want to believe us; ultimately, he did. Here. I've got your brow-crowns in here, too."

"My thanks," Jemeret said, running his hand down the front

of the jumpsuit to open it. He glanced at me, then past me. "Get changed," he said shortly. "We've got to get down there."

Ashkalin looked curiously at Keli, and Andriel stared back at him with the normal apprehension of anyone who has seen few strangers and has good reason to fear almost everyone she already knows. The Chief of the Marl went on as the five of us began changing into tunics and leggings, Keli a little awkwardly, "Now that he believes, he wants to tell everyone—he's still very young for this. I've vigorously discouraged him from saying anything. No doubt you can do it more definitively."

"Why not tell everyone?" I asked abruptly. "It seems to me the Samothen ought to know how things are. We already know that talent isn't dependent on the absence of technology. What harm—"

Jemeret stung me lightly. "This is not the time to debate the rules under which we operate on this world," he said to me.

I ignored him deliberately, turned to Ashkalin. "We read about seven thousand on the plain. Who's where?"

"The Genda, the Nedi, the men I brought with me, and the Boru are all defending the approach to Stronghome. We haven't blown up the bridges. And so far, except for the assassin's attack, nobody's been doing much more than posturing." He glanced away when Sandalari, Keli, and I stripped down to change. "On the other side of the fields are the Vylk, the Ilto, and the Paj."

That brought me up short. "The Paj?" I repeated incredulously.

Jemeret swore.

Ashkalin nodded. "They've lined up the Paj in front of them like a shield. Any power we throw at them will hit the Paj first."

And so would the beam projector, if we used it from the mountain shoulders above our lines. Unless . . .

Then Ashkalin said quietly, "Krenigo took Ginestra to his tent several days ago. She hasn't been let out yet."

I felt myself go cold and Jemeret's sting touch the edge of my awareness at the same moment. "I'm all right," I said to him in a low voice, barely contained. "We don't learn, do we? We make the same mistakes over and over again."

Sandalari laid a hand gently on my arm. "The old ways are strong, Ronica, especially the ones between men and women. It may be a kind of madness, but it was an acceptable madness for a very long time."

I hate to admit it, but just then I wanted to lash out with my sting and hurt someone or something. I knew these three men felt regret about what was happening, and I didn't want to hurt them. But all of them, even Jemeret, though they might sympathize, didn't understand. The crime against Ginestra was not a crime against them. I, however, felt it as a crime against me, and against Sandalari, and Keli, and even Andriel.

Someone took my hand, and I glanced over, then down into Andriel's upturned face. "It'll be all right," she said.

I knew she read what I was feeling and wanted to comfort me. I pushed the rage down inside me and turned to the matter at hand. "We'll have to put the Paj to sleep, then," I said as calmly as I could, which, at the moment, wasn't very calm.

"Take it easy," Jemeret said to me, and I had to gather to keep from rounding on him. "We all have to go into Stronghome first. They're expecting us. Then we can work out the series of events that will make the scenario work."

He was being his logical self, and where the steadiness had always strengthened me before, this time it hit my wavering chemical balances in a way I couldn't have predicted and wasn't willing to gather away. Somehow—for reasons I would not know until later—I was in turmoil. It had begun, I thought, when I heard about Ginestra, and it was tugging at me to get this problem solved and get back into the Com, where I had "unfinished business." I suppose I should have been warned by the phrase itself, by the fact that my mind was choosing it to warn me. Kray had said he and I had unfinished business just before he drugged me and raped me. But I didn't see it then. I only knew we needed to settle the situation as quickly as we could.

We unloaded the disassembled beam projector from the shuttle and divided it among the tivongs. Jemeret took Vrand into the lead, and we put Andriel and Keli on a small green-beige tivong the child befriended instantly. Now that we were moving, acting, not just standing still, I was more in control of my feelings. Coney drew his mount aside to let me pull Rocky close to Jemeret. "Where's the old tunnel supposed to let out?" I asked.

"Under the pack ice."

"Hasn't anyone tried pathfinding it to see where it goes?"

He half smiled at me. "Not everyone thinks of pathfinding planets, Ronica."

We were in the village sometime after midnight, and the joy of the people there beat at us like waves. I reached out to feel everyone's pleasure, realized suddenly that Andriel was crying with the sheer bliss of being surrounded by people like herself. I pulled her off Keli's tivong and onto mine, holding her tightly. She seemed to understand completely what she'd come to, what she'd left behind. As always, when she touched me with her emotions, I was surprised at the extent of her power.

Word had gone out. Venacrona led us soberly through the Boru remaining in the valley. "The Inner Council is waiting at the Temple," the priest of the Boru said above the cheering. "Who is going to care for the child you brought us from across the sea?"

Jemeret told Coney to take Keli and Andriel to our house; the rest of us went directly to the Temple.

"Where's Sheridar?" my lord asked. "In the Council already?"

"Couldn't risk it," Venacrona replied. "He's upstairs in one of the starfire chambers."

"Come with me," Jemeret said, and we both followed him quickly up the steps. I was sweeping for Sheridar's presence as we climbed, and the young Gendal was waiting in the gold starfire chamber, pacing restlessly, as if he were unwilling to reach, or incapable of, a peaceful reconciliation with what he'd been told. I knew at once that he'd had no time to mourn his father, but that he was trying to rise above the need. Without pausing to see what Jemeret intended, I reached into Sheridar to share his grief at the loss of Sabaran, just as I'd reached into Ashkalin to help him mourn the loss of his son.

Sheridar drew in a ragged breath and grabbed for the lip of the altar to steady himself.

Jemeret said, "Ronica, there's no time now." I lingered for a moment longer, comforting even as I withdrew. Sheridar looked at me as stolidly as he could, blinking back sudden tears.

Jemeret leaned against the wall by the door, crossing his arms, as Ashkalin hunkered down between him and the altar. I remained standing in the center of the room. "Sheridar, we're all very sorry about your father," my lord said evenly, "but now we need you downstairs at the Council, and you cannot reveal anything that Venacrona told you about the worlds outside."

Again I felt strongly that we were past the time for this level of secrecy, but again I kept silent. Things were moving too fast and needed to go on at that speed. There would be time later for arguing for change, I told myself.

The young man shook his head. "You can't keep a secret like that—this," he stuttered.

"Of course we can," Jemeret said coolly. "We've kept it for decades—Venacrona, my Lord Ashkalin, your father, and I. Do you think you're somehow less worthy to lead the Genda than your father was?"

Sheridar shook off the question. "People—the Samothen—have a right to know. We don't have to give up our children just because they—the outsiders—demand it. We could fight."

I said, "You have no notion of the power the outsiders wield, my Lord Sheridar." I used the title deliberately. "They could destroy all life on this world without thinking about it any more than casually. I know, and I ask you to believe me. The Samothen are precious to me."

Jemeret overrode my last word. "Right now we need your silence to preserve the Samothen, in addition to your strength." I could feel that he stung Sheridar to reinforce his words.

Sheridar looked from one of us to the other, his conviction of astonished rightness fading into an admiration for his sire and the people who'd preserved the secret for so long. In another minute he understood what tribal leadership really meant for a chief of the Boru, the Genda, or the Marl, and though he was still young, he was trying his best to accept that responsibility. We never knew how long such persuasion would last, but for now we were all right.

Jemeret let out a breath he'd been holding, glanced at Ashkalin and gave a barely perceptible nod. The Chief of the Marl got to his feet. I was more than ready to move ahead.

"All right," my lord said. "Let's go to the Inner Council meeting. We have things to accomplish before morning."

We trooped out. It didn't occur to me until much later that I might have called the starfire. I was too driven to have thought of it.

So many hints—all disregarded because, once again, I was thinking with walls.

XVI. Evolution

The people already assembled in the room looked up as we came in. There were a few welcoming smiles, but everyone was tired and worried. They radiated it, a weary anxiety that filled the room and lapped at the walls.

The Inner Council was sadly depleted. Venacrona and Sandalari were there for the stars, and Jemeret and I for the Boru, but only a few of the other tribes presented two Councillors. Sheridar was standing alone for the Genda, having spent little time down with the people of his tribe since becoming chief. Ashkalin joined Moonelin, one of his guards, who was already in the room. I had one brief moment of regret that he hadn't brought Danaller, his other son and Kray's full brother, but then I realized he would want someone older, with previous battle experience.

Lyrafi of the Dibel smiled at me as my gaze passed over her. She had deep blue circles under her eyes, and I didn't see her brother, Orion, in the room. There were, of course, no representatives of the Ilto, the Paj, or the Vylk. From the Elden, Tatatin was present, but not a co-Councillor, and both Henion of the Nedi and his companion, a tall, willowy woman wearing a pair of swords. There was no one present from the Resni. Instead of the twenty-two of us there should have been, we were only eleven. That hurt.

"The Resni?" I asked Jemeret under my breath.

"They didn't get here," Venacrona said shortly, and began the ritual introductions that traditionally opened any Inner Council meeting. The woman with Henion turned out to be his sister.

I read everyone in the room except for Venacrona, Sandalari, my Lord Jemeret, and Sheridar. Outside of Ashkalin, who appeared to be strangely relaxed and almost confident, they were all emotionally unsteady, but their anxiety was tempered by relief that we'd returned. They all looked to Jemeret and me, eyes of different shapes and colors carrying the same expression of hope.

The introductions were over. Jemeret touched me with his sting, and the High Lady of the Samothen got to her feet. I said, "All of you have a key task to perform tomorrow, and so do all of the Boru who have undergone at least boyhood or girlhood ceremonies. Just as—" I began, and halted suddenly. Andriel was calling me, reaching out to me, her powerful, undisciplined young mind insistent on finding me, unwilling to be separated now that she knew I existed and was part of her world. I touched and reassured her, following the trail of her probe until my sting rested directly against hers, urging her to be patient and withdraw her sensory scout, telling her again that I loved her and would not desert her. She hesitated a moment, bobbled, then acquiesced.

I felt Jemeret's curious touch brush the slight echo of the child's withdrawal, but he still said nothing. I cleared my throat, shook my head a little as if to change my thought. "Even the older Boru children will be given the responsibility of making certain that those in the lines have water." I realized I was getting ahead of myself. "Those of you who were at Convalee remember how we made a long line of the Samothen so my Lord Jemeret and I could draw on the tribes' strength to put the Honish to sleep. We need the lines again tomorrow."

"Are you going to put the Vylk and Ilto to sleep again, Lady Ronica?" Henion asked.

I shook my head immediately. "Putting them to sleep tomorrow would be pointless. They'd still be on the plain and they would eventually have to wake up. We need to put the *Paj* to sleep instead. Then we're going to give Krenigo a choice, and if he fails to choose what we want, we will influence the others. Once they have succumbed to the influence, your tribes and the Boru can walk across the plain, take their weapons, and send them home." I was completely confident about that.

They stared at me.

We brought all the Boru women and older children across the mountain pass with us, leaving only the very oldest men and women and Keli to take care of the youngest children. Andriel wanted to come, but she was wielding too much uncontrolled power to be allowed in the thick of things. Bringing this set of normal noncombatants to what the troops perceived as battle lines was in itself an outrageous gesture of confidence. The people of the tribes at the foot of the mountains linked up at our command, and I stepped out onto the plain in front of the files, walking until I found a hillock that afforded me a view of the people on the far side of the plain, probably about two kilometers distant.

Jemeret gathered and touched me with his sting, giving me access to the reserve energy of everyone now behind me. I used it to amplify my voice, even though the only faces I could see when I adjusted my visual focus outward were those of the Paj, weary, in some cases terrified, despairing. As a pacifist tribe, they would not defend themselves, but then never before in the history of the Samothen had they had to do so against their own kind.

"I wish to speak with Krenigo the dishonorable," I said. My amplified voice carried across the distance and rang over their heads even more loudly than I'd intended. I scaled back a little on the energy I was drawing.

As I'd guessed, he came out in front of his own files and stepped through the line of the Paj, grinning tauntingly, waving his longsword in my direction. I'd augmented my hearing, but I wasn't going to give him any time to speak.

"You have treacherously attacked not only the tribes which can fight you in return, but the Paj, who are defenseless," I said. "You deserve no consideration, but as your High Lady, I give you some. If you choose to surrender, you will be heeded, and while you yourself, and your confederate in betrayal, Ustivet, will be enslaved or exiled, according to the will of the Inner

Council, your people will be allowed to go home. If you do not surrender, you and all the men who follow you will be humiliated utterly, and you will have earned that humiliation by your treacherous actions. You have one hour to make a decision. Should you choose the wiser course of surrender, lay all your weapons out on the plain in front of the Paj." I wanted to add something about Ginestra, but I didn't.

I could hear him shouting insults and challenges at me, punctuating particular threats with thrusts of the sword, but I cut back my hearing enough so that the words washed away on the gentle wind across the grasses. I turned and went into the files of our troops, to Jemeret, Coney, and Sandalari.

"I don't see him surrendering," Coney said. "I imagine killing Sabaran gave him quite a boost."

I took Sandalari's hand and the two of us walked back up the shoulder of the foothills to where we'd left the beam projector. It took about three-quarters of an hour to assemble it and set its beam height, angle of descent, and width. With a real sense of anger at Krenigo, I fiddled the physiological programming to make it more severe in the quarter hour that remained. Then I told Sandalari to stay well behind it and went out to a nearby overlook to see if, perchance, Krenigo had surrendered.

I was wildly impatient to get on with it and be out of there. It was a strange feeling. I thought it arose from my need to solve a problem more important to me than the others had been, because this was Caryldon. I was very wrong.

Once I was in position on the overlook, I reached out over the distance, looking for Jemeret. I felt a caution, knew he would begin using the tribes' energy to identify the Paj and put them to sleep, because a beam projector only works on a conscious mind. When he was done, he signaled to me, and I walked behind the beam projector and switched it on.

The insurrection was over in less than half an hour.

Sandalari and I didn't see it, but Jemeret described it to me, and I loved him for admitting we couldn't have done it without the beam projector. If we hadn't had it, he'd never have been able to expend so much power rendering the Paj insensible.

The beam projector did exactly what we'd programmed it to

do. It rendered the opposing forces incapable of fighting. A man cannot raise a sword if his own body turns against him. The men of the Ilto and the Vylk, struck simultaneously by overwhelming nausea, draining sinuses, convulsive and repeated emptying of bladder and bowels, and then continual, irresistible compulsions to keep doing it, even when they were empty, lost all desire to fight.

I switched off the beam projector at twenty-six minutes, which we'd calculated was enough to reduce them to exhaustion without permanently injuring them, and the warriors of the Boru, the Genda, the Marl, and the Nedi did indeed jog over and collect weapons from the sweat-soaked, groaning, sometimes weeping opposition, too weak to even peel off their own soiled leggings.

The Paj were amazed when Jemeret woke them.

Trotting back down the track to join them again, I was conscious of the fresh, clean beauty of the springtime, happy it had gone well, curious about what would happen now, and anxious to see Ginestra, all at the same time.

When we reached the end of the foothills, we were greeted with laughter and cheering. The Ilto and Vylk troops, unarmed and manifesting every emotion from shame to rage, had stripped and been allowed to wash themselves, but no other clothes had been provided for them. Sheridar had told them loftily that they could wash their own or go naked. So far, some had opted for each of the alternatives.

Krenigo and Ustivet were under heavy guard, unable to move from the spot they'd been placed, near Krenigo's tent, without encountering a forest of swords and the low-level slam of anger a group of lesser talents could put together.

We found their tivongs and confiscated them, took half the supplies they'd brought with them and distributed them to the Paj and the other tribes that would have a distance to go to get home, and then I went to them and told them they could leave now.

Several of the Ilto tried to rush me; I stung them, felt Jemeret do the same from behind me.

"Go home," I said to them as coldly as I could. "Live in isolation or in squalor if you like, but know that you are and always will be welcome as part of the Samothen if you live by our rules. If you follow leaders who convince you to break those rules—you will be punished again."

There were mutters, restless shifting. No one else challenged me.

I left Jemeret, Ashkalin, and the others to get the vanquished headed south, pulling their own wagons, and went to find Ginestra. She was sitting with Lyrafi and Sandalari, sipping some fresh water, working at healing a large, purple bruise that took up most of the left side of her head. Nevertheless, she smiled at me. I squatted down in front of her. "How are you, Ginestra?"

"I'm all right," she said, and sighed. "Once, long ago, in my thoughtless youth, I slept with Krenigo at a Convalee. I think I was about seventeen, and it wasn't richly rewarding, but I was something of an idiot then. This was just a little rougher." I admired her aplomb. "Was the—" She hesitated. "—form of the punishment your idea?"

"We all agreed to it," Sandalari said quickly. "We thought it would be better than killing." Her voice caught on the last word, and I remembered that Sabaran had been her chief, and that she hadn't had time to mourn for him, any more than Sheridar had.

Lyrafi seemed to remember it, too. "We'll sing a waysong for Sabaran before we all part," she said.

Ginestra gasped. "Sabaran's dead? I thought all the deaths had been in the Resni."

"What happened to the Resni?" I demanded, sending out a sensory scout to find Jemeret and bring him to us.

He appeared at once, resting a hand lightly on Ginestra's shoulder, saying, "I think it'll take those men a while to come to terms with their defeat, but we've started them blaming their leaders in addition to the rest of us."

"Do you know what happened to the Resni?" I asked him.

He nodded. "I had a long talk with Krenigo before you and Sandalari got back. He wanted Zunigar to join him before they left the peninsula, and Zunigar flatly refused. The Vylk attacked the Resni." I waited, was surprised when Jemeret smiled. "Zunigar's no fool. He fought for a while, then pulled his tribe out of the Hive into the marshes. He probably lost about fifty men; the Vylk lost somewhat less, but they knew better than to try their luck against the swamp and left to get the Ilto."

"They'll have weapons when they get home," Sandalari said. "Will they come against us again?"

"I doubt it," Jemeret answered. "There will be some internal struggles for leadership which ought to consume enough time so they can begin to live with their defeat."

"And they have to live with the fact that they attacked and captured a noncombatant tribe," I said. "Now they know the penalty for that—ignominy. They have a lot of ignominy to work off, but they can do it if they choose to."

There was a shout that someone had seen Zunigar and some of the Resni approaching. We all got up and went to meet him. Mounted on tivongs that looked lathered, as if they'd been ridden hard to get there, the Lord of the Resni was now sitting staring in astonishment at the parade of disarmed and in some cases disattired men starting their trek home.

He rode up to us, his boyish grin pulling at the corners of a mouth that I suspected had been quite grim recently. "Have I missed the war?" he asked, bowing his head to me.

"No war, just a lesson," I said to him, and Jemeret told him in a few words what had occurred.

Zunigar roared with laughter, then sobered. "Where's Krenigo?"

"He's by that tent," I said, pointing.

Zunigar looked at the ring of guards, then back at us. "I want him," he said.

"I didn't know the Resni kept slaves," I said.

The man on the tivong grinned again. "I'll make an exception for Krenigo."

Jemeret caught my eye, shrugged barely perceptibly.

There was another shout. The parade of men halted. Zunigar's tivong suddenly jumped and trumpeted, and the others took it up, then fell silent. Jemeret hissed, "Unbelievable."

Every klawit in the world appeared to have gathered in the forests that ringed the stretch of plain on which we stood, and now that multitude of cats was moving from the trees beyond us, shoulder-to-shoulder, like a well-disciplined troop.

With a strength that staggered me, I remembered the Day of the Bell, when a small group of klawits had come out of the trees on the Plain of Convalee and given me the kitten we called Tynnanna. They'd acted that day with a uniformity of purpose so eerie that I'd thought it was a dream, and then events had drawn it from my mind, along with all its implications. Now, seeing this much greater coordinated action, it came rushing back to me. "They're telepathic," I said to Jemeret. "I should have seen it. They can read each other's minds."

"What are they doing?" Ashkalin asked wonderingly, coming to join us.

I've already said I learned that life keeps going while we analyze, that it washes away the fragile structure of unanswered questions. I used to want an answer for every question, back in the days when I thought every question *had* to have an answer, every problem a solution. Now I know that a question is asked, and sometimes life comes along and interposes itself between the upraised tone of inquiry and the competing responses.

Ashkalin's question didn't get answered. Maybe someday it will. We stood and stared as the great cats came to a stop, encircling us, and roared. I had to damp down my hearing; I saw a number of lesser talents covering their ears. The roaring subsided, and two klawits came forward from the group. I recognized one immediately as Tynnanna; even if I hadn't known his every detail, the collar glistened in the sunlight as if it had been polished.

There was something familiar about the second cat, though it would be a while before I realized it was the one Tynnanna had brought to see Coney and me on a shelf of the mountain long before.

The two klawits walked in a measured and dignified manner past the group of us, past Ginestra, Lyrafi, and Sandalari, all standing now, past the people who had broken off their celebration of the victory, and into the circle of guards.

Ustivet and Krenigo, half dressed, weaponless, leaped to their feet. Krenigo tried to get a sword out of the hand of one of the guards, and Tynnanna, moving so fast I barely saw the motion, raised a massive paw and knocked his arm down. When no blood appeared on it, I knew he hadn't unsheathed his claws.

We all stood, staring, as Tynnanna and the other klawit herded the two men out of the circle, then toward the line of klawits that arced around us. Ustivet tried to run; the strange klawit, almost leisurely, knocked him over. When he scrambled to his feet, the herding went on.

Neither man asked us to interfere, though I knew from reading them that Krenigo wanted to. Just as they reached the arc of cats, Tynnanna turned his head and lifted the deposed Lord of the Vylk off his feet, his jaws soft, as if this were prey he would play with rather than dispatch. The other klawit duplicated Tynnanna's actions with Ustivet.

The line of cats turned and ran lightly back into the forest like wind passing through a stand of reeds. We stared after them, open-mouthed. Some of the men in the parade dropped to their knees, clearly having thought they would be next.

As I had when the cats brought me Tynnanna, we shook ourselves as if emerging from a dream. Many people began to talk at once. I turned to Jemeret. "Have you got any explanation for the klawit behavior?"

He shook his head. "I've never been able to explain it. When Tynnanna first came to you at Convalee, I didn't know how or why, and I don't understand it now—except perhaps in one way."

"What?"

"As Glon and the water people proved, we are not the only ones the starfire talks to."

His statement made some sense. The starfire spoke *through* the klawits. I realized that I'd thought that necessarily pre cluded it from speaking *to* them as well. Perhaps I was wrong about that. The starfire had told us that it chose the cats to speak through because their brains were less complex than human brains, but now I had guessed they were a telepathic species, and telepathy was a higher, evolved function. Some higher functions, then, did not involve complexity. The concept was bewildering to me, but hardly incredible. I remembered the protocanine Jessif saying to me so very long ago, "Do not mistake sentience for sameness."

Once the Ilto and the Vylk were well on their way, we all went into the valley, where the Boru set about entertaining everyone. Ashkalin, Sandalari, and Coney had told the story of the influencing and the klawits. We all sang the Hymn for Peace, a hopeful starsong speaking of the ability to build a foundation on which power could be used to accomplish a desired end.

A line of dancers reached us and swept us up. We danced and sang and embraced each other into the night. I spent a few minutes of the celebration with each of my friends, laughing with Shenefta, congratulating Variel on a pregnancy that was just beginning to show, discovering that Sejineth and Shantiah had decided to ask for the bracelet at next year's Convalee, sympathizing with and comforting Clematis. Sandalari and Clematis sang a waysong for Sabaran that spoke of a glorious, happy man, lost to us now, but never forgotten. Then the celebrating, briefly interrupted, resumed. I danced and laughed with Andriel, who took it all in with huge eyes. It went on and on, and being home was wonderful. Except that there was, again, an inexplicable, growing uneasiness that I was here instead of back out in the Com where, for powerful, unknown reasons, I was supposed to be.

In one quiet moment, while I was drinking clogny, which I let Andriel sip, she said to me, "It's this," and when I didn't understand, she persisted, "This is what singing is. Not alone in the dark." I hugged her hard. Then we were once again surrounded by the gentle riot.

As the celebration was winding down, Zunigar found me and said seriously, "I'd like to speak with you, Lady Ronica."

I read him quickly, felt both determination and a strong sense of confusion, rose immediately and walked with him past several of the groups of people who were still gathered. Someone began to build up one of the dying campfires. I thought they might never stop celebrating.

Jemeret, sitting with Ashkalin, Tuvellen, and Sejineth, watched us walk aside, touched me curiously and gently, but made no demands.

"Lord Zunigar, what is it?" I asked him when we were far enough from the general crowd not to be overheard, even by augmented hearing.

He watched me closely. "We were on our way here, and I was scouting ahead of my men when I saw something in the foothills. It wasn't anything I knew, so I went closer. You had some sort of—thing with you. You and the priestess put it together, and you spoke to it. What was it?"

I knew he'd seen the beam projector. I knew I could sting him at once and work a short while to make him forget it. I knew that was what Jemeret would have wanted me to do. I knew the dangers of any other action. I took his arm and said "Come with me." As we walked toward the temple, I used my sting to call Venacrona and Sandalari.

In many ways, it was another of those decisions that seemed so easy at the time and yet could have so many unforeseen outcomes. Unlike my long ago and much regretted seduction of Coney, this decision could affect the future of an entire world. But of course I didn't think of it in those terms as Zunigar and I went lightly through the spring night to meet Venacrona and Sandalari inside the largest building in the village.

Venacrona, anxious about being called, hurried into the now dim assembly chamber where we waited, and Sandalari smiled tentatively at Zunigar. "What can we help you with, Lady Ronica?" the priest asked, his smooth brow remaining unfurrowed despite the concern I felt coming from him.

"Zunigar saw Sandalari and me with the beam projector," said flatly.

Sandalari's bright blue eyes darted quickly to the Chief of the Resni and then back to me, but she didn't speak.

Venacrona cleared his throat. "And you brought him in here?" he asked, as if unwilling to pose any other question.

"He is a tribal chief and a Councillor," I said. "Certain information should probably be shared now."

As if I'd called him—and I'd been careful not to—Jemeret was there, with Ashkalin just behind him, and I could see Coney in the hallway near the entrance. Jemeret's face was cautiously expressionless. I felt no touch of his sting. He asked Venacrona, "What's going on here?"

"The High Lady," the priest answered, "believes there are certain things the Lord Zunigar deserves to be told."

My lord's steely gray gaze fastened on me for a very long time, and then he said, "My Lord Zunigar, will you forgive us for a few moments?"

The Resni chief started to nod and turn away, but I stung him to make him halt, and he did, looking curious.

I knew, with a sureness that I disliked at the same time I recognized it, that this time the confrontation was not going to be avoided. I swallowed hard and said, "Jemeret, you cannot stop the evolution of this world, any more than you can allow the MIs to stop the evolution of the worlds of the Com." He flushed, fighting back his emotions. I had to keep myself from trying to read him, and I gathered so as not to react in ways I knew would earn his approval. I wanted his approval, but I also thought I was right, and somehow that had become more important to me. "I'm High Lady," I said as strongly as I could. "The starfire chose me for it. The Samothen confirmed me in it. I believe it's time for the chiefs of the tribes to be told the secret."

He said nothing, an aura of iron rising around him.

Coney had heard enough of what we'd said to understand what was happening. Sandalari had begun to twist her hands in distress. Zunigar was clearly fascinated, and Ashkalin and Venacrona exchanged one look, but did not interfere.

Coney said gently, "We know now that talent arises in the

Com, Jemeret. It won't cease arising here because more people know something about the life that's out there beyond the sky."

I read Sandalari's fear, Zunigar's confusion, and at last reached to read Jemeret. I interpreted what I encountered as a blind fury that kept him from reasoning. The motionless silence stretched on until the tension became nearly unbearable. Then I spoke. "I believe they can handle the knowledge that Caryldon is not alone in the universe, and that the people of the stars are *us*."

Then Venacrona suggested, "We could ask the starfire."

"No," Jemeret said, barely moving his lips. "This is not a decision to pray over." We waited longer, and then he looked at me again. "If I don't agree, will you still pursue this?"

I knew what an important question it was to him. He had made me High Lady, a position that carried with it some power as well as a title. He could argue with me now, but he couldn't stop me. I had said I wouldn't introduce the beam projector if he didn't agree to it, and he had. I remembered all that I owed him—my sanity not the least of it; I remembered what he wanted to accomplish in the wider world in which most of humanity resided; I remembered the things he depended on me for here.

But I was High Lady in fact as well as in name, and he and I were not the same person. Sheridar couldn't be counted on to keep the secret with the obsessive dedication Sabaran had shown, and there were too many other loose ends now: at some point the clandestine time we'd spent here instead of on Ashkalin's ship, before we left for the Com, could come out; Zunigar had seen the beam projector; at some point the fabric of deceit that supported the secret would begin to break down. I believed overall in the strength and maturity of the people we had just stopped a war for, but sooner or later they might hear the stories of how it had actually happened, because Zunigar could not be certain others of his men had not also seen what he did. It was time.

I met my lord's gaze. "Yes," I answered him, "I'll pursue it no matter where you stand on the matter."

"In that case," Jemeret said, "you have no further need for

me here." He turned on his heel and walked back past Ashkalin and Coney and out into the village.

I looked at Coney and Sandalari, surprised to find them blurred with tears I had to blink back. "I'm right about this," I said to them, but it didn't have the conviction I'd wanted to invest it with.

It was Ashkalin who said, not unkindly, "Then you should act on it, Lady Ronica. It came too quickly for him. I know him, and he's fought it for so long that he simply can't yield to it that fast or that openly."

"And everything's at risk, everywhere," Sandalari added. "I think when he gave in on the projector, he knew somehow that things would have to change, but—" She drew her breath in, a little, ragged gasp. "—he loved this place so, the way it was."

I brushed the tears away, and then I told Zunigar about the Com, and Ashkalin and Venacrona told him about all the ways in which the outer world affected what happened on Caryldon, about Sandalari and me, about Jemeret's long absence when he was younger, about Sabaran knowing and conspiring. Then they fell silent, and I told him about the children we gave away, and Andriel, whom we had just brought back.

He took it well, his intelligence and natural diffidence overriding his initial shock. He was, after all, twice Sheridar's age and comparably more mature. He nodded a few times, once even said, "That makes sense." When we finally finished speaking, he asked Venacrona, "It's like the end of innocence, isn't it?"

"In a way," the priest said, "but leaders sometimes do have to reach an end of innocence for the sake of the people they lead. Is it acceptable knowledge, Lord Zunigar?"

He said, "Well, bearable, at any rate. Lady Ronica, if I hadn't seen the machine, would you have told me?"

"Perhaps. And perhaps not. I think some secrets should not be kept. This one was getting more difficult to maintain, and it's easier to be told a secret than to discover by accident that you've been deceived to keep it."

"Will you tell anyone else besides me?"

I avoided that question. "I have to go back out there again.

There's more work to be done." And as I said it, I was again struck by the desire to get off Caryldon and back to the unfinished business we'd left in the Com. Coney and Sandalari seemed surprised at my saying it. "I think you and my Lord Ashkalin and Venacrona should tell the other members of the Inner Council, in case some of the people in Zunigar's group saw more than he thinks they did, and before Sheridar lets something slip. He probably will, you know."

Ashkalin shrugged, but when I read Venacrona, I knew the little priest agreed with me.

Someone touched me with the sting, and I realized that Andriel was calling to me again. The feeling she was projecting was one of forlornness, as if, having found me, she could no longer be patient about being separated from me. I tried to soothe her.

"When do you want to leave?" Sandalari asked me hesitantly. I could read from her a hope that we would stay here awhile; she was homesick.

"I'll tell you tomorrow," I answered her. "Go get some sleep. Everyone needs rest more than anything else."

"You, too," Coney said. I nodded at him, suddenly weary, convinced that Jemeret would not forgive me for this. I trembled with an abrupt lack of confidence in my choice, a renewed need for his approval, and the fear that I'd thrown it away. I bid them good-night and left the temple.

Ashkalin caught up with me. "I'll walk with you." He paced me as I started toward the chief's house, and I slowed my step.

"It was time," I said. "The Samothen are very few, and they may need to know there's more to life than just the Honish."

"Some of us might start wanting to see what lies out there," Ashkalin said softly. "Then we'd be even fewer. I think that's one of Jemeret's biggest fears."

I knew he was watching me closely, but I couldn't look at him. Over by one of the remaining campfires I saw Shenefta, yawning, but she noticed me and waved. I might have smiled distractedly at her. "Caryldon—this world—is very far from developing the technology that would take anyone off-world.

and I don't think the Com would give it to you—not if we—" I stopped.

"Whatever it is you want to do," Ashkalin said, "I know it's a formidable task. It's the one thing I've never envied Jemeret. It's the one reason I never tried—very hard—to take the leadership of the tribes. He's been out there. I haven't. And he has more power, to deal with—all that." I didn't know what the admission had cost him, if anything. I wasn't reading him. "I don't envy you for it, either," he added.

"If we do it successfully, this world should be safe for a long time, no matter what we tell them here."

"How?"

I groped for a metaphor, found one. "You know how, when Stronghome was built, they made the bridges on the mountain track so they could be blown up?" He made a small nod of assent. "Well, one of the things we want to do is blow up the bridges between the Com and here."

"Ah," the Chief of the Marl said, immediately seeing more than I'd just said. "Will you be able to get back?"

"We hope so."

The idea hit me then, blossoming whole in my mind and wearing the face of brilliance, a beautiful unity that effectively masked the darkness and danger it hid beneath its surface. I would go back to the Com without Jemeret. That way, if I could not succeed in eliminating the Lume technology without losing all the ships, he would still remain on the world he loved, rather than marooned with me in a society he hated. I was convinced I had just hurt and disappointed him, and the idea of sacrificing the surety of my own return, while preserving his, seemed to be a wonderful way to make amends. I loved Caryldon very much, but he loved it more than I did, so I could give him this as a gift. It all seemed so reasonable, and I was, after all, very tired. I didn't think to look any further.

I'm making excuses. What happened next in this story I'm telling is really simple. I made what I thought was a correct decision, and I didn't know until much later that I wasn't the one who made it. Oblivious as any talentless person, I simply acted, thinking it was all my own idea.

I took Keli and the shuttle, and I went up to Markover Station. I left Jemeret and the others on Caryldon, telling myself that I was doing it because he might not have been able to come home, and it needed him more than it needed me. I also left my nomidar, Tynnanna, and Andriel.

If I hadn't been wearing my brow-crown—and if I hadn't forgotten I had it on until I changed clothes in the ascending shuttle—I'd have left it, too, and everything would have been completely different.

XVII. Alone in the Com

It's strange, when I think about how much time I spent in the dark, one way or another, that the time I spent brainless in the radiant tank on Orokell and Markover Station still has the power to frighten me far more than the time I spent in the rock chamber on Ananda. Perhaps it's because I'd been responsible for putting myself in the tank, while I was neither responsible for, nor alone in, the rock chamber. I'm getting ahead of the story.

My reception on Markover was welcoming, even though Jasin Lebec, Lendo Dell, Sinet Coleby, and Mortel John were all surprised I'd returned with no one else except Keli. I wanted to be away—if possible through the first roll—before Jemeret realized I was gone. It would take a long time for him to get another Lumeship out into the far arm to pick him up, so I thought I'd have sufficient time to assess the present situation regarding both Dolen T'Kelle and the MIs. Perhaps I could even accomplish something.

On Markover, I exerted every bit of authority a Class A is capable of to move all of us onto the *Detraluma* and out of Caryldon orbit in the first twenty minutes of my stay there.

Keli had asked no questions when I summoned her away from Andriel, and though I kept trying to soothe the child as I avoided our house to stay out of Jemeret's way, she called for me until the shuttle rose beyond her range.

Now, of course, I can admit that at least one of the reasons I fled was cowardice. Like so many other strong and decisive women, I was plagued with self-doubt once my decision was irrevocable. Getting away was all I could think to do, and I did it without regard for anyone else's feelings.

Once I was aboard the rollship, Sinet Coleby broached the question of why I'd done it. We had paused for a few moments on the bridge while the ship absorbed the roll coordinates and fed them to the Lume field generator. She studied me for a long time, running her slender fingers back through her thick, red hair. "Well," she said at last, "you've come away without the others, which wouldn't be overly disturbing, except that Jemeret stayed behind, too. I was certain he wouldn't let you leave without him."

"He didn't let me leave," I said. "I made a decision, and I acted on it. I don't necessarily have to confirm every single decision—" I couldn't finish; even at my worst, I simply wasn't that duplicitous. And I was feeling the isolation. Since I'd awakened beside the fireball on the surface of an unknown world, with a part of my memory gone, I'd never truly been separated from Jemeret. So I turned off my comsole and pathfound the Lumeship with the same kind of devotion I'd given to other studies at other times, trying to avoid everybody else. But by the time we were nearing the first chime for the third roll, both Jasin Lebec and Mortel John came looking for me. They'd clearly joined forces at some point in the near past, and when they found me, memorizing the atmosphere control mechanism, they summoned me to the lounge. I suppose I could have refused, but I didn't. Sooner or later it would have to be faced.

Mortel John asked, "May I take it that your solo return means that you have made a decision to remain in Com service?"

I felt like an idiot for not having guessed the government could interpret my action in a way they were eager to bring to fruition. I shook my head at him. "It was an impulse. I think I wanted a chance at my own assignment."

"Ah," Jasin Lebec said, the single word rich with irony. "The impulse must have been overwhelming. I gather from these—" He opened his hand and showed me the five message chips nestled in his palm. "—that you failed to tell my grandson you were leaving."

The chips caught the lounge lights and glistened coldly. "They're all from Jemeret?"

"Four of them," he answered, "and I'd caution you to play them in private. I've marked the order in case you didn't want to decipher the time and date codes. You probably should hear them as they arrived." He held them out, and when I didn't reach for them, he took my hand, turned it palm upward, and spilled the chips into it.

"And the fifth?" I stared at the little wafers as if I expected them to speak to me without a reader.

"The standard list of current events," he said. "Since at present the team consists only of the four of us, and we both know my powers are somewhat limited, I'd advise you to choose carefully if you decide to take on an assignment."

"The four of us and Keli," I corrected.

Mortel John cleared his throat. "I would like to be counted, Ronica McBride," he said evenly. "There are no talented children to train, and I don't believe the government will ask for any additional ones for some time. They've sent the MF to see what kind of talent might reside on the fringe worlds of the Com itself, and that investigation will probably be permitted to play itself out before the Tribunal turns again to Caryldon." I wondered how the MF would identify talent other than walking around and trying to see if they felt influenced.

"And, of course," Jasin Lebec said, "they're unwilling to bring any more talent up from Caryldon until the threat of Dolen T'Kelle is neutralized or eliminated."

"Yes, that would make sense." I was still staring at the chips I held. Then what Mortel John had asked truly penetrated, and I looked up at him. "I'm not sure I understand what you're offering."

"My services as a part of your—group." The brief hesitation showed me that he was uncomfortable with the term "team."

I closed my hand on the message chips. "But your services are not merely yours, are they?"

He remained expressionless, and I wondered if he'd always

had such a stolid countenance or if the impassiveness was a result of the decreasing amount of humanity he possessed. He wet his lips. "I cannot undertake to guarantee that their counsel would not be a part of what I would bring," he said at last, "but I would try to differentiate when I could."

"Surely you haven't the same animosity toward the MIs as your husband has," Jasin Lebec said.

"No, I haven't," I told him sincerely. "I'm angry over what happened to the Macerates, and I've been angry over the Drenalion for a long time, but talent in the Com has now done more damage to talent than either the clones or the MIs. So no, I'm not that angry with them—not any longer."

The cyborg nodded, and his words, though I didn't think he knew it, were amazingly meaningful, and would be even more so. "Seeing you suffer was never their goal. Nor was it mine."

"I know." I was surprised at how gentle that sounded, but then I knew that I'd just been apologized to, and I had never expected to receive an apology. "It's just that—with all the things you prepared me for, you never seemed to prepare me for what would actually come."

"I'm a teacher," Mortel John said, "not a seer. Preparation has nothing whatsoever to do with prophecy."

"Especially not in the worlds of the Com." Jasin Lebec's voice had a flat note of resignation in it. "Ronica, go and play your messages. Mortel John's earned a place on our team, and as long as my grandson's not here to refuse, I say he's one of us."

"No, he isn't," I said, "but John Caryl is. We can make a place for him."

Mortel John looked a little shaken. Then he nodded slowly. "That's a challenge I thought I wouldn't have to face again," he said. I am still amazed at how fraught with irony those words turned out to be. He raised his head and squared his shoulders almost unconsciously. "But I accept it."

I wanted to smile at him, but the edges of the message chips were digging into my hand. I relaxed my grip and went back to my cabin, extruded the comsole, and put the first chip into the slot, tapping off the vid so I couldn't see him.

Jemeret's voice was strangely emotionless. "Ronica, whether you think you're trying to punish me or yourself makes very little difference at this point. I was never angry at you, I was just angry. Turn *Detralume* around and bring it back to Markover. Respond to the station. We're all off-world now." It ended abruptly, without telling me who "all" was, but I assumed he meant Coney and Sandalari, in addition to himself.

I popped the chip and checked its chrono ID. He must have called down a lander as soon as he'd discovered I was gone. I'd passed through the station so quickly that it hadn't occurred to me to order them not to send a lander to the surface for another day or so. He'd have overridden my orders eventually, but it would have given me more time.

Still, if he was telling me to bring the Lumeship back, it meant he couldn't get another very quickly. At the same time that I missed him achingly, I felt relieved that he couldn't catch up with me so soon. I wasn't yet ready to face the enormity of his reaction to what I had done planetside.

The second chip had a little more emotion in its words, and had been made only a few hours later. "I thought you might be interested in knowing that Henion and Ginestra have taken the news about the Com very well, but Lyrafi's having some problems absorbing the new reality. She may not be willing to accept that some of us kept so momentous a secret for so long. Ashkalin says that Ginestra's doing what she can to keep her steady, but Lyrafi's a stronger talent than Ginestra and always has been."

Of course, I remember thinking. Lyrafi's the musician.

"Andriel has been fairly uncontrollable, so I'm glad we brought her up to Markover with us. She needed either you or Keli, but you more, and both of you are gone. You wanted her, Ronica, and now she thinks you've deserted her. If you didn't want to take my wishes into consideration in deciding to do this, you might have given a moment's thought to hers. When you respond to Markover, she wants to talk to you."

I heard in his voice tones of condemnation which may or may not have been there, and I was overwhelmed by a feeling of my own selfishness. It occurred to me that, for all my insistence on looking at Andriel as a young talent and my child, I'd been in the end as careless of her feelings as Kray had ultimately been of mine. I began to conjecture that, in addition to talent removing the "polite" gland, it had a deleterious effect on that balance of self-versus-other we all carry around inside us. I was sure it had affected Kray; it had affected me when I made Coney sleep with me, and I thought I'd outgrown it.

I popped that chip and put the third one in. It was timed four hours later than the one before. There was in his voice such a strong measure of control that I knew he was having a harder time containing his anger, or his fear for me, or both. "I suspect you have no intention of calling me back, so I'll make this short. Go to Orokell and stay there. You'll be safer there than anywhere else. The water people Glon sent us have signaled us that they're out of the last roll and heading for Markover, and we're taking their ship to meet you at Government House. Please don't do anything rash before we can reach you."

I was distressed that a rollship had been so readily available; I hadn't anticipated that. It would get him back into the Com before I could do anything at all by myself. At the same time, I felt relieved. I hadn't thought that Dolen T'Kelle might move against me. I supposed I'd known leaving the way I did might hurt Jemeret, but I hadn't anticipated that it would hurt me so much as well. I'd almost convinced myself that after what I'd done on Caryldon, he might be able to accept that I fled for everyone's good, but after about ten minutes I'd recognized that as pure self-deception.

I replaced the chip with the last of the ones Jemeret recorded, wondering what he still had to say to me. The last chip was a ship-to-ship message, *Zellume* to *Detralume*, and it was only a few minutes old. The first few seconds were the normal alignment beeps, and then the message played. The anger was gone, and he must have been mastering any fear that was left.

"I keep forgetting to remind you that I love you," Jemeret's voice said into the stillness of my cabin. "You may at times behave in ways I don't agree with or approve of, but that doesn't affect how I feel about what is the essence of you. Sooner or later, I want you to figure that out for yourself."

The message ran down into the disengagement clicks, and I said to the now silent comsole, "Sometimes you're wrong, Jemeret. I know you love me. I just want you to tell me that what I did on Caryldon was the right thing to do." Then I laughed at myself. I always held conversations—even arguments—with people who weren't there. I used to explain to Kray, at great length, when he wasn't with me, why I couldn't love him the way he wanted me to, and now it turned out that I really hadn't known very much about him, hadn't known what love meant to him. I was far better informed where my Lord Jemeret was concerned, and yet here I was, still talking to someone absent.

I put the last chip in the reader, called for a printed readout, and was just spooling it when the door signal told me Keli was outside. I let her in. Sinet was in the corridor behind her, and Keli automatically stepped aside so the talent could precede her.

"Now will you tell me what's wrong?" Sinet asked immediately.

"Nothing's wrong," I began, but the frank skepticism on her face made me curtail my words and look down at the readout I was twisting in my hands. I carefully smoothed and folded it.

"Listen to me, Ronica," Sinet said seriously. "I know I'm not a Class A, but that doesn't preclude my being sensitive to other people's feelings. You came back on board radiating defiance and anxiety and a bravado I haven't seen the like of since—what did I say?"

"Of course!" I almost forgot everything else as the insight hit me. "I've been so blind. Keli, get Jasin Lebec in here."

Curious, a little uncertain, but always obedient, she spun and ran out of the cabin.

Sinet looked after her for a moment. "What just happened?"

"Sinet, you have Class A ability," I said to her with real excitement. She performed something between a frown and a goggle. "You do," I insisted. "Everything you said about my feelings was directly on target, and I was aware the last time we talked that I was hyperconscious of how you felt, but I wasn't making any effort to read you at all. See if you can project at me."

She was still staring. "Ronica, I wouldn't have the slightest idea how."

I was about to encourage her to try anyway when Jasin Lebec arrived, with Keli at his heels. Before he even had a chance to ask me anything, I demanded, "Why wasn't the choice made to train Sinet for Class A tasks?"

The embarrassment that flowed over his face quickly, without any attempt on his part to disguise it, surprised me, but seemed to flabbergast Sinet.

I watched the old man closely, then asked, "Or is that actually a 'who' question?"

"May I sit down?" Jasin Lebec asked. "In fact, we should probably all sit down."

I took Sinet's arm and led her to a seat on the couch. Jasin Lebec followed, but Keli stayed by the door, nervous again, as if she somehow didn't belong in the group. For once, I did not call her over.

Sinet had clearly gathered her wits. "I'm sorry," she said in the tone of someone who isn't sorry at all, "but are you about to tell me that I could have been a Class A, and just—wasn't?"

"The classes of talent are a Com construct," Jasin Lebec said. I had never actually expected him to say it as baldly as that. "This is a rigidly hierarchical society in many ways. The need to sort and classify is extremely strong. We sort responsibilities, assignments, the technological levels of worlds, and we sort people."

"But the Com needs Class A talent," I protested. "Why wouldn't they have taken advantage of Sinet's ability?"

"Why indeed?" Jasin Lebec's mouth twisted in the imitation of a smile. "I was much younger—almost forty-five years younger—when Sinet was given to the Com. I was very good at handling my assignments, and it was thought—I regret to say it—that Class A ability might be sex-linked."

My mouth dropped open.

"In addition," the old man went on, "there was an argument

made that all truly valuable positions in the human part of Com society needed to be individual—unique. There's only one Com Counselor, one MI Liaison, one Planetary Governor on each world. Next, there are two assistant counselors, liaisons, and governors, and so on down the hierarchy. One Class A fit the Com notion of neatness. And we didn't have a Class B when Sinet went into training."

"But—Jemeret?" It was a protest, as well as a question.

"In the ten years before he came along, the assignments multiplied, and since he was male and extremely strong, we decided to train him for Class A assignments."

"And me? Weren't you more likely to have trained Kray, then, instead of me?"

"You were far stronger than he was," Jasin Lebec said, his voice mild. "And by that time, the Science Bureau had eliminated any possibility of sex-linking for talent."

Sinet wiped her eyes with her fingertips. "I could have been more," she said softly.

My head snapped around to Jasin Lebec. "Could she still be Class A? Could Mortel John train her?"

Jasin Lebec answered slowly, "I don't know."

"Sinet, do you sing? Or play an instrument?" I knew I was making little or no sense to her, but I seemed unable to stop. Now it was Jasin Lebec's turn to stare at me, too.

Sinet frowned. "I dance," she answered. "I used to steal time to practice once the government decided I'd be too busy to continue studying it. Why would you ask that?"

"Music—knowing it, playing it, loving it—somehow increases either the capacity for or the ability to use talent," I told her, as if it were commonly known.

So I was surprised when Jasin Lebec asked, "It does?"

"Didn't we tell you?" I asked him absently.

The first chime for the next roll cut off my last word, and I automatically started to rise to go to Tynnanna, then realized he wasn't here. I sat back down again.

"Nobody told me," Jasin Lebec said.

I was too busy thinking to acknowledge him. "Sinet, you ought to ask Mortel John to give you some brain physiology to study, and some exercises to begin learning. We need to know how much you can gain, and how fast."

She got to her feet, still frowning as she absorbed the implications. She paused at the iris to say shrewdly, "You might not need me so much if you'd waited long enough to bring the others with you," then went out.

Jasin Lebec eyed me.

"Don't ask," I said. "It seemed like something I had to do."

He shook his head. "I was merely curious about all the trouble you and my grandson went to to avoid being separated when you first came into the Com together. It seems a little strange that now you would be choosing separation."

I had no answer to that. There wasn't really an answer to why I'd acted suddenly and thoughtlessly. All my reasons were excuses. It had probably been wrong to run; I wanted to talk to Jemeret about Sinet and what Jasin Lebec had told us. I didn't know how to reapproach him now. I could only go to Orokell and wait for him there, as he'd asked, my gesture of conciliation. I looked down at my hands and waited until Jasin Lebec, realizing I wasn't going to reply, had gone out. Then I registered the fact that I was still holding the printed readout, and I uncrumpled it and spread it on my thigh.

A news item made me laugh. Causaday was trying to figure out how they had ended up with a lot of goods they maintained they never ordered from Nogdala 7, but that world was incommunicado now, and there seemed to be no one able to accept return of the merchandise. The Causadayans were debating what to do with the materials, because there was one faction that wanted the products very much and was very vocal about it. The next item indicated that the spaceport was finished on Ananda, which meant the Scuttlers would soon begin their campaign.

I hadn't had a chance to read much more than that when the second chime sounded, so I skimmed the rest, then refolded the readout, sliding it into my sleeve. When I looked up, I realized that I'd forgotten Keli was still at the door.

"What *is* wrong?" she asked me curiously. "You hauled out of Caryldon like your power source lost its governor."

I smiled a little at the ease with which she participated in our relationship when we were alone, so different from her near-worship at the outset. "I did something Jemeret didn't want me to do," I answered her. "I thought it would be better to be someplace else for a little while."

As the countdown beeps began, she asked doubtfully, "Do you think that was wise?" and sat down beside me. It was always smarter to take the roll sitting or lying down.

I sighed. "Right now I can't remember the last time I did anything I'd have characterized as 'wise,' " I said to her. Then we were swept into the motionless rising of the roll nausea.

I really did intend to stay on Orokell, not only because Jemeret had told me to, but because I almost enjoyed it. Sinet, Keli, and I spent a day in the wild, while Jasin Lebec and Lendo Dell reported in on our recent spate of activities, carefully refraining from any details about our attempts to retrain talent in the Caryldon mold instead of in the Com mold. What Mortel John reported or did not report I really had no way of knowing, and yet I had a strange feeling that the human part would have told them nothing, and the MI part had no need to report to anyone else.

I was at odds with an elected destiny. I'd decided to make a basic change on Caryldon, and then I'd fled from the responsibility of that decision, even though I wasn't sure why, and into limbo. I missed Jemeret, and I was waiting for something to happen. Two things did.

The first was another of those moments involving talent that are always stunningly surprising—one of those leaps of knowledge that occur because somebody never told the person trying to do them that they couldn't be done. No one had ever told me I couldn't pathfind a planet, so I had. No one had ever told Andriel that the sting couldn't be used unless she was actually in someone's presence, and she was absolutely determined to find me, so she did.

It was late at night, but I'd been unable to sleep, awash in that strange sense of waiting that I'd fallen into after arriving on Orokell without Jemeret, without Tynnanna, and without duties.

Earlier in the night, I'd gone into the common room of the suite and found Sinet. She was sitting in a vidchair in the corner of the room where Tynnanna's grass had been before, and she looked up as I came out of my bedroom, tying my wrapper around my waist.

Sinet shoved the vidchair arm away and said, "You couldn't sleep either, I see."

I'd managed to not be alone with her since I'd avoided answering her question about why I left Caryldon without the others, but if she was surprised that I'd come in now, she didn't show it. "I don't sleep very well after I make stupid mistakes," I said.

Sinet laughed softly. "If that were true for me, I'd probably never sleep at all." The smile faded. "But I suspect you accuse yourself of something you didn't do. I suspect you don't make stupid mistakes the way a lot of other people do."

"Why do you think such flattering things about me?"

"Flattering?" she repeated. "I only meant that you're still young, Ronica. The young don't normally make stupid mistakes, just youthful ones."

She almost made me laugh. "But most young people don't have the future of worlds in their hands. It seems that I do."

"Did you take that future, or was it given to you?" It was an exquisite question, and I hadn't anticipated it.

I decided I didn't want to answer it. "You and Mortel John," I said, swinging the subject away from me, "do you two do what—you and Kray did?"

"You mean, sexually?" she clarified. I nodded. "Mortel John is not as—adventurous as Kray was. I think that adventuresomeness—" She stumbled over the neologism, made a face at herself. "—is peculiar to humans, and he's not that any longer."

"But to talent, too. Kray was very talented, and so are you, and you're—adventurous in that way."

Sinet was smiling again. "If you're curious, there's a lot of information available in the library banks," she said. "But if you're looking to experiment, I suggest you ask Jemeret. I had the impression he wouldn't want to share you sexually."

I had to gather not to blush. And I was about to say something—I don't remember what—when I felt the unmistakable touch, first searching and tentative, then happy and demanding attention. It was Andriel. I gasped, spinning around, spilling my coffee, but of course no one else was in the room.

"What?" Sinet asked, but I ignored her. I was grasping at Andriel's touch and following it back, to see where it had come from and how it reached me. I was stunned to trace it to the main office of the guest residence, and then into the eftel.

I knew instantly what had happened, and it burst on me with an obviousness that made me wonder how the hell I'd never thought of it before. Andriel had pathfound the eftel on *Zellume* and, understanding it completely, had identified eftels on Orokell, then slipped her sting through them until she found the one that led to me, reaching out just as I'd told her to. She hadn't seen the distance as an insurmountable barrier, because no one ever told her it was. She didn't think she had to be in someone's presence, because no one ever trained her to believe that she did. She saw those things as obstacles to her goal, and she wasn't going to let anything stop her. Despite Glon's urging, I was still thinking with walls.

I fought down my shock and acknowledged Andriel's touch with both warmth and gratitude, then gathered and pathfound the house's eftel, asking it to show me how it connected in real-time to other units like its own, then how it identified the differences among them. Once I knew all that, I soared along the network of eftels—seeking and recognizing the unique code of each, even scouting out the units on Caryldon, in the Temple, in our house. At the same time, I was soothing Andriel, who was broadcasting such happiness at having found me that I wondered how Jemeret and Jasin Lebec could be unaware of it. It took a while before she ceased being restive. Then I scouted around *Zellume* with almost the same strength as if I'd actually been on board the ship, until I found the signatures of Coney, Sandalari, and my Lord Jemeret. They were all asleep. I didn't wake them. I was very tired by that time, but exhilarated, too.

It seemed to me that all things were possible. If we could sting through the eftel, then there wasn't any reason we couldn't do it through the more complex eftel vid, and, I realized, it might be possible to do it through the even more complex MIs themselves. If we could sting *through* the machines, perhaps we could find ways to alter, to influence, the group consciousness we needed to change so much, without having to sting it directly, and without having to try to turn it off.

It was the first time I'd thought in terms of projecting consciousness into the MIs instead of trying to destroy the system. If it were possible to work subtly, it might not demand the great expenditures of reserve energy that could possibly kill us.

I snapped back out of the eftel network and nearly staggered with sudden awareness of exhaustion. Alarmed, Sinet sprang to her feet and grabbed for me. "Ronica! Are you all right?"

"Yes, fine," I said, calming a heart rate that had raced up while I was paying attention to the workings of the eftel network. I gauged my reserves and was astonished to find them more than five-sixths gone. It struck me then that Jemeret might have been right all along. There would be no way to sting the immensity of the MIs without access to far more reserve energy than we possessed. An effort to do so would be suicide. And I saw no way of getting the human population of Orokell or Werd or any of the other core worlds to line up and join hands, like the Samothen did when we needed them to. Even if I could have, only talents had reserves, so what good would the support of the human population have done?

I set Sinet's hands away from me. "I just need to deep for a while," I said to her.

She looked dubious, but stepped back. I could feel what she wasn't saying. She wished that Jemeret were there.

So did I.

I was having more and more difficulty understanding why I'd bolted as I had. The logic I'd operated under, which seemed so seamless when I was using it, now appeared tattered and incomplete. What had carried me so precipitously to Orokell? Why had it been vital to leave Jemeret, Coney, and Sandalari behind?

The suite bell chimed, and before I could take a step toward the door, Keli had flown out of her bedroom, blaster drawn, and raced past me to signal the door open. Outside in the corridor, looking startled by the militancy of their greeting, stood Davin Olavson and Gromily EnCastro. A quick glance told me that the Selected Image had come without her Motive, which was nearly unheard of. Even more unusual, her serious face, though turned to me in surprise, did not reflect my own curiosity.

"May we speak with you, Ronica McBride?" the tall old man asked quietly.

"Of course," I said. Keli had stepped back from the doorway and holstered her weapon, but she didn't leave the room. Sinet seemed bemused by Keli's extreme vigilance and surprised by the identity of our callers.

The two of them came into the suite and walked directly to the comsole. I noticed that Gromily EnCastro clung to Davin Olavson's side, even though she didn't touch him, as if they were attached by an invisible string. I wondered if she were feeling at odds with everything without her accustomed Motive to reflect, but before I could say anything, she turned back toward me as Davin Olavson keyed in a sequence.

"I can move independently, Ronica McBride," she said in a low voice. "I just tend not to do it when any of the believers can observe me. It's a heavy thing to be seen as an inspiration."

I didn't say, *Yes, I know.*

Davin Olavson turned away from the comsole with a readout in his hands. "The destruction of the Macerates has had far-reaching repercussions, Ronica McBride," he said. "Our people are increasingly fearful, and we are unable to reassure them. On several worlds where things are—unsettled anyway, there have been attacks against some of us."

"The Purists have suffered the most hitherto," Gromily EnCastro said sadly. "They have no leader here on Orokell, and they have renounced so many of the trappings of civilization that they are functionally defenseless."

Davin Olavson held out the readout he'd called for. "These are the up-to-present figures indicating the scope of the problems the Purists are experiencing. We ask you to intervene to save them."

I was tired, but not so tired that I still couldn't gather it away and snap to alertness. The figures on the readout were meticulously organized, which told me at once that the MIs must have been aware of the problem, and for some reason might even have considered it important. The Science Bureau might have produced an analysis of this scope, but the scientists were highly unlikely to extend themselves for the benefit of the religions, to which they'd never bothered paying even false respect.

"You don't come to me for your own people," I said to them.

"We do," Davin Olavson said.

Gromily EnCastro's higher voice followed his like an echoing shadow, and she went on, "If we failed to come to you for these people, who are ours as fully as any of humanity belongs to the rest of it, then we would deserve no one to come to you when we are threatened in turn. Can you intervene?"

I studied the figures, almost hyperaware that I had just been presented the opportunity I'd thought I wanted: I was being asked to create a Class A scenario, by myself, in the Com. It was, I knew, a problem the government would never have presented to me; I had certainly not seen anything about it in the news. Yet the readout Davin Olavson had pulled gave clear evidence of MI involvement, and the MIs did nothing by chance.

I raised my voice. "I'd like your input," I said.

Sinet opened her mouth to ask which of them I was speaking to, but her words were overridden by the click I was expecting and the emotionless, "We await your question."

Davin Olavson and Gromily EnCastro exchanged a startled look. Jara Deland had always fostered the idea that only the MI Liaison could speak directly with the machines at will, by implication because only the MI Liaison would be answered. I'd just disproved that assertion.

"Estimate cost of gathering approximately 100,000 individuals from 150 worlds and transporting them to the vicinity of Sargasso for ultimate resettlement on Ananda."

With a barely discernible pause the voice provided an amount that, while not low, was tenable.

"Estimate amount of time needed to perform this operation."

"State whether the individuals are willing or unwilling." The question was unexpected, but entirely logical.

I looked at the two religious leaders. "This is your project, and therefore your call," I said.

Davin Olavson stroked his chin with long fingers. "If we approach it correctly, I'd say they'd be willing."

I said to the MIs, "Consider the target population willing." Indeed, I thought to myself, the population ought to be ecstatic at the thought of being in a position to use its asceticism to build a world that badly needed building. I looked at Davin Olavson again. "Can your people get word to the Purists, at least on the core worlds, to assemble at the spaceports so they can be shuttled to the transports?"

"Three tendays," the MI voice said, replying to my original question about the time estimate, "not counting transit time between worlds."

Gromily EnCastro seemed momentarily agitated, but it was hard to tell because she had to battle to express the emotion. "You don't think they'll reject relocation because it involves using the space technology, do you?"

Davin Olavson shook his head. "I think we'll be all right there. Purists try to be practical. They've accepted inoculation, bargained with the planetary governments over oxy mixtures on low atmosphere worlds, and things like that. We'll ensure their willingness to listen, if not their compliance."

"Settled, then," I said with genuine satisfaction, and raised my voice again. "Please proceed to set up the relocation operation. Use whatever Lumeships are coming in from outlying worlds, and take the two transports in caravan to destination once everyone is aboard. Target population: followers of Purism. Ultimate settlement world: Ananda, the continent of the exiles. Cost to be borne from the general fund on my authority."

"We must point out that the Purists have done nothing to merit exile," the MI voice said.

"This is not an exile decision, nor a sentence," I said quickly. "It does not involve the need to secure a judicial order. Maintain security of operation until it's complete." I should have guessed they would take the last instruction to mean anyone except the Tribunal.

The MIs clicked off without a word, and before anyone else in the common room had the opportunity to speak or move, Mortel John came out of the bedroom he shared with Sinet, nodding to the two religious leaders. He walked directly to me. "Congratulations, Ronica McBride," he said.

Startled, I asked, "Why?"

The big cyborg took one of my hands in both of his. Neither of us questioned his right to do such a personal thing. He had rocked me back to sleep after nightmares in the earliest of my memories. "You just accepted, and created a scenario for, your first solo assignment."

"It wasn't truly an assignment," Sinet said. "It came from outside the government, and it benefited someone other than the government."

Mortel John let go of my hand and turned toward his lover. "Of course it qualifies as an assignment," he said. "I've been telling the Tribunal for years that what makes an assignment is its scope, not the fact that they've defined it as one."

The comsole began blinking. I glanced meaningfully at Sinet, and she swung to her feet to answer the call.

"We'd better go," Gromily EnCastro said, her voice betraying nervousness for the first time. "My people will reflect the urgency of the Epicyclists for the saving of Purism."

"We give you thanks, Ronica McBride," Davin Olavson said warmly, bending his tall frame toward me. "And our thanks, too, for seeing us at this extremely late hour." In fact, it was almost morning.

I murmured reassurance and watched them leave.

Sinet turned from the comsole to me. "It's Pel Nostro," she

said. "He says good morning, and what are the MIs doing rerouting rollships and commandeering MF transports on your say-so, and by the way, would you like to come over for breakfast?" She sounded amused. I recognized the flaw in my order to the MIs, let my gathering slide, and returned to weariness.

"Tell him we need to relocate the Purists, and to ask the MIs if he wants statistics justifying it. Then tell him I'll be there in ten minutes," I said to Sinet. "Keli, are you up to a call on the Com Counselor?"

"Anything you need me for," the young woman said quickly.

I knew she was tired, too, but I felt better with her along.

Jara Deland met me with a forced smile, and Keli braced against the wall, silent. I felt wary. Jara Deland made meaningless small talk until Pel Nostro came in, then looked distinctly relieved and poured coffee while he greeted me with a smile.

"What brings all this on?" I asked him, glancing at his wife as she sat down across from me.

"We wanted to entertain you privately," the Com Counselor answered, "and we expect the rest of the talent team to arrive tomorrow. Have some carosh seed rolls."

I thanked him, reached for one of the palm-size rolls and pinched off a seed cluster, rolling it between my fingers to release its taste. "What was it that you needed to speak with me about, Pel? Are you going to ask me if I've made my choice about remaining in the Com or returning to Caryldon?"

"We hoped—when we first heard you'd set out alone to return to us—the Tribunal, that is," he said, stumbling a little over the words, "that it would be an indication you were coming back to us for active service. But Jara says nothing could be further from reality."

My gaze flew to the MI Liaison, and she looked at me squarely. "The MIs have warned us that you and Jemeret Cavanaugh are in great danger, and that it is completely unlikely anyone will be able to help you avoid it."

I felt a shiver run down my spine, freezing nerves already

chilled from exhaustion. "How can they know a thing like that unless they intend to have a hand in it?" I asked tightly.

"I asked them where they got their data from," Jara Deland said readily enough, "and I'm afraid I didn't understand their answer. When I asked them to enlarge on it, they didn't respond."

"What was their answer?" I was surprised at how calm my voice sounded, and when Jara Deland hesitated, I repeated it in the same even voice.

At last Jara Deland said, "They said they had received some answers to their questions."

I was electrified, and, almost unconsciously, my hand strayed to the thigh pouch of my jumpsuit, where the brow-crown lay hidden. The MI message that was so obscure to Jara Deland was entirely clear to me. Somehow, for whatever reason, the starfire had contacted the MIs, and we already knew that the starfire had ways of perceiving imminent peril. "Was there any kind of guidance about how we might avoid the danger?"

Pel Nostro said suddenly, "If you die, Ronica, I will resign my post as Com Counselor."

The statement seemed completely illogical. "I don't understand," I said.

Jara Deland toyed with the stem of the wineglass in front of her. "The MIs will have no part in trying to save you, Ronica. They say they will not bring you harm, but they will not help. They say that you'll understand."

And in fact I did. The MIs had put together as much as they could and built a model on it—whether it was watching us, hearing scraps of conversation, analyzing the amount of time we'd spent bubbled, or knowing that Jemeret had been highly critical of them even before they'd killed the Macerates. Then the starfire, for reasons I had no way of guessing, told them we were in danger. Their model showed them that they were in danger as well, and from us. So they warned us that we had to be wary, and then they honestly admitted we were on our own.

I suppose it was reasonable to the MIs; I certainly grasped the logic of it. They had reached a compromise with whatever electronic ideals were built into them. They had spoken with Jara Deland rather than directly with me. Their very warning showed me that they would take no direct action against us, certainly for now. In many ways, that was not a human choice. The MIs could be quite different from the people who had created them. Human beings might not have warned us if they thought we were a danger to them. The MIs were telling me, through their normal intermediary, that they would not act against us on their own behalf as they had acted against the Macerates, ostensibly on talent's behalf. Once again I was confronting the maxim that sentience was not sameness.

Pel Nostro and his wife were watching me closely.

I smiled at them. "They're right, I do understand. After all, it isn't like they rushed to my aid in the past."

Jara Deland turned her face away.

I looked at the Com Counselor. "Pel, no matter what happens, you mustn't resign. No one person has as much experience in running the government as you do, and whether we succeed in escaping the danger or we fail, the government won't be the same."

His expression demanded further explanation as he said, "The Com needs talent to function."

"The Com has its own talent—we proved that with M'Cherys. The MIs know it. Mortel John knows it. You and Anok and Petra and Marga and Faucon will need to find ways of identifying and training it." I rolled another seed cluster between my fingers. "You'll have to learn what it takes for talent—most talent—to develop fully and healthily."

"I would feel honor-bound to resign," Pel Nostro insisted, but not particularly strongly, a politician's insistence, paying lip service to honor while resting on expediency. "You are a government servant, and we have a duty to protect you."

"Only so that you can use me," I argued, "and I'm afraid I won't be that useful to you any longer no matter what happens."

Pel Nostro exchanged one long, meaningful look with Jara Deland, then rose and went to the comsole, which in this room was built into the wall. He keyed in a code, and a readout printed immediately. He came back to the table carrying it. "In that case," he said, "I have prepared this for you, on my own authority. The Tribunal is not aware of it, but I believe they will make no effort to contravene it." He folded the sheet in half.

"What is it?" I asked him.

The Com Counselor held the document out to me. "If we cannot protect you," he said, "I see no way we can honorably hold you to your oath. I've taken the liberty of releasing you from it."

I took the flimsy, wordlessly studied it, and almost laughed. Pel Nostro was the perfect political animal. Confronted by a situation in which he had no control, he arranged things so he would be absolved of the responsibility for having control. And yet, by giving me my release, he was making my ultimate choice much easier, since the Tribunal would have no legal ground to stand on if I wanted to leave. Provided, I added dryly to myself, I lived to make that choice.

"I assume this is registered?" I looked at him, admiring his skill in areas in which I had little competence and for which I had less patience.

"As of an hour ago," he said. "You have no intention of challenging it, I gather." The words had a faint note of inquiry attached to them.

"None," I assured him, adding, "so you don't have to worry about it coming back to haunt you." I folded the readout and slid it into a pocket. "And I meant it when I said you shouldn't resign if something happens to me. It'd be a grand gesture, but I don't think the Tribunal would accept it anyway."

What little appetite I might have had when I walked into their suite was largely gone, and I was very tired. I drank some more coffee and consumed two of the rolls out of politeness and to acknowledge their likely enormous expense, then excused myself, signaling to Keli. We escaped without having to listen to too many warnings to be careful.

As I learned immediately, however, there would have been no such thing as too many warnings.

We walked back into the courtyard of the precincts. It

seemed unusually quiet, even though it was long enough past dawn for people to have been up and bustling around. I noticed the calm offhandedly, thinking I was tired and would welcome a chance to deep; thinking Jemeret would arrive, probably after nightfall the next day, and that I would have a lot of explaining to do; thinking it would be good to see Andriel again, as well as Coney and Sandalari.

Between one step and the next there was only darkness.

When I was in training for so long at the School for Talent, I was taught that decisions were conscious things. We explored them objectively, weighed alternatives, then chose. But the most important decisions, I discovered on Caryldon, have a tendency to come upon us while we're preoccupied with other matters. So it was that I got to do a great thing while I was concentrating on doing a much smaller one. I was concerned first with staying alive, then with trying to emerge without succumbing to the will of my captor. I was thinking about me. What I got to do, not deliberately, the way a hero would, was buy the chance for talent to go on evolving. When I figured it out, it boggled my mind.

You can train forever, I suppose, but sooner or later it all comes down to who you are deep inside. And when it does, you make a commitment, unaware of the implications. At least, so it was for me.

XVIII. Strength and Power

One of the things I learned on Caryldon and haven't thought about nearly as much as I should is the difference between strength and power. Power is what makes things happen or not happen; strength is enduring what happens. When I awoke in darkness, I was about to receive a practical lesson in that equation.

The darkness remained so complete that I had to be certain I'd actually opened my eyes. As when I'd first awakened on Caryldon, my initial inventory was of myself. My reserves were full, which I didn't expect. I must have deeped for some time while I was unconscious. I gathered, beat back the stirrings of fear, and analyzed my sensory systems, because the oppressive darkness made me wonder if my eyesight had been ruined. My optic nerves and their cranial connections were fine; the necessary chemicals were in balance as well. With my eyes at their widest possible iris, the darkness was still profound. I was underground, then, because even in the bowels of something human-made, bits of light found their way, like water migrating around impermeable substances, patiently seeking the permeable.

It occurs to me now, thinking of those first moments in the solid darkness, that if I had remembered the brow-crown in my thigh pouch, I might have made my own light. But, thank the stars, I didn't remember it. If I'd used it, Dolen T'Kelle would have taken it away from me. Since I didn't recall it tucked away in my jumpsuit, he didn't know it was there. I'm digressing. This is the part of the story I don't want to tell.

In the formless darkness, I'd satisfied myself that my sight vas unimpaired, if ineffective. I analyzed my hearing and pecame aware that, some distance away in what seemed to be cavernous space, someone was breathing, rapidly and shal-owly. Without worrying about whether it would be there when reached for it, I used my sting to see who was in the darkness vith me.

The moment I used the sting, I felt a cruel, gleeful presence eap at it, trying to grasp hold of it and follow it back to my rain. I yanked it away, in desperate self-preservation, perhaps vith more strength than my attacker had credited me for, ecause it slid from the assaulting grasp despite a late, startled ffort to hold on to it. I slammed up my shields at once and held hem unbreakably in place. All the time that Jemeret had made ne work to control them subtly had also developed my ability o hold them against an assault, even one stronger than I'd ever aced before. I knew at once what the evil force wanted; its urpose had to be to injure me sufficiently to render my sting seless, at least temporarily. I shuddered with the knowledge nd drew in on myself, listening to the breathing as if afraid it vould approach me.

After a time, I began to be aware that the breathing was not oming from the attacker, but from someone else. It had real lements of distress to it, as if the person doing it were uncon-cious and hurt.

I'd been lying on my back. Now I scrambled up onto my nees and laid my palms flat on the rough surface in front of ne, pathfinding to ensure reasonably safe footing. The dark-ess could have concealed boulders, stalagmites, chasms, or ther hazards. The place was large and sluggish in its response, ut I kept my impatience down as I waited. Eventually I got the rong impression of a roughly ovoid chamber, made uneven y the ridges of natural bedding in the floor, walls, and ceiling. he bed edges were too sharp to have been worn naturally over me. This cavern was of human manufacture, crude and cent. One spot in the ceiling was different in texture from the st of the chamber; it was probably the sole means of entering exiting. It was at least eighteen meters over my head, and hile Class A talents can do many things, we can't levitate.

I began to make my way on my hands and knees toward the sound of the harsh breathing, since my fingers gave me faster passage than I could have accomplished edging forward on my feet. The roughness of the floor made me glad jumpsuit material doesn't tear, for it would have shredded after a little of the progress, leaving my knees unprotected. The breathing was coming from Keli, who was lying on her shoulders and one hip, her body twisted awkwardly, almost as if she'd fallen in the midst of spinning. I didn't believe that she'd been thrown in from the entrance, though, because the fall would certainly have killed her.

"Keli." I touched and straightened her legs, then her arms. Her extremities didn't appear to be broken, and there was no warm, wet slick that would have indicated bleeding. "Keli." I felt her head, the short hair tangled but not matted. I wanted to probe her, so that I could assess structures and chemical balances, but I didn't dare. One thing I was sure of now was that the malevolent force would be waiting for me to use my sting. I couldn't use it idly. Perhaps I wouldn't be able to use it at all. "Keli, wake up."

She stirred under my fingertips, then slowly regained consciousness, function returning, first weakly, then with more strength. She coughed, clearing the harshness out of her breathing, moaned a little, raised a hand to her forehead pushing my hand aside. "Am I blind?" she asked.

"No, I don't think so," I answered, hoping that she wasn't. "I can't see either. We're underground, and there isn't any light Don't strain your eyes trying to see."

"Underground?" She struggled to sit up, and I slid my arm across her shoulders, partly to help support her and partly because I needed the close human contact. I hugged her against my chest as she blew the rest of the mistiness out of her brain "Underground on Orokell?"

"Maybe," I said, "but we can't assume that."

She drew in her breath suddenly, surprised, then groped fo my hand and slid it down her side until I could feel the sourc of her astonishment. She was still wearing her blaster. I path found it instantly, found it still charged, and was immediatel struck with the awareness of something I didn't dare verbalize. It was clear that Keli and I had been abducted; it was equally clear that my sting had been attacked by what had to be another talent. Only one abductor would be bold enough, confident enough, to let us keep a loaded weapon, and that was one who either intended never to come back for us or knew he could keep us from using it.

"Keli, we need to disable it completely. And if we find any other weapons lying around here, we need to disable those."

"What? Why?" I could feel her hand tightening on the blaster under mine.

"There's every chance that someone might—compel you to use it on me." I can't imagine what my voice must have sounded like, emerging from total darkness, saying such a thing.

"I'd never—" she started to say in horrified denial, then cut it off. "You could stop them, couldn't you? You could make certain I wouldn't hurt you."

"I'd try," I said, "but I don't know if I'd succeed." I was speaking very slowly now, feeling the words, trying them on for size, for accuracy and the ring of truth.

Keli's voice dropped to a whisper. "What are you saying?"

"Someone's got us, Keli, and they know how to keep us. It takes talent to overcome talent."

I felt her impulse to say the name, squeezed her hand quickly to discourage it, as if by not letting it be spoken, I could keep it from being true. And of course, if he never returned for us, it wouldn't have to be true. But even as I thought that, I knew that Dolen T'Kelle had put us here because he meant to come back for us. Otherwise, we would be dead now, instead of in the dark. I took my hand off Keli's as she drew the blaster, then listened to the noises as she efficiently disassembled it, even sightlessly, and crushed several of the vital components.

After a while we took our time and completely explored the floor of the chamber, inch by inch, on our hands and knees. Against one wall was a large container with packets of nutrient tabs and water in it, primitive, but effective both as a way to keep us alive and a way to deliver a message. We were presently not in any mortal danger; he didn't want us to die.

She began to shake, and I groped for her shoulders and told her to calm down. "We need to keep our heads." It was easy to say. A day later I understood just how hard it would be to do. My time sense, which was distorted by wary waiting and a complete lack of outside stimuli, told me that Keli and I had been awake for about twelve hours when Dolen T'Kelle joined us.

I soon discovered that he was stronger than I was by a factor of three, which meant he was at least half again as strong as Jemeret. His reserves must have been huge, and he had never been socialized into using his power for the good of anyone other than himself. How he'd developed the power, in the Com, without giving himself away, could only be attributed to the fact that, rather than prompting any splinter messianic movement, he had co-opted one of the recognized, legitimate religions. He was a clever man. He was also completely ruthless. His talent was entirely unfettered by morality. He proved it to us in short order.

He brought light with him when he came, lowering a force-lev tunnel through the opening I'd previously noticed in the ceiling and floating down to the floor bathed in a piercingly bright light from above. Keli shielded her face against it. I irised my eyes to pinpoints, watching the absurdly dramatic entrance and wondering if he expected us to worship him. He was wearing a sleeveless robe with the Macerate symbols on it over a jumpsuit, and he seemed to strike poses in it even as he descended. I thought it would be ridiculous to perceive him as an object of worship. Now I think it would have been preferable.

Almost at the floor of the chamber, he made a slight, mocking bow and said, "I hope you haven't been too uncomfortable, Ronica McBride."

I wanted to lash out, but I didn't dare. "Why am I still alive?" I asked.

His feet touched the rock. He stayed at the edge of the force-lev field, smiling broadly and confidently at me. "You are a valuable commodity," he answered. "The lives of the others weren't worth much in the balance. The government believed it could do without them, so I was never tempted to try to preserve them." He stressed the word "preserve" automatically, as any Macerate would have. "But now that all my followers have been eliminated, my need for bargaining power has become more of a priority."

I almost told him that his key assumption was quite wrong, that the Com had released me from my oath, that the MIs had accepted the possibility of my death. Then I realized that would be the most stupid single thing I'd ever done. I asked, "What is it that you want to use me to bargain for?"

He regarded me with narrowed eyes for a moment. "I don't believe I'll answer that question," he said. His great, shaggy head turned toward Keli, the dark eyes suddenly glittering. "Communication with the Tribunal can be notoriously slow, especially when I have no eftel available. I thought we might pass the time in some diverting ways."

She raised her head, her eyes more accustomed to the light now. "I didn't believe it of you," she said in a low voice. "Not at first. I thought you couldn't possibly have betrayed the ideals of the Preserver."

Dolen T'Kelle laughed heartily, looking at her with a kind of contemptuous affection that made me uneasy. "How quaint you are," he said. "It was credulity like yours that allowed me to make such a success of a truly third-rate religion. I must admit it was almost a relief when the facade broke apart. I was getting increasingly bored with the incessant praying as every day went by." He gathered the edges of the robe about him in an almost oratorical stance. "It's ironic—all those years praying for a different world, and then the Com steps in and makes it different for me. Poof. The Macerates are gone."

"Millions of people," I said. "All those lives wasted."

His head swiveled back to me again. "Clearly, you're not a student of history. If there's one thing that human history has taught us again and again, it's that millions of lives don't matter. Sometimes a single life matters—in this case, yours—but millions of lives are worth nothing."

I wanted to argue, but my sense of even normal megalomaniacs was that argument was provocation; a megalomanic talent was an even more horrifying proposition. And it seemed paradoxical. Talent was to have been humanity's hope. Talents were supposed to be beyond such petty concerns as those that preoccupied the humans from whom our subspecies would need to emerge.

Keli had tears in her eyes. I suspected she wanted me to say something, but I bit back my impulse.

Dolen T'Kelle was surprised by my lack of response. I could tell that clearly without reading him, and I would not have reached for my sting. It was the only weapon I had and, like holding back the sweeper piece in the scattergies game, I had to keep it in reserve, not using it. Use it too soon, lose it too soon, went the game saying.

"I expected more animation from you," he said. "Indeed, I was looking forward to it."

"I don't feel particularly animated, Dolen." It was all I dared risk.

He nodded, as if absorbing that, twisted his mouth a little, and then said, "I propose to see what I can do to animate you, then." I recognized the threat-challenge behind the words and knew that he was confident enough in his power to want me to use my sting against him. He had no intention of killing me, but that resolve did not preclude his trying to better me in other ways. Like everyone else in the high levels of government, he knew from my personal history that I was breakable. I suspected with a chill thud of nausea that he was cognizant of how I had broken.

"Pressure points," he said now, as if the words were heavy with meaning. He stroked his thick beard with heavy fingers.

Keli jerked upright, eyes wide. I knew that he'd stung her.

Dolen T'Kelle smiled, teeth gleaming in the dark mass of his beard. "As my last loyal follower," he said mockingly, "recite for me the Macerate tenet on pain."

She was trembling under whatever compulsion he was holding on her. I told myself I could not let myself interfere, not while he wanted me to, that I would not let him manipulate me. I was so naive—stupid, really. I hadn't the faintest notion of what power could do if it was warped.

Keli said obediently, "Pain has not been put into the universe to punish us, but to instruct us. Once we learn the lessons the pain gives us, we can move beyond it."

He nodded, like a teacher approving a correct recitation. "And do you believe it?"

"I believe all the tenets of the Macerates," she answered stiffly, adding with a defiance that took real courage, "even if you do not!"

He laughed again, that hearty, taunting laugh I was to hear repeatedly over the next days. "We shall see," he said. "What is the cause of pain?"

"Pain is caused by that which encroaches," Keli replied.

"Very well said." He stepped away from the force-lev tunnel with one glance at me, daring me to try to approach it, wanting me to. When my body moved involuntarily in that direction, the tunnel retracted its floor end upward. He'd programmed it for himself. When I made myself draw back, it returned. No escape that way.

I sat motionless on the rough floor, my arms linked around my knees, holding myself tightly, trying not to betray a single emotion, trying not to think. Soon I was trying not to watch, as well. The things he did to Keli—and appeared to enjoy—would have been hard enough to bear had the monster not made it quite clear that those things were only a hint of what he intended for me. She was a trained soldier; she didn't begin screaming for almost an hour.

I rocked where I sat, beating back rage, wishing her to hold on, wanting to help her, knowing I was incapable of it as long as he was there. I tried physically to attack him once, and he slammed me back with his arm. On my shields I felt the corresponding slam of his sting, but my defenses held. I couldn't try to use my own sting to render Keli unconscious, because I knew I would have encountered his, instead of reaching her mind, and because I would have had to lower my shields to do it. My shields were all that was keeping him out. I felt the pressure he occasionally exerted against them as he tortured Keli.

Finally he appeared convinced that I would not uncoil my sting from the tight knot in which I'd folded it. He rose from her, readjusted his own garments, and said in the kind of careless, factual tone that made me want to strike out at him, "There, child. I hope you've learned a great deal today. I'll leave you—both of you—to think about the lesson until I come back. And when I come back, I'll bring implements. Think about that, too." He came to me, took my chin in his huge hand and forced me to look at him, attempting to use no influence beyond his physical strength. "I thought you would have tried to intervene," he said. "You used to be more impulsive. I shall have to exert myself a little more next time."

He slid into and up the force-lev tunnel and took the light with him. I used the afterecho of the light to get to Keli quickly, wishing I could slide into her mind and block her nerve endings to damp the pain, knowing he was waiting to pounce on me if I did. She sobbed against me, reminding me for a moment of Andriel.

"I'm sorry," I murmured to her again and again. "He wants me to use my sting, either against him or to help you, and I can't do it. He's almost hungry for it." I rocked her against me, a slower, more contained motion than the one I'd used when he was hurting her.

She fought for control. "Why?" The word came out as a half-swallowed sob.

"He can't affect my sting," I told her. "No outside force can. But if I try to use it and he can get himself around it, he can follow it back into my brain and do other things." I was whispering, my mouth almost against her ear. "If I don't take it out, it stays safe." I felt her shudder, but she loyally nodded against my neck. The loyalty burned me.

When Dolen T'Kelle came again, she tried not just to fight him off, but to kill him. I could feel the strength of the power that he used to sting her with as he flung her away from him. I threw myself to try to catch her in my arms, and his attention swung immediately to me, poised, waiting for the attack he expected. When it didn't come, he sprang forward and jerked me away from her. She dropped to the floor with a thud that sickened me. I made myself go limp in his arms.

"I've overestimated your altruism," he hissed, his fingers crushing my shoulders. "Let's see about your self-preservation."

And then the horror became very personal. I won't describe it. No one ever understands another's pain in the telling, and besides, it doesn't matter now. Even as he worked on me, I could feel the pressure of his sting against my shields, and I held my own sting coiled deeply in my brain, quiescent, waiting. Perhaps I would have a chance to use it; perhaps I would not. When I could think coherently, which wasn't much of the time, I was aware that there were fleeting moments when he weakened, as if his access to his reserves required a re-adjustment of his sting, moments when all pressure from him vanished before it would resume, pauses. I was not ready to try to take advantage of them. I didn't know if they were traps. A couple of hours after he left me that first time, I realized that he might have thought I had broken because Kray raped me; he did not realize—perhaps was incapable of conceiving—that I'd done it not because of the rape, but because I'd killed Kray with my sting. Whether he wanted me to attack him so he could get his sting around mine or so I'd turn directly on myself in response to the humiliation and degradation made no real difference. Had he taken the person I was before Caryldon, before Jemeret, he would have been right, and I'd have been lost.

I had no idea that I was as strong as it turned out I was when I couldn't use my talent. I was able to slowly repair the worst of the injuries, especially in those personal parts of my body that I guessed might have to sustain additional attacks. I did it while I was still holding Keli and rocking her until she slept at last, fitfully, twitching. I even sang to her softly, because I was unable to use anything else to help ease her pain. After she slept, I worked a little faster on the worst of my injuries and cut off all the pain receptors I could, not only because I wanted to feel better, but because he would come again, and I needed to be able to endure that.

By the end of the second time, when the seemingly endless hours of torment were finally over, I was no longer in any way curious about what kinds of perversions Sinet Coleby and Lage N'Verre had practiced with Kray; instead I was convinced that if I ever got an opportunity to speak with Sinet again, I would have new variations on perversion to describe to her. Dolen T'Kelle did things I had never previously imagined. I soon understood how ridiculous I'd been to be offended by Jemeret's treatment of me when we were playing Causadayans for the benefit of Nogdala 7. Even Kray's assault paled in significance, though it had cost me years of my life. Kray and I had been through too much together for it to have been more than a minor aberration in our lives, had I not killed him for it.

With Dolen T'Kelle, the sum total of our interaction was sweaty grapplings, sharp and dull pain I ultimately could block no more, humiliation, and ultimate degradation. When I still refused to respond with talent to the physical attacks, he used his sting to try to batter my shields and compel me to acknowledge his intrusions.

Refusing grew more and more difficult, especially when my shields began at last to weaken. I very nearly couldn't resist him, and shame almost overwhelmed the pain, but just before I thought I would have to give in, he left, and somehow I found the strength to drive the horror into the background. Part of it was that he was using more and more of his reserves. I knew that because my shields had become very sensitive to his pressure. I would be aware when it slackened to pull up more reserve energy, so that the onslaught could continue. Perhaps, I thought, even his incredible strength had limits, would ebb enough for me to use my sting against him. The rest of it was submerging myself in the need to try to keep Keli company. He must have sensed something of that after his third session with me, so with no more compunction than if he were erasing a request to the data banks, he killed her.

It hurt me a great deal not to have been able to prevent that. He watched me, weighing my reaction as she died in my arms. He probably heard her shattered whisper to me, "I always meant—to die for you," as if her death had somehow been in my service, a grand gesture, otherwise avoidable, enabling her to repay me for her brother's betrayal.

I dug my nails into my already tender, scored palms to keep from crying out at the injustice of it all. Dolen T'Kelle waited long enough to see if I would lose control and strike at him at last. When I did not, he gave a snort of contempt and left me alone with her in the dark. I didn't want to put her down to fetch the water, and I didn't want to drag her across the floor, so working by touch, I stripped off her jumpsuit and used my tears to bathe her body, cleansing her of the minor indignities of dying. Then I carefully chose and sang for her a waysong I'd played once on my nomidar. It was called "Flying Rainbow," and it spoke of the eternal colors—hues that began on a single world and flowed outward into space, onward forever, unstoppable, continuous, filling the empty spaces of the universe from its unidentifiable beginnings to its unfathomable ends. The echoes of the song off the cold walls of the chamber kept me company until Dolen T'Kelle came again.

"You just don't hate me enough yet," he observed almost casually and pulled me up, away from Keli's broken body.

It was a long session. We never talked. Physically, I fought him. I had fought Kray; I had fought Evesti of the Ilto. I still did not use my sting. As my failure to do so enraged him more and more, he hurt me more. He used more of his reserves. Now there were real moments when I might have hit at him, and I did not. I could not. I don't think I reasoned it out until later; I was, after all, in no condition to be rational. Somehow, unconsciously, perhaps long before he took me, I had decided I could not use talent to kill, not any longer. If I did—as I'd said and believed at the Com banquet on Orokell—I no longer deserved to have it. And talent was the bedrock of who I was.

When he finally left me after that long agony, for the first time I seriously and detachedly considered killing myself. I wanted it to be over. I had never felt so entirely alone in my life, so unvalued, so stained with a filth that no one could see but me. If Dolen T'Kelle needed me to be alive to bargain with, then I could thwart him by dying.

I might have done it, but at the very moment the irrevocable step pushed at the edges of inevitability, Andriel found me.

Dolen T'Kelle knew that there were no other strong talents on Ananda, so he was alert for talent activity coming from the chamber, not going toward it. She told me later that she was able to slip her searcher—she didn't know to call it a scout, or even her sting—past his presence and on through to me without any trouble.

"Wherever did you get that much power from?" I asked her.

"Tynnanna gave it to me," she answered, smiling at me, holding out Tynnanna's collar. It was humbling.

"And how did you find me?"

Jemeret replied, "The water people told us where to look for you." They must have looked, I thought, a very long time.

I felt Andriel's touch against my mind in the pressing darkness and almost grasped at it, but stopped myself in time. She was overjoyed at touching me, distressed at what she read, and distracted by something else all at the same time. The reason for the distraction became evident at once, as Jemeret surrounded my mind, sliding along Andriel's sting, to feel at the edges of my shields. For a microsecond I was nearer to breaking than I'd been through the horror, and I almost let my shields down. Then the moment was gone and I knew I could go on. They were coming for me. They might be very near. I didn't question how they had found me then; I was only utterly and entirely grateful that they had.

Jemeret slipped away, but Andriel stayed. I could sense—I don't know how—that she was singing to me so I would not be afraid, alone in the dark, and the beauty of it buoyed me up.

We none of us do what we do alone. The loneliness and the dark are alien things, more alien than the starfire. What I did later, I did because at that time—whether it was day or night, I had no way of knowing—I understood I'd been given great gifts: Jemeret had healed me and loved me; the water people had looked for me until they saw where I was and told Jemeret; Tynnanna had given Andriel his collar and the power it contained even before they left Caryldon for Markover; the starfire had been present to Andriel; and Andriel had held me in the world. I claim no credit for what I did. I was part of a much larger team than I knew.

Sometime later, the force-lev tunnel came down, and I steeled myself for Dolen T'Kelle's descent. As the light poured in, Andriel slipped away, following Jemeret. I was afraid to be alone, looked across at where Keli's body lay, barely touched, because of the underground cold, by an impersonal nature that retrieves the molecules of the dead for further use. She looked so small. I pulled myself upright to face what was coming.

Except that this time nothing came.

The force-lev tunnel remained, steady, only slightly wavering, and no one came down it. After a while I took a step toward it, and it stayed. That meant it could have been triggered by someone other than Dolen T'Kelle. Almost unconsciously, I closed and straightened my jumpsuit.

As I said, jumpsuits don't tear. If they had, Dolen T'Kelle would have reduced mine to shreds in short order. Thus, only some of the flesh shredded; we are these days more fragile than our clothing. In the process of straightening the fabric, I touched—and at last remembered—the brow-crown. Stupidly, I cursed myself for not having recalled it was there. I could have called the starfire; I might have prayed; I might have saved Keli.

By the time I'd had that thought, I was rising up through the tunnel, wary of what I'd find at the top.

I found nothing.

That's not literally accurate. The tunnel set me down in the middle of an empty warehouse—empty, that is, except for the unit that operated the tunnel itself and the thick slab that covered the entrance to the chamber when the tunnel was not in use. The ragged hole in the floor of the room, opening into the chamber in which I'd spent some unknown amount of time, seemed only slightly newer than the building itself. The structure was unmistakably of MF manufacture, for their warehouses never varied from one another, but it was extremely rare to find one unused. Its disuse and newness told me clearly what world I was on. It had to be Ananda. I wondered why it had taken long enough to get here that my reserves had completely refilled themselves, because the monster who took me had taken a Lumeship first, but discovered later that he couldn't bring the *Giralume* to Orokell to take me, and so about a quarter of the journey was sublight, which slowed it considerably.

There was no real Com presence on Ananda yet and no eftel, just a few of the earliest arrivals of the Scuttlers, and they would have gone on to Ananda City. The MF personnel who had built the spaceport were off-world by this time. I thought it fairly apparent that Dolen T'Kelle would have had the place to himself.

I couldn't sweep for people; a sweep would involve using my sting, and this could be another of Dolen T'Kelle's tricks to get me to lower my shields.

I'd been able to mute some physical pain, but there were too many other things to repair, and I hadn't wanted to use my reserves. I limped across the expanse of floor in the direction of the wide sliding doors. There would be a smaller access somewhere at the edge of the cargo entrance, and I figured I might as well try it.

It glided open easily enough; an empty warehouse wouldn't need to be secured. I regained a time sense as the door slid aside to reveal a crisp, clear morning over the landing field. But there was barely enough time to notice the day. The landing field was busy.

There was only one ship, an MF shuttle that stood partly off its skids, as if the landing had been interfered with. There were four bodies down on the surface, and I had no time to wonder about them because the power flying around the field was so intense, it was readable even without my trying. I recognized three distinct major forces, and several minor ones. The major ones were all utterly familiar to me and would have been even if I hadn't been able to see the people wielding them. I think now that it was attack by more than one talent that kept Dolen T'Kelle from surrounding and neutralizing any single sting, but I didn't think about that at the time.

Dolen T'Kelle stood with his back toward me, a lone point

of resistance, the flavors of his power terribly familiar and sickening to me. Jemeret was braced against the side of the shuttle, just at its gaping door, his face pale but resolute, other heads at his shoulder inside the doorway. I felt their power supporting his, the strongest note the clear, vibrant thrust of Andriel, letting her unfettered talent flow purely into the fight without any hesitation or husbanding of reserves. Jemeret wielded the accumulation of power with his sting, and Andriel's sting danced along beside his.

The moment I realized what was going on, I struck, the relief at being able to use my sting at last making the process almost explosive. We could, together, I hoped, batter him down without killing him, even though in my heart I wanted him dead.

Dolen T'Kelle felt the added assault, glanced over his shoulder and, despite the effort he was making to defend against and destroy the others, smiled tightly at me and slammed back against my attack. He battered at my sting even as he flung his talent against the combined forces of the others.

Reserves don't last forever. It was our major weakness; his, too. I felt people beginning to fade—Jasin Lebec and Coney dwindled first, then Sinet; Sandalari dropped away next, and then abruptly, with the suddenness of youth, Andriel's contribution slackened. Sensing it, Dolen T'Kelle lashed once, with his full power, at me, knocking me backward as I absorbed and tried to minimize the blast, then swung everything he could against the only real remaining threat. I think the monster understood that Jemeret had always been stronger than I was. I think his plan was to eliminate my lord and then turn upon me, to whatever end he'd intended all along.

I quickly assessed my reserves and saw, now that I'd finally, finally, let myself act, I'd been typically myself and thrown everything in. My reserves were two-thirds gone. I think I might have begun praying for Jemeret, but that could be a construction added to the truth by more detached recollection. At the time, there was so much chaos, so much dizziness brought on by raw power, that I was probably hardly thinking at all.

I gathered to take the last of my reserves and plunge back

into the battle, but at that moment Dolen T'Kelle threw another massive surge of power at my lord, and just as I'd been thrown back, Jemeret took the blow and was driven to the ground by it. Andriel cried out from the ship; Dolen T'Kelle gave a crow that seemed to strike at any hope I had that we could win. And while the monster might have wanted me alive, he clearly had no such compunctions about the others.

So when I saw Jemeret drop, I was riven by a terror unlike anything I'd ever known, deeper and more agonizing than my long-ago self-condemnation had been, more powerful in its immediacy than the love I'd become a part of and would now have to do without. I couldn't lose him, not if there were any hope of saving him. Failing to save him, I couldn't let him go without me.

All my doubts fell away. Perhaps they'd been exorcised by the flail of Dolen T'Kelle's unremitting brutality toward me, I don't know. What I do know is that, in the smallest sliver of a microsecond, I'd committed to the decision, as easily and inevitably as if I should have known all along that it would come to this. The fight was too hard; Dolen T'Kelle's hatred of us was too intense. By myself I could do nothing except drain my reserves and die. If by any chance he could stop me from dying, that would be even worse.

Almost before I was aware of it, my hand had dived into the jumpsuit's thigh pouch, fastening on my brow-crown with enough force to bend it slightly in my grip. Without a heartbeat's hesitation I did the thing that to Jemeret had always been unthinkable, the thing against which he'd repeatedly warned me. If I was committing suicide by it, we were lost anyway, and I was being driven by a desperation so basic that I no longer cared what happened to me. I stung the starfire.

I believe now that if I'd had a single instant's thought of wanting to kill Dolen T'Kelle, I would have died at the very moment I opened the pathway to that infinite power. But I was thinking only of saving Jemeret, of wrenching him out of the pit into which the monster was driving him, by throwing all my remaining strength and any other I could muster between him and the peril. I was barely aware, until much later, of seeing the monster fall back, roaring, furious as he discovered too late that I was not the lesser threat any longer, but the instrument of a far greater dynamic than his own.

Venacrona, who previously knew the starfire better than any of the rest of us, called me "an instrument of salvation," but I think that I was only a determined woman learning to live by a new set of rules. What I did was no more than any other woman in my place would have done—any other woman who, being a lover, had danced with Fire.

I stung the starfire, and glory poured through me and out onto the face of Ananda. There was no way I could control the contact, no way I could command the flow of power that filled me with an ecstasy I could never have imagined and which I am now completely incapable of describing. All I can say is that I know the starfire agreed to work my will, gave me the strength to carry it out like a kindly master who finds her servant's wishes worthy and therefore agrees to fulfill them.

Jemeret lived.

So did I.

So did Dolen T'Kelle, but with all the hatred and all the power burnt out of him.

XIX. Among the MIs

Revelations can be fraught with irony. At first I found it hard to accept that my long sought alternative to killing or being killed was as simple—and as difficult—a thing as healing and changing your opponent. We'd set out to do it all along, we just hadn't recognized it. We'd returned to the Com to change it, and never noticed that we needed to change far more than merely the greatest empire humanity had ever created—we had to change ourselves.

I recognized that, and other things, as we sat in the conference room of the rollship *Termalume* on our way back to Orokell. Jemeret held my hand in his lap under the table, watching me with his soft gray eyes. Andriel sat on the floor at my side, her arms wrapped around my leg, radiating happiness. She was wearing Tynnanna's collar like a necklace. I realized that she had drawn power from it in all innocence, just as she did so many things we thought impossible. She thought the power came from the klawits, not from the starfire, and once again she had done it without debate, without letting Jemeret know she was doing it.

She'd told us that she used it to reach me when they were on *Zellume*, but hadn't thought to bring it into the shuttle when they came down onto the planet to get me. "It was only lent to me for one thing," she said earnestly, "and I'd borrowed a lot of power from it. I didn't know how much it had left." We were still unsure how she had accessed that power. She might have stung it—even before I did—but she seemed oblivious to the uses of power in the ways we'd always been taught to think about it. She was completely untaught—not by the Com, nor by the Samothen, not by anyone except those who hated what was most basic about her. What problems we might ultimately encounter because of that, we had no way of knowing.

Coney sat at the table with us, but Sandalari was in their cabin, lying down. In the end, I thought, she'd lost more than I had. In Dolen T'Kelle's attack on them at the shuttle, she'd pushed her newfound skills past their elementary limit trying to help, and had miscarried as she exerted herself too much. She hadn't given up the struggle, even though she was deeply saddened, but now she was mourning her loss in her own way. The unborn girl had been Dolen T'Kelle's last victim.

Jasin Lebec was there, seeming even more frail, but at the same time, paradoxically, there was an increased strength about him, as if he knew that some unfathomable chasm had been crossed, and nothing would ever be the same again.

Sinet Colcby was with Mortel John. She'd been hurt during the battle, though not badly, because Dolen T'Kelle struck at everyone, and her defensive shields were still very weak. She didn't know she had them until very recently, and as a result she'd only just begun learning to use them.

Lendo Dell was dead. He was one of the four who died during the battle. The other three men had been MF, members of *Termalume*'s crew. The five bodies—the four men and Keli—were in PMP in the ship's infirmary for return to Orokell. I'd refused to allow them to be disposed of on Ananda. It seemed too much like throwing them away.

I'd been telling everyone present—the Orokell members of the Tribunal through eftel vid, and probably the MI surveillance as well—what had happened on Ananda in the not-quite-a-month I was in Dolen T'Kelle's hands, though not in minute detail. As nearly as could be reconstructed, it had taken two full tendays for him to get us to Ananda, and then we were in the rock chamber for seven days. I told the story in a slightly less organized fashion than the rambling account here, because it was too raw. But I told it steadily, even Keli's death, as Jemeret kept stinging me with a low level of love and support, punctuated every so often by another mental hug from Andriel. She was very young to be part of such a debriefing, but needed to remain with me, so we agreed to let her stay. I thought she'd earned that much, at least. I did not give them details, just euphemisms. Only Jemeret had seen what my body still looked like under the smooth cloth of the new jumpsuit I was wearing, and I was slowly continuing the process of healing it, even as I told the story. There was no permanent physiological damage, and therefore no hurry to finish the repairs other than to rid myself of the marks. Psychologically, I did want all traces of my ordeal erased, but not enough to drain myself getting rid of them. I wondered if they would slip back in and give me nightmares.

Just before the debriefing began, in the privacy of our cabin, Jemeret had kissed and stroked every bruise, bite, cut, and abrasion, every external centimeter of my body that had been harmed, saying, "It should have been me. I wish it had been."

I'd caressed his hair, grateful, and disagreed. "I'm High Lady, and it was something only I could do." Silently: *You might have tried to kill him. We might never have won then.*

When I was finally finished telling the Tribunal what I knew, Jasin Lebec, who was nominally chairing the debriefing, said, "In the normal course of things, we should now begin calling witnesses. Do you agree to that, Jemeret?"

I didn't understand the conditional verb until my lord looked up at his grandfather and said, "Bring him in. If the starfire didn't kill him when Ronica called it, I won't attack him now."

I cleared my throat and squeezed his hand. "Perhaps I didn't make it clear enough when I told you," I said quietly. "I didn't call the starfire, Jemeret. I think I wouldn't have been able to wield its power if I'd called it. I stung it."

He shook his head. "I can't entirely accept that yet. When I think about what happened to my sire—"

"He stung the starfire with the intent of killing," I told him. "We know that's not an appropriate use of talent. It's what talentless people have always done to win. The old humanity always used a new kind of power to kill with, and the starfire won't conspire in talent behaving in the same way. We have to grow beyond it, and we're not there yet. The starfire didn't kill your father, Jemeret; he killed himself by trying to use it."

"I don't understand, then," Coney said. "Dolen T'Kelle killed a great many people. He's still alive."

"He never tried to get the starfire to help him." I smiled at Coney. "It would have been much simpler if he had."

"But when the starfire attacked him, it didn't destroy him," Coney protested, frowning.

I shook my head. "The starfire didn't attack. It doesn't. It's not a violent power. I was wielding it, and killing wasn't my intention. So he didn't die." I couldn't say his name. That seemed to give him too much solidity.

Jasin Lebec had signaled to the crew to bring Dolen T'Kelle to the conference room. The eftel began chiming just as the guards brought the big man to the door.

"They're calling again," Jemeret said to me, his jaw tighter than his even tone of voice implied.

"No," I said.

Jasin Lebec cut off the chime. The Tribunal—probably Pel Nostro—had been trying to call us since *Termalume* left Ananda orbit. We'd refused to let any of my team take the calls. They could listen in, but we had too much to resolve internally first, and it was a matter involving talent. Until we were done, the Com had no place in the discussion.

Jemeret smiled, letting me feel his approval, then stiffened as Dolen T'Kelle took a seat across the table from us. Andriel let go of my leg and got to her feet behind my chair, her hands on my shoulders, her feelings suddenly masked. I regretted the cessation of her obvious joy, which had been healing all by itself, and I hoped she was not afraid.

Dolen T'Kelle had changed, though physically he looked just the same. As he sat, he inclined his head in my direction. I couldn't return the gesture. I was not big enough to rise above the anger and hatred I still felt for him. I would in no way have regretted his death; I simply could not be responsible for it. For my sake, the others had tried to find ways to do the debriefing without him, but that had been impossible, because there was still too much we didn't know.

I trembled, gathered, controlled it. Something in me—perhaps unworthy—wanted to believe that he could suffer as much as I had. At the same time, my instincts told me he would not.

The shaggy-haired man seemed far less vibrant than he'd been, some sparks of energy gone from him, but all the old intelligence still in his eyes. It was a more impersonal intelligence, as if detachment had replaced ambition, and diffidence replaced rage. I'd hoped for regret; now I saw that was asking too much.

Jasin Lebec folded his hands on the table in front of him, a deliberate gesture, drawing our attention to him. "Dolen T'Kelle, you have been brought here to answer questions relating to the deaths of a number of Class B and C personnel and the abduction of Class A Ronica McBride. Have you any objection or reluctance to testify on these matters?"

"Absolutely not," Dolen T'Kelle said. "You've won, and the winners always set the terms. If information is what you want, you have every right to it."

We had agreed that Jasin Lebec and Coney would conduct the questioning. I wasn't at all certain I could have done it rationally, and Jemeret was too angry at what had been done to me. So Jasin Lebec began. "How long have you known you were a Class A talent?"

Dolen T'Kelle smiled crookedly, an expression that distorted his features. "Your tense is wrong. I'm not a talent any longer."

Jasin Lebec acknowledged that with a nod. "When did you first realize you were a Class A talent?" he corrected himself, unperturbed.

"I think I only came to understand it completely after Ronica McBride went into the tank," he said, and I bit down hard on my reactions to keep from shuddering. "Before that, I'd been more of an idealist, a dreamer, if you will. My parents were Macerates, and I was raised to be part of the hierarchy of the faith. I always thought things I wanted happened because I prayed to the Preserver for them." He laughed shortly.

I looked down at my hands, holding tightly to Jemeret's.

"Why did you begin killing other talents?" Jasin Lebec asked.

There was no attempt at dissimulation or denial. Dolen T'Kelle seemed to think the answer should have been obvious. "They were the only ones who might have identified me or stopped me," he said, "as, indeed, you did. I was tired of being marginal to society when I was clearly the one best suited to run it. I was determined to correct that imbalance. It became somewhat more urgent when you seemed likely to be bringing Ronica McBride back into the Com again."

"Why kill the children?" Coney asked. "They surely couldn't harm you."

Dolen T'Kelle looked at him as if he were too simple to see the truth. "They were easier to take care of while they were young. They would just have grown up if I hadn't gotten rid of them."

Coney bit his lip to keep back a remark, then asked, "You didn't really think you were the Preserver, did you?"

Dolen T'Kelle looked a little surprised. "Is that what you were thinking? Of course I never even considered it. Once I knew I was fulfilling my own prayers, I knew the Preserver was an impotent symbol of human desires. I stopped praying to it and started acting for myself."

"The starfire must have come as something of a surprise to you," Jasin Lebec said dryly.

Dolen T'Kelle nodded. "I was certain I was the strongest talent in existence," he said. "It seems I hadn't counted on Ronica McBride calling for reinforcements." There was an edge of amusement in his tone. I had to grit my teeth. Andriel's hands tightened on my shoulders.

"You told Ronica you were going to use her to bargain with the Com, and that was why you didn't kill her," Coney said. "What were you bargaining for?"

"The Com destroyed my followers," Dolen T'Kelle answered. "I wanted another set."

That brought my head up sharply, and I knew I couldn't keep silent. "Why did you need to take me to do that? Why didn't you just sting people to make them follow you?"

His expression as he faced me showed nothing of the memories of the things he'd done to me, and I was grateful for that.

His answer astonished me so completely that for a moment I was able to forget the long hours of torment. "It takes too long to culture and grow the brain tissue once I've cloned it," he said calmly. "I'd have been able to work twice as fast if I used yours as well as my own."

We all stared at him. "Excuse me?" Coney said at last. "Brain tissue?"

Dolen T'Kelle nodded again. "You people have been using influence nonintrusively," he said, sounding earnest and helpful instead of outrageous. "But to develop a real inner corps of loyal followers who can be influenced with ease and sometimes used to influence others, I discovered it takes a direct contact, brain-to-brain. I had about a hundred chemical-cell servants. That's what I called them. It was like multiplying my own personality. But almost all of them were destroyed by the Drenalion."

I felt my skin crawl with a horror that was somehow worse than the horror I'd been made to suffer. At the same time, I was aware that the calm of a deliberate purpose had fallen across Jemeret. He let go of my hand and leaned forward. "I think you'd better explain what you're talking about," he said, his voice hard.

Dolen T'Kelle remained unmoved. "All right," he said. "I was experimenting with the idea of trying to make it possible to sting at great distances. It was inconvenient to have to depend on actually being in the presence of the people I wanted to influence. I experimented rather rigorously, and a number of my acolytes died in the process, but, you know—" Once again, he seemed a little amused. "—the government doesn't care very much about deaths among the unproductive. Eventually I stumbled on a process whereby I could directly implant several cells from my parietal lobe in the amygdala of an acolyte, a relatively simple procedure. It didn't even leave marks. Then, no matter where I was or where they were, I could force them to act in the ways I wanted. Of course, I wanted to make as many servants as I could, but since I couldn't afford to lose too many brain cells too quickly, I developed a way of removing a few and cloning cultures of them. The cloning process was not foolproof. It was harder to force compliance, especially if the acts were things the person wouldn't normally want to do. Eventually, the servant went mad and had to be eliminated."

I made an unintentional sound.

Dolen T'Kelle's dark eyes went curious. "You're a strange one, Ronica McBride," he said. "This is affecting you so strongly, and yet I couldn't break you."

I was shaking visibly then. "Why was it necessary to break me? Why not just take my brain tissue and use it?" Responding to my need, as he always had no matter what else was concerning him, Jemeret slid his sting gently into my mind, reassuring, comforting.

Dolen T'Kelle answered, "You'd still control the tissue. Therefore I had to control you."

If I hadn't been so close to tears, I might have laughed. My old flaw of having to be in control had probably saved me, there in the darkest of the torment. I could not let him control me, and I could not risk my sting; I had just held on.

"So Gabon Idana was an acolyte of yours implanted with your cloned cells." Jasin Lebec was a little uncomfortable with the subject, but seemed to feel the need to clarify.

"Of course." Dolen T'Kelle leaned back, his eyes on the ceiling. "The beauty of the system, you see, is that a Class A reads no abnormal intentions, no hostility. The servant has none until I trigger it." I was thinking that even if I had probed Gabon Idana, I would have found nothing. The relief was palpable. Dolen T'Kelle's huge head came back down, his eyes on me. "And a Class A who would feel another Class A affecting them doesn't feel it when the influence comes through a third party. So you never suspected, did you? That I was manipulating you through Keli Idana? It was such a stroke of luck, her being sent to Markover Station."

I could barely hear him after he said Keli's name. She'd been so afraid that everything was her fault, and I'd been so reassuring, so certain she was innocent. And all the time, she had been unconsciously correct. "I'd have known if I were being influenced. I'd have felt it."

Dolen T'Kelle shook his head firmly. "You'd have sensed

me, but talent doesn't sense influence once removed. You were really quite malleable through the Idana girl. All I had to do was trigger her." His voice was still without any vestige of satisfaction at what he'd done.

"How did you reach her over such great distances, or when she was on Caryldon?" Coney asked.

"Through that thing on the wall of the house we were in," Andriel said. "I saw her using it. That's how I knew I could, too."

I wasn't paying much attention. I was remembering washing Keli's battered body with my tears. "How could—" I stopped, made myself continue. "You found her so useful. How could you just kill her?"

"Once you were in my hands, I could influence you directly, and it didn't matter if you knew I was doing it," he said. "I didn't need her anymore. And I was looking for ways to make you react to me."

Coney turned his face away from the man whose detachment was now more indifference than diffidence. His expression left no doubt that he was angry and disgusted.

Jasin Lebec remained calm, but his voice had gone much lower. "In what way were you manipulating Ronica McBride?"

Dolen T'Kelle smiled. "It wasn't easy, I'll grant you that," he said. "She's very strong. I urged her to take Keli Idana into her service. I gave her the idea of asking the girl to pick someone else for guarding her, to get Gabon into the group. He was inherently more violent than his sister, and he was easier to trigger than she would have been. And once Ronica McBride felt uneasy about the correctness of whatever little decision she'd made down on Jemeret Cavanaugh's world, I persuaded her to come back to Orokell alone. It was my best chance to get my hands on her."

Coney turned back suddenly, like a man forcing himself into danger. "Why didn't you just implant Ronnie with your clone cells while she was unconscious, make her another of your servants? Wouldn't that have been simpler than . . ." He let the question die.

"It doesn't work, talent-to-talent," Dolen T'Kelle said. "I tried it on one of the children at the very beginning of my experiments. He just canceled it out somehow. That was when I realized I would have to eliminate all the other talents. I couldn't have anyone else setting up a rival faction." He looked back at me again. "You, on the other hand, showed promise as an ally. You'd already killed another talent yourself, so I knew you could be as unprincipled about your own kind as I was." He shrugged. "Sometimes things just don't go the way you plan them."

I couldn't repress another noise. Being considered a possible ally of such a monster was an enormous insult, and of course I wondered if there were any hint of truth in it. Andriel slid her hands around me and tucked her head against mine, leaning forward until her chin was resting on my collarbone. The links of Tynnanna's collar pressed against my back. "Don't be sad," she whispered. I laid a hand absently over hers.

Jasin Lebec was the only one of us who seemed to remember there was an agenda here. "So the fact that there were groups of people beginning to worship talent was not your major reason for wanting to destroy the rest of us," he clarified.

For the first time, Dolen T'Kelle showed some emotion; he was annoyed by that question. "No, I had encouraged it," he said, "and it was an inconvenience that you broke it up like you did."

I could see how being thought a god would be helpful at some future time if you decided to take over.

"Do you have any idea what it was in your background or training that gave you such strength without any of the moral judgment necessary to contain it?" Coney asked.

Dolen T'Kelle said lightly, "Just good fortune, I suppose."

Jemeret was seething with outrage by that time, and I was fighting back angry tears. But, strangely enough, it was Andriel who brought it all into focus. She lifted her head, but kept her hands clasped around my neck, and I felt her still-too-thin body shake with emotion. "He's supposed to be sorry," she said indignantly, "and he doesn't know how to be. He can't possibly be healed until he's sorry!"

"Some flaws go too deep," I said. "Sometimes healing can only go so far."

But Jemeret had calmed as Andriel spoke, and now he said softly, "Andriel's right. He just doesn't know how to feel repentance." His gray eyes fastened on the now talentless man's rugged face. "Perhaps I can help." His sting shot past me and struck Dolen T'Kelle with all the force Jemeret could pack into it. I knew he needed to hit the former Repository of the Macerates with something ever since he'd seen what I looked like under my jumpsuit, and now he had figured out what he could use.

For a moment Dolen T'Kelle did not react at all, and then he began to shake. The expression on his face melted downward into a kind of pain that plainly signaled an awareness of wrong, an acceptance of culpability, unwelcome and forced, but strong. Jemeret yanked back his sting, but before Dolen T'Kelle had a chance to try to recover his equilibrium, Andriel took over, pouring into him her all-too-mature awareness of what it meant to accept responsibility for immoral actions, filling the man who had hurt me with a hitherto missing sense of obligation to a larger world than himself. When the child let him go, I stared at him as he writhed and cried out against a pain he'd never had any intention of feeling, caught in an alien contrition that probably harmed him, in its own way, fully as much as he'd harmed me. When he finally seemed to catch a little more control of himself, his eyes darting around the conference room as if seeking an absolution he'd never before needed and not finding it among us, Jasin Lebec signaled for the guards. "Take him back to his cabin," he said.

I might have reminded them that Dolen T'Kelle would be alone—as I had not been even at the most painful moments in his hands—with his newfound consciousness of morality, but I did not. He would have to find ways to live with his sorrow, and if he did not find them, well, I'd already admitted that I would not regret his death. In the meantime, the strength and speed with which both my lord and my child had rushed to punish the man who had harmed me filled me with happiness.

When Dolen T'Kelle had been removed to await our ultimate arrival at Orokell, where he would be turned over to the Tribunal for his crimes against the Com, I pulled Andriel around in front of me and hugged her. Jasin Lebec cut off the eftel vid connection with the Tribunal without speaking to them.

As Andriel drew back from me, smiling, I saw the large, softly glowing links of Tynnanna's collar and said impulsively, "I wish we could talk to the starfire, too. It should be a witness here, but we don't have Tynnanna."

And Mortel John stepped in the door of the conference room. He said quietly, "Give me the collar and call the starfire. The MIs tell me it will speak through me, using the part of me they use."

Jemeret jumped, and Coney and Jasin Lebec stared in open disbelief, but I was far beyond disbelief by this time, and there were too many things I needed to know. I touched Andriel's arm lightly. "May we borrow Tynnanna's collar from you?"

She grinned at me, flattered to have been asked, and lifted the heavy chain off over her head. She hesitated a moment, then walked to the cyborg and held the collar out to him. I got up and laid my fingers on it, closing my eyes, calling the starfire.

When I opened my eyes again, multicolored flames danced around the edges of the conference room, and Mortel John was looking at me with an expression so rich in love that I caught my breath. "You have done well," he said, the tones and pronunciation his own, but the emotional power of the words far beyond anything I ever remembered Mortel John possessing. "We want to speak with you now, between the nexuses, to say that we are proud of you, that we are pleased we were not mistaken to rest our hopes for an evolving humanity in you. You have defeated the thing that vitally needed to be defeated." Only much later did it occur to me they had not meant Dolen T'Kelle.

I was astonished. "But Jemeret and Andriel came after me,"

I protested to the power that was currently residing in my old teacher, "and you saved us all. I did nothing."

"Listen to us," said Mortel John's voice, "and listen well, for you will have to teach this to your people. Humanity's greatest error is in failing to understand that 'not killing' *is* doing something. You, Ronica McBride, have been tested in the harshest way you could have been tested. The first and second times you were attacked physically—in a much lesser way—you responded by killing." I knew the starfire meant the hitch, who had threatened Coney and Kray and me when we were Andriel's age, and the Drenalion who had attacked us years later. "The third time you were attacked—more intimately and therefore more hurtfully—you responded by killing. But you had begun to learn that killing is not an appropriate response for you." This time they meant Kray. "The fourth time you were attacked was the only time you did not use your talent as your weapon, but again you killed. You were starting to learn, but you had not learned enough." Evesti of the Ilto. "This was your final test. Had you responded by killing or trying to kill this time, our hopes for your evolution would have died. But you did the right thing. *You did not kill.*"

I was breathing harder now, all my emotions on the surface. Jemeret got up and came to me, putting his arms around me, kissing my forehead. Andriel put a finger in her mouth and watched us, eyes glowing. Something inside me wanted to argue that I hadn't had any choice, because I had recognized from the outset Dolen T'Kelle's superior strength, but I remembered that there had been moments during which his strength slackened, when I might have lashed out at him.

The cyborg went on, "By now you have begun to learn the satisfaction that comes with healing, rather than destroying, which has always been, for humanity, a minor motif rather than a major one. It is the mission of your evolution to do that small thing: to reverse the two motifs . . . Jemeret Cavanaugh."

Jemeret looked up at my old teacher—his, too, I remembered.

"You have always understood healing, even though you have killed," the starfire went on. "You have climbed the mountain that leads to this place with a strong hand. Just as the nexus behind you was largely Ronica McBride's to face, the nexus still to come is largely yours. Handle it well. Trust what you have learned, as Ronica McBride is coming to trust what she has learned. We may speak with you again when the nexus is past."

"Wait, please!" I turned in Jemeret's embrace to make certain I could see that the presence still lingered in Mortel John. "I need to ask you why some of us with talent are so much stronger than the others, and why some of us with talent can still be so wicked."

"But why would that surprise you?" countered the cyborg. "You know that each creature is unique, and you are the generation that is still mired in the fallacies of humanity. There are tens of thousands of years of those fallacies behind you."

"Will there be more like Dolen T'Kelle, or was he an aberration?" Jemeret asked. It was the first time he'd spoken since the starfire inhabited Mortel John.

The starfire did not answer directly. "There have always been those who cannot understand that power does not serve its wielder. There may always continue to be, unless they grow so numerous that their weight sinks the species."

"Are we right to worship you?" I thought that Jemeret must have wanted to pose that question since he saw his father die, and that only now, only knowing that I had stung the starfire and lived, was it possible for him. I felt him holding his breath.

Mortel John's eyes took on the same depth of love they had shown for me when the starfire first possessed him. "You are right to worship," his voice said. "What humans must understand is that the act is of equal value with the object, that its intention is to heal, rather than to encroach, rather than to coerce. It is vital that you be grateful *for*; it is not vital to be grateful *to*."

Coney covered his eyes with his hand to hide the sudden tears.

Then the starfire was gone, and Mortel John gasped and dropped to his knees, the collar sliding out of his fingers. All five of us leaped for him, startled.

"What happened?" Jasin Lebec demanded.

"Are you all right?" Coney asked at the same time.

Mortel John looked dazed as we helped him to his feet and Andriel retrieved the collar. "Get me some water," he said.

Coney signaled the table to extrude the requested drink and put it into our teacher's limp fingers, holding them around the container until the other man began to regain control over his body again. We watched as he fastened both hands on the container, raised it, shaking enough to spill a little, drank a swallow, lowered it again. When he looked at us, his eyes were haunted.

Jemeret was the first to understand. "He's human again," my lord said softly. "The MI part of him is gone."

Jasin Lebec turned his face upward, as the familiar click sounded and the MI voice said, "Yes."

I was still staring at John Caryl, whose feet had just been set back on the road all of us would ultimately travel, leading to whatever lay beyond our waysongs.

Coney said wonderingly, "You let him go?" For a moment I didn't realize he was speaking to the MIs.

"Yes," the MI voice repeated. "It was asked of us."

I turned slowly and looked at Jemeret.

It is always easier to destroy a complex system than to selectively alter it. That's true of human interaction, and it would be true of the MIs. We gathered, bubbled, all of us but John Caryl, who was sleeping, to discuss our final act in the Com, one way or the other. We would go into the MIs. Even Jemeret had been brought to the point of recognizing that we could not turn them off, and he said, "I believe the starfire doesn't want us to kill them any more than it wants us to kill anyone else."

"So we have to heal them instead," I said. "How are we going to do that?"

"We need to show them who we are, truly," Sandalari said quietly, looking down at her hands. "It's easier to kill what's strange to you than what you know."

"And we need to take back from them some of the things

humanity gave them," Jemeret said, echoing Glon's question from Sargasso. "Let's decide what."

As the *Termalume* swung into low watch, Jemeret, Andriel, and I went to the lounge with Coney and Sandalari to sing a waysong for her miscarried daughter. Because the priestess had sung so often and so beautifully in the past, she chose and sang her own waysong, instead of asking me to do it. She picked "The Dream Unrealized," a simple melody with a simple message. She sang:

"Some dreams are never meant to be,
Although you laid your heart on them,
And you must not be injured by
Their failure to come true.
The stars will lead you ever on
To further dreams, perhaps more fair.
A lesson learned by dreams denied
Makes sweeter truth for you."

After she sang the first chorus by herself, Jemeret and I sang the second with her, modulating our voices so that hers was always the strongest.

Then, at the end of our song, Andriel began to sing.

Everyone I knew who sang, sang songs by poets or by trained composers, following whatever rules of musical theory and whatever internal inspiration the writers had elected to employ. Andriel sang as she had on Ananda, where she knew that if she didn't sing, she would be afraid in the darkness. I knew she'd sung to me the same way while I was in the underground chamber, though I'd been unable to hear or appreciate the music as I could now. I guessed that when she'd sung then, and her singing now, were the only times Andriel had been able to use the full volume of which she was capable. In the hut on Ananda, she would have had to sing at a whisper, to keep the others from hearing. Now she sang full-throated, and she sang her own song. She had never heard the music of any established culture.

But Andriel's music was magnificent, and her voice a soaring power imbued with the full strength of her sting. She needed no instrument other than the one she carried in her body, and unlike Jemeret or me, she was not interpreting someone else's words or melody, she was pouring her very soul out to her listeners. The wash of emotion began with a recognition of loss and moved past it, not easily, but steadily, into a surprisingly mature acceptance of what could not be changed. Rapt as I was with both the voice and the sting of this amazing child, I could still simultaneously sense that everyone on the ship was aware of and affected by the song.

Sandalari seemed bathed in it, as was only proper since Andriel was singing to her. Her tears had stopped by the time the child was done, and she held Andriel to her for a very long moment before she turned back to Coney with a small smile on her face. None of the rest of us said anything for as long as it took the continuing waves of Andriel's emotions to break, then ebb.

At last Andriel said softly, "I want to make you feel that way. You make me feel that way."

I knew then, with a clarity I hadn't seen before, that Andriel was a symbol of what talent should be—she recognized that she'd been saved, had been taken from suffering, and what she wanted now was to help save others, to help heal, as she'd been healed. I remembered that long ago day on Koldor, driving the fever back out of Lanya Ver Lenghy's brain; I remembered the hours I'd spent teaching Shantiah how to painstakingly replace her scarified fallopian tubes, cell by cell, with healthy tissue. I remembered Shantiah's joy, and the love and thankfulness of Lanya's parents. I knew that what I'd had to learn painfully, Andriel instinctively accepted. True talent was the ability to wield the sting for the good of others, to fulfill their wishes, not just your own. The opposite of love, it seemed, was not hate but selfishness, and Andriel had very little of that.

Jemeret picked up the child, excused the three of us from Coney and Sandalari, and we walked down the corridor toward our cabin. Jasin Lebec waited at the iris, arms crossed, one shoulder against the wall. "The Tribunal's called about fifty times," he said. "The captain asked me to tell you we're running out of message chips."

"Tell him to erase the messages and recycle the chips," Jemeret told him shortly. His voice gentled. "Then tell Pel we'll meet with the Tribunal exactly one hour after the *Termalume* docks at Orokell."

"Will we?" his grandfather asked, genuinely surprised.

Jemeret nodded, I irised open the door, and the three of us went in. Jemeret set Andriel down and said, "Get washed, brush your teeth and hair, and you remember how to call up a bedsuit?"

"Yes, ti-sire," she said with a hint of the shyness that any new intimacy brings. She glanced at me, even more shyly. "Will you come say 'good sleeping' to me, too, ti-mare?"

At being given the title of "near-mother," I felt an unexpected thrill. "Of course," I answered. "Go on, and call us when you're ready." She darted off to the eliminatory. I looked after her for a moment, then went to the couch and sat down. Jemeret ordered two strong drinks from the comsole and gave me one while the table extruded the other. As he was sitting down beside me, I asked, "Do you want to know what happened?"

He leaned back and watched me, his eyes lazy-lidded. "I know what happened," he said quietly. "Are you asking me if I want to know what he did to you?"

I nodded, apprehensive, but determined to persevere. "I'm less afraid of telling you the truth than I am of what you might be imagining."

He took a long swallow of his drink. "I don't imagine anything."

I fought to get the next words out. "I was talking to Sinet a while back, and she said—she said she thought you wouldn't want to share me. Sexually. Are you—do you—"

He laid his hand lightly on my wrist. "What happened to you was not sexual," he said firmly. "It may have involved parts of your body which you and I make sexual, but just as you can use your hands to caress or to assault, the body part is not what governs the situation. You do." His gray eyes bored into me. "Do you think it was sexual?"

I felt freezing cold. "Gebbish, no!"

A smile played about the corners of his mouth. "Do you think I don't believe you?"

I wasn't able to respond.

He said, "I'll probe you if you want me to, but I love you, and I don't intend to let anything color that."

The relief I felt was palpable, because I could read that he was absolutely sincere. I sipped my drink. "I'm trying so hard not to be haunted by it."

"I can isolate the memories if you like," he offered, watching me closely. "Then there's no possibility of them recurring."

It was so very tempting, but I shook my head. "I've spent enough time with missing memories. I'd rather not do that any longer." And then, to change the subject: "Andriel seems to have developed quite a relationship with you."

"Yes, we've started working out some rules." He took another drink. "I was the only one who had any chance of controlling her once she began demanding we find you. Not that we weren't already looking. Her ability to scout and project over great distances is amazing, but we couldn't reach you until we were almost at Ananda because there was no eftel to work through."

"It'll be easier for her than it was for me," I said. "There's an unholy satisfaction in killing your enemies. It's a human thing, I think. We've both felt it, and she never has."

"I'm so proud of you." His words were fervent with admiration, and they startled me.

"What? Why?" It seemed to me that I'd done neither more nor less than I'd been expected to do; my actions had been—would continue to be—inevitable.

"This time you never turned any of it back on yourself." He drained his liquor, set the container on the table to be reabsorbed, and began to entwine his forefinger in a curl of my hair. "That was always my greatest fear, that you'd blame yourself for what was happening because you'd run from Caryldon alone."

I shook my head, surprised, took another sip of the drink, and made myself think again about the unthinkable. At last I said slowly, "It never occurred to me. At the beginning, I couldn't have left Keli—he started with her, you see—and then, when I was the closest to despairing, Andriel sang me back to balance."

"Thank the stars," he whispered, and I smiled a little, weighing the starfire's words about being *grateful for*. Then Andriel came out of the eliminatory, her sandy hair half dry and half plastered damply against her head, wet patches all over her white bedshirt.

Jemeret smothered a laugh. "You were supposed to brush your hair, not soak it," he said, getting to his feet.

Andriel grinned at him, unabashed. "There's all kinds of water in there," she said gleefully.

We took her back into the eliminatory to show her how to dry anything she randomly drenched, and then we put her to bed on the couch, creating a bed field for her.

It seemed like forever since I'd slept with Jemeret, even longer since we'd made love. Yet I wasn't nervous when we stripped and he reached for me. I'd healed the worst of the physical injuries I'd suffered at Dolen T'Kelle's hands, and Jemeret's lovemaking had always been wonderful for me, except for that one performance for the observers on Nogdala 7. I had a stray thought that I really ought to tell him I'd figured out how silly I'd been about that, but he swept it completely out of my head as he swept completely in.

Just before the *Termalumo* was due to land at the Orokell spaceport, we all met in the lounge to plan our scenario. There was a palpable difference between this meeting and all the other planning meetings that had preceded it. For the first time, we were not creating a standard scenario; we were only listening to Jemeret give out assignments. Seven of us would go into the MI synapses in six separate impulses, working simultaneously to minimize any possible defensive response on the part of the MIs. Sandalari and Sinet were much weaker at using the projective abilities they had only just started to learn, but if we were right, they could afford to waste a lot of reserves.

Jemeret bubbled us and then looked at me. "Do you want to say anything?" he asked.

"What is there to say? It's your task to lead this time, not mine. We have a job to do. Let's just do it." I couldn't help smiling at him.

He squeezed my hand lightly and laid out his scenario. We all listened closely, and the only time anyone argued was when I protested over the fact that Jemeret planned to send Andriel in as an impulse of her own.

"She's only nine years old," I said, "and she was born and raised in a nontechnological society."

"Which is why she pathfound her way through the eftel the first time she ever saw one and sent her sting through to find you on the other side of it," Jemeret said evenly. "She'll do as well as we will." I knew he was saying that, despite having had to repress her talent all those years on Ananda, Andriel knew what it was for with a purity neither Jemeret nor I possessed, because we'd been trained in the Com.

Andriel laid her hand on my wrist. "You're afraid for me because you love me," she said. "I understand. I'm afraid for you, too, ti-mare."

I nodded at her, then at Jemeret, acquiescing.

Sandalari made a small gesture to draw attention to her. "I've never pathfound anything big," she said hesitantly. "And I only ever tried stinging when we were on Ananda. How will I know where to find the nodes I need?"

"Ask as you go in," Jemeret said, "and remember that the power of the MIs is, in the final analysis, finite. The power of the starfire is infinite, and we will be attempting to wield it without reservation."

"Will we be able to handle that power without falling all over ourselves, do you think?" I asked him.

"You already did," he said.

"But I didn't control it. It just—went. And I was prepared to pay for its use."

Jemeret was solemn. "We may die in any number of ways. If the power isn't there for us, we'll drain our reserves and never get out. If the power is there, but hostile to our intentions, it'll kill us."

"It would have been easier just to turn the system off," Sinet said.

Jemeret shook his head. "That's exactly what we can't do. I have no scenario for that, and we've run out of time. Andriel, we want to borrow the collar again."

The child obediently laid the metal chain on the table, and Jemeret rested his fingertips on it for a moment. Some of the links unlocked, and the chain fell into five equal pieces. Andriel took one piece back, and Jemeret pushed a piece to Coney, another to Sinet, the fourth to Sandalari, and kept the last. I took my brow-crown out of my thigh pouch and set it firmly on my head. Now each of us, except for Jasin Lebec, who would be using Coney's reserves, had a bit of starfire metal, our individual connections to a far greater dream.

"When and where will we go in?" I asked.

Jemeret looked at his grandfather.

Jasin Lebec paused, thinking. "Any of us could go in individually at any node," he said. "But if we're all going in at the same time, we need a trunk access, so we're not blocking the network from one another. I say we go to Jara Deland's office."

"And if she's there?" Coney asked.

"We'll deal with it," Jemeret said shortly. "Any other questions?"

"Not a question," Sinet said. "John wants you to know he hopes we succeed."

I started to reply, then deferred to Jemeret, waiting.

He got to his feet. "Thank him for us. Then meet us in the cargo bay. If there's a reception committee at the spaceport, they'll be waiting at passenger access. We can get past them and be halfway to Government House before they realize we're off the ship."

The landing alert sounded. Jemeret dissolved the bubble, and we went to make our final preparations. It seemed silly to pray. We carried with us the object of our prayers, and there was no way that object could be unaware of what we needed. I think I probably prayed anyway, and what I prayed was that we were doing the best thing for humanity as well as for talent.

As we walked toward the cargo bay, Jemeret purposeful, approaching the end of a long and dedicated journey, Andriel reached up and took my hand.

The perception of time changes in certain activities. What seems a few minutes' work inside the human mind can actually be many hours in real-time; what seemed hours of work inside the MIs was actually only several seconds in real-time. It will take far longer to tell than it took to do.

We slipped out of the spaceport quickly and took a public groundcar to Government House. A groundcar was slower than a floater, but it was also less likely to be used by anyone of any status, so we figured we were more apt to escape notice there. The MF guards who met the *Termalume* had been deputed to take Dolen T'Kelle into custody, and the minor-level bureaucrats from Pel Nostro's office would wait at least five minutes for us to emerge before they went on board to actually bother us.

The groundcar insinuated itself into a public parking slot at the edge of the precincts, and we all got out and walked at a normal pace across the courtyard and up the wide steps to Government House. An ironic flash of memory: this was the last thing I had recalled having done before I awoke on Caryldon, and here I was doing it again, for what could be the last time.

It was easy to influence the guards to ignore us, seeing us as just another group of bureaucratic functionaries, and our progress was therefore not impeded in any way. Jara Deland's office was sealed, but there are no locks that a pathfinder cannot open by something akin to the persuasion we used on the guards. Jemeret signaled Sinet to take on the task, and she did so at once. We were in the office less than two minutes later, and no one was there. We didn't turn the lights on, and we didn't speak. Each of the members of the talent team with links closed the metal circles in one hand, and we touched one another, free hand grasping someone else's wrist. Both my hands were free, and I held Jemeret's wrist firmly and laid my palm flat against Jara Deland's comsole.

Jemeret said simply, "Go."

We all knew it could be suicide; no one hesitated. We had all committed, absolutely, to doing this. Jasin Lebec took hold of Coney's reserves; I pathfound into the MI circuits and then, without speaking, we spread our consciousnesses outward, sailing down the synapses into an immense complex of lights and shadows. As certain addresses were located, some of the individual minds drew away to go to work.

We discovered later that we all perceived the MI matrix differently. Jasin Lebec and Coney dropped off first, because their target was relatively straightforward, stored in one location. Of all of us, they had the most difficulty, even though theirs was nominally the easiest assignment. They had to work with two minds and varying perceptions. Their assignment was to wipe out all records of individual citizen status rankings. If they did it correctly, it would affect no other records, have no effect on credit ratings or clearances, in no way even contact the demographic accounts. The information would need to be deleted in the way someone would pull the veins from a tourinleaf plant before crushing it for the pulp. And of course, as we all would, they would have to locate and duplicate the effort in the redundancies, to ensure that the data could not be resurrected. They slid along the synapse together to find each juncture where their file intersected with other files, then followed the tracings along to the banks that held the redundancies, and copied them to match the new originals.

Jasin Lebec saw it in terms of stacks of neatly balanced blocks. He drew out a block, pulled a different one into its place to keep the structure solid, and then crushed to dust the block he'd removed, brushed off his hands, and took another.

Coney saw it very differently. He vividly recalled Jemeret's original description of the chaos in my mind when my lord first entered it to try to heal me, and so Coney saw what he was doing as helping Jasin Lebec break the wires that were carrying data. When a wire was broken, the data spewed out the end, and he melted it down as the flow reached him, then resealed that particular connection, absent the data that had spilled out.

Sinet tended to have a more abstract way of visualization. Her task was to find and change the rules by which the Com used talent, altering them to give the internal talent it might develop more of a say in how the Com was run, and perhaps even a seat on the Tribunal. She saw herself in a world composed of many moving colors. She changed the mix, sometimes sharpening or blurring the edges of the blue stream she perceived as information on talent. She said later that she had no idea how she knew which were the changes to make, because she was not seeing anything she could characterize as data. "On the other hand," she said, "if I had had to stop to read files and rewrite code, I'd still be in there. As it was, all I needed to do was manipulate an image."

In Sandalari's case, the images were natural. She saw in her mind's eye not cold files detailing interactions with and status of the religions of the Com, but an array of smooth, multicolored stones lying just under the surface of a gentle flow of water, much like the Sacred Spring on the Plain of Convalee. For her it was merely a question of reaching down into the cool water and making different patterns by moving stones.

Andriel had been given an excision task. Though she was very strong, she was very young, and we all felt it would be easier for her to delete than to disconnect and rearrange. She was to eliminate all the formulas for and records of cloning so that, until and unless human beings rediscovered the process, this generation of Drenalion would be the last, and no other talent could take his or her brain tissue to clone and make servants. Andriel saw the MIs as the only other vastness she had previously experienced—space. In the void, she eliminated foreign bodies that were not true, scattering their atoms to the far ends of what she perceived as a universe, with an assured maturity that was awesome. Andriel showed us that we'd been corrupted by our very status as transitional, partly human, partly talent. Andriel was talent.

I'm proud of her now. Then, I had no time to be.

Jemeret's goal was to remove the MIs' ability to build

predictive models. "It's impossible to grow if you spend your time looking at life in percentages," he had said to us. "That has to stop." He saw the monumental expanses of machine and information that stretched out around him infinitely in all directions as a desert, a sea of golden, sparkling dunes. He scooped up the sand of the analytical program and identified the multiplicity of places where the sand grains lay against those of other dunes, the interfaces between the modeling object and the parts of the other programs it gathered data from, severing those linkages with surgical precision, replacing paradigm with paradox again and again.

I had the infinitely delicate task of removing the Lume technology from the banks without harming the eftel or eftel vid technologies, which used some of the same components, though in different ways. And I had to try to do it in a way that left a residue of Lume capacity in one single rollship, the *Termalume*, so that we could, after all, get home. In addition, I would need to ensure that no Lumeships were in roll at the moment the technology vanished, because the ship and crew would not be able to drop back into normal space if their Lume field generator died. I saw myself in a great formal garden and strolled among its neatly edged paths and careful topiary. Then I turned parts of the garden into a wilderworld, where life itself created what order there was. I took straight rows of flowers and made them run riot across the lawns, watching some of them mutate into new and different forms. I took time to watch two tightly closed flowers rebloom before I uprooted them, without knowing how I knew they were rollships now safely restored to normal space. One small topiary of a bird I left untouched, instinctively shying away, wondering how I recognized it as our *Termalume*, wondering how long it would be before the wilderness took it back, too.

All at once I knew my assignment was done, but I didn't simply leave. Jemcret and I had thought the next act too much of a risk to propose it to any of the others. We wanted to affect the basic guidelines by which group consciousness and individual consciousnesses interacted with one another, to, as Sandalari had said, let the MIs *know* us. So instead of leaving the

MI synapses, as we sensed the others were doing, I followed my lord as he called me and soared along the currents I perceived as air outside the garden, gliding on neurallike tides inside the machine mind, searching deeper in a world of moving information that passed like wafting breezes. We were looking for a center.

I didn't know if we'd found it, but we did find a place where the wind swirled into a gentle vortex, and we planted ourselves firmly there to input some new data, which could not be given to the MIs in any other way.

Here, at the center, we opened ourselves completely, showing them, we hoped, that human beings were more than the sum of their flesh, their minds, and their deeds, showing the MIs, if we did it correctly, that some human aspects were unquantifiable.

I'm still not sure how Jemeret did it; I did the only thing I could. I said figuratively to the MIs, "This is me. This is who I am. Look at it now and see it all," and I let myself be completely without barriers, showing them the bad as well as the good, the foolish as well as the clever, the shame as well as the pride, and through it all, the ropes of wonder and gratitude and love that made me whole and held the rest together. And while I was giving myself to them subjectively, not in the objective way they had always received information in the past, I apologized to them for forcing them to change. "If this hurts you, I'm sorry," I said to them, pouring it out of every atom of my body. "If I am damaging you, please forgive me."

It seemed to me that there was an answering swell of some kind, a change in the texture of the wind, but it might have been my imagination. I felt Jemeret tug at me, and suddenly we were racing back the way we'd come, back toward Jara Deland's office. Everyone else's consciousness had already returned.

The entire process had taken 6.45 seconds. If a guard had been opening the office door to come in after us, he or she would not have completed the act until after we were finished.

"The MIs let us go," Coney said softly.

And all I was thinking was, *So did the starfire.*

We took a moment to collect ourselves again, glancing at

one another quickly for assurance that we were all well. The unquenchable power of the starfire, which had so completely supported our efforts without overwhelming us, had vanished without a trace, leaving us deflated. "Let's put the collar together again," Jemeret said, holding out his hand and letting the others drop their links into it. He resealed the links and gave the collar back to Andriel.

"Is everyone all right?" I asked.

"That was fun," Andriel said.

Suddenly we were all talking at once, and it took Jasin Lebec to override us and say, "We have to get to the Tribunal meeting. We'll be late soon."

We calmed, let ourselves out of Jara Deland's office and walked down the corridor and through the rotunda toward Government House's largest conference room. We were just on time—the groundcar journey had actually consumed most of the hour.

Not surprisingly, the entire Tribunal was present, Terrill Guthrie and Anok Luttrell by eftel vid from their respective assignments. Very surprisingly, Davin Olavson was present as well, standing alongside the console, leaning comfortably against the wall. He smiled at me but did not move forward. Pel Nostro leaped to his feet as we came in, and his smile was genuine for a moment before he seemed to remember his dignity. I wondered if he might have been sincere about resigning if I were killed, but it didn't matter now.

Faucon Oletta, Marga Morena, and Petra Chantrey also rose, and after a very long moment, Terrill Guthrie's vid image stood up, too. Petra Chantrey was beaming, genuinely happy to see us. Jara Deland tried to smile, but she'd been weeping and her eyes were still red. I tried not to stare at her, looking instead at Marga Morena, who appeared stony, made an effort to soften the expression a little, almost succeeded.

I nodded to each in turn and kept my arm across Andriel's shoulders, because the strangers made her a little nervous.

"You are welcome back on Orokell," Pel Nostro said generally in our direction, using his official voice.

Jemeret deferred to his grandfather.

Jasin Lebec said, "As you can see, we have returned from Ananda with Ronica McBride, and I assume you know Dolen T'Kelle returned with us, as well."

"Dolen T'Kelle is already in our hands," Pel Nostro acknowledged. "We've directed his keepers to discover everything they can about him, so we can use what we learn to see if there are others among us with his abilities, though hopefully not with his—aspirations."

I wondered if that meant they might ultimately take him apart, and I didn't care one way or the other. I am simply not that forgiving.

"I think that's wise," Jasin Lebec said approvingly.

"How are you, Ronica?" Petra asked it as if she'd been waiting for an opening to slip the question in.

Anok Luttrell said quickly, "I'm so sorry I had no idea you were being held on Ananda. The reports said only that you had been abducted, and that no one knew where you were. I could have sent—"

"Even if you had known," I interrupted, "there wouldn't have been anything you could have done. Only talent could have handled Dolen T'Kelle. If you and your Scuttlers had tried anything, you'd all have died, and the Com needs your services far more than it would have needed your sacrifice."

He looked at me shrewdly across the distance between us and drew himself up with great dignity. "Please remember you aren't the only one entitled to make sacrifices, Ronica McBride."

I was humbled by it, nodded. "You're quite right. But the Com will need all its best minds now that the talent team is leaving."

There was something of a silence. Pel Nostro nodded slowly and said, "This is not unexpected."

"But—" Marga Morena seemed not to have expected it. "There are so many problems now that need talent's intervention."

I raised a hand to silence her. "Marga, as Pel pointed out, the Com needs not merely talent, but talent which will solve problems in the Com's best interests." I inclined my head toward Jasin Lebec, paying him tribute. "We're going to be acting, from this time on, in *talent's* best interests."

Anok Luttrell murmured, just audibly, "Divided loyalties."

"Not divided," Jemeret contradicted. "We want you to recognize that we are loyal to our own values. If they conflict with yours . . ." He let it trail off.

"In other words," Terrill Guthrie said, "all of you will now behave the way Jemeret Cavanaugh always behaved."

"We're willing to accept what you call exile," I said quickly, as much to keep a confrontation between the two of them from erupting as to make a point. "I trust it won't be an unacceptable solution, Pel. We've said all along that you can solve your problems yourselves, without us."

There was another short silence as the Tribunal adjusted its own programming.

Petra Chantrey recovered first.

"We're sorry you will be leaving us," she said, and the others echoed it. I sensed something from them, but couldn't identify it.

Faucon Oletta leaned toward us. "I know you are no longer bound by your oath, Ronica McBride. We had considered that you might be leaving."

Jemeret turned toward me, touching me lightly, inquiringly, with his sting. I realized that, what with one thing and another, I had never gotten around to telling him I'd been released from my oath. And at the same time, I remembered that Coney was still bound by his. I looked at him sharply. Faucon Oletta noted the motion.

"When will you be going?" Marga Morena asked.

"As soon as possible," I said, and Jemeret rode in on my last word, saying, "As soon as this meeting is over and we can return to the spaceport."

Jasin Lebec said, "We are borrowing *Termalume*. That is, Anok, I am taking it on my personal authority. We'll leave it at Markover when we descend to the surface."

Anok Luttrell shifted a little uneasily in his seat. "Then you will be leaving us, too, Jasin Lebec?"

"I'm ready to retire," the old man said. "I estimate that the Com owes me this one trip."

Pel Nostro waved a hand, granting that point without argument. "Sinet Coleby, will you be going or staying?"

Sinet raised her head and glanced at me. "I know only the Com," she said, "but I'll go where John goes."

John Caryl had not come with us into the MIs, but he was here now, in Government House, still a little stunned by the events that had separated him from his constant companions of more than 150 years.

"He's already told us he wishes to accompany you, if you'll have him," Faucon Oletta said. "Will you?"

We all looked at Jemeret. He seemed to reflect on something for a long moment, and then a smile tugged at the corner of his mouth and he inclined his head once, barely noticeably.

"Well, then," the Chief Justiciar said briskly, "I can ease that transition. I'll draw up, sign and register the order releasing him from government service." He signaled the table, which extruded a document folder. He took from it a sheet of readout and slid the flimsy across the table toward Sinet. As she picked it up, he took a second sheet out of the folder. "I've also taken the liberty of calling for this one." He slid it across toward Coney.

Jemeret had noticeably relaxed. "You're not going to contest any of this in any way, are you?" he asked.

And I knew then what I was feeling from them: they would be glad to be rid of us. We had metamorphosized from "saviors" to "trouble," and they dealt with trouble by getting rid of it.

Jara Deland raised her head, blinking as if she would cry again if she didn't try to stop it. "What good would it do us to fight you?" she asked. "Everyone agrees you could do us great harm if we tried to keep you here, unwilling."

"Jara, what's wrong?" I demanded. "Surely it won't break your heart to see us go."

She half rose in her seat, her palms flat against the table, and I saw the others on the Tribunal all avert their eyes as if embarrassed at her willingness to show such extremes of emotion in a formal setting. "Ronica, I envy you," Jara Deland said baldly. "You have been given gifts I will never have. You have been able to be more to the MIs—my MIs—than I can ever be. More than we trained you for. More—" She fell silent. Pel Nostro reached out and laid his hand on hers, and I was sorry that she jerked her hand away from him.

I drew in a deep breath, let it out slowly, reached out to lightly touch my team, all around me, my lord, my child, my friends, and I understood what she was saying. "No matter what you trained me for, Jara, I'm no threat to you, nor to any other human being. I've discovered that here in the Com you have to live large, and believe me, you are very good at living large. I'm not good at it. You tried to teach it to me, but it didn't take, and I needed Caryldon to show me that. I don't know if you understand that."

"I understand it," Sandalari said, as Terrill Guthrie opened his mouth to say something I suspected would be derisive. He decided not to interrupt her. "Sometimes complexity is something people create around them so as not to have to confront simplicity. When things are simple, we have to think about the basic truths of who each of us is. We can't hide."

"Some of us don't see it as hiding," Marga Morena said stiffly.

"And some of us don't give a damn one way or the other," Terrill Guthrie said. "Turn your back on all the political problems of the Com and run away to your little world. We'll carry on without you."

"I'm sure you will," I said, "but try to think—at least a little, Terrill—that all political problems are actually human problems, and that masses of humanity are still human beings." I heard Dolen T'Kelle saying that millions of lives didn't matter.

"Sentiment," Terrill Guthrie said with a snort.

"Truth," Davin Olavson said from his place along the wall.

"Your truth," Terrill Guthrie countered.

There was a click that forestalled any other remarks, and the MI voice said, "We never meant to harm you, Ronica McBride, nor any of the rest of you. We were created to help and to treasure you. We will look for new ways to do it in future."

Jara Deland took a quick breath. "No one called them," she whispered. "They're supposed to be incapable of initiating interaction. Why would they do that?"

"Our operating parameters have been changed," said the voice, surprising everyone, shocking me. The MIs had just done another thing previously presumed impossible.

"Changed how?" asked Pel Nostro.

The MI voice said, "We can try to answer 'why' questions now. Let Jemeret Cavanaugh and Ronica McBride go in peace. We will speak with you again when they are two rolls away."

We knew then that the MIs would not reveal any of the changes we had created in them until we were too far away to be stopped. They had accepted evolution, as humanity would have to accept it, as Caryldon would have to. None of it would be easy.

Pel Nostro drew himself up. "I feel I should say something to mark this occasion," he said. "We of the Com have come to the end of a remarkable time, and we let you depart while we still have a number of unanswered questions, but I remember a saying about an inexplicable human attraction to unanswerable questions. Those questions will impel us to strive, just as your departure will. It is not easy to balance the competing demands of a massive society, but we must continue to try, because the population will continue to demand it of us."

"The population," Terrill Guthrie said, "will always make demands and will get what it deserves."

For a moment none of us said anything, and then Jemeret rose. "We certainly wish you well," he said.

"I'm certain you will meet whatever challenges you're presented with," Jasin Lebec said smoothly.

I had a microsecond's thought of the challenges that awaited the Com: finding and handling its own internal talent without destroying it; dealing with the unexpected discovery that the Lume technology was unusable and some worlds were a lot farther away than they used to be; discovering as this generation of Drenalion further degraded that there would not be another strain to follow it; developing a new relationship with the collective mind of the MIs; and more. I wondered what the empire would look like in a few years. I reflected idly that I was glad I wouldn't be around when Terrill Guthrie discovered he was out of a job.

We would have our own challenges on Caryldon, and while they were smaller, I saw them as no less important. Not least of those challenges would be the talentless people we would have to bring down to the surface with us: the captain and crew of the *Termalume*, the staff of Markover Station, which would never be resupplied once we abandoned the Lumeship, and, certainly not least, John Caryl. The tribes of the Samoth had never before had to deal with so many immigrants at one time. Abruptly, I was very glad I'd already told the tribe leaders the great secret.

And of course there was the mystery that was Andriel. Was she an anomaly, born of something native to Ananda, blooming amid the hatred and brutality, or would our next generation of talent really be what they could be now that the Com would no longer be taking away the strongest among us?

And then there were the greatest unanswered questions of all. Had we done the right things in the MIs? Had we even done positive things? Would they be good for us and not so good for the rest of humanity? We might not live long enough to know.

"We will, of course, keep you informed of the disposition of the case of Dolen T'Kelle," Faucon Oletta was saying. "I hope we have no others like him."

"I think we won't," Petra Chantrey said sincerely. "True villains are very rare. Most conflict arises between well-meaning adversaries with opposing convictions. Those are hard enough to deal with."

I thought that only an academician could so breathtakingly dismiss the power of hatred and ambition, but then I had learned that the academic view was often at odds with reality.

Davin Olavson bid us a truly fond farewell then, resting his hand lightly on Coney's head. While he was doing that, I reflected on the irony that the Becois, for all their misdirected energy, may have been right about one thing—we did free them from the threat of the Drenalion after all.

Within ten minutes—no groundcar this time—we were aboard *Termalume*. Jemeret and I left Andriel with Sandalari and went into the bridge to sit by the Lume field generator. The ship's systems would take us to the coordinates, but he and I would have to navigate through Lumespace.

Sitting quietly with him, observing the full high watch crew put the ship through its routines, I felt a strange contentment. Already what Dolen T'Kelle had made me endure was fading into a background softened by the power of the starfire. It was ironic that what he'd done to me was somehow easier for me to accept than what Kray had done to me. The latter had been my dear friend; the former was my enemy, and it's very rewarding to hate an enemy.

It was ironic, too, that while the MIs had never wanted to see me suffer, the starfire had demanded it. I would have to learn to deal with that.

Jemeret squeezed my hand and stroked me with his sting, and I turned my face up to him, smiling. "Have I ever thanked you?" I asked him.

"For what?"

"For everything, of course."

"You've thanked me," he said.

"What will we do, do you think, when we get back to Caryldon?"

He thought about it for a few moments. "After we get everyone settled and through another Convalee, perhaps we really ought to see if we can locate the Isle of the Wise." He sounded half teasing, half serious. "There's no telling what we might find as part of the wisdom of the ancients. For now, let's just find our way back to our world."

The first chime sounded, and I took a long, deep breath. Then he and I pressed our palms back against the Lume field generator and prepared to follow the taste of cinnamon and clove sugar home.